T0357811

Bailey Hannah's Wells Ranch Series

Alive and Wells

Seeing Red

Change of Hart

Seeing Red

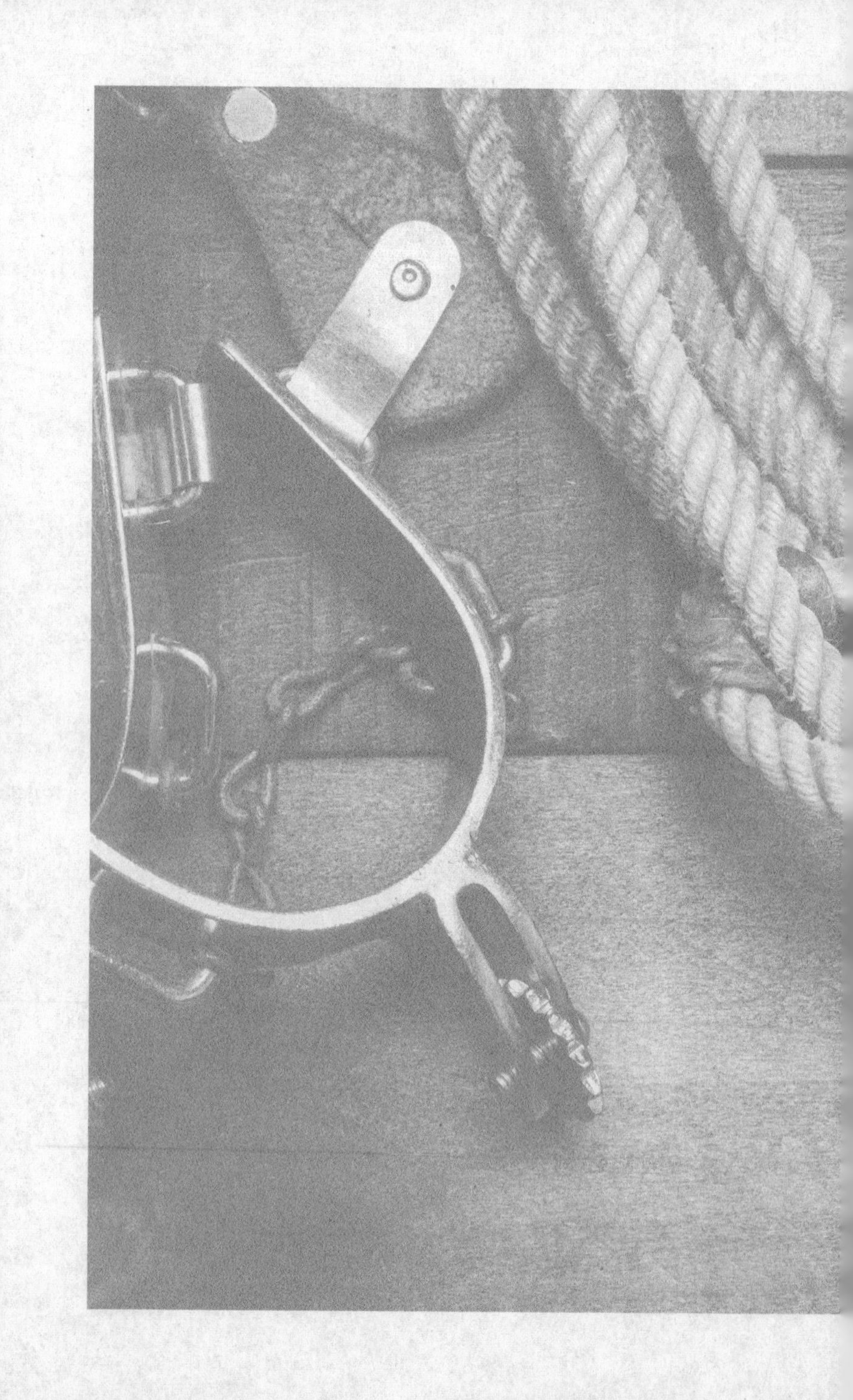

Seeing Red

A Wells Ranch Novel

Bailey Hannah

DELL BOOKS
NEW YORK

Dell
An imprint of Random House
A division of Penguin Random House LLC
1745 Broadway, New York, NY 10019
randomhousebooks.com
penguinrandomhouse.com

A Dell Trade Paperback Original

Published in the United States by Dell, an imprint of Random House, a division of Penguin Random House LLC, 1745 Broadway, New York, NY 10019.

DELL and the D colophon are registered trademarks of Penguin Random House LLC.

This work was originally self-published by the author in Canada in 2024.

ISBN 978-0-593-98400-0
Ebook ISBN 978-1-738-10763-6

Printed in the United States of America on acid-free paper

2 4 6 8 9 7 5 3 1

Title-page art by Michael Flippo/Adobe Stock

The authorized representative in the EU for product safety and compliance is Penguin Random House Ireland, Morrison Chambers, 32 Nassau Street, Dublin D02 YH68, Ireland, https://eu-contact.penguin.ie.

For all of us who thought we'd have
everything figured out in our twenties.
It's okay if you need more time to find yourself.
And if you're really stressed about it, you can always
fuck a tattooed cowboy on the hood of your ex's car.
See if that helps.

Author's Note

This story is about an accidental pregnancy following a one-night stand. Please note: while every effort was made to ensure accuracy and sensitivity, not every pregnancy/childbirth experience is the same, so some details may not be accurate to your own experience. The same is true of Cassidy's experience with PCOS and Hashimoto's. Don't come for me about the baby size references, though—they're taken from pregnancy tracking apps/websites, and any pregnant person who has looked at the fruit-based size references weekly will attest that they never make sense.

If reading about pregnancy in detail is not for you, you can safely skip this book and continue to read the following books within the Wells Ranch series without missing any crucial information. As always, take care of yourself.

Go easy on Cass <3. She's pregnant and hormonal for most of this book.

Oh! Can't forget to mention that the author is not responsible for any unplanned pregnancies that occur as a result of reading this book. Double up on that birth control, friends.

CONTENT/TRIGGER WARNINGS:

- Pregnancy (main trope in book): includes depictions of morning sickness and basic medical procedures related to pregnancy

- Abortion (brief mention)
- Childbirth (on page)
- Chronic illness: Hashimoto's disease and polycystic ovarian syndrome (on page)
- Body image issues (on page)
- Medical fatphobia (on page)
- Physical violence (on page)
- Alcoholic parent/alcoholism (discussed)
- Alcohol consumption (on page)
- Vomit (on page)
- Parental sickness/death (discussed, not shown)
- Alzheimer's disease (discussed, not shown)
- Parental abandonment (discussed, not shown)
- Domestic violence (discussed, not shown)
- Past child abuse (discussed in detail)
- Troubled parent–adult child relationship (discussed)
- Marijuana consumption (brief mention)
- Ranching activities: calving (discussion)
- Explicit sex scenes including cum play, sex toy use, degradation, breeding, hand necklace (not breath play/choking)

Seeing Red

Cassidy

If there's one thing men have, it's the fucking audacity. Bringing the girl he cheated on me with to *my* hometown rodeo is next level. My beer bottle slams into the sticky picnic table with such intensity, it's astounding it doesn't break. Although, if it broke, I'd have something to cut my ex-boyfriend's arrogant face with. And that scenario doesn't sound half bad.

"I'm getting another," I yell at one of my best friends, Shelby, over the Brooks & Dunn cover band. "I'm gonna get stabby if I have to watch them make out for another second."

"I could go for another." Shelby nods and swallows the last of her beer with a gulp. "Quit watching them; your wallowing days are supposed to be over, girl. Screw him. Fight fire with fire—get yourself a man for the night."

"Minor problem, Shelb. I'm not interested in a single guy here."

Normally, I don't date. Not because I'm a goody two-shoes, although a lot of people in town seem to believe I am. I simply have a strict set of rules. Just like ninety-nine percent of the two thousand residents, I've lived in Wells Canyon since I was a baby. All I want is someone who hasn't known me since I was in diapers, doesn't spend every Friday night at my dad's bar, and hasn't slept with either of my best friends. My bar for men is so damn low it may as well be in hell, yet none of the single men at this barn dance check all three boxes.

Failing to see the giant red flags he was waving, I agreed to the fateful first date with Derek over a year ago, simply because he checked the boxes. Then everything went to shit. My best friends see that as a sign I should give it up and date a local. *Vehemently disagree.*

"Well, we're here to get you out of your funk, and letting him under your skin all night won't help. Forget about him."

"Yeah, easier said than done. There's only, like, a hundred people here and he's tall. Sort of makes it impossible to forget about him."

In the two weeks since breaking up with Derek, I've had my ups and downs. The past five days have definitely been rock bottom. I've been wearing the same pajamas the entire time—not just at night. *All day.* Eating cereal out of a mixing bowl and drinking room-temperature sangria. Quite often at the same time. I essentially morphed into a college frat boy stuck in a depression spiral because he wasn't allowed to spend spring break in Florida. I may have even gone down a little *Girls Gone Wild* YouTube rabbit hole. If all that isn't the lowest of the low, I don't know what is.

I've been desperate for a reckless night out—something to get back to feeling myself—so this rodeo couldn't have come soon enough. Then my motherfucking ex-boyfriend had to turn up and kill my vibe.

Approaching the bar, I lose all of Shelby's attention the moment she spots her crush of the month, Denver Wells, one of the ranchers at Wells Ranch, the local cattle empire. He's cute enough, with short brown hair, dimples, and a lean, muscular body. Plus, he's a saddle bronc rider, which seems to impress most girls around here. And Denny's actually a pretty nice guy, but again, I have rules for a reason.

In typical fashion, Shelby orders two bottles of beer and vanishes into the crowd without a word. All I can see from my mediocre 5'6" height is the peak of her rhinestone cowboy hat bobbing among the throng of people in front of the stage as she works her way toward Denny's picnic table at the far right. Shelby's been boy crazy for as long as I've known her, and even though I don't fully understand it, I love that for her.

I grab my drinks and step aside to take in the rodeo beer gardens, breathing in the cool spring air. It's just a square patch of cement, corralled off with livestock panels and neon orange snow fencing, keeping the chaos controlled as if we're an unruly herd of cattle. One way in and out, past the singular cop in town and his team of volunteer bouncers. It smells more like horse crap than I typically enjoy, but I'll take that over what this group of dirty cowboys, drunks, and perfume-drenched women would smell like if we weren't out in the open air.

Scanning the crowd, I don't see anyone I'm interested in hanging out with. I suppose Denver and his ranch hands aren't the worst group to socialize with for the night. At least they don't make lewd comments or try to touch my ass when I serve them at the bar, and a few are pretty easy on the eyes. All in all, they're a chill enough group of guys, so I follow the footsteps of my slutty best friend.

Weaving between a group of drunken line dancers, I'm only stopped by five people wanting to chat. Impressive considering I can name almost every single person here. Although I feel the pitiful stare of every set of eyes, the whispers of gossip about my relationship crumbling. Another blatant reminder of why I don't date locally.

Finally, I reach my destination, coming across Shelby straddling Denny on the end of a picnic table—tongues already down each other's throats.

Jesus, she really wasn't wasting any time.

Again, love that for her, but I can't imagine making out with a guy in a place like this. News travels faster than head lice in Wells Canyon, and the rumors are just as irritating. Everyone from my dad to my kindergarten teacher to my hairdresser would know about it within minutes. A lesson I learned the hard way, after I made out with Steven Gregoire outside the corner store in the tenth grade and was forced into a disturbing sex talk from my dad the moment I walked through the front door. Never made that mistake again, which is likely why most people around here think I'm a goody-two-shoes prude.

My pair of amber bottles clunk against the rickety wood table when I sit across from Red, one of the Wells Ranch cowboys and, arguably, my least favorite of the bunch. If I had a dollar for every time I had to kick him out of the bar for fighting, I'd at least be able to pay for my drinks tonight. And if I had another dollar for every time he's annoyed me since elementary school, I could retire and move to the Caribbean.

"You know, you don't need to bring me beer when you aren't working, Cass. But thank you, I'm touched." Red makes a move like he's going to grab one of my drinks, and I reflexively slap his muscular, heavily tattooed forearm.

"Do it, and I'll cut you."

He laughs and adjusts the faded Stetson covering his shaggy auburn hair. His nickname isn't exactly the most creative I've ever heard—it was even more on the nose when he was a little kid, with hair so red he looked like he belonged in the Weasley family. Now it has more brown to it, but the occasional time I've seen him with facial hair, it's very apparent that he's a true redhead through and through.

"So impolite when you're off the clock," he says with a smirk.

"Yeah, well, you aren't going to tip me here, are ya? No need to feign niceness."

For a long while we sit in silence, awkwardly pretending our best friends aren't making out a foot away and watching the crappy Brooks & Dunn cover band run through "Play Something Country" for the fourth time this evening. You'd think we were at a real concert with the way all the drunk girls bounce in front of the stage. It's guaranteed that one of them flashes their tits at the band before the night's through. If Shelby wasn't suctioned to Denver, I would bet money on her being the one to do it.

"Isn't that your boyfriend?" Red's head gestures toward where Derek and *Alyssa* must be. I don't dare follow his gaze, my stomach cramping with a warning not to peek unless I want to feel downright murderous again. Suffering from a sudden case of restless leg syndrome, I bounce my knee and keep my focus trained on Red, his tongue tucked into his cheek as he narrows his eyes at them.

"Ex," I correct him. "We broke up a couple of weeks ago."

"Want me to punch him?"

"No, Red. I don't." I'd love to say yes—I'd love the thrill of watching Derek get a tiny piece of what he deserves—but it's not worth whatever will happen after the initial hit.

"Want to get even? Make him jealous? We can make out right next to them."

"Honestly, *fuck off.* I'm just trying to listen to music and drink in peace, okay? Why don't you go ask a girl to dance or get in a fistfight or do literally anything other than bug me."

"Well, I don't dance. The sole person I'm thinking about fighting is your ex, which you already shot down. And I was sitting here first."

Plopping my elbow onto the table, I sink my head into my hand to block him from view—effectively blocking Derek as well. Two annoying birds, one stone. A moment later, the table shifts as Red finally takes the hint and leaves.

Not nearly enough time has passed before his presence returns. At least this time, he comes bearing gifts, sliding a shot of tequila and another beer over to me. And I'm not one to turn down free drinks, even if I'm not partial to the guy buying them for me.

Hoisting up his own shot glass with a wink, he says, "Cheers to you not dating that fuckin' nerd anymore."

Jesus Christ. But also . . . hear, hear!

I throw back the shot, chasing it with multiple chugs of beer. Painfully aware of Red's stare, which is burning my insides with more sting than the tequila. He sets his empty bottle on the table and lazily spins it with a wrist flick. Over and over and over.

Thud, clink, rattle, rattle, thud, clink, rattle.

Until the sound of glass on the rough wood surface may as well be an accompaniment for the band, which I'm watching with intent. Desperate to look anywhere other than at the cowboy sitting across from me or at the ex-boyfriend somewhere in the crowd. Hoping if I pretend hard enough to like the shitty cover music, I can get lost in the atmosphere and potentially salvage the night.

"Hey, Cass." Red's grating voice pierces the air just when I've nearly forgotten about him sitting across from me.

I roll my neck with an irritated exhale. "What now, Red?"

"Look at that. Looks like I landed on you in Spin the Bottle. Better kiss me and make your ex jealous—he keeps looking over here."

"You're an idiot," I say with a scoff.

"Not a fan? *Oh, right.* From what I remember, Seven Minutes in Heaven is more your game, isn't it?"

This goddamn town. Suggest a group of us play it *one fucking time* at a birthday party in the eighth grade, and it's still brought up nearly two decades later.

"Are you thirteen?" I consider ditching the overpriced beer and heading home to throw my pajamas back on. This entire night is a waste of time. I hate knowing I put effort into looking pretty so I could sit at a picnic table with Chase "Red"

Thompson—a boy I've disliked since middle school. Stuck watching my ex-boyfriend make out with the beautiful, raven-haired woman he was sleeping with for at least half of our year-long relationship.

"Is that what you're into? Because that's fucked up, Cass." He snorts a laugh, straightening his hat. "Might need to report you."

"I meant because those are both children's games, you idiot." I gulp my beer. And gulp. And gulp.

"I'm just sayin', everybody but us seems to be making out. And it *would* piss him off. But if a simple kiss is too childish for you, there are lots of adult things we could do." He raises a daring eyebrow.

"The fuck is wrong with you?" Leaning over the table, I smack the cowboy hat from his head. He lets out a hearty chuckle, bending to swipe the hat from the ground and shaking out his thick hair. The commotion's enough to break apart Shelby and Denny, who, until this point, might as well have had their lips superglued together.

"Hey, Shelb. I'm gonna walk home," I say now that I finally have a sliver of her attention. Swinging a leg over the bench and standing up, I feel the alcohol wash through my bloodstream. The world's a little hazy, lights around the stage are blown out rather than crisp, and my legs feel like they're enveloped in thick mud. Chugging back my beer in an effort to leave faster might not have been my best move.

"No, don't!" she protests, pushing away from Denny to catch my elbow. "You're supposed to be finding a guy to help you get over Derek tonight."

"And I told you there are zero prospects here."

Shelby looks from me to Red, then meets my eyes with a shrug. "I mean . . . not *zero* prospects."

"Fuck all of this. *Definitely fuck that.* I'm going home. Night, guys."

"Night, Cass. Love you," Denny calls after me.

Shelby's playful squeal rings out as he presumably grabs her, pulling her back in for another consuming kiss.

I stagger through the crowd of drunk people, aiming to keep myself on two feet while I come to grips with exactly how intoxicated I am. That's the problem with throwing them back while you're comfortably seated. As soon as you stand, the Earth tilts on its axis, and you find yourself struggling to remain upright.

Unfortunately for me, small-town rodeos are too much like a family reunion to allow for a quick escape. I'm pulled in every direction by people I know. From Jerry, the middle-aged bar regular who always begs me to line dance with him, to my old high school principal. Debbie from the post office corners me to ask if I can catsit while she goes to Vegas—and who am I to say no when she shows me the little visor hat she had made for the tabby? Everybody and their damn dog are here, inconveniently blocking the lone route out of this hellhole.

After barely escaping the clutches of a group of girls I graduated with, I'm nearly home free. I'd run if I thought my coordination was good enough. As I'm plodding past the row of porta potties and keeping my eye on the exit gate straight ahead, an unpleasant voice sends shivers down my spine.

"Cass . . . hey."

My shoulders fall, and I shut my eyes—but only for half a second because it instantly makes the world feel like it's spinning out of control.

"Hey, Derek." I turn to face him. Thankfully, he's without his mistress.

"How are you doing?" He assesses my body with a raised brow. All the words he's leaving unsaid play on repeat in my mind. Sure, I've put on five pounds since we broke up, but the struggle to zip my denim miniskirt was enough of a blow to my ego for one day. I don't need him to make me feel even worse, and I know it's taking everything he has to refrain from commenting on my appearance. It drives him batty that I'm mostly okay with being in a size twelve body. I'll certainly be even more content with my size now that I won't hear his negative comments all the time.

"Fine. Great, in fact. I'm doing fan-fucking-tastic," I say sarcastically. "Having fun tonight?"

What I mean is, *Why the hell are you at a rodeo in my town weeks after making me feel like the biggest idiot on the planet?*

"Yeah. Alyssa had never been to a rodeo, so—"

Thanks to years waitressing in my dad's bar, my customer service voice is flawless and not affected at all by my alcohol consumption. "That's . . . *super*. Great. So glad that, uh, you brought her here. I'm going to go, so . . . *super* nice seeing you."

"Hope you aren't going home early because I'm here."

"No. Not at all. I'm not going home. I was coming over to use the bathroom." I don't know why I'm lying, or why it continues to spew out of me. "I'm actually here with somebody, too. We're having a super fun time."

Why do I keep saying "super"? Maybe the alcohol is affecting my speech after all.

"Oh? I saw you talking to Red. Don't tell me you're with *that* guy? Jesus, Cass. Slumming it with the local cowboys? Sheesh . . . Even for you, that's fucked up."

Even for me?

My brain and mouth are no longer working together, and words tumble out before I get the chance to think about them. "You know what? It's not nearly as fucked up as bringing the girl you cheated with to this rodeo."

"Cass, I'm just saying—"

"Don't say another word to me, because the cowboy I'm 'slumming it with' would love an excuse to kick the shit out of you. Have a *super* night."

Instead of continuing on my journey home, I shoulder-check Derek and march back over to the picnic table, ignoring the alarm bells and red alerts firing in my brain. I know the idea forming in my drunk mind is a terrible one. I also know that after a year of putting up with that asshole, I don't care. I need to do *something* to expel the rage pulsing in my veins.

He wronged me in a way that made me feel like a fool. I went months before realizing he had a new girlfriend and I'd been relegated to side-chick. But I didn't scream, cry, throw his shit on the lawn, slash his car tires, or do any of the things my favorite country songs say he deserves. No, I broke up with him civilly, handing over all his belongings with a tight-lipped smile while she watched from the passenger seat of his car.

I don't want to be the bigger, more mature, emotionally intelligent person anymore. Not tonight. I deserve to make a terrible decision or two for once in my goddamn life.

Shelby and Denny are nowhere to be seen—though I can make an educated guess about where they've gone. But Red's still sitting at the picnic table, downing beer and watching the crappy band play. Honestly, from where I stand, he's not bad looking. If I didn't know anything about his personality, I might find him attractive. Fuckable, even. With tousled red-brown hair under his cowboy hat, tattoos covering both arms, bulky muscles earned from hard farmwork, faded denim stretched across powerful thighs, and playful, cobalt-blue eyes. It's just too bad about the rest of him.

My hands slam down on the table, making him jump. I'm not sure at all what my game plan is, only that it's fueled by alcohol and hatred. And Red is exactly the kind of guy to go along with it. "Offer still stand to piss off my ex?"

"Why? See something you like, Cass?" His eyebrows raise with a cocky grin lighting his stupid face.

"I might've, but then you spoke. Now I'm filled with regrets. Where's Colt or . . . literally anybody single, attractive, and less annoying than you?" This was a dumb plan. Just because Derek dislikes Red and thinks I'm "slumming it" by hanging out with the cowboys from Wells Ranch doesn't mean I should hook up with one to get back at him. What am I even proving by doing that? Admittedly, my logic is lacking. "Y'know . . . never mind."

"Don't know where Colt is. But I'm free to help and know a good way you can shut my mouth up."

Massaging my temples, I scan the beer gardens. As if I'm being personally mocked by God, the singular pole light illuminating the dark dance floor shines directly on Derek and Alyssa. Grabbing the bottle from Red's hand, I take a long pull. It goes down like water, and I no longer give a single fuck whether my plan makes sense.

"Lose the chew." I point to the bulge sitting in his bottom lip. "I refuse to kiss anybody with chewing tobacco in their mouth."

Before I can finish getting the words out, he's swiping his finger under his lip and flicking the dark brown tobacco onto the ground. "Anything else?"

"Two rules: you don't say anything stupid and we never speak of this again. Deal?"

He throws back the last of his beer and stands. "Deal, sweetheart."

I sigh. "Three rules. Don't call me sweetheart."

Cassidy

Thick T-shirt fabric balled in my fist, I tug him along behind me until we're close enough to Derek that he's sure to see us, but far enough away to make it seem unintentional. Standing closer to him than ever before, I slide my hands across the coarse stubble on Red's face and kiss him. A soft brush of our lips. It's not a great kiss by any means. Probably not even a convincing one—it feels icky and wrong, like when a family member accidentally kisses you on the lips instead of the cheek. When we pull apart, I swear I hear Derek's laugh.

So kissing isn't enough, then.

"Let's go." I grab Red's hand, and he follows without hesitation—unexpectedly smart enough to adhere to my rule about not saying anything stupid. Fingers interlaced with mine, he obediently walks out of the beer garden, past the closed vendor booths, and through the rows of parked vehicles.

"I get that I'm not supposed to say anything stupid, but I'm starting to worry you're about to murder me."

"I know you brought condoms. Where's your truck?"

He stops in his tracks and stares at me. "What the fuck is happening?"

Truthfully, I'm not sure what's happening either. I'm just riding the high, doing whatever my jacked-up emotions and the liquor are telling me to do. "Um . . . Well, if you agree to it, I was going to see if you'd fuck me on the hood of my ex's car. Payback, you know?"

Red throws his head back with a gut-busting laugh. "Holy. Shit. I don't know, Cass. That's wild."

"I asked you because you're the most unhinged man I know. If you won't, then point me in the direction of someone who will." My cheeks flame, burning my entire body from the inside out. I hadn't considered whether he might turn me down. *Shit.* I press a finger to my eye to hold back the embarrassed tears.

"I don't think you want to do this."

"You don't know what the fuck I want. You're here because I didn't want somebody who would try and talk me out of it. I just . . ." I'm starting to lose momentum now. "I forced myself to get dressed and put makeup on to come here, stupidly thinking I'd have a fun night. Then he shows up with the girl he's been cheating with for months, Shelby ditches me, and I'm stuck spending the night with you. I ran into Derek on my way out earlier, and he acted like I'm an ugly, pitiful loser. I hate it. I want to do something to get back at him—I don't even care if he ever finds out about it. Just, for once, I want to feel like I have a little bit of fucking power. I'm so tired of being the mature, polite, responsible one."

"He was wrong. You're beautiful."

"Thanks for the fake flattery. You're right, asking you to do this was unhinged and *so* not me. I don't do this kind of thing. I'm gonna head home."

He holds my shoulders, preventing me from spinning around to leave. "I'm not trying to kiss your ass. You do look beautiful. Not pitiful at all . . . even with your red face and crazy eyes. If you're serious about this . . ." He studies me in the faint glow of distant headlights, and the way his eyes bore into mine makes something in my heart trip up. Like he can see right through me. My head barely moves with a subconscious nod. "*Fuck*—okay, I'll do it. But we're making sure we leave behind enough evidence that he knows."

All I can do is nod again like a bobblehead.

"Oh, and Cass? If your dad finds out about this somehow, you're taking the blame because I refuse to be banned from the only bar in town."

"Oh my God. I can assure you he's the last person who would ever know about this. Glad to see your priorities are straight though, Red."

"You're one to talk." He smirks as his hands finally leave my shoulders.

"If we're doing this, I need you to fuck me like you hate me. Don't tell me I'm beautiful again or pretend like this is more than a quick revenge fuck."

"You think I was planning on making love on the hood of your ex's car?" He snorts. "Be right back."

In the time it takes for him to walk to his truck and back, my thoughts oscillate until I'm feeling dizzy. A little nauseous, even. This is probably a stupid idea . . . but wouldn't it be nice to know I kind of got him back? Red has more red flags than most guys I know . . . but he's also the one guy here who might be willing to do this. Simultaneously trying to talk myself into and out of this reckless plan, I locate Derek's obnoxious red car and lean against it with an anxious exhale.

This is just two people about to have purely transactional sex—he gets to come, and I get to feel like I stuck it to my ex. I exclusively see him at rodeos and the bar, where he's too busy with his friends and other women to give a shit about me. So there are minimal opportunities for things to get awkward, right?

"So, where are we doing this?" His voice forces me out of my spiraling thoughts.

"Oh, um . . . right here." I point to the hood I'm resting

on. My heart races as he steps forward, his rough hands falling to my bare knees.

"You sure you want—"

"Yes. Like you hate me, remember?" I allow my thighs to drift apart, making room for him to get even closer. Goosebumps prickle up in the wake of his fingers, leaving me shuddering as his callused hands stroke my legs.

Our eyes are locked, the whites of his gleaming in the moonlight. "Breathe, Cass."

I inhale deeply and, when he nods, let out a long exhale. The way he's staring into my soul sends a trickle of warmth down my spine, settling beneath my pelvic bone with a haunting ache. Feeling his hand slip farther up my leg, under the relaxed denim of my vintage Levi's skirt, I look down to make sure I'm not imagining it. Obviously, this was all my idea, but I didn't expect my body to react the way it is. The way *Red,* of all people, is making my underwear wet with a light stroke of my inner thigh should be criminal.

"Cute bracelet." I smile at him, trying to ease the sexual tension between us by shifting focus to the thin barbed wire wrapped around his wrist.

Of course he has barbed wire on his wrist.

"You like it? Got you a necklace to match." His hand leaves my leg and, for a split second, I'm longing for him to put it back. He shifts so the glow of a distant pole light catches, and I can see what he's trying to show me. Below the dense forest of black ink trees sprawling up his forearm, there's a tattoo along the back of his hand, running from thumb to index finger.

Barbed wire.

Before I can question what he means, his hand slips around my neck like a collar.

A barbed wire necklace.

"Fits perfectly, Cass. Looks sexy as hell, too."

My breath catches in my throat, stuck right at the spot where his fingers are pressed into my flesh. An involuntary whimper escapes my parted lips and, although it's dark, there's no missing the way his nostrils flare.

Fighting to maintain my composure, I snarl, "What did I tell you about not saying dumb shit? Please, let's just get this over with."

"Jesus, you really know how to turn a man on, don't you?" With a dramatic eye roll, he lets his hand fall back to my thigh, sending a course of heat up to my groin. "If you don't want to do this, say so and I'll stop."

"No, I do. Keep going."

Hesitant eyes narrow in on mine, not buying a word I'm saying. To prove I'm not having doubts, I lace my arms around his neck and smash my lips against his. They're surprisingly soft and warm, melding with mine. *Were they this soft when I kissed them earlier?* The hair at the nape of his neck's the perfect length to twirl around my fingers. Holding a steady hand on either side of my face, Red kisses back with an ardent groan. It's sloppy and frantic and hungry and—to my astonishment—*fucking good.* Nothing like the tense, uncomfortable kiss we shared earlier. His hands run through my hair, and a bite of my bottom lip forces another whimper from somewhere deep in my chest.

When his hand reaches under my skirt, I roll my hips into him. My core tightens, begging for attention while the seconds drag even slower than his hand. I hate that I want him to touch me but, *fucking hell,* I do.

His finger traces the cut of my underwear, then nudges it aside so the tight fabric catches my sensitive clit. Electrical currents shoot out in every direction, and I can't help the moan that Red stifles with his mouth. Repeating with the other edge, he lets my underwear gather between my labia. Even the slightest motion is enough to drag the thin cotton over my clit. Without thinking about what I'm doing, my hips rock gently on the car's hood, shifting the fabric. Inching me toward bliss.

Red breaks our kiss, staggering backward a step. He hasn't even properly touched me yet, but he's watching. Intently.

"Fuck, Cass. *Fuck.*" His gravelly voice sounds desperate and, for some ungodly reason, that makes me even more wet. I want him to want me. I want him to keep studying me with pure lust. So I spread my legs farther, pulling the thong fully to the side, and plunge two fingers deep inside myself.

So much for a quick revenge fuck. Now I'm masturbating on the hood of my ex's car while Red, the insufferable cowboy, watches with a carnal look in his eye. Sobering up just enough to realize what I'm doing, I blush and rip away my hand.

"I didn't tell you to stop. Keep going." He grips his cock through his jeans, rubbing the bulge slowly and never taking his gaze off my body. "I want to watch Wells Canyon's sweetheart make herself come right out in the open. Touch yourself, Cassidy. Play with your pretty little cunt for me."

I swallow hard. I should say no. Tell him to go screw himself. Of all people, he shouldn't affect me like this. He shouldn't have me *wanting* to do anything he asks.

With soaked fingers, I find my clit, stroking with a featherlight touch and frenzied intensity. I arch my back, letting my blond hair cascade down to the shiny red metal, and prop a cowboy boot up on the hood to keep from sliding, praying it leaves a nasty scratch. Red moves to hold my legs steady and wide open, and I watch him watching me.

"That's it—fuck your hand right here in public. You fooled me, Cass. I thought you were just a cocktease but you're a total fucking slut, aren't you?"

"No." The word comes out hoarse, less than a whisper. I'm not. Not usually. I don't know what the hell is happening to me right now. "Just tonight."

"Just for me."

"No." *Yes. But I'm not about to unpack why right now.* "Fuck you."

His chest heaves, and his face is flushed. Staring me down, he gnaws at his cheek, letting out a small groan now and then. His hand tightens on my shin like it's taking everything in him to refrain from touching me anywhere else. With Derek, I would be self-conscious but, extra five pounds or not, Red's making me feel like the sexiest goddamn woman alive.

"Oh my God," I moan as warm liquid rushes through me, and my fingers slow to a lazy circle, riding out the storm. Red's wide pupils reflect the moonlight and, without hesitation, he reaches out to feel the mess I made. Lightly running a finger across my entrance and up to my swollen clit, sending an exhilarating shiver up the length of my spine.

"Holy fuck. Look at you—that's the hottest thing I've ever seen." He slips a cool finger inside, stealing my breath. Instead of thrusting, like so many guys seem to do, he carefully draws the pad of his middle finger in a beckoning motion. Another finger slips in, and his eyes darken at my whimper.

"Making those sounds with only my fingers—you'll be screaming when I really fill you."

"God, you're *such* a douchebag."

"And you're going to look so fucking good stretched around my cock." He withdraws his fingers, leaving a void I'm desperate to feel him fill. Fingers, tongue, cock . . . I'll take anything. Not that I can ever confess that truth.

"Does that mean you're finally going to fuck me now?" I flop back onto the hood. The cold metal's shocking at first, then pleasant as I fight to catch my breath, waiting for him to put on the condom.

When I caught Derek cheating, my best friend since toddlerhood, Blair, told me there's no such thing as a truly original experience. I guess knowing millions of people have caught their boyfriend cheating was supposed to make me feel better. Staring up at the starry, endless sky, I wonder how many other people have had revenge sex on the hood of their ex's car with a guy they don't particularly like. Certainly feels original.

"Jesus Christ," I gasp—in spite of myself—when I glance down and see his cock. For a perfectly average-sized man, he's packing anything but an average-sized dick. Truly, I had been hoping it would be tiny or misshapen or something, so I could add that to the list of reasons why he's firmly on my "do not touch" list. Now I'm starting to wonder if him being a hotheaded prick will be enough to keep me from wanting this one-night stand to happen again. "I thought guys who act like total douchebags usually have tiny dicks."

"So you thought I was a douchebag with a small dick, and *that's* why you chose me to help make your ex jealous? Something isn't adding up here."

"Shut the fuck up, Red." I slide farther down the hood and grip his thick cock. And I do mean *thick*. Hopefully, he's smart enough to take this as an invitation to shut up and make better use of the limited time we have.

"You need to work on your dirty talk, sweetheart."

"I thought we agreed not to use that word."

"I'll call you whatever I want when you're the one begging for my cock."

"I'm not—" I start to protest, and he shakes his head in disbelief, then glances down to where I'm subconsciously tugging his dick in my direction. I drop it like a hot potato, and heat rushes to take up residence in my cheeks.

I can't believe I'm begging Red to fuck me. . . .

"I would *never* beg for your dick. I was just trying to determine if it'll fit."

Should not *have said that.*

He smirks. "Oh, it might be a tight fit, but I'm sure you can take it."

Positioning himself between my legs, he grabs hold of my thigh with one hand and fists his cock with the other. By the time he's notching the head at my entrance, I'm struggling to breathe. Waiting anxiously. Aching for him to fill me. Praying to feel him stretch me with his massive cock and slam balls deep.

He aggressively drags his shaft across my pussy, spreading my wetness down the length of him. The puddle between my legs is destroying any hope of hiding my attraction to him. My knees fall open wider, and he nudges the tip inside me—just enough that it causes intense pressure to collect between my hips.

Centimeter by goddamn centimeter, he pushes into me with a satiated look. "*Breathe,* Cass. I'm not even close to all the way in—you need to relax."

Not even close?

"What?" I gulp and focus on anything but the fact that Red's cock is so deep inside of me he might be touching my lungs. The way it's rearranging my internal organs would explain my sudden inability to breathe, though.

"Relax and take a breath." He groans. "Almost there, sweetheart."

On my exhale, his blunt fingernails dig into the extra padding around my hips, and he plunges deep. My bare ass slides against the metal hood, bunching my skirt around my waist. In a punishing thrust, he bottoms out, balls slapping against my damp skin, and I wrap my legs around his waist to force him deeper. With each pump, the tip hits the spot that has me writhing. I want all of him—every fucking inch. And I kind of hate how badly I want him, but then I prop myself on my elbows and watch as his cock drives into me, and I don't hate it at all. He's stretching and filling every bit of me, over and over. With each powerful thrust, the edge of my thong drags along his shaft and catches on my clit in a burst of stunning fireworks. His movement's slow and steady. And absolutely incredible.

"*Fuck,* you're so fucking tight. How the hell are you this tight, Cass?" He groans, his head tipping back so the muscles working in his throat are highlighted. His Adam's apple bobs in the dim light as he thrusts forward again. "*God*—I don't think I'm going to be able to make this last."

He leaves me panting and empty when he pulls out, bending down to run his flat tongue up my center, lapping me up. My breath hitches, and I knock the cowboy hat from his head to grip a handful of hair. My fingers weave around the soft strands, holding the fuck on like I'm about to ride a bull—even though I'm the one bucking when he hits my clit with the perfect amount of pressure and light suction. His hand's firmly planted on my stomach, restricting my movement. No amount of squirming or fighting will get me out from under the intense pleasure. When I wiggle, my spine's only pressed harder into the rigid metal hood.

"Red, you don't have to—" My words are cut off by his free hand smacking down on my mouth. I try to talk, despite the palm suffocating me, but it's no use.

I don't do this. I don't come when guys go down on me. It's too wet. Too messy. Too much.

But he's leaving me no choice. Every muscle stiffens in concert, and I feel all of my blood rush to my cheeks, then drain entirely as an orgasm tears through me. His large, warm hand quiets my moan, and his tongue draws out my pleasure until I'm quivering under him.

"Now I won't feel so bad when I come too quickly. At least I can say I got you off," he says, licking his bottom lip. My arousal glistens in his stubble, and his eyes tear me apart. I'm not entirely naked, but his gaze is enough to make me feel as though I am.

He seems proud. I'm horrified. It's one thing to have sex

with Red Thompson. It's another to know I came in and around his mouth. And the sated look in his hooded eyes is nearly making me feel *good* about doing it—like there was pleasure in it for him, too.

Fuck, there's something wrong with me for liking this. I wasn't supposed to *enjoy* having sex with him. This was supposed to be a means to an end; I assumed I'd be going home to make up for the subpar experience with my vibrator. Then I'd never think of this moment again.

Thank God he leaves little time for my brain to spiral itself off the deep end. Red sinks his cock back into me with a strangled moan, and his thumb draws circles on my clit until I'm right there again. This time he's right there with me.

"You like fucking me, don't you? You like feeling me deep in your tight cunt."

"Not . . . at . . . all." I struggle to get the words out between whimpers.

"Liar. Gonna come again for me, Cass?"

"You wish," I say through gritted teeth.

"Mmm, I think you are. I think you're gonna drench my cock like you did my face."

"Make me." I stare into his eyes, feeling a rush as he presses harder against my clit. *Please, make me.*

My nails drag across the hood, scratching the paint, as I desperately search for something to hold on to. Anything to keep me from floating above my body. My orgasm surges around his cock at the same time he drops his head with a final grunt. His face is flushed and his body shudders in one smooth wave.

"Fuck," we whisper in unison, seemingly both unsure whether we mean *Fuck, that was amazing* or *Fuck, what did we just do?*

Red

Denny has to shut one eye to drunkenly focus on what I'm saying. I don't understand my best friend's method, but he swears it helps him hear better. Though I've told him about having sex with Cass three times on the walk back to the truck, he's still struggling to make sense of it. I'm not convinced the fourth time's the charm.

"You. As in . . . *you*"—his index finger draws a sloppy circle around my face—"hooked up with Cassidy Bowman? Nah, I don't buy it. I've never heard of her sleeping with *anybody*. She's definitely too much of a good girl to hook up with you."

He climbs into the box of my pickup, and I hand him our sleeping bags. The biggest downside to living out at the ranch is that either somebody needs to buck up and be the designated driver, or we sleep in the truck bed. Tonight, it's the latter. No fancy driving apps available in a tiny town like Wells Canyon. There's technically one taxi, but the driver is drunk off his ass anytime after seven p.m. and too hungover to drive before ten a.m. Not to mention, I'd hate to see what he'd charge to take us that far—too rich for my blood.

"Give me one reason why I would lie about this shit." I smack him with my sleeping bag before unrolling it. As soon as my boots are off, I slip into the extremely uncomfortable makeshift bed. This was tolerable a decade ago. . . . Now I'm fully aware my thirty-three-year-old ass is going to wake up with a stiff neck and pounding headache.

"Okayyyy. How the hell did this happen then?" Denny wiggles down into his sleeping bag, sending a tremor through the entire truck box. "*Why* did it happen? You know if Dave finds out, we'll be fucked. We'll be banned from the bar and be forced to drive to Sheridan to drink. I love you, but I'll be real pissed if that happens."

"Why would he find out?"

"Dunno. He and Cass are pretty close, though."

"You think she's telling *her dad* about every guy she fucks? Who does that? I swear, man, some of the things you say—were you dropped as a baby? Drop-*kicked*, maybe?"

"I've fallen off my fair share of unbroken animals. Hit my head a few times—is what it is. Anyway, *why* and *how* did you and her become a thing?"

I drag a palm down my face, stopping briefly on my chin to stroke the coarse stubble, which was soaked with her cum a few hours ago. "She wanted to get back at her shitty ex-boyfriend for cheating on her, so I fucked her on the hood of his car. She scratched the shit out of it with her boots, too."

He shoots up, suddenly invested in the story. There's a slight wobble as he sits there, although it could be me who's wobbling. The world does seem to be spinning faster than usual.

"No shit. Did you stick around to see his reaction?" Denny asks.

"Fuck no. Shit got awkward immediately after, and she went home. I had some more drinks, played a round of lawn darts, and now I'm here."

"*Cool, cool, cool.* We're totally not allowed back at the Horseshoe. You had to be an awkward motherfucker, and now Cass is gonna barricade the door."

I let out a long exhale, knowing he could very well be

right. At the same moment my brain was exploding with thoughts of fucking Cass over and over again, she was obviously having an entirely different post-orgasm experience. She was right—I'm a douchebag. After a lifetime of daydreams about her, I was too lost in reliving the way her pussy fit me, the way her body reacted to my touch, and the feel of her hands on my skin to notice her leaving until it was too late to stop her.

A week later, it's the moment of truth. I haven't talked to Cass since the rodeo because that was the deal. We're never going to talk about what happened between us again. If only I could find a way to quit *thinking* about it.

Denny flings open the double doors with a dramatic display. "Guess you didn't fuck it up too bad."

I knew she wouldn't *actually* lock us out. Doing that would mean admitting something happened between us.

No, instead she's perfectly normal. As if I haven't been balls deep inside her or watched her eyes roll back as she came on my cock. I know I was drunk that night, but I was coherent enough to know we had amazing sex. It wasn't all in my head. I would die of alcohol poisoning before being too intoxicated to remember how it felt to have her. Her smell, her taste, her sounds. No amount of drinking could make me forget her coming on my face like a goddamn porn star. It was the hottest thing I've ever experienced.

"Hey, boys." She sets down six mugs of beer before we've even settled into our seats, predicting exactly what time we'd arrive and what we'd want without fail. We're in our usual spot against the back wall—just far enough away from the dance floor that annoying drunk girls don't ask us to dance, but close enough we can check them out.

"Cass, have I told you before how much I appreciate being

allowed in this fine establishment?" Genuinely meaning every word, Denny grabs hold of her forearm as she leans across the table to hand Colt a beer.

"Okay, how many road pops did you chug on the drive here?" she asks with a laugh, but her eyes cut to me, brutally slicing through my flesh. The only reason she isn't *literally* cutting me is because her dad, Dave, is twenty feet away and there'd be a lot of explaining to do.

She walks away, hair flowing behind her, and I stare without shame. I've always known she's gorgeous, but she also wasn't an option. Cassidy Bowman is so far out of my league, but I've tortured myself for years watching her from afar. Even in high school, she was pretty, had a huge group of friends, got perfect grades . . . entirely fucking untouchable for someone like me.

Until the night she wasn't.

The sight of Cass from across the busy bar quenches my thirst better than any amount of four-dollar beer, and I let myself drink her in. Everything from the golden waves bouncing on her shoulders to the perfectly heart-shaped ass in tight, wet-dream-worthy denim. I soak up her juicy, thick curves—tits barely contained by the low cut of her shirt and hips I want to sink my teeth into. I like that she's not stick thin; I could grab and bite and rough her up without worrying about breaking her.

With my brain stuck in an unending loop of fantasies about her, the hours fly by. Until it's sometime after midnight, and I've lost count of how many beers deep I am. It's Cassidy's fault. Both for looking so good I had to keep bringing her back to the table—even though she all but ignored me—and for not cutting me off.

As I stumble to the bathroom, my fingers drag along the hallway's textured wallpaper. My knees threaten to buckle when a bass drop rattles through the old floorboards. This is the problem with staying here past midnight. The classic country music switches to dance party garbage right around the same time I become too drunk to tolerate the kind of crowd that likes this noise. I push through the cheesy saloon-style bathroom door and firmly hold a palm to the wall above the urinal.

I'm stuck somewhere between needing to take a deep breath to stop from gagging and knowing the smell of piss and urinal pucks will make me hurl. So I breathe strictly through my mouth and pee as fast as humanly possible.

"Hey, man, we're getting ready to head out." Colt drums his fingers on the doorframe.

"Yeah, give me a minute," I reply, zipping my fly as I stumble toward the trough-style sink to wash my hands.

A splash of cold water on my face helps snap me out of it. I don't vomit when I drink—I do a lot of other dumb shit, but I can hold my liquor. After a forceful exhale and a few blinks to clear my blurred vision, I stroll back out to the bar floor.

I turn the corner just in time to see some drunk dipshit grope Cassidy's plump ass. She turns like she's going to slap him, and I can't fucking wait to watch her ruin this man's life. But, to my horror, he's hit with nothing more than a scowl and a few words I can't make out.

That won't be enough to teach him a lesson.

I see red.

The deep red haze washes over me, glossing my eyes and itching the lizard part of my brain that wants to throw the punch and worry about consequences later. I guess I hit him. Probably even a few times. It's hard to tell when you're in a blackout state. Between my heartbeat pounding in my skull and the obnoxiously loud electronica music, I can't hear anybody around me. The ass-grabbing pervert hits back and, while I'm sure I'll feel it when I come down from the adrenaline rush, I don't even wince at his fist making contact with my jaw. My brain shuts down, and I'm swinging, going through the motions until I'm snapped out of it by Denny and Colt grabbing my shoulders to haul me away from the scrap.

"Get the fuck out of here before you're all banned." Cassidy's voice rings out over the commotion happening in my head. Then, most likely directed at me, she adds, "Seriously, what the fuck is wrong with you?"

"Me?" I shout. "Fuck is wrong with *that guy*?" I point and glare at the ugly, pervy motherfucker nursing his tender jaw.

Cass follows us out the front doors, leaving Dave behind the bar shaking his head. He's not even fazed. Fights are a regular enough occurrence, and it's not uncommon for me to be involved in one way or another. At least I have that on my side. If he suspected I was trying to defend his daughter for any reason other than enjoying a good scrap, I'd be a dead man.

"Let me have a word with him," Cass snaps at the rest of the crew.

Unsurprisingly, they back off immediately, moving to linger by the tailgate of a truck a few stalls over.

"Are you trying to accomplish something by showing up here acting jealous and possessive? *Jesus Christ.*" She combs a hand through her hair, dropping her voice to barely more than a whisper. "We hooked up once and it will *never* happen again. We were drunk and made a stupid decision—nothing more. Pull this white knight shit one more time, and you won't be allowed back here."

"So I'm supposed to let—"

She cuts me off with a sneer. "You're supposed to ignore me like usual. Treat me like I'm any random server at a bar. Let *me* deal with the assholes."

Easier said than fucking done. I've never ignored her. I've paid more attention to Cassidy than I can ever admit. Have since the day I met the sassy six-year-old version of her on the playground over twenty years ago. Maybe I've made it seem like I don't see her, but we wouldn't have hooked up in the first place if I usually ignored her.

She sighs, turning to walk back inside. "Go fuck somebody else and forget about me, *please*."

Cassidy

Six weeks after the rodeo

I telepathically threaten my best friend, Blair, while pacing my kitchen. When her smiling face appears on the video call, I burst into tears for approximately the thirteenth time this morning. Truthfully, I'm shocked I have tears left to shed.

"Hey, oh my God." Her face blanches at the sight of me. "Sorry I missed all your calls. I've been swamped at work. What's going on?"

I scrub my hands over my face, smearing mascara and snot. A rattling, painful breath overinflates my lungs, and there's no option but to scream to release it. A bloodcurdling, peel-the-wallpaper type of scream.

"Cass. What the fuck is going on? Is somebody dead? What's happening?"

"I don't even know. You're the medical professional, so please tell me." I bite my lip, frantically wiping my blurry eyes with my free hand, and tap my phone screen to switch to the rear-facing camera. Showing her the half dozen pregnancy tests I've peed on so far today.

"Cassidy!"

"That's why I've called you eighty billion times. I'm freaking the fuck out here."

"Holy fucking shit! I don't think you needed to take

that many tests, but kudos to you for being so well hydrated. No need for my medical advice, Cass. You're definitely pregnant."

Obviously, I knew that. The second pink line showed up within minutes for each test. *Super pregnant.* So pregnant I didn't need to wait the full time span on the instructions for confirmation. So pregnant the test line is somehow darker than the control. But hearing her say it out loud hits me like a ton of bricks.

"What do I do?" I ask her, while also talking to myself.

"Well, okay . . . speaking as your nurse practitioner, you have options. Do you know what they are?"

"Yeah, yeah. In theory, I do. I just need you to tell me which one to pick."

She laughs under her breath. "You need to decide for yourself. I mean, if you really want input, you could always tell Derek . . . but only if you want to. It's not his decision, at the end of the day."

Derek. She assumes I'm pregnant with Derek's baby. Of course she does. That's what everybody will assume. And I could've easily convinced myself that was the case, except I got my period the day after we broke up. The phone hits the table, and I bury my head in my hands.

"Except . . ." I scrunch my nose up and catch her staring back with wide eyes. "He isn't the sperm donor, so there's no sense involving him."

"You've been holding out on me? You found a rebound guy and didn't bother to tell me about it? Here I thought we were best friends, asshole. Who's the guy?"

"I can't tell you. It's the most embarrassing thing. I drank a lot, and it was a moment of weakness—I mean, *clearly,* I was ovulating at the time. So we'll chalk it up to primal instinct."

"Cassidy Marie Bowman. Tell me this instant. I've been

your best friend for close to thirty years and I demand to know who you slept with to get over your moldy muffin of an ex."

I don't know if the nausea is morning sickness or anxiety induced, but I take a long sip of water to get rid of the bad taste in my mouth. And to delay the inevitable.

"Nobody can know this, okay?"

"Sure. Unless you decide to keep the baby . . . then I think people will find out."

I cover my mouth with my hand, letting the word trickle out from between my fingers. "Red."

"Thompson? Are you messing with me? What the hell were you thinking?"

"I told you. *Ovulation.* I was at the mercy of thousands of years of human instinct and a few too many beers."

"Wait . . . hold up. Didn't you have a crush on him at one point? Maybe that's why you chose him to hook up with. Do you secretly have a crush on him still?"

"Don't you dare. I was twelve and collected crushes as a hobby. I had a crush on Max from *A Goofy Movie,* for Christ's sake. Briefly liking Red when I was a dumb kid means absolutely nothing."

"Oh my God, I forgot about your Max phase." She laughs so intensely it turns into nothing but a wheeze. "To be fair . . . I kind of get Red's allure. He's always been hot for a ginger, and puberty did good things for him. I think it's honestly better than if you were pregnant with Derek's baby. Fuck that cheating prick. Red might have a temper and be rough around the edges and be a bit of a manwhore and—"

"You're not doing a great job selling him. I know I fucked up. Derek and Alyssa came to the rodeo. He said some rude shit. Ugh, and he looked at me like *I* was the pathetic one between us." My blood pressure rises thinking about the interaction. "Red was available and willing to help me get back at him, so we fucked on the hood of Derek's car. Left behind some scratches in the paint, and I think he actually hung the condom off the side mirror afterward."

Blair cackles. Doubling over with laughter and accidentally dropping her phone on the hospital floor.

"Fuck, that's incredible. Did I just become team Red?" When she picks the phone back up, tears brim her lower lids and she's massaging her cheek muscles. "Okay. Anyway, my point stands. If you want input, I guess you'll have to talk to Red then."

"I'd feel better if you didn't chuckle every time you say his name." I pick up test after test, staring at the taunting parallel lines, pacing the small space between my kitchen and living room. "I'm not talking to him about this."

"It's your choice anyway, babe. How are you feeling? Any nasty pregnancy symptoms?"

"My tits hurt so bad I want to chop them off, I'm sleeping fourteen hours a day and could use more, throwing up multiple times per day, and Red is the father. Guess you could say I'm living the dream."

Living in full delusion, I told myself it was a stomach bug for the first three days. Then decided it had to be a PCOS flare-up. Until there was no denying the reality of what was happening.

"With any luck, you'll feel a bit better in a few weeks . . . until all the other symptoms start, anyway. Then it'll go to shit again."

"Thanks for that little ray of hope, you jerk."

"Cass . . . you don't have to keep it."

"Yeah." I swallow the saliva suddenly pooling in the back of my throat. "It's just . . . I don't know if I can do that—no offense."

"Hey, I said it's your decision. Just because I made a different choice doesn't mean I'm trying to sway you. Remember that, even with your PCOS and Hashimoto's, if it happened once it can happen again. You don't have to have a baby *right now,* if you don't want to. But if you want to, then I'll support the crap out of your decision."

"Yeah . . . I'll think about it."

"Good. I gotta run and finish my shift. Keep me updated on everything, please? I wish I could be there with you in person so we could co-parent. Sister wives without a husband." She glances up from the phone screen and frowns at something in the distance. "I love you. Call me later, yeah?"

"Love you." I tap to hang up and fling myself onto the plush gray sofa.

Fuck.

There are options. Just because I'm thirty-one years old doesn't mean I'm in a place where I'm prepared to have a baby. This was supposed to be something I did once I had my shit together. With somebody I care about. In a situation where the whole town wouldn't talk about me. I wanted a well-thought-out plan to follow, not a future full of unknowns and chaos.

I also have two endocrine disorders I was told would make it harder for me to get pregnant—and stay pregnant. One messes with my thyroid, and the other my ovaries. Basically, some part of my body is hurting at any given moment, no matter what I do I'll never be skinny, and my hair is consistently either falling out or growing in places I'd prefer it didn't. The only thing worse than living with Hashimoto's disease and polycystic ovary syndrome is the years I spent suffering without explanation. At least now things are fairly well managed with medication.

After hearing the diagnosis spiel from my doctor, I naively thought it would take months or years of trying to conceive, not a spur-of-the-moment hookup and a defective condom. Clearly I've been fed a load of horseshit, based on the tests strewn across my kitchen table.

Even still, I can't shake the fear of infertility I've had since the day I was diagnosed five years ago. Anxiety grabs hold of the reins, veering me toward the decision that seems to be the most obvious choice. Even if it's also the most terrifying.

I'm having a baby.

My head hits the steering wheel with a sob outside of the doctor's office in Sheridan following blood confirmation and an official approximation of how far along I am.

Eight weeks.

In the days since those two pink lines, I haven't left my bed . . . except to throw up. It worked well enough to tell my dad I had the flu. Thankfully, because I'm a server in his bar, he insisted I stay far away. Which means I've been left alone to think. Crying, panicking, binge-watching bad early-2000s reality television, and trying—though failing miserably—to come up with a solid plan for how to handle this. Waiting impatiently for the blood work to confirm what my boobs and digestive system were already telling me.

It's real. I'm pregnant.

It's actually happening.

Pulling out of the parking lot, I'm armed with an ultrasound booked for next week, a container of prenatal vitamins, and a sample of ginger candies to curb nausea. I chuck three into my mouth and immediately dry heave at the taste, spitting them out on the highway back to Wells Canyon. Not long after, I toss the entire container out the window because simply looking at the plastic bottle makes me want to vomit.

I make the drive home on autopilot, vision blurred and head foggy. Scared shitless, I pull my car into its usual spot outside the Horseshoe. So early in the day, the parking lot is empty save for heat waves radiating off the dark cement and my dad's old Ford. My legs shake so violently, it's a struggle to get out of the car and walk into the Horseshoe. Like a shadow of a girl, I float outside my body—attached but not fully me.

The August mid-morning sun beats down on my shoulders while I catch my breath, staring up at the neon bar sign hanging above the entrance.

Maybe this doesn't need to be done right now. It could wait another day or two. It might be fun to turn up with a baby in approximately thirty-one weeks. Metaphorically hard-launch a baby like all the trendy people do online when they get a new boyfriend. Then again, I can't afford to feed myself if I don't work, and my dad will storm my house if I stay holed up for too long. I need to tell him sooner rather than later. Rip the bandage off.

Dad's stocking the shelves when I drag my sorry ass through the front doors and sit on a worn wooden bar stool. The same bar stool I've perched on at least a million times. Scribbling in coloring books as a toddler, doing homework as a kid, eating French fries and texting friends as a teenager, and drinking after a long shift in my twenties. Raised by a single dad with strict rules about me going out, I spent an inordinate amount of time in the bar when I was underage; this bar stool and Dad's spinny chair in his office were my usual babysitters.

It's not a fancy establishment, but it's home. With mismatched chairs, a couch that probably should've been burned twenty years ago, and a TV with a faulty volume control that makes it either deafening or muted. Not a single inch of the small wooden dance floor is without a scuff or dent. The far corner—next to the Pull Tab machine and unplugged jukebox—may as well be sporting a RESERVED placard because nobody sits there but Wells Ranch cowboys.

Today, the familiar scent of alcohol, fried food, and Bar Keepers Friend cleanser make my stomach turn. But I know if I turn around and leave, I'll never work up the courage to tell my dad what's going on.

"Hey, kiddo. If you're still feeling crappy you gotta get

outta here. I can't risk getting people sick." Judging by the concern on his face, I must look at least half as terrible as I feel.

"I'm fine, Dad. Well . . . I'm not fine. But I'm not contagious."

Tossing his cleaning rag down, he rushes around the end of the bar to rub slow circles on my back. "Are you having a bad PCOS flare-up? Do we need to take you to the doctor? I can shut things down for the night and drive—"

"Dad. I just came from the doctor," I interrupt, speaking around the uncomfortable lump in my throat. The longer I sit here, shaking and letting him coddle me, the harder it's going to be to say what I came here to say. "I'm not having a flare-up. I got blood work done today to check my medication dosages, and it's all good. My endocrinologist is actually going to be keeping an extra close eye on me for the next while because . . ." I close my eyes and let out an exhale. "Because I'm pregnant."

His shoulders drop, taking my heart along with them. *Fuck.* For at least a full minute, he's completely silent. And I wish he would scream at me or throw something. Anger would be less heavy than pure disappointment.

"I'm sorry. I didn't mean for . . . I think I'm going to—no, *I know* I'm keeping it. So . . . *surprise.*" Jazz hands do nothing to turn this into exciting news; I tuck my wiggling fingers into my armpits and stare at him.

"Oh, Cassie." He sighs. "I don't know what to say. . . . This isn't what I wanted for you, but I guess that doesn't matter now, does it?" His massive hand rubs across my forearm, and I fall into him. Like a little girl, holding tight to my daddy's chest and soaking his shirt with my tears. "It'll be okay. You'll be okay. Have you talked to Derek?"

"No." He doesn't need to know Derek's not the father. One shocking piece of news at a time. We can cover that in a separate conversation down the road. "I'm not going to."

"And you're sure that you're going to . . ." The words come out hoarse, dying off before he finishes saying what I think he wants to say.

I mutter against the clean-smelling shirt fabric, "Yes, I'm sure. I'm keeping the baby."

"Well, against all odds, I raised a beautiful, strong woman on my own. I have no doubt you'll do an amazing job without that cheating bastard. And you have my help—always." He kisses the top of my head, patting my hair until I stop weeping.

"Thanks, Dad." I dab at the corners of my eyes with my sleeve. "Good thing I have the best parent to learn from."

"And, on the upside, this means I get to be a grandpa. I gotta admit, that's pretty cool. Even if I'm *way* too young to be a grandpa." He lightly nudges me with his elbow.

Sniffling, I smile for the first time. "Yeah, pretty cool."

"Are you doing okay, kiddo?"

I snort. "Not at all. I'm freaking the hell out on top of feeling terrible all the time—seriously, why call it morning sickness when it's an all-day thing?"

"Your mom was sick as a dog with you, too. It'll get better and, I can tell you firsthand, it'll be so worth it. This baby is going to be the best thing that's ever happened to you—ask me how I know. Let's have some ice cream. That always helps when you're feeling down."

I gag. "Hard pass."

Red

Ten weeks after the rodeo

"Atta girl, Heathen." I hand over half of my apple to my red mare, then start brushing her sweat-soaked body in the dusky barn. She didn't try to throw me today, which is wildly out of character for her. Deserving of a treat, for once. Although the way she side-eyes me while chewing makes me wonder if stroking her ego was a smart idea—bet any money I'll spend half the day tomorrow putting her back in her place.

When I'm finished, I turn her out with the rest of the horses for the night. Shaking my head as she immediately flops to the ground and rolls. The mane I just spent five minutes brushing is now full of dirt and twigs. *Fuckin' horse.*

A deep voice rings out in the darkness when I'm halfway between the barn and the bunkhouse. "Wait up."

Spinning in the dusty gravel, I see Denny hoofing it toward me.

"What's up?" I look him up and down. He's acting like he's about to piss his pants, jittery and with a strange look in his eye.

"I've been waiting to talk to you all day, man." He catches his breath, sucking back a devilish smile. "Have you heard anything from Cassidy lately?"

Cassidy? Why would I have talked to her? "Bowman? Can't say I have."

"Might want to. Apparently, the girls heard a rumor in town." I assume he means his two older brothers' girls: Jackson's wife, Kate, and Austin's fiancée, Cecily. "I mean, you guys only hooked up the one time at the rodeo, right? I'm sure you're fine."

"Spit it out, man." My heart's thundering against my ribcage. Despite a sneaking suspicion of what he's trying to get at, I need to hear him say it.

"Maybe it's a bullshit rumor, but she might be pregnant. . . ." I don't hear the rest of what he says—it turns to gibberish. My brain's liquifying, unable to think of any words except one. *Pregnant.* I drag a palm across my stubbled jaw and stare blankly at Denny.

"It can't be yours, though." His words suddenly become sharp and crisp again. "No news is good news. She would've told you."

"Right." Would she have told me? She didn't want anybody to know we hooked up in the first place. Admitting she's pregnant with *my baby* would make it awfully hard to deny we fucked.

"You wrapped it up, right?"

"Yeah, of course."

"Then I'm sure you're good, man. Don't stress about it." He slaps me on the shoulder and strolls into the bunkhouse like he didn't just drop a fucking atom bomb into my lap.

If only it were easy to simply *not stress about it.* For the rest of the night, the rumor consumes every thought. I go to bed early because my eyes can't focus well enough to differentiate between a club and a spade during poker with the other ranch hands. Then I dream about Cass turning up on my doorstep with a baby. And it's the first thing on my mind as I splash cold water over my face in the morning. I can't even enjoy my coffee; my stomach's churning as if I chugged back a two-six of vodka last night. Assuming it's mine, she's close to three months along already.

Shit. Does that mean she decided to keep it?

As we sit around the massive kitchen table up at the ranch's "big house," Jackson assesses me in the same way he does an unbroken horse, with an intimate understanding of exactly what's going on between the ears. I fall smack-dab in the middle of him and Denny in age, so the three of us caused nothing but trouble around the ranch as kids. We may not be related by blood, but they're more of a family to me than the four biological brothers I have. Growing up on a rural cattle ranch with a permanently exhausted mother and a drunk, violent dad forces you to find your chosen family pretty early.

Jackson clears his throat. "Denny talked to you, I assume?" Thankfully, the kitchen's busy enough for nobody to give a shit about our conversation.

"Sure did." I swallow the bile rising in my throat.

"You good to work today?"

Not a fucking chance. I don't even think I have the wherewithal to tack up my horse, something I've done half a million times.

"No. Not at all, man. Once I'm out there, it'll be fine, though."

"Aus," Jackson calls to the oldest of the three brothers, who's drinking coffee at the far end of the weathered wooden table. "Red's off today. He needs to go handle something. I'll work in his place."

Austin glances up at us with a skeptical side-eye. "Okay. You good, Red?"

Whatever magical touch Cecily has that mellowed out his harsh attitude over the last year, I like it. The old Austin wouldn't have been so quick to give a ranch hand the day off when we're arguably in the busiest season for cattle ranching. With the amount of work to be done, he'd have all twenty of us working sixteen-hour days, seven days a week, if it was legal.

"I'll let you know in a few hours, boss."

"Sounds a bit inauspicious."

"Don't know what that means, but . . . if there's anything to share, I'll tell you guys later."

Cassidy's house is easy enough to find by process of elimination. Like sorting cattle. Wells Canyon has about two thousand residents, and I know where at least half of them live, so I home in on the houses I don't know. I wind my piece-of-shit Dodge down the quiet streets, reading mailbox names and searching for her crappy little blue car. Thankfully, I've seen it parked outside the Horseshoe enough times to spot it from a mile away, in the driveway of a small white rancher with a bright-yellow door.

This is fucking stupid. I can't show up at her house at seven a.m. and ask if she's pregnant with my baby out of the blue. Who the fuck does that? It's completely unhinged.

We had sex *one time.* Even if she is pregnant—which I don't know for sure—the odds of it being mine are incredibly low. I should drive back to Wells Ranch and pretend this didn't happen. Not knowing one way or the other will eat me alive, but enough whiskey can cure that problem.

Then again, I came all this way. And as soon as she confirms this was all a misunderstanding, we can carry on. She can tell me I'm being the world's biggest moron, slap me, and we'll never talk about any of this again. Like she wanted.

Doesn't matter that I saw her in a new light that night. Not just the funny little girl from elementary school. Not just the popular and smart girl who wouldn't even look in my direction in high school. Not just the snarky, pretty waitress from the Horseshoe. She's fucking gorgeous. A sexual goddess. Absolute perfection. And she wanted me, even though she tried so damn hard to pretend like she didn't.

Doesn't matter that I'd do practically anything to have her again. There are three ways this can go:

1. She's pregnant with my kid and didn't want me to find out.
2. She's pregnant with Derek's kid, and they're back together.
3. She's not pregnant, and I'm about to ask if she is, which is a good way to get punched in the face. You *never* ask a woman if she's pregnant.

And, sitting on the street in front of her house, it dawns on me that I have no idea if she lives alone. If her dad, Dave Bowman, answers the door, I'm as good as dead. If her cheating ex-boyfriend opens the door, he's going to try to kick my ass—and fail, for sure. Even still, I've never let the fear of being punched in the face stop me from making bad decisions before, so I shut the truck down with a shudder, stride up to her front door, and ring the bell.

"What the fuck are you doing here?" she asks with half-closed eyes, squinting to adjust to the early morning light. She's in a pink pajama set, hair piled on top of her head, and not wearing any makeup. *Shit. I woke her up*. Not a great start. Admittedly, sometimes I forget not everybody starts their day at four o'clock in the morning.

A few wavy strands of hair fall over her face, and she reaches up to tuck them behind her ear. We simultaneously realize she's wearing a thin tank top with no bra, and her arms quickly fold over her chest. But not before I capture details about the size and texture of her puffy nipples through the light pink fabric. It seems silly she'd be worried about that when I've licked her pussy before but, then again, it was dark and I didn't get to see much of her. Certainly not as much as I'd have liked to.

"Care to explain why you showed up here and woke me up, asshole?" Her bare foot taps on the wood floor inside the entry.

"Uh—" *Shit. What am I doing here?* "I just heard some things and, y'know, small-town bullshit. But it's kind of fucking me up, so I was hoping you could clear the air."

She nods slowly. "Okay, um . . . want to elaborate on what kind of things you heard?"

She's seriously going to make me say it.

I scratch the back of my neck, mentally preparing for the slap or kick to the groin inevitably coming my way. "That you're pregnant."

"Fuck." The word comes out on a wispy breath. The skinny strap on her tank top is a cunt hair away from slipping off her freckled shoulder. And it takes all I have not to reach out to fix it.

"So you are then?" I tuck my tongue into my cheek and release a long breath. It's absolutely insane my knees haven't given out, but somehow I'm still standing. I do need to lean against the doorframe to stay that way, though. I stammer, "Okay. Wow."

"Come sit." She steps back from the door and, in a daze, I stumble my way into the small living room. Then I find myself sitting on her couch, gawking at her, waiting for one of two leftover outcomes. And I'm completely fucked up over which one I'd prefer. I didn't think I wanted a kid right now . . . possibly ever. I'm not cut out to be a parent—my childhood was too fucked up, my life now is too wild, my future is too uncertain. But also, her ex is a complete tool and doesn't deserve her any more than I do.

"Don't love that rumors are already flying, but I guess there's no way it would stay a secret forever." She pulls a thick buffalo-plaid blanket over her bare legs on the gray recliner opposite me. "I'm sorry I didn't tell you. I've known for a few weeks, and it's been a lot to process."

"Uh . . . okay. So then—it's mine then? You're sure?" No clue how I'm able to form words. My heart's seized up, all the air in the room is gone, and my jaw's hanging like it's broken. Not to mention the painful burning in my eyes, as if I'm trapped in a dust storm.

"Yeah, I'm sure." Her nose scrunches, no doubt hating having to admit it.

"Well, *fuck,*" I blurt out. And I immediately regret it, because it feels like that's not the way I should react in this situation.

"Yeah." She pinches the bridge of her nose and stares at the ceiling like she's trying not to cry. *Shit.* Now I *really* regret not having a more positive reaction. "I don't expect or want anything from you. It was my stupid idea that got me into this mess, and I'll handle it on my own."

I gulp. "Handle it? Like . . ."

"Bad wording. No, I'm not getting an abortion. It's my choice and—"

I hold a hand up to stop her. "Okay, I'm not trying to fight you on it."

"Shut up and let me explain. Everything I've ever been told is that I might have a hard time getting pregnant because of some medical stuff I have going on." She slowly twirls a piece of hair around her finger and watches out the window. "Even though this isn't exactly *ideal,* I don't know if this might be my only opportunity. I'm keeping the baby, but I don't need your help or your money or anything—don't worry about that."

My fingernails are gnawed to stubs by the time I work up a response. "No, Cass. If you say it's mine, then I'm right here with you. I want to be here, involved as much as I can be. I'll pay for shit, change fucking diapers, whatever you need. At least, until your dad skins me alive."

"He doesn't know . . . about you. He assumed it's Derek's, and I didn't correct him."

Good. *Great.* I don't know why the thought of Dave believing his daughter got knocked up by her shitty ex gives me heartburn, but it does.

"Yeah, well, you need to tell him. Because it's about to become *real fucking obvious* who your baby daddy actually is. I'm not sitting back and letting everybody think you're pregnant with that dipshit's baby."

"Fuck off, Red. You don't get to saunter in here and tell me what to do. We aren't friends, we aren't in a relationship. We had one drunk hookup because I was pissed off at my ex-boyfriend. That doesn't mean I suddenly like you. I'm not a complete thundercunt, so I'll let you buy shit for the baby, if you seriously want to be involved. *That's it.*"

"Fuck that. If I'm in, I'm all the way in. I'm not just going to be the father who buys the odd box of diapers and visits on Christmas. You think you hate me now? Watch how annoying I can be if you don't accept my help."

"Fine." She takes a deep breath. The Cass I know doesn't give in to me that easily. "But there's going to be ground rules. For one, you need to give me time to talk to my dad, okay? Don't go charging into the Horseshoe on a bender, thinking you'll be my white knight. I'll tell him when I'm ready. Two, don't get it twisted and think you can boss me around now."

I've never given a shit about following rules. I remember Jackson saying he turned into a total softie when Odessa, his five-year-old daughter, was born. Apparently, this is a little taste of that because, *fucking hell,* I'm looking across the small, neatly decorated living room at the future mother of my child. And, out of nowhere, I'm inclined to follow every single rule she lays out for me.

"Okay. Fine. Deal."

She relaxes into the recliner, losing the sharpness in her expression and smoothing a hand over her hair. I finally take a moment to truly see her. She looks . . . beautiful, don't get me wrong, but also tired, pale, and like she's had better days.

"How are you feeling?" I ask. She starts to object—despite appearing drained, she's still got some wild horse spirit, unwilling to let me ask a simple question without a fight. I cut her off. "*Easy.* The next eighteen years are gonna really blow if you can't let me say anything without pushback. I get it, I'm not your boyfriend and I'm not trying to be. But asking a pregnant person how they're feeling is a normal fucking question, Cass."

"Sorry, I'm just cranky and tired. I literally could sleep for sixteen hours a day and it wouldn't be enough. I'm going for blood work in a couple of days and, hopefully, a dosage change will help with the fatigue." She purses her lips in thought. "Um, and I'm puking my guts out multiple times a day. Did you know 'morning sickness' can happen all the time? *I didn't.* Apparently it should stop soon, though."

"You've been to the doctor? Had an ultrasound?"

"Oh, yeah." She stands up and walks into the connected kitchen, returning seconds later with a paper in hand. Just when I think this entire thing can't feel more terrifying than it already does, I see a blip of grayish white on a black background and my stomach twists like I'm on a Tilt-A-Whirl. "It doesn't look like much yet, but that's the baby. And, uh, healthy heartbeat and everything. My due date is March tenth."

"Can I come next time? To your doctor's appointment or ultrasound?"

"Well, there's no more ultrasounds for another couple of months. Sorry. If you want to keep that, you can. The ultrasound tech printed off two, and I was going to give it to my dad but . . . if you want—"

"I do. Thanks." I smile at her, delicately slipping the paper into the front pocket of my flannel button-up. "Um . . . not to pry but, dosage change? Are you okay?"

She rolls her eyes with a groan. "Jesus. Didn't know we were going to get all up in my business this morning. *Yes, I'm fine.* I have Hashimoto's disease and polycystic ovary syndrome—they're chronic illnesses. Both are pretty well managed, for the most part. Um . . . except, I guess I should tell you I also have a higher risk of miscarriage. So I'd prefer we keep this quiet for now, despite the rumors."

Twenty minutes ago, I was driving around silently praying she'd say the pregnancy rumor was false. Funny how quickly that changed. Now the thought of her losing this baby has my heart slamming into my chest. I'd be in less agony if I ripped the stupid organ out and stomped on it with my boot.

"Of course, Cass. Listen, I know you think I'm a fuckup and I'm probably the last person in the world you wanted to have a kid with. But I'm here if you need help with *anything*."

"I don't need help, Red. I do need you to leave before I throw up in front of you. I haven't eaten yet, and my body likes to punish me for delaying breakfast by throwing up."

"Do you want me to make break—"

"Go!" she screams, already halfway down the hall.

It doesn't feel right to leave, but it also doesn't feel right to stay. So I shut her front door softly behind me, then drive back to the ranch with one hand on the steering wheel and the other over my chest pocket, holding the most important photo of my life secure.

Cassidy

Twelve weeks pregnant (baby is the size of an Oreo)*

I wish somebody had told me getting pregnant meant people bothering you whenever you're trying to sleep. Though, to be fair, I'm almost always trying to sleep. First it was Red yesterday morning. Then Shelby during my midday nap. Blair called five times after bedtime. And my dad turned up early this morning with breakfast burritos that smelled so strongly of eggs, I vomited in the kitchen sink.

Whoever the fuck is at my door at nine p.m. on my night off can die a slow, painful, miserable . . .

"Red? What do you want?"

He smiles sheepishly at me, backlit by the orange glow of a streetlamp, and holds up a brown paper bag. "Fuck. I woke you up again, didn't I?"

"If it wasn't you, it would be somebody else. Why are you here?" My attention shifts from his face to the bag and back again.

"Can I come in? I got you some stuff."

My eyebrows knit together in confusion. Too tired to argue, I step aside and follow him into the living room. The

---

* Pregnancy weeks are counted by the number of weeks since the mother's last menstrual period.

bag lands on the coffee table with a heavy *thunk,* and he gestures at me to open it.

"I hope you aren't mad, but I told Jackson and Kate last night. Kate gave me a list of some things you might find helpful. I wasn't planning on getting over here this late. We're finishing up haying this week, and today ended up being longer than . . . anyway, take a look."

What the hell? What part of our conversation yesterday made it seem like *this* is what I want from him? I don't need him to buy me shit. I don't need him to be showing up at my house unexpectedly. *I don't need him.*

I do love presents, though, and I suppose there's no harm in taking a peek. Reaching in, my fingers pinch around the first thing they touch.

A massive bag of Jolly Ranchers?

"Kate said the ginger candies were disgusting, but apparently Jolly Ranchers can help when you feel nauseous, too. Plus, it's a bit less obvious, since you don't want everybody to know yet." He leans forward, his elbows resting on his knees, watching me hesitantly.

I swallow hard. Ironic how the mention of anti-nausea candies makes me want to hurl. "Yeah, Kate's right. *Terrible.* I threw those ginger candies out the window somewhere on the highway."

Continuing on, I find bath bombs, Epsom salts, belly butter, an eye mask, sparkling grape juice, junk food. . . . It's like I'm working my way through Mary Poppins's magical bag with how much stuff he brought. Red's watching with a smile. Giving me the same look I remember my dad having on Christmas morning when I was a kid—eager for my reaction while expecting absolutely nothing in return.

"Red, what the actual fuck? This is too much. I can't accept all this. I told you, we aren't friends and we aren't together. It's really inappropriate for you to buy me presents."

"Well, I can't take it back and I don't know anybody else

who can use whatever the hell belly butter is. Anyway, Kate made the shopping list, so pretend it's from her, if that makes you feel less weird about it."

"Thank you." Stupid pregnancy hormones. I hate that I have to blink up to the ceiling to stop myself from crying. What bizarre timeline am I living in where Red has the ability to do something that makes me feel anything other than exasperation?

"I'll let you get to sleep now. I thought you should have this stuff sooner rather than later." His hands run along the tops of his denim-clad tree-trunk thighs as he moves to stand.

"Maybe we should swap numbers? So you don't wake me up with another surprise visit. Plus, you know, in case anything happens that I need to tell you about." I hold my phone out, Red quickly following suit. With a few simple taps of a finger, I have a phone number I wouldn't have ever expected to need or want.

Popping a green apple Jolly Rancher into my mouth, I bus my last table of the night and try to ignore the uneasy feeling in my gut. It's not nausea because the candies are working surprisingly well—granted, I'll likely have thirty cavities by the time I pop this kid out, but that's a later-Cassidy problem. No, the uneasiness is because this might be the first Friday night in history when none of the Wells Ranch cowboys came into the bar.

"I still can't believe you made this." Shelby swivels on the bar stool, carefully examining the tooled leather purse. Her fingers glide across the floral design and a smile lights her face; the look makes the hours I spent worthwhile. "I wish you'd sell them at rodeos and stuff."

"Nah, strictly gifts for friends and family. Sorry again about giving you your birthday present so late, by the way. I don't have the energy to do anything, and I've been so sick. But Red gave me a big bag of Jolly Ranchers"—I produce a handful from my pocket to show her—"and they surprisingly help a lot with the morning sickness. That's the reason I was able to finish the purse today."

"Hold on." Shelby sets the leather bag down and narrows her eyes in my direction. "He's bringing you presents? You left that part out when you said you told him about being the dad."

"Kate Wells told him to bring stuff, I guess. I told him I didn't want it—I don't want anything from him—but he wouldn't listen."

She pulls a face. "You're mad about him giving you presents?"

"Not mad. Just . . . I didn't even know if I was *ever* going to tell him the baby is his. I only did it because he showed up at my house asking and I'm not a complete monster. Not because I want him to be a dad."

"Like it or not, he is the dad. Sperm donor, at the very least. I say you roll with it. Let him spoil you, if that's what he wants to do. Shit, I'd be fully taking advantage of this. You basically own his soul now. Use and abuse that man."

"Lord help whoever knocks you up one day." I laugh. "I've known him since we were kids—this is all bullshit. He's absolutely not the dad type."

"Worst-case scenario, this is a short-lived thing and he suddenly disappears one day. You didn't want him around in the first place, so I fail to see a downside."

"Yeah . . ."

Except I know what it's like to have a parent around sporadically. I know what it's like to have somebody be present in your life and then leave without a word. The constant wondering if you did something to make them go. If there's anything you could've done to make them want to stay. My mom left when I was one. Turned up for three and four. Disappeared. Came back when I was six. Left a week before my seventh birthday. So on and so forth, right through to when she asked to have my birthday money to buy music festival tickets when I was thirteen. Dad lost his shit, and *poof,* she vanished for good. Now I have a secret burner account to keep tabs on her social media—still wondering from time to time if she misses me. If she ever missed me.

"Anyway, enough about him. Are we still on for the indoor rodeo?" Shelby leans on the bar, watching me close out the till. "I can pick you up."

Shit. Going to the indoor rodeo an hour away in Sheridan sounded like an amazing idea a couple months ago. But Cass then and Cass now are two *very* different people.

My shoulders drop with a groan. "I don't know, Shelb. I'm not sure I'm up to it. I'd much rather binge-watch *Gossip Girl* and fall asleep by seven p.m. on my nights off."

"Girl, you only have a few months before you'll be stuck at home all the damn time. You should get out and enjoy yourself." She bats her eyelashes at me. "And in the spring, I'm going to be so sad without my rodeo partner. We need to make the most of it. *Please. For me.*"

"Ugh, fine. Pick me up. But we're not staying out late."

I lick my lips, sucking the ever-loving life out of my watermelon-flavored candy and trying to ignore the man eating a hot dog with fried onions just behind us in the rodeo stands. If I dwell on it, the poor woman in front of me is going to be wearing the chocolate milkshake currently sloshing in my stomach.

"I always get so nervous when guys we know are up." Shelby grimaces and points across the arena to the bucking chutes. Specifically, pointing to where Denver Wells is seated on the back of a saddle bronc, readying himself for the gate to open.

"Oh, for sure," I mumble, my eyes snagging on something

that makes me significantly more nervous than Denny riding a bucking horse.

Just behind him, there's an unmistakable mop of auburn hair flipping out from under a dusty cowboy hat. He's leaning on the back of the chute in a fitted black T-shirt. Muscular tattooed arms draped over the top rail as he says something to Denny with a smile.

Gross, Cass.

I blame pregnancy hormones, a crushing fear he's going to tell everybody here I'm pregnant with his baby, and the fact that he basically saved my life with these Jolly Ranchers. That's the only reason why I'm hung up on him for so long I miss Denny's winning ride. I'm forced out of my trance when Shelby jumps up, yanking me by the arm, to cheer and whistle loudly.

My thoughts are still foggy—probably the pregnancy brain I keep hearing about—when the rodeo ends and we head to the bar. I buy two drinks on autopilot, unsure how I can temporarily forget I'm pregnant after spending the entire night fighting nausea and struggling to stay awake. When Shelby drags me toward Denny and Red, I'm glad to at least have people to give these to before I reflexively take a sip.

"Cass, have I told you how much I love you lately?" Denny simpers and grabs the silver can I'm holding out. "Seriously, you're the best girl around."

Smoke nearly pours out of Shelby's ears. As if this hasn't been the dynamic between the two of us since high school. If Denny notices how jealous she is, he doesn't care. Unsurprising. She may be smitten with him, but we all know Denny doesn't date exclusively.

"Yeah, yeah. No amount of flattery is going to get me to buy you more than one beer. This is a celebratory drink because you won. Don't get used to it." I sit down next to Shelby, sliding the second beer across to Red. "I bought two instinctively and then remembered I can't drink, so here."

"Making sure we're hydrated even on your day off. Do we still have to tip you?" Red winks, and I furrow my eyebrows at him, refusing to do anything that might be an indication of how warm my chest suddenly feels.

"Tip: shut up, Red." I roll my eyes, biting back a smile. "This is why I don't do nice things for you idiots. You can't simply say 'thank you' and move along."

"You love us." Denny takes a swig, sliding closer to Red to make room for another of his cowboys, Colt.

"Tolerate, not love. And I barely do that."

"Anyway," Shelby pipes up, clearly growing annoyed by her lack of involvement in the banter. "Cheers to Denny on his win."

Their beer cans clink together and then into my giant metal water bottle—something that's basically become an extra appendage since I got pregnant considering it's never more than two feet away from me. I'm viscerally aware of Red's eyes on me as I pop a green apple Jolly Rancher in my mouth. As much as I didn't want to give him the satisfaction of knowing I'm using any part of his present, it's more important that I don't throw up in the middle of the conversation. Seconds later, my phone vibrates in my back pocket.

Red: Are they helping?

Cass: Helping . . . rot my teeth? Yes. Make me gain a ton of weight? Yes. Stop the nausea? Yes.

Red: I'll hook you up with more when you get low

Cass: You make it sound like they come from a dealer on the street corner. I can buy my own.

Red: He's in the alley, actually.

And he'll be pissed if we get our
supply somewhere else
Red: I don't think he's the kind of
guy we want to make mad

I look from the phone over to him, startled to find him looking right back at me. A small laugh blows from my nose, and I shake my head.

Cass: Well, we can't risk pissing
alley-guy off.
Cass: I'm probably good for a few
more days
Red: I'll drop some off at your
house tomorrow night.
Cass: If you wake me up, you're
dead, asshole.

I slip my phone back into my pocket and try to join the conversation. Between it being past my bedtime and the weird emotions around Red, I don't have it in me to focus on whatever small-town gossip the rest of the group is discussing. But I do my best, listening to Shelby shamelessly flirt with Denver. Slogging through Colt's ramblings about some pickup truck he might buy. And glancing over at Red only when I absolutely can't help myself.

Starting to think I might legitimately fall asleep sitting up, I work up the nerve to turn to Shelby. "I'm about ready to go home."

Her face drops. "Already? Really? Can you tough it out for another hour or so?"

"Shelb, come on. It's not even early—it's eleven o'clock. You agreed on the way here that we could leave whenever I wanted."

She groans like the old alcoholics at the Horseshoe when I announce last call.

"I can drive you home," Red offers.

"No. I'm fine, I'll go whenever Shelby's ready." I shoot my best friend a threatening sideways glance before turning back to Red. "You've been drinking, anyway."

"This is the same beer you gave me." He slides the still-full can across the table to me.

"There. Done. Just catch a ride with Red. Love you, girly." Shelby claps her hands together. "Come dance with me, Denny."

What happened to sisterly solidarity? Shelby's officially off the best-friend list.

She leans in before skipping away and whispers, "You *own* his soul. Take advantage."

"Fuck my life." I stand and reluctantly follow Red out of the stuffy rodeo dance hall and into the cool night.

Our first breath of what should be fresh mountain air is tainted by a group of smokers huddled outside the main entrance. Cigarette smoke swirls through the air, filling my nostrils in one fell swoop.

Gag reflex activated.

There's no time to get privacy. Or be graceful about this. Before I've even inhaled a second breath, I'm keeled over, losing the water and French fries and chocolate shake into the white hydrangeas lining the pathway. The collective stare of a dozen smokers burns holes across my backside, leaving me feeling—and smelling, probably—like a piece of burnt garbage.

My hands find their way to my knees for support as a second wave of nausea hits hard and strong. Blond strands curtain my face, blowing straight into the line of fire, thanks to a small breeze.

Fuck. This is why I wear my hair up all the time.

A fraction of a second before the rest of my stomach empties across the lava rocks and plants, Red sweeps my hair into a makeshift ponytail. Holding it safely out of the way with one hand, he rubs slow circles on my lower back with his other. Despite how tempted I am to smack him away, I can't bring myself to. Even after the puking ends, I don't force the removal of his firm touch.

"You okay?" he asks, watching my face worriedly.

"Yeah. But . . . can we get away from the smoke?" I fight to get the words out without breathing through my nose, wiping away the tears drying on my cheeks.

"Shit. Of course." He ushers me forward, hand still unmoved. Even through my coat, it's burning my skin in the best possible way—a calming presence. I hate it, and I need it. And I hate how badly I need it.

We walk toward his truck, and his arm quickly falls away from my body. As it should.

"Sure you're good?" he asks, opening the passenger door for me.

I nod slowly, dabbing at the wetness still clinging to my eyelashes. "All good. Just want to go home and brush my teeth."

He starts his crappy truck and watches me as I shiver relentlessly. "I know you've been dead set on disliking me, but don't you think it might be easier in the long run if we just be friends?" Reaching into the backseat, he pulls out a thick Carhartt work coat and spreads it over my lap. "And then you don't need to pretend like accepting a ride home from me is physically painful."

"Bold of you to assume I was pretending." I pull the jacket up to my chin like a blanket. "Not to be dramatic but the Jolly Ranchers are life-changing, which makes it really hard to dislike you. Also, I don't have to scrub vomit from my hair tonight, thanks to you. So I guess we can be friends."

"Glad I could help." His large hands flex on the steering wheel as he turns out of the dirt parking lot and onto a dark, winding road.

"You guys weren't at the bar last night." I kick myself as soon as I say it. It makes it sound like I was *hoping* he'd show up, and that obviously wasn't the case.

"Figured I shouldn't risk blowing your cover. And I don't trust myself to stay quiet."

That's not the answer I was looking for. Reasoning revolving around the ranch or Denny's rodeo today would've sat better with me. I'd almost prefer he break the news to my dad, because that would mean Red doesn't suddenly care about what I tell him to do. Just like he hasn't given a shit about rules for the twenty-plus years I've known him.

"What happened to your macho 'it's gonna be real fucking obvious who your baby daddy is' bullshit?" Kicking my boots off, I tuck my feet directly against the warm floor vent. "Don't turn into a softie on me now."

"Spent enough time around Kate while she was pregnant and crazy to know it's a bad idea to piss you off."

The blue dash lights emit enough light to give me an opportunity to study the roped muscle in his arms, watch his thumbs tapping along to the quiet music, and notice his tongue darting out to lick his bottom lip. But it's dark enough that I'm pretty sure he can't see me watching him in my periphery.

"Are you saying I'm crazy?"

He snorts. "If you weren't, we wouldn't be here."

A fire ignites inside my chest, and my mouth opens before I have time to think about what I'm saying. "Actually, if you could put a condom on properly, we wouldn't be here." I turn and glare at him. "It's a miracle you don't have a dozen illegitimate children . . . unless you do?" My voice breaks at the end of my sentence, eyes burning with an irritating hormonal urge to cry at the thought of him having a bunch of other kids out there. I hate the way pregnancy has me constantly on the verge of a breakdown over the stupidest things. Thankfully, I'm becoming quite skilled at pushing it away just before the tears fall.

"Shit, I pissed off the crazy pregnant lady." The outline of his illuminated lips crooks into a smile. "No kids . . . Well, I guess I have one now, eh? That feels fucked up to say."

"I've known for weeks and it still feels that way." I pull his coat tighter around myself, fighting off the chill only a long, boiling hot bath will get rid of. And apparently, I'm not allowed to have those anymore. Sounds like I'll be cold straight through to spring. "Eventually it'll be real, whether we like it or not. And then what are we going to do?"

"We've got options. Shotgun weddings can be lovely," he says.

"Did this shitty truck teleport us back to 1940? Next you'll suggest shipping me off to a home for unwed mothers."

"Hey, just throwing shit at the wall."

"You trust my dad pointing a gun at you? Not sure if that's courageous or dumb." I cock an eyebrow. "I bet he'd shoot anyway."

"True." His fingers drum on the steering wheel as he thinks. "Okay . . . We can co-parent and share the baby."

"Don't you live in a *bunkhouse* with other ranch hands, like you're permanently at Boy Scout camp? You think you're going to bring a baby there? Besides, that won't work with breastfeeding."

He laughs quietly, shaking his head. "It's not like being at summer camp. But, yeah, I see your point. Guess I'll have to move in with you."

"Immediately no. I have zero interest in living with you." With a deep breath, I question my sanity as I mull over what I'm about to offer. "What if I allow you to come over anytime you want to see the baby?"

"So I'll live with you but pretend I don't, because I'm going to be there every hour I'm not at work, sweetheart."

I wonder if I can convince him to leave me alone for the next six months on the grounds that it's unhealthy to be so stressed out when I'm pregnant.

"You agreed to not call me that. It's condescending."

"Oh, I thought you changed your mind. Last time I called you sweetheart, you grabbed my cock. Mixed messages, Cass."

There's the Red I know and . . . *tolerate*. At least the crude remark eases my worry he's gone soft.

"Yeah, well, now I'm painfully sober and more likely to cut it off than anything." I lean against the window, but the cold glass only makes me shiver harder.

"You cold?" He turns briefly to look me up and down before returning his gaze to the dark road. The empty stretch of highway is lit solely by our headlights, thanks to the overcast skies. "Adjust the temperature, if you want."

"Always, thanks to my crappy thyroid. I'm used to it, though." Tilting the seat back a bit, I shut my eyes and think warm thoughts. A beach chair in the Caribbean sun. A pool float on the lake during summer. A tanning bed.

Apparently, I fell asleep. Because the next thing I know, I'm being gently shaken awake. There's drool on my cheek, and Red's watching me with a thin-lipped smile. I quickly wipe the back of my hand across my mouth and blink until my vision has adjusted.

"Sorry, I was considering carrying you inside, but I was scared you'd wake up and murder me."

"I would've." I yawn. "Thank you for bringing me home."

"Anytime, Cass. I told you I'd help you with anything you need."

My eyes meet his in an unsettling way, and I blindly feel for the door handle. "Red, please stop being a decent guy. It's freaking me out."

"Want me to come in and show you how not-decent I can be, sweetheart?"

"Fuck off." I shut his door and head inside, keeping my stupid, giddy smile well out of sight. Like the cute lead in a nineties rom-com, I fling my back against the front door the second it closes. I think I might have the tiniest crush on him, and that is *so fucked up*.

Red

Fifteen weeks (baby is the size of a cinnamon roll)

"So, my biggest concern is whether we're going to be allowed anywhere near the Horseshoe ever again." Denny pulls open the barbed wire gate, allowing Rob, Colt, and me through on horseback. The sunset's casting heavy shadows across the ranch, bringing along the crispness of autumn. After a long day of moving heifers and mending fences, beers with the boys would be a great way to unwind, but staying on Cassidy's good side is more important.

"Of course that's your biggest concern." Reaching down from my mount, I smack his hat off as I ride by. "Dave doesn't know anything yet, and I told Cassidy I'd give her time. So if you go there and run your mouth, I'll rip you limb from limb. If Cass doesn't get to you first."

"Does he not know she's pregnant, or not know you're the one who did it?" Colt asks.

"I thought there was an unspoken rule not to touch Cassidy Bowman so we could happily maintain our watering hole?" Denny shouts, trotting to catch up to us. "You took that rule and swung way too hard in the opposite direction."

I shrug, packing my chewing tobacco with a few flicks of my wrist. "Never met a rule I didn't love breaking."

Especially that one. I'd face any consequences a million

times over, with a shit-eating grin, for breaking the rule not to touch Cass. I can't begin to count the number of times I've thought about all the things I would do to her, given the chance and more privacy than we had that night.

"And, Colt, he knows she's pregnant, but he thinks the baby is her ex-boyfriend's," I clarify.

"Smart. Let him keep thinking that so he doesn't hunt you down and string you up." Colt shoots finger guns in my direction.

Up ahead, Rob clears his throat to hide a laugh. He's a bitter, ugly, middle-aged ranch hand who's decent enough at cowboying and poker, but dog shit at everything else.

"What's that, Rob?" I challenge him.

"Why not let everybody keep thinking it's not yours, and you can be off the hook entirely? Seems like a win for everyone that way."

If I wasn't currently on a horse, I would hit him. Actually—*fuck it*—I ride up next to him and punch him in the upper arm. *Hard.* Enough that he sharply inhales through his teeth. "Because I'm not a fucking deadbeat."

"Clearly she doesn't want anybody to know it's yours. What's the reason for that, jackass? Think maybe she's embarrassed? Can't say I blame her," he snarks.

I rip the reins from his hands, veering his mare into mine, my fist landing squarely on his jaw. I wish he wasn't such a good rider. It would make my fucking day to see him fall off the back of his horse and be left to walk home. *Asshole.*

"Jesus, Red. Chill." Denny rides up on the other side of me and wrestles the reins out of my grasp, then chucks them back over to Rob. "He was trying to rile you up."

"Well, it fucking worked." I shake Denny's hand away from my shoulder. Even Heathen side-passes to get away from him.

"Clearly." He shakes his head. "Come have dinner at the big house tonight, get away from the assholes in the bunks. I don't think the girls will want to clean up a bloodbath there tomorrow."

The ride back is silent, save for hooves on the compact trail and birdsong. We untack and turn the horses out without anybody saying a word, going through the motions surrounded solely by the occasional braying and clanging of the tack room door. It's not until Denny and I are halfway down the dark gravel path to the big house that somebody talks.

"Rob was talking out of his ass earlier. I don't think Cass is trying to make it seem like the baby is Derek's," Denny says without taking his eyes off of the farmhouse up ahead.

I don't know if she wishes it was Derek's. But I do know, for sure, that she wishes it wasn't mine.

"Nah, I don't think he was wrong. Still pisses me off to hear him say it, though."

"She must think you're a hot piece of ass or she wouldn't have banged you to begin with." Denny laughs, and I smack him in the chest, which does nothing but make him laugh harder. "Just sayin'. She's a real fuckin' idiot for pretending the baby's his instead of yours."

"Den, I love you like a brother. That's the only reason I'm not knocking you out. Watch what you say about the mother of my child."

"*Holy.* Already got the protective dad thing going on, eh?" Denny smiles, shaking his head. "You guys will figure it out, I'm sure. She's going to realize you're not half as much of a piece of shit as Derek. Love ya, bro."

He wraps an arm around my shoulder as we walk up the front porch stairs, and I don't even bother shrugging it off. Through the front door to the big house—the sprawling white farmhouse where Jackson and Kate live with their five-year-old, Odessa, and one-year-old, Rhett. It's also always been the one place on the ranch where everybody hangs out; the big house's kitchen is always open.

Odessa comes out of nowhere, barreling into my legs with

a hug, then proceeds to chase Denny down the hall. She giggles as he runs just fast enough that her fingertips graze his back but can't quite grab hold of his shirt, untamed brown hair flying behind her. If my kid is anywhere half as cool as her, I think I'll manage fine. Maybe they'll give me some gray hair, but I work best with people who are a bit wild. Back in April, Odessa passed the country-kid rite of passage by falling off a calf she decided to ride bareback, breaking her tiny wrist. Instead of being scared away, she hopped back on three days later and had to go get her cast replaced because it was caked in cow crap.

"Hey, didn't know you were coming," Kate calls over from the table where she's breastfeeding Rhett. "Grab a plate and dish up."

I've had my own permanent spot at the Wells kitchen table since I was a kid. My dad was a cowboy with a bad temper and a drinking problem, and Mom was too tired to care about anything except cigarettes and *Days of Our Lives*. Back then, Wells Ranch employed half as many cowboys as it does now, so my family had one of the four-bedroom bunkhouses. By the time I was eight, I preferred the safety of joining the Wells family for dinner over spending any time with my own parents and siblings. That's when Grandpa Charlie Wells pulled up a chair right between Denny and Jackson and declared it my spot. I don't usually intrude on their family dinners anymore, but the seat's still mine anytime I want it.

"You see there's a snowfall warning for tomorrow night?" Jackson scoops a heaping pile of mashed potatoes onto his plate.

"Mhm, shouldn't be too bad," Austin replies. If there's one thing ranchers love to talk about, it's the weather. It even gets the normally silent of the three brothers to talk. "Still gets pretty warm during the day. Even if things freeze up, they'll thaw by mid-morning."

Denny swallows a bite and adds, "Should fix that broken

water heater in the back pen before it gets much colder, though. If it freezes, we'll be hauling water multiple times a day."

Tuning out their conversation, I watch Kate place baby Rhett into his high chair. His chubby hands immediately dig into the mashed potatoes, bringing a fistful to his mouth. The majority of it squishes between his tiny fingers and lands with a splatter on his tray, which I can't help but smile at. A quiet laugh slips from my lips as his dirty hand moves to smear food through the fine blond hair on top of his head.

It's mind-blowing to think this is my future. Well . . . sort of. I don't have a house, or a wife, or a biological family to have nightly dinners with. Regardless, at some point in the not-so-distant future, I'm going to have a baby covered in mashed potatoes. I like that.

Realizing I've been watching him so intently my eyes are dry, I blink and turn to Austin. "How's the house coming along, boss?"

Cecily answers for him. "Foundation's officially done. They're trying to get as much done as they can before winter. Then it'll be pretty slow going."

At least there's a small chance I could move into their current place shortly after the baby's born. It's not the perfect solution, but I can make it work. Try to save money and maybe build a bedroom addition in a couple of years.

"Tell them to hurry up so you can fill it with babies, then all our kids can be running around together here," Kate says with a chipper voice. She's been laying it on thick with these two for months. "Wasn't expecting Red to be the first one to give my kids a cousin. If Denny beats you two to the punch, I'm going to lose my mind."

Denny laughs and clunks his beer bottle on the worn wood tabletop. "Absolutely no risk of that. I do a better job of putting on my raincoat than this guy."

"You're really testing how much I like you today, aren't

ya?" I snag his beer, turning away to chug it while he laughs and jokingly punches me in the shoulder.

"It's not even raining, Uncle Denny." Odessa's face scrunches up as she contemplates the picture window behind us, confirming not a single drop of rain has fallen outside.

"Okay, enough. Odessa, eat your dinner. Boys, behave or get out." Kate glares in our direction. Somehow I'm always lumped in when Denny says something he shouldn't. Maybe it's because I'm quick to throw the first punch when somebody chirps him back. "Anyway, how's Cass doing?"

"Oh, um . . ." I swallow the food in my mouth. "She's okay. I saw her yesterday, and she's apparently not feeling as sick. So that's good."

"Except bringing her candy was your one excuse to see her. Now she'll have no need for you." Denny smirks. Seriously, I'm going to beat the crap out of him as soon as we get outside.

"Fu—" I start, but Kate's glare stops me from telling him where to go and how to get there. "She's pregnant with *my* kid. I don't need an excuse beyond that."

"Well, if she's not sick anymore, you could bring her food," Cecily suggests with a shrug, pointing her fork across the table. "Kate basically drank her weight in chocolate milk. I'm sure Cass will have something she's craving soon enough."

"Speaking of which, you should invite her here for dinner." Kate's back to being giddy again. I think she wants us all to live in a big commune here on the ranch, with a million feral farm kids running around while the women drink iced tea on the porch. Or beer, knowing Kate.

I'm not sure what kind of life Cassidy dreams about. I *am* sure that whatever her dreams are, they don't include me. A few months ago, I would've scoffed at the idea of her even looking in my direction. A future where Cass and I are together? Absolutely fucking not. *Keep dreaming.*

But now? I would die for the opportunity to prove I'm at least worth taking a chance on.

By the time dinner is finished, all I can think about is how I'll convince Cass to agree to have dinner with me. Never mind on the ranch with everyone, like Kate suggested—that can come later. I'd prefer only me and her.

Denny's lucky my hands are too busy texting Cass to fight him on our way back to the bunkhouse. Come to think of it—Rob's a lucky bastard, too. Aside from a quick nod hello when I walk through the front door, I ignore the guys playing cards and drinking beer around the dining table, retreating to my room because all I want to do is lie in bed and talk to her.

Red: Now that you aren't so sick, having any cravings?

Cass: Um . . . potatoes. Mashed, roasted, baked, any and all ways.

Red: Should've seen Jackson & Kate's baby at dinner tonight. He was basically just a big potato. Covered in mash from head to toe.

Red: It was surprisingly cute

Cass: Getting baby fever? Quit being a big softie

Cass: Besides, I'm sure it's cute until you're the one cleaning up after them

Red: Maybe we should practice.

Cass: I'm nervous to ask what fucked up plan you have for practicing that

Red: If I cover myself in potato would you lick it off, sweetheart?

Cass: You do know that's not how

we'd be cleaning the baby off, right?
Red: Answer the question, Cass
Cass: I mean . . . probably
Cass: But it has nothing to do with you and everything to do with how badly I'm wanting potatoes.
Red: Great, I'll make you dinner tomorrow
Cass: Can't, I'm at the bar. Feel free to drop off a baked potato, though. Just don't come in with it on your dick or something.
Red: I'll save that idea for another day.
Red: Sunday? For dinner . . . not dick potato. Unless you change your mind and want it served like that.
Cass: Dinner, sure. Dick potato, NO.

Potatoes, I can do. Potatoes are easy. Nearly impossible to fuck up. Work for breakfast, lunch, or dinner. Pair well with nearly everything.

That's my in.

"You know this is absolutely insane, right?" Denny peers over my shoulder as I'm hunched over the quartz island, peeling what may be my thousandth potato. You could tell me I've peeled and diced that many, and I would believe it. I've lost count, but my hands hurt and there's so much potato starch built up under my nails I could likely starch a couple pairs of blue jeans.

"Shut up, it's sweet." Cecily walks past to get to the coffee maker, flicking the back of Denny's head on the way. *Yup, she was a good addition to the family.* It's like she was reading my mind with that move.

"Thank you, Filly." I smile at her. "And fuck you, Denny. I told her I'd make dinner, and she texted me last night to say bring potatoes or die. Also, there may have been some texts over the last few days about *other* things involving them. So I'm making the damn potatoes."

"Christ, you two are into some fucked-up shit." Denny cocks an eyebrow. "I wouldn't even know where to begin with potatoes in the bedroom. Then again, I also wouldn't bang a girl on her ex-boyfriend's car for revenge."

"You absolutely would," Austin retorts, without looking up from his magazine.

"Okay." Denny shrugs his shoulders with a devilish grin. "You're not wrong. But this other kinky stuff? Not for me."

"You're setting the bar too high, too early, Red. Driving over thirty kilometers multiple times per week to bring her candy and food, after spending fourteen hours on horseback. Now you're making her this gourmet meal." Jackson plunks down into his chair with a loud exhale. "You're screwing all of us. Next guy with a pregnant wife around here is going to have a *hard* time keeping up."

Denny makes a discreet whipping noise, dodging Cecily by slipping around to the other side of the island with a chuckle.

The peeler lands in the kitchen sink with a clang, and everybody's eyes are on me. I can sense it—they're waiting anxiously to see if I'll fly off the handle. But I'm not even mad. Today, the snide comments hurt, but tell me I'm doing something *right*.

"That's the difference, man." I rinse the potato starch from my hands. "She's not my wife. Not my girlfriend. Hell, until a couple of weeks ago, she wouldn't even say we were friends. If she wanted to, she could cut me out entirely. She could leave me off the goddamn birth certificate. The only way I'd get to be involved at all is by fighting with her in court. Making four different potato dishes in an effort to keep her happy is *way fucking easier.*"

Well, I ruined the mood in a different way. And now, instead of looking at me with contempt, they're staring at me like I'm something to feel sad for. *Great.* I massage my temple and lean against the counter. The surface is cool, and the chill permeating through my shirt helps ease my somersaulting stomach.

"You don't genuinely think she would do that . . . do you?" Cecily asks.

Austin, Jackson, and Denny sit there watching me in silent horror. To be fair, we talk every day but we never really *talk*. I definitely haven't said anything to them about this shit, even though it's been weighing on me for weeks.

"How the fuck should I know? I've known her practically my entire life, but I don't *know* her. Not well enough to know what she'll do if I screw this up. So, yeah, I offered her dinner and she agreed. I'm gonna do a good job—definitely not going to take it for granted. That's all there is to it, and you guys can make fun of me all you want about it."

I don't know if Cecily is kicking Austin under the table or if she's done some serious witchcraft on him recently, but he clears his throat and speaks up before anybody else. "You're doing a good job, man. She's going to see that. Don't let these assholes convince you otherwise."

Beryl, the ranch's main kitchen employee—and pseudo mother to us all—strolls into the kitchen and immediately gets to work helping me. Thank God because I can barely feel my fingertips and I'm not even halfway through.

Before long, it's only Beryl, Cecily, and me standing around the huge island, quietly peeling, slicing, and dicing potatoes. Normally, my day off wouldn't be spent in the kitchen with the ladies. Shooting guns, drinking beer, rodeoing, four-by-fouring my shitty pickup, or catching up on sleep are how I tend to enjoy my free time. With all of that bound to change in a few months, I'm thinking of today as a practice round. To determine if I can survive a workweek without doing anything to blow off steam.

Standing with our shoulders nearly touching, Beryl holds a potato in one hand and slices perfect thin wafers for the scalloped potatoes. Something I would've absolutely fucked up, if left to do it alone. I watch intently—it feels like this is a skill I should master. If this dinner works, I'll cook potatoes every day for the rest of time. Doubt Beryl will want to be my permanent slicer.

"You better bring this girl by sometime, honey. She must be pretty special for you to do all of this." Beryl missed my entire speech earlier, and I'm not giving it again.

"No, no. The *baby* is very demanding. That's who this is all for."

Cecily chuckles. "Nothing at all to do with having a crush on the pretty blonde, eh?"

"Nope, because I'm not risking fucking this up by thinking with the wrong head. We're only friends, nothing more."

Beryl smiles. "I swear, you boys all strut around here like a rooster parade, but the minute a good woman practically falls into your lap, you lose your heads. *Both of them.* Think with your heart—not either head—and you won't mess it up."

Cassidy

Sixteen weeks (baby is the size of a can of pop)

Red: I have scalloped, baked, mashed, AND roasted for tonight.
Cass: Weird way to propose, but yes.

"Cassidy Bowman, you're *flirting* with him." Blair's voice echoes through my bathroom over speakerphone. "I bet you're shaving your legs in that bath, aren't you?"

"It's friendly banter, that's all. And if it comes off a bit flirty, it's not my fault. I blame this weird-ass body of mine." I drag the razor up my calf as silently as possible. I don't need her judging me for shaving. It doesn't mean anything. I have to shave all the damn time thanks to my PCOS. "It's like the moment I stopped wanting to vomit every two seconds, my body decided I need orgasms just as often. I'm taking a break from bingeing *Gossip Girl* because the vivid dreams I've been having about Chuck Bass are making me blush every time he shows up on the screen."

"Then I don't understand why you don't hook up with your baby daddy. Are you worried about getting double-pregnant? Or his dick hitting the baby? What's your reasoning?"

"I really love hearing a nurse practitioner say all of that. *Very* reassuring about both our education and healthcare systems."

I doubt Red would turn me down, but things have been so *nice.* He's been so nice. Honestly, I've maybe been taking advantage of it a little bit because he seems to do anything I ask of him. The last thing I want to do is mess things up to scratch an itch. An itch a vibrator handles perfectly well. Most of the time.

"For the record, I know neither of those can happen. . . . Well, superfetation *technically* can, but it's pretty rare. Anyway, I'm trying to gauge where *your* head is at. You're the one who mentioned your text messages with him. Sue me for assuming that was because you wanted to hear my thoughts."

"Go on," I say in an unenthused tone.

"How many days in the last week has he stopped by your house?"

"Three, I think? Four, if you count the day he dropped off food here when I was at work. Mostly he stops by briefly to drop off snacks he thinks I might like or dinner when I'm working late. He's making sure I'm eating enough because I've been so sick—nothing more."

"How often do you text?"

"Pretty often . . . probably every day. But we're trying to become friends. Y'know, for the sake of the child we're going to have together."

"He's attractive, feeds you, and is at your house all the time, anyway. Why are you not jumping all over this opportunity?"

"Because, for one, it's *Red.* For two, it'll ruin any possibility of us having a nontoxic co-parenting relationship. I'm trying to keep this all professional. I can't be trusted with oxytocin—you know this. I'm so delusional, if a guy is sort of nice to me I fall in love with him. I mean . . . *clearly,* because I refuse to believe staying in a relationship with Derek for a year was the result of anything but delusion."

She wheezes out a *yes* around her laughter.

"Add in raging pregnancy hormones, and I'm fucked. I'll fall for him because he cooked me potatoes, then realize how crazy I'm being a few months from now, everything will implode, and we'll still have to co-parent. So it's staying strictly professional between us."

"Ah, yes. Talking about eating mashed potatoes off of each other is *super* professional." I swear I can hear her rolling her eyes. "So if you're not going to hook up with Red, why don't you go out on some dates? Go enjoy your hot body and childless freedom."

"I'm already a blimp. I'm so bloated and gross."

"You sent me the tiniest bump pic yesterday. I know that's not true, dummy. Chuck Bass and your vibrator aren't going to tide you over forever."

"They don't need to work *forever.* Just long enough to get me through this strange pregnancy symptom. Maybe a few weeks or months. I'm sure I'll be too tired and uncomfortable to want anybody near me eventually."

She laughs. "Right. So you technically *could* hook up and then go back to being whatever you two currently are when you're no longer horny."

"Red is not even under consideration, and you know my feelings about dating guys around here. So I don't really know what you expect me to do."

"That was a dumb rule even before you got pregnant. If you're never going to date guys living within one hundred kilometers of Wells Canyon, move away."

I pull the drain plug and wrap a towel around myself, grabbing moisturizer from the cupboard and homing in on my legs. Only because I don't want dry skin. Literally no other reason.

"Well, moving's no longer an option. So . . ." As if I need

a reminder that now there's absolutely zero chance of me leaving my hometown.

When I face the mirror, I look a bit puffier all over, but mostly like myself. All of the throwing up during the first thirteen weeks actually caused me to drop ten pounds. Nothing hurts quite like having the doctor declare I had at least that much I could stand to lose. I sobbed and ate French fries for the entire hour-long drive home. Thankfully, Red hadn't been available to join me for *that* appointment.

It's when I study myself from the side that it becomes more obvious. Not too noticeable to anybody except me—mostly looks like I ate a big meal. With the weather getting cooler, I should be able to hide my growing stomach with sweatshirts and layers. Even still, the little bump is a reminder that I'm running on borrowed time before my being pregnant will be more than just a rumor . . . and everybody in town will know Red's the father. Which is exactly why we need to be a united front. Two friends with a baby. Nothing more. *Ever.*

"You're still coming down after Christmas, right?" Blair asks. "I don't have the desire to spend a full two weeks with my parents."

I finish meticulously coating my stomach in the moisturizer Red gave me. Doesn't matter that Blair told me stretch marks are mostly determined by genetics—I'm doing *everything* in my power to prevent them.

"Duh. Now that I'm not constantly vomiting, I'm no longer completely housebound. It'll be like a little babymoon."

"Since you want to be difficult about Red, I'm making sure you get laid when you're here. That'll be my early push present."

"Jesus Christ. I'm going to be massively pregnant by then. Go get laid yourself." A shock of cold air rushes across my body when I open the bathroom door and pad over to the closet.

"Yeah, yeah. I'm too busy for dating."

I roll my eyes, sure she can sense it even though she can't see me, and shove my legs into a pair of jeans. "Oh, for fuck's sake. I can't button my favorite jeans—the ones that make my ass look amazing. I told you I'm a blimp."

"You were going to wear amazing-ass jeans to have dinner—*at your house*—with a guy you have zero intentions of sleeping with? Seems a little suspect."

"I'm hanging up now." I chuck the jeans into the back of my closet with a groan and fall back onto the bed, listening to my best friend giggle maniacally on the other end.

"Good call. Better go get prettied up for your date. Wear leggings. They're comfy, don't make it seem like you're trying too hard, and make your ass look great. Guys *love* them. Bye, babe. Love you."

I genuinely thought he was kidding. But, arms loaded with cloth grocery bags, Red shuffles past me in the doorway and strides toward the kitchen, seemingly quite serious about his offer to cook me dinner. When he suggested it, I assumed he'd get the girls back at Wells Ranch to make something.

"I premade some of the stuff, but I need your kitchen to finish up."

"Are you sure you're capable of cooking?" I follow and start unbagging the groceries next to him. Thankfully, he seems to have brought everything he could ever possibly need, clearly anticipating that I'd lack even the most basic of ingredients. I squint to read the label on a fresh green herb I don't recognize. "I refuse to believe you can even pronounce *tarragon*."

"Pronounce it, cook with it. Hell, I can *spell it,* which I'm sure shocks you," he says as he washes his hands and gets right to work. "I might've played hooky in high school more often than I should've. Definitely wasn't a perfect, straight-A student like you were, but I'm not a complete dumbass."

"Didn't say you were." Thought it, maybe. Implied it, definitely. "I don't have the faintest idea what to use tarragon in." I hop onto the counter and settle in.

"Good thing you're not the one cooking then."

"Why are *you* cooking? I heard the word *potato* and agreed instinctively, but you didn't need to come over and actually cook dinner."

"Whatever my baby wants, my baby gets."

Thank God he doesn't look up from cutting radishes, because his words send my heart into a fluttery overdrive, and my jaw hangs slack. Then it dawns on me. He's talking about the *literal baby* in my uterus, and I'm an idiot. An embarrassed warmth prickles up my chest and neck.

"Oh . . . um. Right. Of course." I fumble my words, sliding off the counter to go bury my stupid, flushed face in the fridge while I pretend to search for something. Anything to keep him from noticing how weird I feel.

It's the pregnancy. *It is.* If I weren't teeming with hormones, there's nothing Red could say to trigger a reaction like this.

Either oblivious to my humiliation or wanting to save me from myself, Red clears his throat. "Did you ever have cooking class with Mrs. Carr?"

"Every single year from grade eight through twelve."

"Remember the way she pronounced *oregano*?"

Laughter bursts out of me. "Oh. My. God. I forgot all about or-ah-*gah*-no. She was trying to fancy up one of the most common herbs ever. And that's not even the way Italians say it."

"School couldn't afford any nicer ingredients, so just make up your own, I guess." He pauses his chopping to beam at me.

"She loved making up pronunciations, period," I say. "I feel bad for anyone who might've ordered a tiramisu at a restaurant after taking her class."

The way we laugh together feels like we've been friends

our entire lives, not two people who have barely interacted while existing inside the same small-town bubble for all these years. My cheeks ache, and my heart could burst as I lean against the counter next to him, giggling like a schoolgirl with a crush.

I watch him work intently—slicing, dicing, doing whatever that maneuver is where you flip food around in a frying pan. "I guess it should come as no surprise I took her cooking class for years and still can't cook to save my life. I can turn the oven on, but that's about where my abilities end."

"That was the one class I didn't skip. If I wasn't on the ranch, I'd probably try to find work in a kitchen or something. I like cooking . . . and eating." He aggressively slaps his stomach, which sounds firm. Muscled. Not at all like my squishy belly. "Good thing 'bout being a cowboy is you don't need to be ripped to get ladies. Dirty jeans and a hat make 'em feral."

Easy to say when, based on how muscular his arms are and how solid the stomach-slap sounded, he *is* ripped.

"Maybe if the only girls you're interested in are buckle bunnies."

"Worked on you, didn't it?" He winks.

"*Alcohol* worked on me. Turns out, enough beer and tequila can make me overlook the filthy jeans, sweaty cowboy hat, and arrogant personality."

I look him over, taking full advantage of his back being turned to me. No dusty jeans or hat in sight. Just clean, fitted Wranglers with a Skoal ring permanently marked in the back pocket, a flannel button-up with the sleeves rolled up his forearms, and thick, tousled mahogany hair.

"If you weren't pregnant with my kid, I'd offer you a shot right now, Cass. See if you'd overlook some things again."

"If I wasn't pregnant with your kid, I never would've let you into my house." I take a slow sip of water and watch the muscle in his forearm as he adjusts the dial on my gas range. The dark veins branching under his tattooed skin send blood directly to the area between my legs.

Shit, this was a bad idea considering how horny I've been lately.

"Guess it's a good thing I knocked you up, then."

Yup. Bad idea.

Instead of jumping him, I busy myself by setting the table. Reminding myself over and over that I'm turned on because I'm pregnant. Hormones, increased blood flow, and finally feeling less nauseous and tired. That's the only reason why I can't stop staring at him like something I want to sink my teeth into. Hooking up might seem worth it now but, when my sex drive slows to normal, it's bound to fall apart. Which is the last thing I want to deal with when I'm going to be stuck co-parenting with this guy.

"Red?" I sit down as he shuffles serving dishes around on my small kitchen table, struggling to find room for all the food he's prepared. "I've been meaning to talk to you about something. We probably should've covered this when you told me you're all in but, honestly, I didn't even think you'd stick around this long. I just . . . um, I need to know that when you say you're all in, you know what that means. You're promising to be here for the baby, kid, teen, and adult. It's not as simple as being here until you don't want to be or until they turn eighteen. Even if things are shitty between us or the kid turns into a menace."

"I know what I signed up for, y'know? No need to explain."

I shouldn't have to explain it. But I do. Because apparently nobody had this conversation with my mom when they should've, and I refuse to let my baby deal with the same unreliability I did.

I let out a strained exhale. "I'm sure you're aware it's always been me and Dad. My mom was in and out of my life for most of my childhood. Sometimes I think I would've been better off if she had stayed away altogether. I won't put my child through that. So if you have any doubts, leave now and let me do this on my own."

His face twists. "Not getting rid of me that easy, sweetheart."

Lost in thought, I hardly register that he just called me *sweetheart* again.

"Does that mean you understand and plan on being here? Or . . ."

"Aren't you supposed to be the smart one?" He smiles and slices through a piece of steak. "You're stuck with me, as much as I'm sure you hate that. Get used to it."

I'm surprised to find I don't hate it. Not at all.

And by the time we're standing side by side washing the dinner dishes, I'm *enjoying* hanging out with him. The conversation has been easy and fun. We've covered important topics like which people we hated in high school, the worst baby names we've ever heard, and whether my kitchen is organized correctly—obviously it is, and Red is enjoying himself too much getting me riled up over it.

"Please. *Please* explain why the oven mitts, of all things, don't go in this drawer next to the oven," he says—thoroughly tattooed, muscular, *all-man,* and talking to me through a makeshift oven mitt puppet. Even if this was a conversation worth taking seriously, there's no way I could when I'm hung up on the idea of sticking googly eyes on that mitt before the next time he comes over.

Is there going to be a next time? My breathing stutters—I definitely want there to be a next time.

"Because that drawer is the only one big enough to fit my Ziploc bag organizer," I answer matter-of-factly, putting away our clean plates.

He blinks at me, both his mouth and the puppet's agape.

"They come in boxes. Why can't they just be left that way and put somewhere else?"

"Well, this is more organized. But also, it's about the *aesthetic.* Something I wouldn't expect you to understand, considering you live in a bunkhouse, and your closet is probably a sea of Carhartt and Wrangler." I swipe the mitt from his hand and tuck it into the drawer where it belongs.

He leans against the counter with raised eyebrows and a goofy grin. "You're something else, Cassidy."

It's the way my name rolls off his tongue, or the playful gleam in his eyes, or the way he's made me laugh more tonight than Derek did in an entire year, or the corded muscle in his forearms. Or it could be—probably is—a combination that makes my heart race. And while he has no reason to stay, I don't think I want him to leave quite yet.

"Do you want to hang out for a bit longer?" I nod my head in the direction of the living room on the other side of the archway.

"Yeah, for sure."

"I have a doctor's appointment next week, by the way. No pressure at all, but you said you wanted to know these things." We settle onto the plush gray couch, and I wrap a blanket around myself, wiggling my toes to ensure they're fully tucked in. "I understand if you have work to do. I know midweek isn't the most convenient. And, like . . . it's not a very *exciting* appointment. They basically just check my blood pressure and ask how I'm feeling."

"No. I'll talk to Austin, but I'm sure I can make it work, if you want me to come."

"I felt like a potato-shaped lump of trash after my last appointment, and it would be nice to know if the doctor's a dickhead, or if I'm hormonal and crazy. I need a third party there to confirm." Also, something is terribly wrong with me. Maybe I have brain cancer on top of being pregnant because the possibility of spending hours in the car together actually sounds exciting.

Plus, it would be wonderful not to endure the sad looks when I'm alone at my appointment *again*. I bet we can make a somewhat convincing couple.

See? I'm sick.

"You're definitely at least one of those two things." He flashes me a teasing smile. "Sure you want me there? Because if he's a dickhead, I'll kick the shit out of him."

I swat my hand at him—getting nowhere close because we're sitting on opposite ends of my couch. "And then we'll be banned from the hospital and I won't have anywhere within three hours to deliver a baby."

"I've pulled enough calves, I'm sure we'll manage."

My jaw drops, and I brave the cold, swinging a leg out from under the blanket to kick him hard in the thigh. "Shut the fuck up. You ever say shit like that again, I'll castrate you."

He's laughing. A gut-busting, wheezy laugh I've never heard before. As annoyed as I want to be at him, I can't help the smile bursting at the seams.

"Shut up." I nudge him with my toes again. "Serious, Red. No fighting my doctor. You can be pissed off all you want, but we'll vent about it on the drive home like normal people."

"Okay, okay. Stop kicking me with your damn ice cube feet."

"Promise you won't." I point a threatening finger in his direction, narrowing my eyes with a serious intent despite the smile I can't shake.

"Yes, Cass, I promise. Even if he's a tool."

I retreat back under the covers, and Red reaches over to carefully tuck the blanket around my toes. All I can do is stare at him and clasp my hands, gripping hard to stop myself from launching into his stupid, annoying, cute, sexy lap.

Fuck.

Glancing at the clock above the fireplace, he scrubs a

hand across his chiseled jaw. "I should get going. Four a.m. comes sooner than I ever want it to. I'll text you after I talk to Austin."

"Okay. Night." I watch him stand up, refusing to budge from my comfy seat. Partially because I'm a terrible hostess, but mostly because I know I would kiss him if I gave him a proper goodbye.

Red

Seventeen weeks (baby is the size of a potato)

Fences to mend, tractors to repair, and Austin's never-ending shitlist of chores to be done before we bring the cattle home for the winter. From May until October, all twenty thousand head live out on grazing land in the mountains surrounding Wells Ranch. The cattle drives bringing them to and from the ranch are a multiple-day, all-hands-on-deck affair. Since the first time I was allowed to help out when I was twelve, those have easily been my favorite days on the ranch. The shit that makes me proud to be part of this place. Except now the idea of spending multiple days next week without Cass—even without the ability to text her—sounds like hell to me.

As I'd hoped, potatoes were my in. Even with little downtime, and a lot of heckling from the guys, I've been playing around with potato recipes every chance I get. Both because it's fun to fuck around with different recipes and because Cassidy's face *lights up* every single time. Not to mention, the soft moan at the back of her throat when she takes the first bite has been giving me some great spank bank material. So any night when she isn't working late at the bar, I bring dinner and we eat together at her cartoonishly small table.

But being invited to her doctor's appointment feels like

the real deal. Despite what Kate and Cecily constantly yammer in my ear, I haven't been convinced the dinners are enough. She could be using me for food—in fact, she's stated that's what she's doing multiple times.

I need something to help convince me she actually wants me to be the dad. Wants me around, period. Lately, it seems like she's content with keeping me a secret forever, and I've been bottling my emotions—the frustration, the hurt, the anger.

The highway's quiet, but not nearly as quiet as the first ten minutes of the drive have been. My thumb taps repeatedly on the steering wheel, playing to the beat of "Guitars, Cadillacs." Something about the silence makes it impossible to keep my thoughts contained.

"So, are you *ever* going to tell your dad?"

Likely not the best time for this conversation, but it's a fair fucking question if you ask me. She's almost halfway through the pregnancy, has known about it for months, and is still happily going along pretending *Derek*—the rotten scumbag—is the father, while I'm over here busting my ass for her.

"Lose the tone." She shoots a look in my direction. "I told you I will when I'm ready."

"Great. So never then." I don't even bother hiding the snark in my voice.

"Jesus Christ. I didn't invite you to come today so you can treat me like shit." Turning to look out the passenger window, she huffs. She has more to say—I know it.

"Why did you invite me, Cass? Shouldn't Derek be here with you?" My volume steadily climbs until I can't hear the soothing sounds of Dwight Yoakam over my voice. Every momentary thought of self-doubt bubbles to the surface and runs like a river from my mouth. "Is the baby mine or his? You're lying to *somebody*, Cass. And if you aren't sure who the dad is, then fucking say that. I don't give a shit if you say you slept with a dozen other guys. But if the baby's mine, I'm not going to be your dirty secret forever."

"You think if there was any uncertainty, I would've gotten you involved? I could have easily carried on pretending nothing happened between you and me. The baby *is* yours. I just . . . it's complicated telling my dad, okay? You know what our shitty town's like."

I probably should've known this would all come back to my family. That's why she doesn't want to tell her dad. Because Dave—like most people—hates me by association. All thanks to my father, Joe Thompson, the raging alcoholic who fucked over plenty of people in Wells Canyon. Drinking, fighting, stealing, crashing cars . . . Dad's bullshit got us run completely out of town when I was fifteen, and even now, more than fifteen years later, he's ruining my life here. I'm still the loser, Cassidy is still the unofficial town princess.

"I get it. You made the choice to have sex with me, keep my baby, tell me I can be involved. I do every single thing you ask of me, but somehow, a cheating cuntbag still seems like a better father figure in the eyes of you and your dad and everybody else."

Most of the people who hate me, or think I'm trash, don't know me. That takes the sting away a little, usually. But this? This fucking sucks. We've been talking every day and acting like friends for weeks, yet Cass still sees me the way everyone else does. Nothing I've done is good enough. I bet nothing ever will be.

"That's not—*shit.*" She buries her head in her hands. "That's not what I'm saying. I don't want to have a baby with Derek. But he and I broke up right before the rodeo, so it's natural for people to assume. I hardly even liked you as a human being then. And you gotta know your reputation is . . . sorry, I *will* tell him. Okay? I'm not withholding shit to intentionally hurt you. My best friends know, your friends know. The only people who don't, *somehow,* are my dad and the rest of town. You might not get it because I don't know what the deal is with your parents, but my dad and I have only ever had each other. And . . ." Her voice is unsteady, and I don't need to look at her to know she's crying, which instantly stops any trace of anger running through my veins. *Damn it.* Now I feel like a dick for bringing this up. "You should've seen how disappointed he was when I first told him."

"You let him think it was Derek's to make him a bit less disappointed."

She sniffles hard, wiping her nose on the sleeve of her sweater and tucking her blond hair behind her ears. "Not intentionally, no. He might think Derek provided the sperm, but as far as my dad is aware, I'm completely on my own. His disappointment is solely in me. I don't want him to think I'm a slut who's running around sleeping with *you* . . . sorry, no offense."

I don't bother replying. What's the use? I already knew she didn't want people finding out about that night—she's made it clear from the beginning. So I turn the stereo dial, cranking classic country music, and neither of us speaks for a painful forty-five minutes.

"Can we please be a united front here today? I think the only thing worse than the sad looks I get when I'm alone in the waiting room would be the looks I'd get if we're fighting," she says, once we're finally out of the suffocating pickup and walking across an empty, sun-filled parking lot. The beautiful day, the birds chirping, and the warm breeze are heckling my sour mood.

"I don't want to fight with you. I just want . . ." *How do I say what I want without seeming pathetic?* That I need some security here. I need to know she won't drop me the moment I'm not at her beck and call.

"What?"

"Never mind. We won't fight. Let's go."

I follow Cass into the sunny white waiting room, and we sit the closest we ever have. I suppose because it would seem weird if we left an empty chair between us. She smells like vanilla, and her knee keeps bumping into mine, sending warm flutters through my chest and sparks under my skin. The couple across from us is holding on to each other like their lives depend on it, and my eyes jump between their hands and ours. Sharing an armrest, we're close enough I could loop my pinky around hers if I didn't think she'd deck me for it. God, I want to try—a broken nose might be worth it. If she has any of the same thoughts, her poker face is way better than mine. Staring forward, I shuffle in my seat, pretending to merely be getting comfortable. My hand brushes against hers, and she doesn't immediately recoil.

Win.

Taking a shot in the dark, I casually flex my hand so my fingers splay across hers—nothing more than regular old stretching happening here. When they relax, my pinky catches on hers and she pulls away, clasping her hands loosely in her lap.

Lose. Fuck.

So we sit in silence, and I cross my arms over my chest to keep from trying to touch her again.

When a nurse comes to bring Cass into the exam room, I'm suddenly very unsure what my role is. Do I stay here? Do I go? What if she needs to—*I don't know*—get undressed or something, and we have to awkwardly explain that I've had my fingers, tongue, and dick inside of her, but I haven't seen her naked?

Then she grabs hold of my arm and tugs me through the swinging gray door.

Not long after, a skinny, middle-aged doctor enters the tiny, sterile room without even bothering to glance at her, and busies himself typing and scrolling on his computer. "So, Cassidy, how have you been feeling?"

My eyes move from his giant, shiny forehead over to Cass,

and I give her a look, letting her know she was right. He's a total dickhead.

She raises her eyebrows at me. "Pretty good, actually. Barely any nausea, not as fatigued."

"Good, good . . ."

For the next minute or so, there's nothing but the sound of the blood pressure cuff. Apparently, this guy has never heard of bedside manner.

"Well, your blood pressure is normal. Your endocrinologist is still handling your medications, correct?" Cass nods, and the doctor's fingers clack on the keyboard. "As you know, you lost some weight during the first trimester. But you're gaining it back quicker than I'd like to see, so be extra mindful of what you're eating from here on out, okay?"

There's an audible cracking, and I can't tell if the sound came from my knuckles or my molars. It's taking every ounce of energy not to hit this asshole. I thought it was common sense not to comment on a woman's weight *ever*, but when she's pregnant and finally just stopped throwing up multiple times a day? That's extra douchey. Yet Cass is shooting daggers in my direction, not his. And the fear of upsetting her keeps me cracking my knuckles over and over instead of doing what I want to do with them. Whatever the doctor and Cass talk about for the rest of the appointment sounds like TV static to me; tunnel vision has me staring at the blood pressure monitor and replaying Cassidy across from me on her couch.

Promise you won't. Yes, Cass, I promise.

My mouth is hot and stale. I could really use a dip of tobacco to calm the drumming in my skull, but I've been leaving my tin in the truck's glove box anytime I'm with Cassidy. If a moment comes when I might get to kiss her again, I'm not risking her turning me away because of some tobacco in my lip.

Thank God it's not long before she's leading me out of the

exam room. I don't even wait for the main office door to click shut before my mouth opens. "Not saying you aren't crazy anyway, but that doctor was a motherfucker."

"The worst." Her voice breaks, and it takes everything in me not to head back inside and have a few words with the doctor. If she starts crying, he's in for it.

"Hey, don't let him bother you. The guy's a prick."

A storm must've passed through while we were inside because massive puddles fill the parking lot and give off a wet soil smell. We walk side by side—taking long leaps over the biggest puddles and speed-walking through the open parking lot, crisp damp air nipping at us.

"He's not totally wrong, though. I probably shouldn't be eating potatoes for every meal. Just because I'm pregnant doesn't mean I need to gain a hundred pounds," she says, hopping over a puddle. "Plus, I'm single and would like *somebody* out there to find me attractive when this is all over."

"*Fuck that.* You'll be a smoke show no matter what." I open the passenger door of my truck for her, staring intently at her rear as she climbs in. She's been wearing leggings a *lot* lately, and the way they hug her ass makes my dick pulse with every glimpse. "We're getting French fries and milkshakes for the drive home, and you're eating it."

She laughs. "No need to lie to spare my feelings. But yeah . . . I need French fries. I've been getting them after every appointment, and baby knows the routine now. That's all I'll think about until I have some."

I'm recklessly tempted to tell her how hard my dick gets from just looking at her. That she's beautiful and cute and sexy as hell. That I seriously doubt her body changing because of *my* baby is going to do anything except turn me on more. But I can't say what I'm thinking, so I shut her door and take a deep breath of the humid air before climbing into the driver's seat.

As with every shared meal, I'm fully affected by the little

moan of pleasure with her first taste. The muscles working in her throat when she swallows the strawberry milkshake send a rush of blood to the area below my belt.

"Did you know the baby's actually the size of a potato right now?" She holds up a French fry as she speaks.

"Very fitting for our little spud." I can't help but smile any time she's within twenty feet of me, but especially anytime we're talking about the baby.

"Little Spud. I like that." She rubs her stomach. "Are you spending Thanksgiving at the ranch?"

"Yeah, the girls tend to go all out for any holiday, so I'm sure we'll have a huge feast. What about you?"

"Me and Dad. Same as always."

I roll my lips, trying on the sentence before saying it. "You could come to the ranch."

"That'll be an easy thing to explain to my dad, I'm sure," she says sarcastically.

She could just tell *her dad about us.* That's an option. But I'm not dumb enough to get into that fight twice in one day, so I zip my mouth shut and focus on the empty road ahead.

After some time, she blurts out, "Do you visit your parents or siblings for Christmas?"

I laugh under my breath, running a hand across the back of my neck. "Definitely not my parents. And my siblings are either equally fucked up or they have their own families. Nah, I usually spend it at the ranch. . . . Just you and your dad for Christmas, too?"

"Yup. But then I'm going to go visit Blair for a couple days."

That's a name I haven't heard in a long time.

"Like . . . Denny's Blair? I didn't know you two were still friends."

"*Denny's Blair?*" She laughs. "Are we fifteen again? Jesus, they dated in high school, and you know better than I that Denny has long since moved on. But yeah, she's still my best friend. She lives in Vancouver, and I usually visit her every couple months. With being so sick, I haven't seen her since she visited her parents at the start of summer."

My stomach flip-flops, fingers tightening around the leather steering wheel. "You're driving to Vancouver in the dead of winter?"

"Yes, I am . . . *Dad.*" She flashes a side-eye at me before shoving a fry in her mouth.

"Is she not coming here to see her parents for Christmas?"

"Oh, she is." She holds up a finger, finishing her mouthful before continuing. "She doesn't like sticking around here any longer than necessary, though. And we'll know the sex before then so I can do some shopping while I'm there. Shit, I guess we've never discussed that—do you want to find out or keep it a surprise?"

"There are two options, Cass. I'm not going to be surprised unless the baby's born with a tail or some shit."

She chucks a fry at me, bursting into a fit of laughter when I fumble trying to catch it and nearly veer the truck off the road.

"We can find out, if that's what you want." I lick the specks of loose salt from my bottom lip. "What do you usually do when you visit Blair?"

"Mmmm . . ." She thinks while sipping her milkshake. "We go out for dinner, shop, go to the bar. So all of that, but without the drinking. And she has some stupid idea about—never mind."

"What?" I watch her in my periphery and steal a French fry.

"Well, she thinks I need to have one last hurrah. Get with someone while I still 'have a hot body.' Although you and I and Dr. Dickhead already know I'm well past that. Plus, I'll be undeniably pregnant by the time I visit her—far from hot."

There's a long pause while I try to keep my blood from boiling over, try not to slam on the fucking brakes and ravage her. For one, because she stupidly thinks she isn't hot. For two, because the thought of another man touching her makes me want to smash my knuckles against the truck dash.

"No. You're not doing that," I say through gritted teeth and around the hot fry lodged in my throat.

"I mean, I wasn't actually planning on it. But now that you're trying to act like my keeper, I'm reconsidering."

I hate the fucking smirk on her face. I'm undecided about whether I want to grab her long braid, wrap it around my fist like a rope, and face-fuck the snarkiness right out of her mouth. Or I could kiss her, doing a much better job than at the rodeo, and glide my hands over her body while I fill her head with compliments about how gorgeous she is.

"Absolutely fucking not. For as long as you're carrying *our* baby, you're not letting any strange men near you. If you're that damn horny, you come to me. Use me. Got it?"

Cass's eyebrows bunch together, and her lips part slightly like she's struggling to find words, so I cut her off. "Before you backhand me, I'm not trying to be your boyfriend. We've fucked without feelings before so, if you need an orgasm, I'll give it to you. No feelings. You don't have to like me to fuck me, and we both know it was great last time—even if you don't want to admit you love my cock. But some random dude's dick will not be inside of you while my baby still is."

"I'm not fucking anything other than my vibrator, but thanks for offering to take one for the team."

Now I'm going to have the image of her using a toy on herself permanently trapped in my brain. I've seen what she looks like when she makes herself come, so it comes to mind too easily. I keep my eyes trained on the road ahead, knowing I'll have an instant hard-on if I look at her. It's difficult enough to keep it from happening, anyway.

I wonder what kind of toy she has. Before I truly knew her, I would've thought maybe something cute and dainty. But after the night of the rodeo, I'm not sure. It could be a fucking Godzilla dick, for all I know. Either way, I really want to know what she's working with. Fuck, I'd *love* to watch it, but that's not an option. At least knowing what she's using would help my imagination when I'm in the shower tonight.

"Wow, that shut you up." She breaks the silence after God knows how long. *How long have I been thinking about Cass riding a silicone dick?* "Mention a toy and you get so insecure you can't function or what?"

"Nah, I've done some team roping, sweetheart. I have no problem working with a teammate. Sometimes you need a header and a heeler."

That shuts *her* up.

At ten p.m., I'm three shower-beers deep and fisting my cock when I work up the nerve to finally ask. Because I'm desperate to fucking know.

Red: What kind of vibrator is it?

Cass: Are you drunk?

Red: Just tell me.

Cass: Hard no.

Red: Are we talking clit, penetration, both?

Cass: You are the human form of a migraine.

Cass: I'm not telling you about my vibrator so you can jerk off thinking about it

Red: Please :(

Red

Nineteen weeks (baby is the size of a hot dog)

I sink into her couch and look up at the mantel clock. I should head home, but I find myself staying later and later each night, even though it makes the early mornings painful. From the moment her front door closes behind me, it's an excruciatingly slow countdown to when I come over again. There aren't many places I'd rather be than on the back of a horse, far from civilization, with nothing but open skies and endless mountains. But these days I spend the entire time itching to get back to the barn, untack, shower, and drive to her house.

My new favorite place on Earth is wherever Cassidy Bowman is.

Nothing could've cleared that up for me like being out of cell service last week. My body was moving cattle with the boys, but my mind was right here with her. When somebody made a funny joke, I wanted to text Cass. While I made dinner, I wondered if she was eating the meals we saved in her fridge. Falling asleep at night, I pictured her watching TV alone. We haven't talked about whether she missed me—not that she would ever break and admit to it, anyway. But the moment we returned to the ranch, my phone went crazy with incoming delayed text messages to the point Colt and Denny both made snippy comments about me being whipped. It seemed she texted me every single random thought that popped into her head over those three days.

Tonight, it's late. I should leave, yet I make no move toward the door. Instead, I tuck her frozen feet under a blanket while she flips on our nightly reality TV binge. I've never been a big television guy but I can get behind sitting here with her every night. Rubbing her feet when she says they're sore, talking about our friends, planning a nursery. And as fucked up as it is, I've unwittingly become invested in all these women competing to date one guy.

"Imagine making it all the way to the hometown episode, then discovering the other person's family is completely off the rails." Cass gathers a section of her golden hair between her fingers like she's creating a paintbrush and begins toying with the ends. "Do you dump them because of that, or just accept the insanity?"

"Who am I to judge? My family's a fucking train wreck. I'd be the one getting dumped after the episode, not the other way around."

"I'm sure your family can't be that bad. Your brothers always seemed like decent guys. I know your dad's a drinker, but your parents are still together, right?"

I snort. "They shouldn't be. My dad's not a good guy, Cass. Way beyond the drinking."

She pauses the TV and turns in her seat, worry filling her pretty blue eyes as she considers my words. "How bad are we talking?"

I waffle between telling her or not. My family situation isn't a secret, per se. Austin, Jackson, and Denver know all of it because they were there. Even still, I usually prefer not to bring this shit up. Although the anxious look on her face tells me she genuinely wants to know. She wants—and probably deserves—the honest answer, as the mother of my child.

"I don't want you to think less of me."

She squints, shaking her head with a small, confused smile. "Why would I think less of you because of your dad?"

Why wouldn't she? That's the better question.

"I don't want you to question who I am as a person." I look down at my lap, sliding my callused palms together until they're fiery. "And I really don't want you to wonder if I'll be the same type of dad he was."

"Never. Promise." The soft kindness in her expression and the quivering corner of her lip ease my worry. A gentle nod encourages me to talk.

I grab her hand and run it over the circular scar on my forearm. It's covered with thick black tattooing in a pine tree design, but you can feel the raised, scarred skin underneath. Her eyes narrow, searching for an explanation of why I'm making her feel an old wound. "This is where he burned me with the twelve-volt lighter in his truck. I was ten and left the window down a crack on a night when it rained . . . so when we got into the truck the next morning, my mom's seat was wet."

"Jesus Christ. Did your mom know he—"

"She was sitting right there." I suck my teeth.

Her shoulders drop, and she blinks up at me with doe-like, watery eyes. I feel bad sharing this with her. Worried that Cass hearing about my shitty upbringing would make her regret letting me be involved with Little Spud, I didn't consider she might feel empathy for me.

"W-why didn't she try to . . ." Her voice trails off, silently answering her own question.

My hand fully covering hers, I move her fingers toward my wrist. "This scar here, I had surgery because I broke my arm when I was twelve. He smacked my mom, and I charged at him. He shoved me pretty hard, and I fell down the front porch steps of the house we lived in at the ranch."

"*God,*" she says under her breath. "I can't imagine."

Good. It's good she can't imagine it. It's good she didn't have to deal with anything like that. It's so fucking good she knows what it's like to have a loving, safe parent, so she can teach me how to be one.

"None of us were safe. When it came down to choosing between us kids and Joe, I guess she thought it was better in the long run to side with him. Keep him happy or whatever."

She tosses the blanket aside and crawls across the couch cushions until she's practically on top of me. Tight against my side, cradling my arm in her hands. She leans in to study my skin, suddenly noticing all the scarring I've done a great job of disguising behind tattooed trees, horses, and heavy shading.

"Is that why you have your tattoos?" she asks in a whisper.

"I got my first at fifteen and, when I realized it was a way I could cover up my past, I started spending every spare dollar on them. Until my body, and my memories of him, were nothing but a canvas for something better."

"That's really sad . . . and beautiful." The pads of her fingertips trace my tattoos, stopping briefly each time she feels the uneven texture of an old injury. I can't even breathe with her hands on me, and the fire in my veins feels like I'm pounding back hard liquor. Her touch is a fucking drug, and it's no wonder why I'm addicted. "Are all these scars from him?"

"No, no. A lot of them are from growing up on a ranch and working on one. I've gotten my fair share of cuts, scrapes, and broken bones just from roughing it with the Wells boys. But I think that only made the shit my dad did less noticeable. Teachers and nurses and doctors couldn't tell when my injuries were from something stupid I did versus something he did."

She licks her lips, blinking away the glassy sheen in her eyes, then presses her cheek to my chest and tucks her arms around me. I breathe in her hair like I'm trying to get high off her scent. Sharing my secrets comes with a weightlessness I've never experienced before. My heart's so light it floats, bouncing against my sternum like a balloon hitting the rafters, her embrace the singular thing keeping me from floating away. And, *fuck*, her hug's infinitely more healing than the liquor and weed I've previously numbed my pain with.

"I'm so sorry. You didn't deserve any of what you went through. And somebody should've stopped it. I wish I'd known the pain you were in."

"It's okay. I learned to stay out of his way, for the most part. And especially when he'd been drinking. Thankfully, the Wells family was always there when I needed to get away."

"Is that why you came back here instead of staying in the city?"

Driven out of town when I was fifteen—after my dad started one too many fights, stole one too many items, and pissed off one too many people—we moved to a shitty two-bedroom apartment in the city.

Though she can't see me, I'm sure she can feel my nod. "My dad struggled to find and keep jobs—turns out, construction sites are slightly more strict about drinking on the job than cattle ranches. We barely scraped by, which made things at home significantly worse, if you can believe that. As soon as I could, I called Grandpa Wells to ask for a job. Coming back to all the terrible memories was hard, but not coming back would've been harder. If he would've said no, I don't know where I'd be today—sure as shit wouldn't be in Vancouver. Only deranged people prefer to live somewhere where you can't see the stars, smell clean air, or jump on a horse and ride for hours without seeing a soul."

She sits up straight, keeping her hands on me. Her painted pink nails run up and down my forearm, igniting my skin like a grass fire that spreads quickly up my arm and explodes in my chest. "I always thought I'd end up in the city."

"Really?" I choke out the question—a piss-poor attempt at masking my concern that she might pack up our baby and leave Wells Canyon. "I have a hard time picturing you anywhere but here."

"Well, don't waste your time trying to imagine it because I'm stuck here now."

"You're not stuck. . . . If you want to move to a city, you can expect me to put up a fight. Anywhere else, I'll come with you."

"You'll come with me, eh? Did you seriously just invite yourself to move in with me again? Starting to worry I'll come home one day and all your stuff will be here." Her cheeky smile's illuminated by the cool glow of the paused television in an otherwise dark room. It sparkles in her eyes and highlights the deeply grooved Cupid's bow above her upper lip.

"We don't have to live together, but I told you I won't be the dad who's never around except for holidays. Living hours away from my kid isn't an option."

"I seriously doubt I'd ever choose to move, anyway. I always said I wanted to, but I've never been able to find a good enough reason to leave. No dreams big or worthy enough to justify leaving my dad here alone." She lets go of my arm, and I feel the loss of her touch all the way down to the marrow in my bones.

"You were easily the smartest kid in our school. I always assumed you'd be a doctor, lawyer, scientist, or something."

She halfheartedly laughs. "I wish that were the case. But I never found my *thing*, y'know?"

"Maybe your thing is having a disturbing amount of knowledge about reality television."

"Too bad I can't figure out a way for that to pay my bills instead of gossiping about it with Blair every week. I'd be living the dream." She lounges back, farther away from me than I like. But we're friends. *Just friends.* That's why she comforted me when she felt I needed it and why she's moved back to her end of the couch now that the moment is over. "For what it's worth, I'm not worried about you being like your dad."

"No?"

"I know you're quick to solve problems with your fists

when it's another guy involved. A few months ago, I might have been a tiny bit concerned. But since I've gotten to know you better, no shot. You're like . . . well, you're somewhat of a growly farm dog."

I recoil. "The fuck?"

She flaps her hand in my direction, silently telling me to calm down because she's laughing too hard to get words out. "*Relax.* I only mean you won't hesitate to fuck somebody up if they mess with the people you care about, but you wouldn't dream of hurting the people you love."

"And you figure you're one of those people?"

She absolutely is. Tops the list, honestly.

She pulls a face. "I'd fucking hope so, considering I'm carrying your child."

"Okay, okay. You're right. I guess I'll pretend being compared to an old farm dog is a compliment."

"Hey, you're the one who added *old,* not me." Her foot taps on the couch as we sit silently for a moment. "Nobody knows this, but I have secret accounts online, so I can keep tabs on my mom."

"Yeah? Why?"

She shrugs, chewing the inside of her cheek like bubble gum. "I guess to see if she's happier . . . without me."

"She's not."

"Mmmm, agree to disagree. She seems pretty happy traveling around in a camper van with a boyfriend closer to our age than hers."

"Everybody seems happy online. I bet she misses you. I can't see how anybody who's ever had the privilege of knowing you wouldn't miss you."

Hell, a few days without her was physically painful. I can't imagine years.

With a huff of disagreement, Cass snuggles down deeper into the plush couch. "Every time I get a fleeting feeling of wanting to leave town, I get scared I'm turning into her."

"You're not," I state matter-of-factly.

"You don't know that. I could be."

"If I'm a growly old farm dog, you're a barn cat. If I keep feeding you, I doubt you'll go anywhere."

"You're an asshole." She kicks me in the thigh playfully.

Cass presses Play, and we return to the show. Well, *she* returns to the show. I'm having a hard time paying attention to whatever Courtney F. and Sara P. are bitching about when the most incredible girl in the world is sitting across from me. Instead, I watch her with complete adoration. One hand resting on the tiny baby bump while the other twirls a loose strand of hair. Some nights, I worry she's going to pull her hair right out with the way she absentmindedly twists it around and around for the two-hour episode.

I've known her for so many years and wasted so much time not trying to *know* her. Or letting her—or anyone—know me. I bared the heaviest part of my soul tonight, and nothing changed in the way she looks at me. She glances over at me from across the couch, and her eyes light up, a crooked smile traipsing across her lips. My only regret is not finding a way to be here with her sooner—*years sooner.*

Cassidy

Twenty-one weeks (baby is the size of a bottle of sriracha)

"Cassie, I told you I have no issues shutting things down here for a few hours to come to the ultrasound with you." My dad runs a rag across the smooth wood bar top.

I hate that I'm lying to him but, for some reason, I can't find it in me to stop. Hindsight is 20/20, and I wish I'd had the balls to confess that Derek isn't the father months ago. Now the lying is so habitual, it honestly feels like it might never end. How can I possibly tell the truth when he's finally stopped being disappointed in me for getting pregnant in the first place? I dread letting him down all over again.

We don't talk about my pregnancy during open hours—I'm trying my best to keep it a secret from the rest of the town—but the hours before opening and after closing the bar are incredible. Dad tells me stories about when my mom was pregnant, we discuss baby names I like, and I show him photos of my nursery inspiration on Pinterest. Those moments feel like I'm experiencing the pregnancy I always assumed I would have—where there's a husband, a dog, a beautiful home, and a planned baby. All the while, I'm lying to my dad and not giving Red the credit he deserves.

"It's fine, honest. Shelby's coming with me, and I promise I'll come over first thing the next morning." The last of the clean glassware stacked under the bar, I stand up with a groan. I have no clue how I'm going to make it through another nineteen-ish weeks when a half shift at the Horseshoe sends blazing flames up my spine. "Besides, if you come, they're going to think you're my rich old husband. I fucking hate when people think we're *together* when we go places. Or, *worse*, they'll think I brought my dad to the ultrasound because I'm a pathetic loser with no boyfriend. No thanks."

"All right, all right. I'm just excited. Uncle Pete gave me some long-handled massager thing for my fiftieth birthday. I'll see if I can find it for you to help with the back pain." He grabs a full tray of dirty dishes and heads toward the kitchen door. "And quit gallivanting around with Shelby all the time—you should be resting."

I make a mental note to buy Shelb something *really* nice for Christmas as a thank-you. She and I haven't actually hung out in weeks, but like a teenager, I'm using my friend as a cover for the fact that I've been hanging out with a boy. Hell, I didn't even do this when I was a teenager because I was painfully uninterested in any of the boys around here.

I'm aware this entire situation is stupid, given I'm thirty-one and pregnant. I could, and arguably should, come clean.

"We're not *gallivanting*. There's nothing to even do in this town, anyway." I shake my head and slump onto my usual stool, stretching over the cool bar top until sweet relief hits my lower back.

Sweet relief, followed by an unusual sensation. I sit up straight with a jolt and focus on the bizarre feeling.

Did my stretching squish my belly in a weird way or something?

After a minute of nothing, it starts up again. I stare at the shelves of alcohol, listening to my dad run the industrial dishwasher for the last cycle of the night, and place a hand instinctively over my stomach.

Holy shit. The sensation's like somebody poured a glass of champagne, bubbles fizzing and bursting in my lower abdomen. Blair's basically my personal pregnancy tracker, filling me in on what to expect each week. And she informed me this would happen sometime around now, even with my anterior placenta. I squeeze my eyes shut, blocking out everything except the ticklish, weird, beautiful feeling. When it stops again, I tamp the dampness from my tear ducts and pull out my phone to text the person I'm most excited to tell.

Cass: I just felt baby kicks.

Cass: At least, I'm 90% sure I did.

Red: Serious??

Cass: If not, then I just cried happy tears over gas.

Red: I hope that's what happened

Cass: You would, asshole

Red: Only because I wanted to be there the first time

Cass: They're too small to feel from the outside. You didn't miss anything.

Cass: I promise you'll be the first

Red's truck has to be at least thirty degrees Celsius when I hop in. His face is flushed and he seems uncomfortable, but it feels so amazing on my chilled bones I have a hard time feeling guilty.

Rubbing my hands along my thighs, I say, "Ready to meet our kid?"

"Fuck no. But I'm excited, too." He looks over at me. "What about you?"

"No words exist to describe the weird mix of feelings I'm experiencing."

A puff of air blows from his nose in agreement. At least if

there's one thing we can both be consistent about, it's feeling overwhelmed. Rather than our usual easy conversation, today's stilted and jittery. As if we drank twelve cups of coffee each before having to sit still in the truck for an hour. I can't speak for him, but all I've had is a single half-caff while I was prepping the bar for Dad this morning.

"Supposed to snow tonight." *Great.* He's resorted to small talk about the weather.

"Yeah, that's what Dad said. Gave me a good lecture about driving in winter conditions, as if I haven't lived in Canada my whole life."

"I know we talked about going out for dinner, but maybe we should skip it so we don't get caught in the storm."

"Oh." Logically, I understand where he's coming from. But I also wanted today to feel more special somehow—not the same as every other typical doctor visit, where I drive home stuffing my face with French fries. "Right, yeah. Good call."

"It's not the same, but I can make dinner."

I plaster on a pretend smile. "As long as we can stop at the store and get some root beer. We're temporarily off the potato train and fully on team ice-cold root beer."

"As if you aren't permanently shivering as it is. But, all right, root beer takes a lot less effort than scalloped potatoes, so I won't complain."

We arrive at the ultrasound clinic without a second to spare, and they bring me into the back immediately, leaving Red, with his tense expression and anxiously bouncing knee, in the front lobby. It's the same ultrasound room I was in last time—complete with vintage landscape paintings lining the walls and an uncomfortable leather exam bed. I don't hate the artwork as much today. Almost as if the little trees and snowcapped mountains became less ugly and foreboding, somehow.

"New paintings?" I ask as I lie back on the bed and Heather, the cheery sonographer, squirts a dollop of warm gel on my stomach. Or maybe it's cold—I'm pretty sure I remember it being cold last time—but my body is in a state of permafrost, so most things feel relatively warm on my skin lately.

"Nope. Been there since long before I started here. Are you wanting to find out the sex or keep it a surprise?"

"Um, yeah. We're finding out." The memory of Red's response to me asking him that question makes my heart skip. Then I close my eyes and try not to let anxiety get the better of me. Although all I want to do is ask if things seem okay every ten seconds.

"I'm looking at the boring stuff right now. Measurements, close-ups . . . a bunch of things that'll look like blurry blobs to you. Just about done here, then I'll grab your husband and show you the fun stuff."

I open my mouth to correct her, but my brain's fried mush, unable to form a thought. I zip my lips shut, tucking my left hand under my thigh to hide the ringless finger, and revel in my pretend life for a moment.

"Perfect. Hang tight and I'll bring him in." She stands and walks out, leaving me alone with my racing pulse and anxiety-ridden thoughts. I pull my clammy left hand out from under me and dry it on my leggings. The deodorant I put on this morning suddenly doesn't seem enough for the amount of stress sweat pouring out of me.

And then, before I've even noticed him entering the room, Red grabs my hand. Letting his other hand fall to my thigh like it's the most natural resting place in the world and sending a rush through my entire body. For what may be the first time in weeks, not a single part of me is cold. I'm scorched. Flushed from head to toe.

"Okay, here's baby."

I'm pretty sure I black out. I can't even be totally sure what I'm looking at, or whether the blurriness is in my eyes or the monitor. But when I finally focus, it's pretty undeniable there's a small human there. Ten fingers, ten toes. A head so big and round, I'm already silently praying for my vagina. We watch a tiny heart beating, the rhythmic sound filling the room. And, just when I think I'm somehow not going to cry during this, I glance over at Red.

"Shut up," he murmurs before I've even said a word, frantically wiping his teary face with the sleeve of his jacket.

"Shit, now you got me crying. You softie." I reach to delicately dab away the tears brimming my eyelids.

The sonographer clears her throat. "All right, I'm going to print off some photos and get the envelope with the sex inside. If there's any concerns or the need for some more scans, your doctor will be in touch." She hands me a damp towel, and I'm made suddenly aware that I'm exposed from just under my breasts to my pubic bone. My belly's not particularly big, but it's also not a cute baby bump yet. Definitely not something I'm interested in showing off. Blair gets "bumpdates," but that's different from Red seeing me this way.

With a steady grip on my hand, he pulls me into a seated position and waits as I clean myself up, the dopey expression never leaving his face. For half a second, I consider kissing him to see what it would feel like to be a couple who *wants* to be in this situation. But I don't because we aren't.

So much of the weight has been lifted when we leave the stuffy exam room and walk into the crisp autumn air. All the awkwardness from the drive here vanished the moment we saw the baby.

"I don't think I can wait to look." Red holds the envelope up to the quickly setting sun, desperately trying to sneak a peek through the thin paper. Light, glittery snow drifts around us, settling on our shoulders and Red's tousled hair.

"Then give it to me if you can't control yourself." I reach out to grab it, and he pulls his arm away, then raises it above his head. Too high for me to ever be able to reach.

"What's the point in waiting?"

"Because it's special," I protest and strain my arm to reach the envelope, but it's no use. "Too special to open in the parking lot of a strip mall next to a KFC and a liquor store."

"What if I grabbed some chicken and beer . . . root beer for you. Isn't Derek from Sheridan? Could go sit on the hood of his car while we eat and open it up—for old times' sake. Would that be special enough, sweetheart?" He smirks down at me, his eyes falling on my lips. A teasing smile and pet name that I've always thought were condescending . . .

Except now I'm starting to think I've been wrong. Maybe I desperately need to be wrong.

"The more time you spend fucking around, the longer we have to wait to open it." I walk away before I do anything stupid like kiss the smug expression right off his face.

My nerves are entirely shot by the time we make it back to the quiet streets of Wells Canyon, having narrowly escaped wreckage at least five times, thanks to a brutal combination of heavy, wet snowfall and roadways coated in black ice. Pair that with a lot of drivers who weren't prepared for the season's first snowfall, and it's a miracle we survived. Neither of us spoke, the music turned low so he could focus. And I picked at a pinhole in the knee of my leggings until it became big enough to fit my thumb. I haven't been in Red's truck often, but tonight was the first time I've seen him keep both hands firmly on the wheel for the entire drive, and that scared me more than anything.

Falling in a heap on the couch, I look over at Red. "I thought I was going to die without ever seeing what's on that paper."

"Hrm, should've listened to my idea." He shrugs, pulling the slightly crinkled white envelope from his back pocket. "What do we need to do to make this fancy enough?"

"I don't care anymore. Just glad we made it home unscathed." I shuffle down the couch until my shoulder bumps into his, tucking my feet underneath me and discreetly enjoying his subtle soapy scent. "Open it."

"Give me a second." He disappears to the kitchen and returns a moment later with a barbecue lighter. Lighting the candles on my mantel and coffee table, he flicks off the overhead light. "*There.* Fancy."

Settling back in next to me, he's close enough I feel the butterflies in his stomach. With snow falling and contented stillness in the air, Red unfolds the paper. His trembling fingers smooth it out over his lap so we can read it together in the dim candlelight. And I'm immediately crying too hard to say anything. Too hard to express my excitement, to check in on how he's feeling, or to tell him he should stop the tender way he's stroking my hair.

"Holy fuck . . . a girl," he whispers—to himself, I think.

I kick myself for not wearing waterproof mascara as I come away from wiping my tears with black streaks across my hands. I know my face is probably a disaster but I'm comforted by looking at the man gently crying next to me. At least we can both be weepy messes together. "Think you can handle a girl?"

"Fuck yeah, I can. We'll paint our nails, then go work cows together."

"*You're* going to paint your nails?" The way I'm blubbering, I feel drunk.

"Abso-fucking-lutely. Painted nails, hair bows, whatever she wants. Not ashamed at all of being wrapped around her finger."

I laugh despite crying even harder with that statement. "My dad rocked painted toenails for *many* years when I was a kid. Poor guy was constantly undergoing makeovers. I can't wait to see you in blue eye shadow, glitter, and red lipstick."

"Been there, done that. Odessa got me good when I was asleep once."

I haven't thought much about Red's relationship with Kate and Jackson's kids. A few months ago, the thought of him interacting with small children would've been laughable. Maybe even a bit horrifying. That was before I got to see this side of him. The version that isn't the teenager who rarely went to class, smoked weed and drank beer on school property, and usually had more passengers in his truck than was legal. Or the guy who's drunk and always ready for a fight down at the Horseshoe. Neither of those is proving to be who he really is.

"Why do you never go by your actual name?" I ask, and his face crumples with confusion.

"Dunno. Got a nickname, and then that's just what everybody called me. I didn't bother fighting it."

Red is the rough cowboy from high school, or the bar, or the rodeo. He'll drink most guys under the table and kick anybody's ass without question. Chase is the guy who makes me any food I'm craving, drives cautiously through blizzards despite being proficient at four-by-fouring, and tucks warm blankets around my bare toes. The one who's crying about having a baby girl while smoothing his work-worn hand over my hair.

"Do you have a preference?"

"Nah. Not really."

"Well, you're going to be a great dad, Chase."

His hand pauses abruptly on my head before tugging me into him. My cheek collides with his firm chest, filling my ear with the thudding of his pulse. My heart's in a flurry, safe and warm with the weight of his arms holding me close.

"I should head out before the weather gets worse." He pulls away from the hug, clearing his face of any prior emotion.

Without a second thought, I blurt out, "Absolutely not. You aren't driving down that shitty dirt road in a snowstorm. You can stay here."

"I'm not sleeping on this dollhouse couch." Technically, it's a perfectly average-sized couch, but I can see why a guy who's hovering somewhere just under six feet tall wouldn't find it comfortable.

"You'd rather end up buried in a snowbank? I'll take the couch, and you can have my bed."

"Oh, good idea, Cass. Like I'm gonna force the pregnant woman to sleep here. I'll take the floor."

"Fine."

Red

Her room's exactly as I expected it—girly, simple, and as neatly organized as the rest of her house. And it smells just like her, of course. The same faint vanilla scent that's still lingering on the work coat she used as a blanket in my truck after the indoor rodeo.

I've never been the type to lie awake for hours at night. Usually, my head hits the pillow, and I'm a goner. But not tonight. Can't even blame it on the floor because I've slept in worse places than Cass's carpeted bedroom floor—with a thick, massive blanket and multiple pillows.

My mind's going a mile a minute, long after we say good night and the room becomes quiet. Judging by the changing angle of the moon as it pokes around the curtain edges, at least an hour has to have passed. I can't stop thinking about a baby girl . . . *my* baby girl. And the beautiful woman who's going to be her mom. Today made things feel real, and it wasn't only because I saw a tiny, fully formed human on a shitty old computer screen. Although, obviously, that made shit *really* real for me.

Cass trusted me to get her home in a blizzard, she curled her body into mine on the couch, and there were so many moments she looked like she wanted me to kiss her. Then again, it could be I'm seeing things that aren't truly there because I'm constantly overwhelmed with the need to kiss her. And I would if I thought it wouldn't fuck things up.

A noise cuts through the still air and my ears perk up. Another moment goes by, and I hear Cass. Moaning. The sweetest, softest noises go straight to my cock, making it jump to life inside my boxers.

Fuck, she must be having a wild dream.

If she knew I was overhearing the soundtrack to her dirty dream, her cheeks would turn the prettiest shade of pink. But the longer it continues, the less sure I am that she's sleeping. The blankets shift on her bed as she squirms underneath.

She couldn't be. My mind runs wild thinking of her touching herself not even six feet away.

"Cass?" I whisper, then hold my breath because she won't stop if she's truly asleep. But the sounds and the motion come to a grinding halt. *Holy fuck.*

I'm not thinking with the right head anymore—my lengthening cock convinces me to shoot my shot. "Need help?"

"Oh my God. Please fuck off," she mutters.

"Sorry, carry on. Just thought I'd offer, since it sounds like you're going to take all goddamn night to come at this rate."

"Yeah, well, I didn't want to use a vibrator and risk waking you up."

I reach down, adjusting the erection in my boxers and trying my hardest not to climb up into her bed. "I'm awake. Go ahead and use it."

Please, please fucking use it.

"Absolutely not. Not when you're here."

"You had no problem touching yourself when you thought I was asleep—which is hot as fuck, by the way. So I'll shut up and act like I'm sleeping." I can't help my mind wandering, wondering what she was thinking about as she pleasured herself. Picturing her on the hood of that car, legs spread wide as her panties shifted against her clit. The way her eyes stared directly into mine, fingers exploring her soft pussy. The way cum fucking *flooded* out of her. I thought squirters were purely a porn thing, but Cass is so fucking real—so sexy it drives me crazy—and I would give anything to be driven to insanity watching her come again.

"I haven't been able to sleep without it lately. I couldn't fall asleep, and I didn't know you were awake, so . . ."

"You need your rest, so just do it, Cass. We've fucked before—I promise not to be weird about it. Pretend I'm not here," I say despite the tightness in my throat and the ache to be in bed with her. No promises I won't jack off to this moment for the rest of my life, though. I swallow hard when her nightstand drawer squeaks open, and my cock's already dripping.

"Do you still want me to tell you what it looks like?"

"Holy fuck, *do I*." Obviously, I'd rather see it—and watch her use it—but I'll settle for this. It's embarrassing how many hours I've spent picturing her doing this since the day she mentioned having a vibrator. "Sure you don't want my help?"

"Shut up or I'll kick you out of here entirely."

"Sorry—go on." I bite my lip and slip my hand beneath the elastic waistband of my boxers. If I'm not allowed up there, I'm at least going to join in from down here.

"So, it's black and has two, umm, sections—the big one goes inside, and a small part vibrates against my clit. The small part has, like, bunny ears . . . um, I guess that's why it's called a rabbit."

"Mmm, wanna walk me through how you use it?"

I hear her let out a long exhale and the comforter on her bed shifts. My hand's wrapped around my cock, stroking slowly to the sound of her voice.

"It mostly does the work for me. Once it's hitting the right spots, I can lie back and enjoy. Normally I'd use lube, but I'm . . ." Her voice trails off.

"Already fucking soaked." *God*, I could come just from thinking about how wet her pussy likely is.

A breathy laugh. "Yeah . . . that." She sucks in a small gasp, then falls silent. I'm desperate to know exactly what she's doing. There's no way I'll be able to lie here not knowing.

"Sweetheart, use your words. Tell me what you're doing. *Please.*" I groan as I spread pre-cum down my shaft, pretending it's her wetness.

"I just slid it in. And now . . ." The drone of her vibrator fills the air, and my grip tightens around my dick. "I'm going to let it work its magic."

The buzzing intensifies, and she whimpers quietly—it sounds muffled, like she's clutching a pillow to her mouth.

"Don't be quiet just 'cause I'm here." I fist my cock, picturing how fucking good she probably looks right now. Her creamy thighs parted, one hand on the vibe and the other gripping her bed for dear life, long hair splayed across her pillow.

She takes my command seriously, letting out a raspy moan that catapults me to the edge. Between her moans of intense pleasure, all I can hear is her panting. I'd forgotten what she smelled like when she's turned on, but the room's so thick with it I can practically taste her. Each whine and whimper has me holding a firm grasp on her bed frame with my free hand. Anything to keep me on the ground instead of jumping up there, pulling the vibrator away, and ramming my cock deep inside.

"God, Cass. You sound so fucking sexy."

Her feet drag across the sheets, shoving her light blue comforter to the foot of the bed. If I sat up, I'd be able to see her. Maybe not in detail—it's pitch black in here, not even lit by the moon—but I'd be able to make out her curves as she thrashes. There's no way she doesn't look fucking incredible. My grip's sloppy and frantic, balls tightening as I hear her fall apart.

"Fuck, *Chase.*" I don't know what it is about hearing my

real name tumble from her lips as she makes herself come, but that does me in. A final pump sends thick ropes of cum shooting onto my bare stomach and thundering chest.

Once I've caught my breath, I tuck my dick back into my boxers and head for the hallway bathroom. It's not until I'm squinting into the mirror at myself that I realize what a mess I'm in. Because—*for fuck's sake*—I don't want to be her friend. Her dirty secret. Her baby daddy. I want more than that. I want to be in her bed, making her come every night so she can sleep. I want to touch her in ways that aren't even sexual—hold hands, stroke her hair, rub her sore back, and keep a hand firmly on her stomach while we sleep. And the only reason she didn't throw a pillow at me and order me to leave her room when I caught her touching herself was because I told her we could fuck without feelings. Which was total bullshit.

"Just sleep in the bed," Cass says when I walk back into the dark bedroom and find my makeshift floor bed gone. The room smells like sex, and her hand patting the empty space next to her has my dick pulsing in my boxers again. "Come on, we masturbated together . . . I think we can share a bed like mature adults."

Can't argue with that, I guess.

"Okay—switch sides."

"Absolutely not. This is my side of the bed." She pulls her hand away from the empty spot. "If you want to try and boss me around, you can stay on the floor. I retract my offer."

"Fine then. I'm sleeping closest to the door one way or the other."

Her face scrunches up like I just said something truly insane. "What are you on about?"

"The guy should always sleep closest to the door, for safety. What if somebody broke in?"

"I've been living here alone for *years*, and you think tonight is the night somebody finally breaks in?" She laughs but slides over anyway. "You're completely out of your mind, but whatever. I'll let you be the strong, protective cowboy hero for tonight. Although, whatever will I do without a big, tough man to save me tomorrow night?"

I want to offer to stay here every night, but I think Cassidy would shove me out of the bed. And this is an opportunity I selfishly don't want to give up.

"Thank you." I slip in next to her, wrapping my arm around her waist. "I'm warning you now—I'm a cuddler."

She groans. "And I'm absolutely *not*. Fuck all the way off."

"I bet you'd like cuddling me, if you tried."

"Nope." She scooches farther over, until her body is nearly hanging off the bed. "I can guarantee I would not. I like to sleep alone—uninhibited, unconfined, free of gross morning breath in my face."

"If I promise not to breathe in your face, will you let me cuddle you?" I chase her across the bed, until there's a ton of space behind me, but she and I are on the edge. My arm hooks around her waist, keeping her close.

"No." She groans dramatically under the weight of my arm. "Who the hell are you? One second you're like '*gotta protect the helpless woman*' and the next you're all '*cuddly-wuddly bear.*'"

There's something about the flirty, cute way she mocks my voice that fills me up every time. I don't even care that she's technically making fun of me; the smile it's paired with is my favorite fucking thing. And I can't help but notice she hasn't made a real effort to move away from my embrace.

"Cuddly-wuddly bear? Sounds cute."

"I'm not a teddy bear kind of girl."

"Too bad." I squeeze tighter. Knowing her feet are cold—they're *always* cold—I reach down and tuck them between my legs. With her in my arms, there's no issue falling asleep when my head hits the pillow.

Red

I wake up to her nails lightly dragging up my arm and across my chest, but I don't dare open my eyes. The room's still dark, though, so it must be early. She traces my tattoos, then brushes over the Wells Ranch brand on my chest. The brand I was eager to get when the Wells family let me come back, despite the hell my dad caused before we left town. The day I should've been walking across the stage for high school graduation, I was already en route back to Wells Canyon. Nervously calling Grandpa Wells as I fled the city. Praying he'd give me a job. Of course, he didn't even hesitate to say yes. And that's when I truly realized these people were more of a family to me than my own blood.

Cassidy's thigh creeps over my leg so her knee nudges my cock.

"Morning," she whispers because I guess she can tell I'm awake. My eyes fly open when her hand drifts lower to the waistband of my boxers. I was right, it's still dark. But the whites of her eyes are shiny as she lies on her side, looking me over.

"Cass," I mutter. "What—"

"No feelings?" Her hips press against my side with need, and she grabs hold of my cock through my boxers.

Fuck. How do I say no to something I've been wanting so goddamn bad, knowing it's not a good idea?

"No feelings." It's easy, apparently—I don't. I just lie. To both myself and her.

Without hesitation, she's straddling me in an oversized T-shirt, only the silhouette of her body visible as she grinds against my quickly hardening cock. Hooking my thumbs under the elastic of my boxers, I tug until my dick springs free. It bobs against her warmth, twitching when I watch her tongue dart out to lick her lips. This might be a bad idea in the long run, but it's incredibly worth it right now.

"Just one time, okay?" Her bare pussy drags slowly, smoothly against me like she's hoping it'll *accidentally* slip in. "One rule though."

I roll my eyes. "You and your fucking rules."

"No kissing. We're finally friends, and I don't want to fuck that up. But I need this. Need you."

Kissing is crossing a line but fucking isn't?

"Okay. No kissing. *Shit* . . . condom? I got tested after you told me you were pregnant, and I haven't been with anybody since you," I say, raising my hips slightly to feel the head of my cock nestle between her wet lips. Hoping to fuck she says she doesn't want to use one. I've never been bare inside a woman before, but I want to with Cass. I want to feel all of her around all of me.

"You haven't been with anyone?" Her eyes widen. I don't know why it comes as a surprise when I've spent nearly every spare moment with her for the past couple months. "The doctor tested me for everything at my first pregnancy check."

"No, I haven't." I barely get the words out before she grips my cock at the base and slides herself down the length of it. A fire spreads through me like I've been electrocuted in the best way. "*Fuuuuck.*"

Good fucking morning.

Her tight, wet pussy clenches around me with every bounce, and I grab at her delicious ass, helping her move up and down with slow, purposeful movement. Even in the dark, with bedhead and a baggy T-shirt, she's goddamn perfect. I'm aching to know what she looks like without the shirt—there's no way my fantasies have been doing justice.

I have the hem raised to her belly button when she stops me. "I don't . . . I think I should leave this on. It's not a great sight under there anymore with the belly and extra pudge in all the wrong places."

"I'm not fucking you without seeing your tits. Not again. *Take it off,*" I demand, giving the shirt a little tug, and, despite the flash of defiance in her eyes, she lets go. I can tell she wants to fight me—it's the same confrontational expression she had that first night. But there's no hiding the fact she *likes* when I boss her around. Flinging the shirt to the bedroom floor, I finally hold her full, round breasts in my hands. As expected, my dreams haven't been nearly as good as the real deal.

"They're still a bit tender so be easy on them, okay?"

I cut to where she's wrapping an arm around her stomach. As much as I want to stare up at this view forever, I throw her onto the bed.

"Don't hide this from me either." I plant a kiss on her bare stomach, my hands cupping either side tenderly. She didn't specify if kissing her body was allowed or not, but I don't give a shit about the rule anyway.

"Looking like I ate an entire horse isn't sexy."

"Are you shitting me? You're growing our baby girl and that's incredible, Cass." I kiss her warm, soft skin again. Any hope of fucking her without feeling anything is long gone. And I think she knows it. "You *never* need to worry about me thinking that's not beautiful. Or that you aren't beautiful."

I drag my tongue up her body and she shudders, sucking in a breath through her teeth and digging her nails into my shoulder as I pull her nipple into my mouth.

"Sorry," she whispers. The bite of her nails in my skin eases as she moves to tangle her hand in my hair. "Everything is super sensitive lately."

"I'll be gentle." Thank God I got it out of my system last night, or there's no way I'd be able to take my time here. Although, again, taking it slow doesn't make pretending this is a meaningless fuck any easier.

I should probably pull away and tell her to have another round with her vibrator. *Alone.* But instead, I lightly lick her hard nipples and smooth two fingers over her wet clit. She tightens the grip around my hair, and her back lifts above the bed, pressing her pussy firmly into the palm of my hand.

"Is this how wet you were last night?" My fingers slide down her soaked entrance.

Biting her lip, she nods.

"What were you thinking about?"

She doesn't answer. Instead turning her face to moan into the pillow as I plunge two fingers deep inside, feeling her walls tighten around them. The heel of my hand presses against her clit, and her body trembles from head to toe at the sensation.

"Now you're going to play shy, huh? You started this, baby. Want to know what I was picturing last night? I was thinking about burying my cock in this tight cunt, feeling you squeeze around me, hearing you moan my name, painting your fucking insides with my cum." She moans and squirms in response, messing up her sheets like she did last night. Her head rocks side to side on the pillow, and I delicately play with her pebbled nipple, drinking in the gorgeous body she's been hiding from me all this time. "Is that what you think about every night when you're lying here making yourself come? Tell me, Cass."

"Yes," she whines. The confession makes my heart race, and my balls feel like they're ready to combust.

"Tell me what you want right now."

"You." She nips at my jaw.

"Gonna have to be more specific if you want me to make you come."

"I want . . . I *need* you to touch me, lick me, fuck me. I want it all."

"Sit on my face, sweetheart," I demand, lying down next to her.

"What?" She blinks at me and, for a second, I worry I've pushed her too far.

"You heard me. Sit that sweet pussy down on my mouth. Wrap those pretty thighs around my head and fuck my face. Let me taste you. Let me look up at your perfect fucking body while you come."

"What if I crush—"

"*Cassidy*, quit being a fucking brat or I won't let you come at all."

With a hard swallow, she pushes up on her hands and swings a leg over my chest. I grip her thighs, moving her exactly where I need her.

"Grab the headboard and hold on," I order. The air between my face and her wet cunt is hot and thick, and I can taste her before she's even lowered down on top of me. When I look up, all I see is Cassidy. I wish she could have this view. See herself the way I do. It's fucking incredible.

"You're so fucking sexy." I run my tongue up her center, then delicately suck my way down either side. "And you taste—*fuck*." She tastes like no other man should ever be allowed to have her. I slide my tongue across her again, circling her clit and making her relax deeper. When I let up for half a second, she pulls away again.

"Quit hovering. *Sit*. Full fucking body weight, sweetheart."

"I can't do that. You heard Dr. Dickhead. I've gained—"

I pinch her clit between my teeth as punishment, disrupting her sentence as she inhales sharply. "If that moron gets in the way of me fully enjoying this pussy, I'm driving to Sheridan the moment we're done here and kicking his ass. *Sit.* Last warning."

She groans but sinks down further. My fingers dig into her plump ass to hold her to my mouth. I'm in heaven, smothered between her soft, wet lips, inhaling her sweet and clean scent. What I would give to eat her out for breakfast every fucking morning.

She wasn't kidding about being sensitive. The lightest flicks over her clit have her grinding against my face, searching for friction, moaning like she's trying not to come already. I suck and kiss her pussy lips, my pre-cum dripping down my shaft as her nails drag across my scalp. Her thighs on either side of my head ripple with tension. *She's close.* Focusing on her swollen clit, I give more pressure until her entire body contracts and relaxes in one drawn-out wave.

"Fuck," I say, licking my lips.

I could wear her like a fucking hockey mask all day, but my dick is so hard it's throbbing. I need to be inside her more than I've ever needed anything. She shimmies down my body, leaving her wetness on my bare chest like she's marking me with her scent.

Good. I want to be hers.

She notches the head of my cock at her entrance, her fingers wrapped around the shaft, and sinks down. Taking inch by goddamn inch, stretching around me with a raspy exhale. Cassidy Bowman is everything.

"Jesus, Cass. Look at you. You're a fucking dream." I grab at the meaty flesh of her hips, the pads of my fingers holding her with a bruising grip, and then I move up to keep her sore boobs from bouncing too hard as she rides the ever-loving hell out of me.

I don't even know where to look—it's all breathtaking. I didn't take enough time to fully appreciate her when we hooked up at the rodeo. I'm not making the same mistake today. There might never be another chance to see her this way, so I let myself get lost in her.

Her face tilted toward the sky, mouthing the words *oh my God* each time she's filled to the hilt. Her full, dense tits overflowing from my hands, with rock-hard nipples dug into my palms. Her perfect, soft, slightly protruding stomach that I want to kiss. Her hand rubbing rapidly over her clit while my cock glides in and out, shiny with her wetness.

"Is this what you've been craving? Ride me harder, sweetheart. Take what you need. Use me."

"Chase," she moans my name—my favorite fucking sound.

Her hips grind into mine, over and over, forcing the sweetest whimpers from her mouth. I'm kissing and sucking any scrap of her I can reach. Letting my hands roam her body like I own it. Nipping her forearm, pressing a soft kiss to her wrist, gently sucking her tits when she leans forward. If she's serious about this being a one-time thing, I'm going to touch and fuck and take every piece of her I can.

"I'm gonna come," she says on an exhale, riding me as if it's her goddamn job. Working hard to draw the next breath as her entire body threatens to fall apart.

"Good, I want to feel you drench my cock. Make a mess of the sheets under us."

Like a good girl, she does exactly that. Her greedy pussy grips me like she never wants to let go, starting to draw an orgasm out of me as I feel her cum run down my shaft and coat my balls.

"Come in me. *Please.* I want to feel you."

That'll do it. I groan, gripping her hips to hold her on my cock while fire courses through my veins. The edges of my vision blur with every frantic pump until I empty inside of her.

She falls onto me with the floppiness of a rag doll, and our chests heave together.

"You're perfect. So fucking perfect, holy shit," I say before pressing my lips to her sweat-soaked forehead. "Lay down and let me clean you up."

My cum and hers trickle down my shaft as I pull out with a shiver. I ease her off of me and slip down the bed, kneeling between her legs and licking my way up each of her thighs. She whimpers softly, her legs shaking with aftershocks. Flattening my tongue, I lick either side of her pussy. Then the center. She bucks when I suck her swollen clit into my mouth.

"Oh God, I can't take more." Her hips lift so I'm buried in her and her thighs tighten around my skull, betraying her mouth. "I'm too sensitive."

"Just making sure you're good and clean." I smile and dive back in for more barely-there swipes of my tongue. Cleaning my own mess. Savoring the tang of our combined cum on her delicate skin. Dragging my nose up her slit to breathe her in. Desperate to commit every piece of her to memory.

"We taste so good together, sweetheart."

Moaning, she arches her back, and a small stream of my cum drips out of her. Without a second thought—knowing it won't make her any more pregnant than she already is—I save it with the tip of my finger and slowly slide it back inside her.

"Chase," she whines. When she looks down at me with sleepy eyes, I press one final kiss on her stomach before taking my space next to her. She tucks into my side, and my hand naturally finds its way to her belly.

"I'm gonna start sleeping here every night. What a way to go to sleep and wake up. *Damn.*" I exhale, letting my heart rate return to normal.

"Sorry, I've been . . . *really* horny lately. Then I woke up to a muscley, tattooed man in my bed and I couldn't stop myself."

"You do that anytime you want, like I told you. If you need it, come to me."

"Friends-with-benefits never works. Haven't you seen any of the hundred different rom-coms about it?" She's back to tracing the tattoos on my arm.

"Do I look like I've watched a *rom-com*?"

She laughs, sweet as honey. "Okay, no . . . Believe me when I say it's a bad idea, though. Somebody always catches feelings, and we can't afford to have this implode on us. Can we go back to how things were before last night?"

The funny thing is last night changed nothing for me. I didn't need to hear her moan my name, see her naked, or bury myself deep inside her to know I'm falling for her. I've never felt love—not really. My mom said it to me, but I didn't feel it. I guess the Wells family is the closest. But I've definitely never had it with a woman and I didn't think I ever would. *This* . . . the way I feel when I'm with Cass, the way I can't go a minute without thinking about her, and the way we just *fit* together. That's gotta be love, right?

"You seriously haven't slept with anybody since we hooked up at the rodeo?" With a wiggle, she's even tighter against my body, a leg slung over mine.

Doesn't like cuddling, my ass.

"That surprises you?"

"I mean . . . yeah, kinda. I thought that's what you and Denny do. Get drunk, get in fights, sleep with tons of women."

I snort. "Sometimes, sure. Mostly the drinking and fighting, though. Denny and I sleep together in a pickup box most nights."

"*Cute,*" she teases, pinching my ribs. "Probably won't surprise you to hear I haven't hooked up with anyone either."

I hadn't put too much thought into it before, but I can't help the calming effect those words have on me. My callused hand brushes over her hair, and I stare down at the golden eyelashes fanned out across her cheek. I count the tiny apricot-hued freckles speckling the bridge of her nose, losing myself in how incredible it is to finally hold her. Technically, since we're supposed to have no feelings, we should get dressed. I should go home. But neither of us moves for at least ten minutes.

We're perfectly content until the sound of Cassidy's front door lock cuts through the silence and throws her from my arms.

"Oh shit—my dad." She springs to her feet.

Fuck. Shit. Fucking shit. It can't be later than seven o'clock. Does he always come here this early in the morning?

"What do you want me to do?" I whisper back.

She's on the brink of tears as she rushes to dress. Any hopes of spending the morning wrapped up with her are long gone. We're both well aware my truck's in her driveway. In hindsight, I should've been parking it down the block this whole time. It's incredible it took this long for him to find out—gossip typically travels fast in a small town. None of that matters anymore. The jig is up. I should be thrilled she finally has to tell Dave the truth, but this isn't the way it was supposed to go.

"Just . . . crap, crap, crap. I guess get dressed and come with me."

I feel around under the sheets for my boxers, then quickly throw my clothes on and follow her down the hall. It's not the first time I've walked into a situation where I'm about to be punched for sleeping with a woman, but it *is* the first time I'm sick to my stomach over it. Could I hold my own against Dave, despite the fact that it looks like he spends hours at the gym daily? Probably. But I already know if he punches me, I have to find a way to stop myself from hitting back. For Cass. For the baby.

"Dad, what are you doing here?" Cass walks in ahead of me and sits opposite him on the couch. I hang back, leaning against the doorframe so I can make a quick exit if I need to. She and I are likely nose blind to the sex smell, but this is a small house . . . no way he doesn't notice it. As if coming out of her bedroom together wasn't bad enough.

"Power's out across town from the storm, so I came to see if you're okay."

Huh. I glance around the room, and it seems he's right. We were too busy creating body heat in her darkened bedroom to notice the chill in the air and the lack of working lights.

"What's *he* doing here?" Dave's head gestures in my direction, but he doesn't actually acknowledge me.

"Um . . ." Cass's eyes cut back and forth between me and her dad. "The roads were bad so he couldn't get back to the ranch."

"Right. But why is he *here*?"

I watch her fiddle with her shirt. She twists the loose fabric around her finger, untwisting, twisting again. Giving a small glimpse of the kissable skin on her lower stomach.

"Well, I didn't tell you the whole truth earlier. . . . Shelby didn't come with me yesterday. Red—uh, Chase—did. The baby isn't Derek's."

Even though his back is to me, the way his big-ass shoulders quickly rise and fall tells me he's *pissed.* I can't say I'm shocked. I knew he wouldn't like finding out Red Thompson had sex with his little princess.

The way he's sitting—hunched over and massaging his temples—brings me back to childhood mornings with my dad hungover on the couch. We'd watch cartoons on mute while he groaned in agony. His fingers clenched his head so tight I thought sure as shit they'd press right through to his brain—my older brother told me the temples were a thin spot, and that's exactly where Dad's pointer fingers were gripping. I was torn about whether that happening would be super badass or terrifying. Maybe it would even kill him. Maybe we'd all finally get to be happy.

"This isn't how I wanted to tell you," she continues. "I was just nervous and kept putting it off. He wanted me to tell you, and that's why he hasn't been to the bar in weeks, because he's been trying to respect my wishes. So be mad or disappointed or upset with me, Dad. It was a rebound thing after Derek, and I was serious when I told you about planning to do this alone. But then Red—Chase—found out, and he's been great."

My heart's damn-near bursting from the amount of times she's called me Chase. Even when her instinct is to say Red—which makes sense given that's what I've gone by since we were kids—she quickly corrects it.

"Like, the Jolly Ranchers? Those were from him. And he's been bringing me dinner multiple nights a week, even though he works all day. He made sure we got home safe in the blizzard last night. So don't hate him."

She's listing facts, but the tone of her voice makes them sound like compliments. It's as close to a woman bragging about me, being proud to have me, as I've ever gotten.

Dave's silence is fucking unnerving. Cass looks at me with impossibly wide eyes, and I wish I'd told her there are already feelings involved on my end. Maybe then she'd be okay with me comforting her in front of him. The tendons in my arms are aching to reach out to her. I want to scoop her up, take her back to bed, and show her how thankful I am that she's not keeping me a secret anymore. Even if coming clean was against her will.

Finally, he clears his throat. "Red, sit."

I keep a wide berth around him, like he's an untamed horse liable to kick or bite, and sit in the recliner. The same one Cass sat in when she told me the baby was mine. Seeing Dave's face, I understand the horror in Cassidy's expression. He's seriously pissed off.

"Not that I wanted Derek to be the father, but I gotta say I'm not fucking happy about this alternative, Cassie." He shakes his head, forcing an exhale through gritted teeth. "Are you together then?"

"No." Cass is quick to answer.

"Christ." He pinches the bridge of his nose between his finger and thumb. "Now what? Are you going to be involved?"

Oh, he's talking to me.

"Yeah—yes." I have no idea why but I'm suddenly tempted to call him sir. "As much as Cass lets me. Obviously, this wasn't planned, but I'm happy it's happening."

"He cried twice about it yesterday." Cass throws me under the bus with a soft smile. "Dad, I know you have your feelings about Chase. But . . . I'm honestly glad it's him instead of Derek."

Oh yeah, she's definitely getting anything she wants to repay her for that.

Dave's eyebrows are drawn together so tightly they create a canyon in the skin between them. His eyes slice between me and Cass. "Let me be clear, Red. I don't trust you. I don't think you're good enough for my daughter, and I have *very* low expectations for you as a father."

"I know I'm not good enough for Cass. Don't need to tell me what I already know." I stare back at Dave's unwavering glare. "I think I'll be a pretty good dad, though."

His nose crinkles with disagreement, huffing. "Mmm—apple doesn't usually fall far from the tree."

"Dad, that's not fair." Cass shakes her head with a sneer.

Fucking typical. It always comes back to my piece-of-shit father.

"He taught me exactly what *not* to do. I'm not him. Not even fucking close."

Dave shrugs, likely not believing me. People don't know half of what went on at home. Joe Thompson in public was a hotheaded, drunk nuisance. *But at home?* When I was six, I figured out how to barricade my dresser against my bedroom door to create a makeshift lock. Growing up on a ranch led to a lot of scars—falling off animals, barbed wire scrapes, and climbing trees all marked up my body. But most people don't know that Wells Ranch wasn't the only source of my injuries. I might drink more than I should sometimes, and I'll be the first to admit I can have a temper, but I'm not a mean drunk. Definitely not abusive.

"If my dad is your main argument against me, what about Cass's mom?" I'm quickly losing control of the heat swirling inside me. I know it's not fair to pull Cass into this with me, but my brain's scrambled and a landslide of words tumble out. "She's nothing like her mom, but I'm automatically the same as my dad?"

"That's different." Dave clocks my clenched fists and raises a brow, clearly thinking he's onto something. Of course he thinks that's different somehow.

"Honestly, fuck off. This is between Cass and me. You can think whatever the hell you want about me—it doesn't change the fact that we're having a baby *together,* and I'm stepping up to the fucking plate. None of this involves you."

"None of this involves me?" Dave yells, rocking forward like he's ready to launch himself at me. "Cassidy is my daughter and—"

"And she's carrying mine!"

My chest rises and falls in a rapid commotion, hot blood pooling in my ears, tension building in my fists.

"Chase! Dad!" Cassidy's pleading voice brings everything to a grinding halt.

"I'm gonna head out. See if the road's cleared back to the ranch." I stand, shaking my clenched hands out and heading for the door. If I stay a second longer, I'll punch my baby's grandfather and lose any chance of being allowed around the baby or Cass.

I'm halfway to my truck when I hear the front door shut and Cass calling my name. She's barefoot, tiptoeing on the balls of her feet through the ankle-deep snow.

"You're gonna get frostbite," I say.

"I just needed to tell you that I'm going to talk to him, okay? It won't be terrible like this forever. He just . . ."

"Thinks I'm a piece of shit. It's fine. I'm used to it. Your feet can't handle getting any colder than they usually are. Go back in, and I'll talk to you later."

"My dad being upset about this doesn't change anything, so you know. We're still friends, and I still want you to do this with me." Her hand smooths over her stomach. "I'll try to talk to him. Can you come over again tonight?"

I want to kiss her, despite the stupid rule she created. But tenderly kissing her in front of her house, with her dad inside, is a boyfriend move. And we've already established I'm *not* that.

"Please, Chase."

A cozy warmth settles over me, despite the snowy weather. "I like that you've been calling me Chase."

"It suits you better. Are you going to come over?"

"I'll be here."

Even though I shouldn't. I'm not the right guy for Cass. For a minute, I was starting to think I could be, but her dad jarred me back to reality. I'm only here because she's too good a person to tell me not to be.

Even still, if she asks, I'll be here.

Cassidy

Tears well as I watch Chase drive away. Turning on my heel, I storm back into the house, slamming the door and parking myself on the recliner. Staring at Dad with a narrowed glare.

"That was uncalled for. You were an asshole to him for no reason."

"Really, Cassidy? *Red Thompson?*"

"Yes, Dad. *Chase Thompson.* We . . . we hooked up one time. And at first, I didn't know if I was going to tell him I was pregnant. But he turned up here because he heard a rumor, and I couldn't lie to him—"

"Yet you can lie to me?" He exhales loudly, cracking his knuckles. "He's a loser, Cass. I don't know what the hell you were doing hanging around him in the first place—you know he's nothing but trouble. Destined for prison or worse."

"You don't know him." I spit the words, unblinking, with a pounding in my skull. Nostrils and eyes burning as I will myself not to cry. "You don't."

"Come on. You're a smart girl—you've gotta be able to see through the bullshit. That's what this is. *Bullshit.* You've been there as often as I have to see the shit he pulls. The drinking, fighting, acting like an idiot with his cowboy buddies. It's exactly how his dad used to be. Same bullshit twenty years later."

Exasperated, I throw my hands in the air, letting them fall against the padded armrests with a resounding thud. "This is why I lied to you, Dad. Because I knew you'd be a *fucking asshole* about it."

My jaw quivers, dispersing droplets of brackish tears across my lap. They pour down my face, thankfully blurring my vision because the last thing I want right now is to see my dad's face.

"So yeah. I told you Shelby was coming to the ultrasound yesterday, but it was Chase. By the way, we're having a girl. Not that you've bothered to ask."

I suck in my lips and look over at him, taken aback by the broad smile gracing his face.

"Wow, Cassie. I'm sorry I didn't ask. I meant to, obviously . . . God, baby girls are the best, you know."

"Yeah, Chase is pretty excited."

"Cassie, I—"

"Save it. You need to go."

I don't bother waiting for him to leave before dragging my feet down the hall and burying myself under the covers. My pillowcases smell faintly like Chase—freshly lit woodstove with a hint of tobacco. I inhale his scent, clutching the pillow for comfort and letting myself fall apart. About being in my thirties and not knowing what the hell I'm doing. About having a one-night stand and getting pregnant. About that guy turning out to be sweeter than I imagined, and how painful it is that nobody else sees it.

An extraordinarily rude beam of sunlight streams through an opening in my curtains, straight onto my eyelids. Blinking away the sleepiness, I slide my hand around in the dark for my phone. Eleven o'clock . . . in the morning, I assume. With a yawn, I pull myself out of bed and saunter down the hall to my office.

While this morning started out as one of the best I've ever had, it quickly devolved. And now I may as well keep the shitty mood going by packing up my leatherworking tools. I flip the light switch, pleasantly surprised to see the power's back on, and stare at the mountain of work in front of me. My dad offered to help weeks ago, but this pregnancy task needs to be done alone. I need the catharsis of putting this stuff away—putting this part of me away.

The lid snaps off a blue plastic tote, and I plop down in the leather desk chair.

There's no need to be sad about giving up this silly little hobby. Think about the baby.

I sigh, carefully packing tools one after another into the various totes I have around the room, then moving on to the meticulously stored leather. I grab a small piece of scrap and hold it to my nose, inhaling deeply—calming my body and easing my emotions. Exhaling with tear-filled eyes and rattling breath.

By the time I'm done, I'm sure I've cried every last tear available to me. I'm numb and tired and starving. Naturally, with Chase cooking here most nights, my fridge is full of ingredients, but nothing helpful for a non-cook like me. He won't be here with dinner for hours, and I'm obviously *not* showing up at the Horseshoe today. Which leaves me with Anette's Bakery down the street. Fantastic cinnamon rolls, awful gossip mill.

But shit. A cinnamon roll would be pretty great.

Two minutes later I'm bundled in winter gear and heading out into the snow. Rather than digging out my car, I opt to trudge through the mid-calf-deep powder. The sun warms my cheeks, despite the air being cold enough my nose tingles and my breath creates dense fog. And kids run past hurling snowballs, clearly thrilled by the early season blizzard.

Anette's Bakery is a small shop on Wells Canyon's tiny Main Street, tucked between a home goods store and the library. Anette has to be at least seventy and has been running the place since long before Dad and I moved to town. On a good day, when the breeze is right, I can smell fresh bread from my front yard a few blocks away.

The door opens with a jingle, and I pull off my mittens, stuffing them in my pockets. Despite the heavy snowfall, the cozy bakery's crowded with people sitting in every overstuffed chair and huddled around the quaint bistro tables. The smell of ground coffee and sprinkled cinnamon floods my nostrils, causing an incessant rumbling in my stomach. I sashay to the counter, where Anette's standing with a flour-covered apron and sparkling grandmotherly eyes.

"Well, good morning, young lady. Long time, no see."

I put on a happy face for her. "Morning, Anette. How are the grandkids?"

"Oh, they're a handful. You here for a cinnamon roll?"

"You know me too well. And a coffee, please."

She smiles and gets right to work, sliding a hot cup of coffee across the counter, followed by a pink box. With a wink, she quietly says, "I put an extra one in there for you. I was so hungry all the time when I was pregnant."

Confirmed: everyone in town knows.

"Oh . . . thank you." I scoop up the box and my coffee, heading to the far end of the counter to add cream and sugar.

Despite the kitchen sounds, coffee grinder, chatter, and the glug of heavy cream splashing into my cup, my ears perk at the mention of my name.

A group of women sits at a table behind me, talking about me. While I don't typically provide good fodder for gossip, the act of gossiping itself is not unusual here—this *is* the place people come to indulge in whisperings about everyone in town. Show up here any day, any time, and pull up a chair if you want to know every diminutive detail of a person's life. Somebody's husband cheating on her with their nanny, two teachers hooking up, the corner store closing for an hour every Thursday morning so the owners can go to couples counseling. The rumors are inescapable and, admittedly, sometimes fun to hear. Until you're part of it.

Today, I'm part of it. But it's not just me . . . it's Chase, too.

"I heard they've been secretly hooking up at the bar for a long time—that's why her boyfriend broke up with her."

"Makes sense. I mean he's *always* at the Horseshoe."

"I'd be so embarrassed to be with a guy like that—always drinking and getting hauled out for fighting."

My bottom lip trembles, and I'm frozen in place, knowing I should leave and go back home. I'm in no state to stand here listening to this after everything else today, but I can't stop myself. White-knuckling the counter with one hand, I continuously stir my coffee. The thud of the spoon against my cardboard cup is so frequent and fast, I might accidentally make whipped cream.

"I mean, he's hot. That's basically all he has going for him."

"Sure, but I would get an abortion so fast if Red Thompson knocked me up."

The metal spoon drops, clinking against the countertop, as I spin around to face them. Three women I've known since high school—which also happens to be when they peaked—stare at me wide-eyed, realizing their hushed whispers weren't quiet enough.

"Cass, hey. Didn't see you there." Sophie, the preppy blond ringleader, stares innocently at me. Growing up, she was the absolute worst. Then she married her high school sweetheart, had three kids by twenty-two, and nowadays spends her free time hating her life while gossiping about everyone else's. "Where's Red?"

Her two friends refuse to face me, taking sips from their lattes to cover cruel smirks. Not Sophie, who's wearing a Stepford smile like her only two brain cells are fighting for third place.

I stare back, unsmiling. "Oh, probably on horseback somewhere at the ranch. *Minding his own fucking business*, like what you should be doing."

"Come on, Cass. You misunderstood, we were joking around."

"Misunderstood what, Sophie? Tell me exactly what's funny about you spreading bullshit rumors and saying I should"—I swallow hard—"get an abortion."

Her petite brunette friend, Ashley, clears her throat. "We didn't mean *you* should."

"Don't forget, I know your husbands. They spend a lot of time at the Horseshoe, too. You're not in a good place to talk shit about Red when *those* are the men crawling into your bed every night."

Cinnamon rolls and coffee secured, I leave their stunned asses behind. I pull out my phone to text Chase, confirming whether he's coming over tonight. The two of us talking, laughing, and relaxing in silence is exactly what I need to get out of my head. I need to look across the couch and see his smile. I need to hear him laugh at something stupid I said. I need his hands firmly massaging my feet and calves and I want them softly touching everywhere else. Friends-with-benefits is risky behavior, but one more night won't hurt.

The front door clicks shut, and I slowly lower the bottle of root beer I'm pouring from, waiting for something to indicate whether it was Chase or Dad who let themselves in. With a hard swallow I lean to peer through the archway, and a glimpse of reddish hair makes the tension in my muscles melt away. The armor I've put on to keep myself sane since getting home from the coffee shop—the only defense preventing me from being a weepy mess on the floor—falls apart the instant he steps into the kitchen.

"Hey. *Hey*, why are you crying?" Chase grabs either side of my face, forcing my eyes to meet his. "Are you okay?"

"Today fucking sucked." I rub away the tears. "I'm sorry about my dad. About the shit he said."

"That's not your problem, Cass. He can think whatever he wants. I expected it."

I expected it, too. Doesn't make it less frustrating, though.

"If you want me here, that's all I care about. All I've wanted since day one is for *you* to say you want me involved. To feel like I'm not just here because you feel obligated to let me be around. I don't care what anybody else thinks about it."

Because I feel obligated? That's *why he thinks he's here?*

"I want you here. Little Spud and I need you here."

His hand slides up to my hair, cradling my skull and pulling me into the hug I desperately needed. The way he holds me tight to his body, enveloping me in the scent of his soap and the warmth of his arms, I think he needs it, too. We cling to each other like Rose and Jack Dawson should've done on the floating door out at sea.

"Thanks for attempting to stand up for me. Even if you tossed me under the bus a bit with the crying shit," he says.

"I can't help that I love knowing how much of a softie you secretly are. You're a crier *and* a cuddler—two facts I wish everybody could know about Chase Thompson."

"I'd rather you not tell the whole town. Got my shitty reputation to uphold and all."

I tamp down the urge to tell him about the stupid women at the coffee shop. I'm aching to talk through it after spending the afternoon with their words on replay in my brain, but it's a conversation best saved for Blair. I won't risk hurting Chase's feelings.

Instead, I lick my lips and keep things light. "Damn, wouldn't want to go fucking with that, would we?"

"Well, if it weren't for my reputation, you wouldn't have begged me to fuck you on Derek's car hood."

"*Begged?*" I raise a brow. "Maybe not, but that's not what's getting you in my bed tonight."

With a disapproving click of his tongue, he says, "Cass, I thought you said it was a one-time thing. Now you're breaking your own rules. This is going to lead to full anarchy."

"Shut up if you want to get your dick wet."

"Oh, do I. But after your crappy day, let me take care of you first. Let me make it better. *Much* better, hopefully."

"It already is."

Red

Twenty-three weeks (baby is the size of a box of Kraft Dinner)

I flick my Skoal can in my hand, absentmindedly packing a dip of chewing tobacco as I stroll into the fairgrounds behind Jackson, Kate, and the kids. Odessa's on Jackson's shoulders, knocking his hat sideways with every other step, and Rhett's fast asleep strapped to Kate's back. I can tack up a horse in minutes—under a minute, if I put my back into it—but there's no shot I could figure out how to work the backpack-type carrier Kate has him in.

Add that to the never-ending list of shit to learn.

The Wells Canyon Winter Fair is the most excitement our town sees outside of rodeo season. Some people might find it odd how excited the whole town gets, considering the primary goal of the fair is for the local 4-H kids to sell their project animals—mostly for meat. But among the food vendors, live music, and bounce houses for the kids, you have just about every person who lives within an hour's drive of Wells Canyon. *That's* the real reason people enjoy it.

The massive hall is filled to the brim with people. At least twenty old-timers are circled up—wearing faded denim and dusty cowboy hats, sitting on folding chairs, and drinking coffee out of Styrofoam cups. Their wives sit similarly a bit farther away. With numbers pinned to the back of their shirts,

4-H kids run amok all over the place. And a few babies are crying in the distance. It's overwhelming as shit.

Weaving through the crowd takes forever, thanks to Austin and his inability to ignore people wanting to talk to him. For a man who barely mutters a single damn word at the dinner table, you bring him into a room with a bunch of other ranchers and he's Mr. Social Butterfly. Well, *kind of.* He still prefers they do the talking while he nods along like a bobblehead.

When we step into the show barn, where some kids are parading around their hand-raised lambs, I finally take a breath. The place smells like various kinds of animal shit, but I prefer that over the suffocating air inside the crowded Agriculture Hall.

My calming exhale is cut short by the blond-haired beauty standing on the opposite side of the show pen. The past two weeks have been the best of my life, without a doubt. I've spent more nights in her bed than my own, touching her and holding her while we sleep. It's the same routine: eat dinner, talk about our day, curl up on the couch to watch TV, fuck. Then she tells me we shouldn't be doing this, that it's only going to ruin our co-parenting relationship once Little Spud comes. She's given the same speech so many times I have it memorized. Yet, when I leave before daybreak to drive back to the ranch, she squeezes my hand and asks if I'm coming back later. And my answer is yes. Forever yes.

When her eyes lock on mine, I forget about the nicotine fix in my hands and the uncomfortable buzzing under my skin from being in such a crowded place. I knew she'd be here, but that doesn't make me any less surprised when she gives a small wave and starts toward us. Under the prying eye of every gossip in town, I wouldn't blame her for outright ignoring me.

"Hey," she says. Her hair's tousled and down, falling across her chest. I know her tits are getting more impressive by the damn day, but nobody else can tell how full they are thanks to the baggy black hoodie—*my hoodie.* Between the loose-fitting fabric and the way her arm's slung across her stomach, you'd never guess she's pregnant. I don't understand her desire to hide it when I'm sure the whole town already knows. But there's no way I was going to win *that* argument last night.

"Nice hoodie." The unopened Skoal can slides easily into the back pocket of my jeans. "I think I have one just like it."

She rolls her eyes at me, a small smile cropping up. "It's a pretty generic black sweatshirt, so probably."

"Cass!" Kate practically shoves me out of the way. "A girl! Oh my God, I'm so excited."

She pulls Cass into a hug, rambling away. "I keep telling Red to give you my number, but I'm going to go out on a limb and guess he hasn't. So please take it. Call me. Text me. Anything you need, got it?"

Cassidy's gaze meets mine from over Kate's shoulder as they separate.

"You better take it. She's known to be a pain in the ass when she doesn't get what she wants," I say, quickly stepping to the side to avoid Kate's swinging arm. "Actually, this was probably a bad idea to get you two together."

"Oh, right. Because we're '*crazy pregnant ladies,*'" Cass says in the deep voice she uses to mock me, handing her phone to Kate. "This asshole had the audacity to say you were crazy when you were pregnant, and that now I am, too."

Just before I'm about to have my ass handed to me on a silver platter, Odessa—who will be getting some very nice Christmas presents this year—throws herself into Cassidy with a thud. Odessa's small arms wrapping around her hips and her huge eyes staring straight up at Cass, it's the perfect distraction.

"Oh. H-hi." Cass stares down at the little girl clung to her.

"You're Uncle Red's girlfriend. Mommy said you have my baby cousin in your tummy." Her small hand draws slow, thoughtful circles over Cass's stomach like she's rubbing a magic lamp.

"Um . . ." Cass starts—her eyes the size of saucers when she looks at me.

"Odessa! Personal bubble, remember?" Kate shakes her head, smiling despite her scolding tone. "Sorry about her. She's pretty excited—we're all excited. Hopefully you don't mind we've been referring to the baby as their cousin. It's really looking like that might be the closest thing to a cousin my kids get." She shoots a sideways glance at Austin and Cecily, who are paying zero attention to our conversation. Luckily.

"Oh, it's fine. I don't have any siblings, so it's nice she'll have some cousins around." Cass slowly peels Odessa off like a piece of old chewing gum. It's clear she's uncomfortable, so I grab the kid and toss her over my shoulder. Her legs kick wildly, tiny cowboy boots whooshing through the stale air.

"C'mon, chicky. Let's go check out the animals and let the *crazy* ladies talk."

Kate reaches out to smack me, but I dodge her at the last second, tripping over my own feet and nearly dropping Odessa in the process.

"*Holy shit*, your mom's trying to get us killed," I say to Odessa, who finds the entire thing hilarious. Draped over my shoulder and giggling away like a maniac. "Told you—absolutely crazy."

"Let's get away!" she shrieks. "Giddy up!"

With an exaggerated jog, I make my way toward Jackson, Austin, and Cecily. Odessa bounces on my shoulder, wheezy laughter filling the air.

"Better not pee your pants from all this laughing." I pinch her sides before plopping her down on the ground. Her laughter's fully silent now, and my cheeks burn with an unrelenting smile. She reaches up, trying to tickle me, and I place my palm on her forehead to hold her at arm's length. "You're a dork."

"No, *you are.*" She huffs before giving up with a sigh. "Can I have some ice cream now?"

When Cass gets home from the fair, I'm already waiting with dinner and one of her stupid reality TV shows lined up. The guys are drinking and having a bonfire tonight—beer pong on the back of Colt's truck, laughing and goofing off, unwinding from the workweek. Typically, I wouldn't miss that fun for anything. Until now. Until her. I'll choose her every time.

"Ugh, you are the *best.*" She places her coat and boots in the closet before sinking into the couch next to me with a groan. "Baked potato, root beer, *and* a bunch of hot singles on a tropical island? What more could a girl ask for?"

"Anybody ever told you you're a bit too easy to please?" I hand her a full plate of food and watch her settle into her spot. Her hair was down when I saw her earlier, but now it's hanging in a slightly messy, loose braid—my favorite.

She swallows a bite, pointing her fork at me. "Consider yourself lucky that I am. It's the only reason you're here."

A joke, but not really.

"How was the rest of the fair?" I change the subject to spare my own feelings.

"Mmm . . . It was good. I helped Shelby with her 4-H kids, mostly." She sets down her plate and turns sideways on the couch to face me, hands clasped in her lap. "How are you so good with kids?"

I laugh. "That's a fucking stretch."

"No, it's not. I saw you with Odessa today. You're so . . . natural."

"Well, probably helps that I see her every day. She's a handful at the best of times."

She purses her lips in thought. Opens her mouth. Closes it.

"I've also known her since she was a baby. Stick me with a strange kid, and I wouldn't know what the hell to do," I add.

"I just . . . *shit,* this is stupid, and I don't want to cry about it. Never mind, let's watch the show."

"No, no, no." I snatch the remote before she can and power off the television altogether. "What's wrong?"

"You were so good with her. I swear I didn't hear a word Kate said to me because I was distracted watching you being a good uncle. And when she came up to me, I froze. It was like I'd never interacted with a tiny human before." She takes a deep, ragged breath. "What if I don't know how to be a mom? Maybe the maternal instinct that should be there is missing entirely? It's not like I grew up with a mother to show me what to do."

"Cass, you're going to be the perfect mom. You don't have any reason to worry."

"But that's probably why my mom left, right?" She swipes her fingers across her eyes, leaving a streak of black mascara on her cheek. I reach out to rub it off with my thumb, and watch the tears pooling in her eyes, threatening to burst the dam. "She obviously didn't have any maternal instincts. She didn't bond with me. That's why it was easy to leave. What if . . ."

The dam breaks.

Whatever we are to each other and whatever I'm supposed to do in this situation—I don't care. I wrap her in my arms, tugging her tight against me. Pressing a kiss to the top of her head. The heavy rise and fall of her chest is absorbed by my body. And I wish I could soak up her pain as easily as my T-shirt soaks up her tears.

"You aren't your mom. I don't have a single doubt about how incredible of a mom you're going to be because you're the best person I've ever met. You stayed late today to help Shelby. If I had to guess, you also stopped by Mrs. Kozensky's house to feed her cats on the way home again."

She nods against my chest. "Told you she's out of town all week."

"You're thoughtful and caring, Cassidy. Plus smart, funny, a bit of a hard-ass—when required. All traits every good mom has." I let my lips discreetly touch the top of her hair again. It's the closest to an intimate kiss I'm willing to risk. But, goddamn, would I love to grab her jaw and force her to look at me, then kiss her until she forgets all about this—until she forgets everything except us.

"But . . ."

"No buts. Even if it takes a little while to figure out, you're going to connect with Little Spud. It'll be so different than having a strange five-year-old attack you. She's gonna be *ours.*"

It hits me at the strangest times. That we're having a baby together. That a piece of me and a piece of her are forever intertwined, attached in the most meaningful way possible.

"Cassidy, if I had to pick somebody to have a baby with, I'd choose you every damn time."

"I'd choose you, too," she mutters softly. Quiet enough I think she didn't mean for me to hear.

"But I also know what you're feeling. . . . You think I never worry about what kind of dad I'll be? I'm terrified of becoming anything like him. We both came from crappy situations. Doesn't mean we're doomed, though. Least I hope not. . . ."

She sniffles. "You're not going to be like your dad, either. I know you aren't."

"I'm gonna bust my ass to make sure I'm the complete opposite. You wanna join me in that?"

"Deal." It's small, but the smile is genuine. Her eyes are blue-green and shining, a perfect replica of the glassy water on the lake above the ranch—I'd love to take her there one day.

I want to show her the lake, and everywhere else, too. Side by side, hand in hand. I love her. I'm madly in love with Cassidy Bowman. And I think—*fuck,* I hope I'm right on this—that she might be starting to feel the same way.

Cassidy

Twenty-four weeks (baby is the size of a package of Oreos)

I stare from the front door as Chase wrestles something plush, gray, and adult-human-sized from the front seat of his truck. "What the fuck is that?"

"Shouldn't have taken it outta the fucking vacuum-sealed package before coming here," he shouts. He tosses the giant object over his shoulder in a firefighter carry position and strolls up to the house. "It's for you."

He throws it down on the couch, and that's when I realize. It's a massive U-shaped pregnancy pillow.

"Are you saying you're already sick of being my pillow?" I wrap my arms around his waist. He holds the back of my head, fingers woven in my hair, and pulls me tighter into the embrace.

"Never. But it's supposedly a 'must-have,' according to Kate."

"I'll have to send her a thank-you text." I step back and watch as his eyes flick to my lips before slowly meandering back up to meet my gaze. "You know you don't need to buy me presents, though."

"Yeah, well . . ." He shrugs. "You need to be comfortable. And I know you like presents."

"You know me too well."

Since the anatomy scan, he's been here almost every night. We eat dinner and watch TV. On nights I work late, he's waiting with snacks when I get home. When one person yawns, that's the cue. The sign to head into my room, strip, and fuck, promising each other it'll be the last time. We fall asleep, and in the morning, he leaves for work. Rinse. Repeat.

I know we're playing with fire. But, *fuck*, we burn so good.

There's a long pause, where I'm staring at him staring at me. I'm pretty certain he wants to kiss me. I'm also pretty certain I want to kiss him. But kissing is too intimate for whatever we are. We don't talk about what happens in my bed under the dark cloak of night. That's different. That's fucking.

"You could always come to the ranch and thank Kate in person," he says.

I can't tell if dinner is crossing a line in our casual arrangement. I suppose it's fine since it's not exactly the same as meeting his family—I already know them. I'm already friends with Denny, and I'm friendly enough with Kate and Cecily.

"Yeah . . . yeah, we could do that." It would be nice to talk with Kate some more, considering everything she told me at the winter fair went in one ear and out the other. Blair's obsessed with texting me pregnancy information, including a weekly announcement of how big the baby is, but she's never experienced it firsthand. "I'd love to hang out with Kate so she can give me tips. By the way, did you know she's bigger than a Furby now?"

That was Blair's disturbing twenty-three-week comparison I've been forgetting to tell Chase about.

His nose wrinkles, face twisting with mock disgust. "The baby or Kate?"

I rap my fingers across his firm bicep. "Stop. You know who I meant."

"Those things were creepy. Don't ever use the word *Furby* when describing our perfect daughter again." While his tone is serious and scolding, there's tension tugging the corner of his lip.

"Well, the poor girl has you for a father so . . ." I shrug, dodging his fingers as he reaches to pinch my side. "I'll love her even if she's born looking like you, though."

"Bullshit. I'm a pretty boy, and you know it."

Okay, fine. I won't actually be the slightest bit mad if our baby looks like him. Don't get me wrong, I'll be irritated about doing all this work to create his carbon copy. But a sweet baby girl with blue eyes and bright-red hair? That's the most adorable thing I can imagine.

"The prettiest boy."

I grab the pregnancy pillow and lug it down the hallway to my room. Collapsing onto the bed, my body turns into jelly thanks to the luxurious, supportive, greatest love of my life. Even with my stomach still relatively small, it's a game changer to take the weight off my back for a moment. There's a chance I may never move. "Oh, I think I'm in love with Kate. This is so comfy. You're excused now—I don't need you anymore."

"I refuse to be replaced by a dildo and a pillow."

"Don't forget takeout." I roll my lips, narrowing my eyes at him. "Yeah, I think I could probably replace you with those three things."

In a swift movement, Chase is hovering over me on the bed. Without hesitation, his hands slip under my shirt to tease my nipples, sending a hot jolt of pleasure radiating through my breasts. He's shimmying my shirt over my head, and I don't bother stopping him. It's hard to feel self-conscious when he constantly looks at me like he's starved for my body.

Sucking my nipple between his teeth, his tongue flits across the hardening bud.

"Can your vibrator or pillow do that?"

"I can probably get my boob in my own mouth now—these things are getting massive. What else you got? Hurry, my interest in you sticking around is expiring." I tap an imaginary watch on my wrist.

His eyes darken, fingertips tracing the curves of my breasts. "You're a fucking brat."

He yanks my yoga pants off, suffocating himself between my legs. Nudging my underwear to the side, he tests how sensitive I am by blowing cool air on my clit.

Fuck him—that's how sensitive it is.

I'm inclined to smack him, instead groaning and flexing my legs in response. Then his tongue makes sharp contact, and I cry out.

"Still want to trade me for the toy?"

I gulp, trying to hide how turned on I am. "I mean . . . maybe. It doesn't talk as much."

"Get it then. Let's see which one you like better." His head motions toward the nightstand. When I don't immediately move, he does, pulling open the drawer and reaching for the rabbit and a bottle of lube. "Jesus, how many toys do you have in here?"

My face grows instantly warm. "Oh, um . . . well . . . they all do different things."

With a smirk, he shakes his head in disbelief. "I can't wait to see you use all of them. Fuck, all this time I had no idea how dirty of a girl you really are."

"What would you have done if you'd known?" I raise an eyebrow. There's not a chance in hell I would've told him, or anybody, about my toy collection. I don't have a drawer full because I'm a sex fiend or anything—it's simply easy to amass a stockpile when you're single and unwilling to date for most of your twenties.

"I would've convinced you to let me fuck you years ago. Now, show me what you like. How do you want to be fucked, Cass?"

I gulp, letting my knees fall apart so I'm spread wide before him, and run my fingers up my pussy. Slick. Soaked. Aside from one short swipe of his tongue, he hasn't even touched me. I grab the lube from him and toss it down on the bedspread. "Um . . . I don't think we'll need that."

"Fucking hell. You're so sexy, spread out and ready like this." He holds out the vibrator, and I reluctantly take it. I want to just tell him to forget this. I'd rather feel his warm body pressing into me than the cold vibrator rubbing against my skin, collecting my wetness.

But my stubborn side wins; I can't let him know how weak he makes me. How badly I want him every second of every day. Goosebumps sprinkle my skin, and I press the tip to my entrance, waiting for a sign of his approval. The long, soft silicone slides in with ease. Despite the instinct to turn my face into the pillow with embarrassment, I remain transfixed, staring at him. At the way he's watching me, his chest barely moving with short, shallow breaths. When I turn it on with a whimper, he licks his lips and groans. Glowing with lust, a muscle in his jaw twitching repeatedly. As usual, it doesn't take long before I'm squirming on the bed. Heat coiling at the base of my spine. All the blood in my body rushing to that spot as I feel the familiar push-pull of an orgasm.

He doesn't let me come, though. Chase grabs the rabbit's base and pulls it out, chucking it across the bed—filling the room with a light buzzing. "You're not coming yet. Not until you've felt my cock and decided if you still think you can replace me with your toy."

"How do you want me? Use me. Tell me what to do." If anybody ever asked, I'd lie until I'm blue in the face, but I crave his rough demands. His possessive control awakens something in me—a sexual rush I've never experienced before. His face lights up with intensity, clearly enjoying being the one to boss me around.

"Flip over," he commands. "Knees and elbows. Ass up."

Without hesitation, I'm flipped around and eagerly waiting. My hips wiggle against my will, needing friction, begging him to fill the ache of emptiness. He tosses his pants aside, the belt buckle hitting the metal footboard with a loud *ping*. Then his cock is slipping between my legs, teasing me, and my breath stops with desperate anticipation. No matter how many times I feel it, the initial stretching when his thick cock fills me is a sin I'll never get enough of.

"Look at you, so needy for the real thing. This cunt always prefers me, doesn't it?" With the tip notched at my entrance, he presses a palm between my shoulder blades, shoving my breasts into the mattress and smashing my cheek into the pillow. He drives into me in one swift motion, filling me to the hilt with a strangled, cursing groan. The grip he has on my hips makes me clench my jaw tight enough to trap my gasp. There are deep purple bruises in my future, for sure. Sore patches of flesh for him to tenderly, apologetically kiss better later.

The first two thrusts are slow, then he picks up the pace. Pumping into me while maintaining a rough grip on my hip with one hand and firm pressure on my spine with the other. His cock's managing to hit every square inch inside me, leaving no part of my body unaffected as sparks fly up my spine.

"This what you want? You want my cock, or the fake one?"

"Mmm . . . It's up for debate," I taunt, looking over my shoulder at him while pretending to weigh my options.

He slaps my ass. Hard. When I bite my lip with a moan, eyes shuttering with pleasure, he does it again. "I'm going to have to fuck the brattiness right out of you, aren't I?"

"Guess so." I shoot him a cheeky smile.

His hand snakes around from my back to grab my breast as he piles into me. Over and over. With a punishing pace. Then his fingers trail upward until he's grabbing my throat, pulling my heavy upper body off the mattress to greet his. I reach out for the headboard to steady myself as his fingers tighten around my neck. I'm arched into him, reveling in his hot breath on my ear.

"*Fuck, Cass.* You're a fucking dream with my hand around your beautiful neck and my cock buried in your tight pussy."

His dirty talk sends a rush up my spine every time. My nails bite into his thigh, eliciting a raspy exhale against my ear. Chase pulls out in an agonizingly slow movement, and I push my ass toward him, subconsciously begging for the pleasure he's withholding.

"Ready to admit you like my cock better than the fake one?"

His rock-hard cock drags across my bare ass. And stubbornness be damned, I need him to fuck me.

"Yes. I want—*need*—your cock," I admit with a yearning rasp.

"That's my good little slut—you'll do anything I tell you, won't you?"

"Mmm, maybe," I lie through my teeth. I would. I'd do anything. I'm already doing things I would've never considered with anybody else and loving every second of it. I want to be his slut. I want to be his dream.

"Brat," he murmurs into my hair as he shoves back inside me.

Fuck. Why does that word make me want him even more?

My bottom lip skates between my front teeth. "You love it."

He responds by tightening his grip. Not choking me—I can breathe relatively well, considering the force of every thrust is radiating up to my lungs. But he's keeping enough pressure on either side of my throat to make it obvious he's in charge here. Knowing I'm at his mercy sends an electrifying tingle through my skin, settling into my core.

"I really do love the necklace," I say between harsh thrusts, which knock the wind out of me every time. I stroke the tattooed back of his hand, the skin I know so intimately after nights spent sleeping with our fingers interlaced on my stomach. He squeezes either side of my neck, tight enough to make my lip quiver.

"It's all yours. Only yours." His rough fingers press into my pulse point, and I gasp. "Now get your hand off mine and touch yourself. Play with your needy cunt for me."

"I have a better idea." One by one, I peel his fingers from my skin and lean over to the drawer, pulling out a bullet-sized vibrator and adding to the hum of buzzing electricity in the air. "You want me to come hard? Use this while you fuck me."

"Who said anything about you coming yet? You think you deserve to come on my cock after being such a pain in the ass?" His hand jumps to my throat again, pulling my back into his chest. His ragged breath is hot in my ear, and I whimper a desperate yes around the pressure of his fingers. "Yeah? Well, you're lucky I'm a nice guy."

"So lucky," I eagerly agree, rolling my hips to feel him deeper.

"Ask nicely. *Maybe* I'll let you come." His grip tightens as he talks. Begging for it isn't an option when I can barely form words past his palm on the column of my neck, but I moan and press my hips deeper into his, letting my body speak my greatest desires.

"Plea—" I gasp as he thrusts into me.

"What was that?" He pulls almost all the way out, then slams back in so my high-pitched sharp inhale fills the room. Leaning in close to nip my shoulder.

When his grip lets up for half a second, I cry out. "Please. *Please.* Let me come."

"Such a needy little slut."

I rock back so his cock is buried deep enough there's a tinge of momentary pain before the overwhelming pleasure. "Chase, I need it. Don't stop."

"Use your toy, baby. I want to feel you come harder than you ever have before."

Swept up in primal momentum, he's fucking me rough and deep and fast. The air's thick with our arousal and sweat. My muscles beg to turn to jelly, struggling to keep me upright, with one hand on the headboard and the other moving the small vibe across my clit.

"That's it. Squirt all over my cock. Make a *fucking* mess of me."

I can't hear. Can't see. Can't feel. Everything goes black, and I fall apart with a drawn-out, hoarse moan. My body convulses in his arms as I truly come harder than I have in my fucking life. With his cock pounding into my pussy, his hand clutching my neck, and his lips on the sliver of skin behind my ear. When it should be done, it's not. The orgasm keeps coming, my cum providing even more lubrication for both his cock and my vibrator. It doesn't stop until I'm on the verge of tears, fully drained, and shaking uncontrollably.

"Good. Fucking. Girl."

Then I drop my hand, thrusting the vibrator between his legs to the hot skin behind his balls. The sensation sends him forward with a shudder that threatens to completely undo the powerful persona he has in bed. He's sloppy and frantic and so clearly about to fall apart.

"Holy fucking shit." He moans, thrusting hard and fast, until he's filling me with warm, thick liquid. His arms shaking, breath faltering. Both panting, we collapse onto the bed in a mess of weary limbs.

That was the last time. It has to be. This is getting too good. I'm becoming addicted. And not only to the pleasure. While the orgasms are amazing, I *could* have orgasms solo. It's everything about him . . . and us.

He pads across to the en suite bathroom and returns a few seconds later with a warm washcloth, wiping my skin delicately. Then he places a halo of kisses around my baby bump before settling in next to me, pulling my leg over his lap.

"Have I told you how happy I am that I knocked you up?"

"Yeah, we'll see if you're still saying that when the sex high wears off."

"Serious, Cass. I am. Even if you never let me touch you

again—which, fuck, I hope that's not the case. I'm happy this happened."

"You wouldn't change things if you could?" I lift my head to look at him, searching for any hint of a lie. Waiting for him to say what he thinks I want to hear. His irises are the picture of a lake on a perfect summer day, when the sun is out and you're floating with a beer in your hand. Not a cloud in the sky, nothing but shimmery vibrant blue reflecting the sun. There's a single freckle just below his eyebrow, and I can't help myself from reaching up to lightly brush my thumb across it.

"Not at all. With the childhood I had, I didn't think I'd ever want kids of my own. But I wouldn't change a second of this. In fact, if I could go back to the rodeo night, I'd skip the condom entirely, to be really sure that we still end up here. Little Spud is the best thing to happen to me. *You* are the best thing to happen to me."

My stomach leaps into my throat.

"You can't say that to a pregnant woman." I sniffle, wiping the tears suddenly brimming my lash line. "You're going to make me fall in love with you if you say nice things like that."

"Oh? Well, good thing I said it then." The muscles in his arm tighten around me. I can't breathe for a second, and it has to be because of his tight grip. Not because I'm briefly picturing a world where I love him. Definitely not that.

I bite back the weird feeling. "Shut up. Trust me, you don't want me falling in love with you. You think I'm needy and annoying now? It would be nothing but dinner requests, cold feet tucked between your warm legs, and crappy reality TV shows."

"That's already my present hell, Cass." His hand rubs slowly over my bare stomach. "Would you change anything?"

"This isn't exactly where I thought I'd be at thirty-one, y'know? But, no, I don't think I would."

I wouldn't. Not the accidental pregnancy. Surprisingly, not the baby daddy.

Before I say anything to cross the "friends-with-benefits-slash-friends-with-a-baby" line I insist on having in place, I change the subject. "Before I forget, I didn't know we were giving each other Christmas gifts today, so it's not wrapped, but I have something for you."

"The pillow isn't a Christmas present. You said not to buy you one because we aren't together." He gives me an easy smile. "And yet . . . you have a Christmas present for me?"

"Okay, I know. But this feels like a necessity." I drag myself from the bed and walk over to the dresser, mindful of his eyes on my naked body. But even with the extra pounds and growing belly, I feel inexplicably comfortable. More confident with him than I ever was with Derek.

"Close your eyes." I pull the present from my drawer and hurry back to the warmth of the bed, snuggling into his strong arms. "Okay . . . open. It's a bracelet. Um . . . I made it because you probably shouldn't hold a baby with barbed wire on your damn wrist. I'm not going to explain to the hospital why a newborn needs a tetanus shot."

He turns the leather band over in his hands, stopping to run his thumb along the tooling, which looks like barbed wire, running the length of the bracelet. "You *made* this?"

"I taught myself leatherworking after high school when everyone was off at college and I was trapped here. It's a fun hobby." I shrug, trying to brush off the expression he's giving me right now. The soft eyes, creases between his eyebrows, and a genuine smile. It's filling my chest like a helium balloon and, if I'm not careful, I might float away on that smile.

"Cass, this is super fucking cool. I can't believe you made . . . actually, I *can* believe it. Is there anything you aren't good at?"

"Did you repress memories of the lasagna I tried to make a couple of days ago? Cooking is not my strong suit."

"Hey, I ate it and I'm still alive. Could've been worse." He laughs, already replacing the metal bracelet with mine. "Good thing I'm here, or our baby would be surviving on Flamin' Hot Cheetos, root beer, and French fries. Seriously, though. This is amazing."

"Thanks." I fumble with fastening the clasp for him. "I should find photos of the heels I made for Blair when she graduated nursing school. Those were super cool."

"You could sell these. Do you sell them?"

"Nah. I've briefly considered it before, but I don't know. . . ." I fiddle with a strand of hair, unable to make eye contact. "It's time-consuming, and I probably should get some more practice first. It's just a little hobby."

"Fuck that. Don't sell yourself short. I'd pay for this. If you made belts, I know at least twenty ranch hands who would buy them from you. You said before that you didn't have a *thing,* but maybe this is it. With how smart you are, I bet you could make a great business out of this."

"Yeah, if I had the time, maybe. And I'm going to have even less time with a baby to take care of. Besides, I packed up all my supplies because my office will have to be a nursery." The way he's watching me anxiously fidget is only making me more flustered. I can't bear to meet his eyes. "Thank you, though. I'm glad you like it."

"I love it." He takes his time spinning it around his wrist. "And I was serious about being here every day. You're gonna be so fucking sick of me, I bet you'll be stoked to have a hobby that gives you a break."

"You *are* best in small doses. . . ."

He leans in. "Mmm, that's not what you say when I'm inside you."

"Okay, see. Now you've officially overstayed your welcome." I shove him playfully in the side, and he wraps himself around me. His tattooed arm drapes across my stomach, and his leg encircles my ankles. He's got me pinned—not that I had any intention of moving, anyway.

"You're stuck with me, sweetheart." He nuzzles into my hair.

"*Great*. How did I get so lucky?"

I told myself I wouldn't do this. I wouldn't fall for him. But suddenly we're talking until midnight, and I'm laughing in his arms. Our bodies knit together like every limb, muscle, and ligament were created to be interwoven. I'm the happiest I've felt in years. And I'm so wonderfully, irrevocably screwed.

Cassidy

Twenty-six weeks (baby is the size of a large soft pretzel)

Cold, icy, muddy slush splashes up the sides of my boots when I jump out of Chase's truck, drenching my socks and cascading a string of expletives from my mouth. I kick myself for not listening to his suggestion to wait in the truck while he grabs a couple last-minute items for dinner.

"You good?" Chase calls from the other side of the truck.

"Soaking fucking wet."

"Fuck, Cass. *Okay.* Should we skip grocery shopping or . . ." He appears at the back of his truck with a shit-eating grin. "You know those are my three favorite words, right?"

"Not like that, asshole. You parked right in a giant puddle and my boots are full of water." I trudge toward him, feeling the sloshing and the squelch of wet socks under my feet with each step.

"Well, that's less fun than what I was picturing. Still, though. We can get back in the truck and strip ya down?" He gestures toward the pickup with his head, the stupid smirk never leaving his lips.

With a laugh, I smack his arm. "Nice try, but only my socks are wet. That's the most I'm taking off."

"Worth a shot. This entire parking lot is like a giant root beer slushy. Where did you expect me to park?" He starts across the crowded parking lot toward the store. "Come on, soggy socks. We should probably get you a snack in here, eh? Don't think you'll make it home without eating something."

We trudge through the root beer slush—which is a pretty accurate description for the grimy parking lot. It dumped snow the whole drive to Sheridan for my doctor's appointment and plow trucks littered the roadways with sand to provide traction. Then the temperature promptly rose just enough to transform the foot of powder into a soupy, muddy mess.

"No snacks, unless it's carrot sticks or some shit. I'm tired of Dr. Dickhead's judgmental sigh. And I'm really sick of his comments on my weight every time." I grab hold of Chase's arm to hop over a flowing stream in the center of the road. The grocery store door opens with a blast of warm, dry air, and Chase's hand falls to my lower back to guide me in ahead of him. Even though Sheridan isn't far from Wells Canyon, and there's always a good chance of running into people we know, it's nice to pretend we're different people here. To interact the way we typically do in the privacy of my house. It's blurring the lines between us, but I can't bring myself to stop it.

"You need to stop listening to that fuckwad," Chase says. "Or let me smack him, like I keep offering. You're pregnant and you need to eat. He doesn't know what the hell he's talking about."

I cock an eyebrow. "Oh, you went to medical school?"

"You get miserable when you're hungry, and stress isn't healthy for Little Spud. I know that much." He grabs my hand and squeezes. "So go to the damn snack aisle and pick something you actually want—not carrots. I'll grab the dinner stuff."

Twist my rubber arm. "Fine, fine. You're taking the blame next time he says something, though."

Moments later, I'm alone under the buzzing fluorescent ceiling lights and deeply lost in an excruciating internal debate about chip flavors. It's easy to pick which one sounds more appealing at the moment, but who's to say that's what I'll still want an hour from now? And if I make the wrong choice, future me will be pissed. Possessing only ketchup chips while craving Flamin' Hot Cheetos is a good way to ruin my entire night.

I could get both, right?

Chase would never comment on it. If anything, he'd cheer me on for ignoring the doctor's very practical medical advice about watching what I eat.

"Hard chip decisions?" A voice startles me, and the bag of Cheetos falls to the floor with a crunch.

I bend over to pick it up, trying to shove down the stirring in my gut and the rapid thumping in my chest. And suddenly he's there. Derek's hand bumps mine, and I snatch the chips, aggressively shoving them back onto the shelf as I stand.

"Derek." I gulp.

"Cass. How are you doing? I haven't seen you in . . ." His eyes scan my body the way they always do, picking me apart piece by piece. Plucking at every insecurity I made the mistake of telling him about. Making me feel the need to cover up. As much as I appreciate that my body is carrying this baby without issue, I can't help but feel self-conscious about the constant changes. The insecurities Chase washes away with a single gaze are quickly rising to the surface under Derek's smug stare.

Thank God I'm wrapped in Chase's hoodie. It's not massive on me, but it does a good job of hiding my growing stomach. And it smells like his soap, which eases the curdling in my stomach.

"I'm honestly great." I smile to myself when I realize I'm telling the truth—I *am* great.

"Oh, good. Y'know, I've been meaning to text you. Alyssa and I broke up."

"My condolences," I snark, rolling my eyes. "Thanks for

letting me know, I guess. Now there's zero need for you to text me."

"Cass, I'm sorry for what happened. I didn't mean to hurt you." He takes a step toward me, and I promptly step back. If he were to touch me, I can't say for sure that my reflex wouldn't be to punch him in the nose.

I scoff. "Apology *not* accepted. Please leave me to my grocery shopping." *Fuck it,* I'll get both kinds of chips—no shot I'm standing here debating my choices while he stares me down.

Do you really need that? All that's for you? Oh, somebody's hungry.

The minuscule comments, which added up to so much more over the year we dated, swirl in my head, making my throat tighten and my nostrils burn. I grab both chip bags, and he clears his throat—the sound I know means the same thing as the comments. It's what he'd do in public anytime I filled my plate at the buffet, got a second helping, or ordered an appetizer with my dinner.

Before he has the chance to say something, I snarl, "I'm pregnant, you piece of shit. I can eat what I want."

"You're . . . *what?*" His face blanches. "Is it . . ."

"No. She's not yours. None of this"—I cradle my free hand under my bump, pulling the hoodie tight enough to reveal my protruding stomach—"has anything to do with you."

Appearing out of nowhere—and with impeccable timing—Chase sidles up next to me. Without thinking, I slip my hand into his back pocket to make it seem like we're a couple. Derek catches the movement, and his nose crinkles. The relaxed weight of Chase's thick arm falls around my waist, tugging me closer to his side. I release the vise grip from my lungs with a heavy exhale. I know we fit together wonderfully when we're horizontal. But vertically, it feels like this spot was made for my body, and I sink into it. Certainly doesn't seem like we're faking being together.

"Problem?" Chase's gruff voice makes the hair on my arms jump to attention.

Derek's nostrils flare, face twisted. "Really, Cass? You're with *Red*? Jesus."

"Devin, right?" Chase asks, knowing damn well that's not his name.

"Derek." Derek's eyes bounce between us. Funny how he doesn't have more to say when there's a man standing at my side.

"Right. Well, look, Cass and I have a long drive home." He tilts his head to look at me. "You got everything you need, sweetheart?"

I swear to God, I could kiss him. "Yup."

"Let's go, then. See you around, Dexter."

I can barely contain my laughter long enough to turn the corner into the next aisle. "Did you see his face? *Fuck me*."

"Later, you horn dog." He winks, and my fingertips playfully smack his bicep. I hook a finger through his belt loop and follow him to the front of the store. A surge of emotion inflates my chest as he quietly snags my favorite chocolate bar from the display next to the cash register.

In the nearly empty parking lot, cast in orange hues from the setting sun, there's no avoiding Derek's tall, skinny frame on our way to the truck. And there's no avoiding him seeing us.

Derek slams his car's trunk and stalks toward us. "Cassidy, can I talk to you for a minute?"

Chase leans over, lips brushing the shell of my ear, and whispers, "Look at the fucking scratch on his hood. Wonder what kind of wild shit happened to put such a big gash in the paint."

I downplay my laugh by turning it into a fake cough, quickly hiding my mouth behind a closed fist. Without Chase, seeing Derek would've had me wanting to curl up in a ball and die. But when his hand presses to the small of my back, stoking the fire deep in my core, I feel like I can conquer the world. Facing a shitty ex-boyfriend is small potatoes.

Dropping my hand from my lips, I focus my attention on Derek. "I'm really not interested in whatever it is you have to say. You already apologized—let's just move on."

"It'll only take a minute."

I cross my arms over my chest. "Fine. I'll give you a minute."

Derek's eyes narrow in on Chase. "Without him."

"Not a chance. Hurry up, your time's quickly running out. *Tick tock.*"

"Cass. Come on. This is awkward."

"So keep whatever awkward bullshit you have to say to yourself, then."

Keeping his mouth zipped—or his pants, evidently—has never been his strong suit. "It's just . . . *him*? You honestly want to be with Red? The number of times I had to listen to you bitch about him and the other local guys in the bar. What the hell, Cass."

Chase shifts his weight from one foot to the other, noticeably tensing in my periphery. Sure, I complained about having to kick him out of the bar a time or two. Yes, that was technically not very long ago. But it feels like years have passed since Derek and I broke up. Without needing to look, my hand locates Chase's forearm like we're magnetized, and my thumb immediately begins drawing slow circles. A silent apology.

"I know I messed up . . . but if you need somebody to take care of you—"

"She has me," Chase cuts him off.

"A dirty, alcoholic cowboy?" The words come out slow and punctuated, with a questioning undertone, like it's the first time he's ever said any of them out loud and he's not quite sure of the pronunciation. "Wow. Yeah, no. I can see why she'd pick you over me. *Quite* the catch."

Chase steps toward him, trying to shake my grasp, but I hold on tighter. My fingernails whitening as they press deep into his flesh. Maybe if I break the skin, it'll disrupt him for long enough to stop him from committing murder.

"Hit me. I dare ya." Derek leers. "Don't worry. I'll look after Cassidy and the baby while you're in prison for assault."

"Chase." I tug on the rolled-up sleeve of his flannel. "*Fuck him.* He's not worth it. Please take me home." With a second *firmer* tug, he breaks his focus on Derek's smug face and turns to me. The harsh lines of his face soften when our eyes meet, and he gives me a nod.

"Let's go home, sweetheart." He firmly interlaces our fingers and holds our joined hands up like a trophy. "Fuck you, Dyson."

"Don't talk to me again," I yell over my shoulder as I walk alongside Chase, letting my hip bump into his at random.

"Dyson?" I ask under my breath as Chase swings open the passenger door and I hop into the seat with a shiver. All the heat that had built up in the truck cab dissipated during our ten-minute grocery shop. "That's a vacuum brand."

"I couldn't think of any other *D* names on the spot," he whispers back, softly closing the door.

The moment he joins me inside the quiet truck cab, I say, "I've got a *D* word you'll like—dick. You're getting yours sucked tonight, Chase Thompson."

"Oh, yeah?" The corner of his mouth lifts, and he glances at me as the engine rumbles to life.

"You made him so uncomfortable, and I loved every second of it." I swipe my hands across the tops of my thighs. "Also, um, I've never thanked you before, but dealing with him in the grocery store reminded me. Thank you for not being an asshole about"—I gesture to my body—"this. Me. My body. I know it's not exactly the same as it was. . . ."

Thankfully, he holds his hand up to stop me from turning into a blubbering mess. "Let's get one thing straight—there's nothing to be an asshole about because your body is fucking flawless. I'm gonna tell you exactly how perfect it is the entire time those gorgeous pink lips are wrapped around my cock tonight, until you stop questioning whether I find you sexy. And, if you still insist on talking shit about yourself, I'll tangle my hands in that blond hair of yours and shove my cock so far down your pretty little throat, you won't be able to say anything at all."

"I wish you would," I tease, though my voice is still thick with unsettled emotion.

"*Jesus.* You're . . . something else." He bites his lip, sending a rush up my spine. I love making him flustered, possibly even more than I love when he's telling me exactly what to do in his commanding, sexy tone.

His forearm rests on the leather center console as we pull onto the main road, so I drag my nails lightly across his tattooed skin. "Thank you for not hitting him."

"A gentleman doesn't throw punches when a lady's right there." He turns the heat dial in response to my incessant, though barely noticeable, shivering.

"You're going to call yourself a gentleman immediately after making that comment about your cock down my throat? *Really?*"

"Yeah, I am. A gentleman knows what his lady wants, and I know for a fact you want me to treat you like a pretty little slut. Don't you, sweetheart?"

He's got me there.

Red

Twenty-nine weeks (baby is the size of a gallon of ice cream)

Growing up, Christmas was an excuse for Dad to day-drink without judgment from people. Everyone adds liquor to their coffee on Christmas morning. You're not an alcoholic for doing it—you're *festive.* Which meant we waited to open presents until he passed out on the couch midafternoon. He'd always wake up in time for dinner and more drinks. If his after-dinner drink was spiced rum, we'd watch Christmas movies and drink hot chocolate like a normal family. If it was whiskey, my brothers and I would retreat to our bedrooms for the night.

When I step into the big house, I'm hit with the sound of laughter and the scent of sugar cookies. It's warm and decorated like something out of a Christmas movie, with garland and lights and even fucking mistletoe hung above the living room entryway. A massive live tree—which Jackson, Kate, and the kids went on horseback to cut down—takes up most of the cozy, firelit room.

I stroll down the hallway toward the busy kitchen. Some of the ranch hands live in town with their families, others go to wherever they came from for the holidays. Those of us with nowhere else to be come here. Because I offered to handle feeding the horses this evening, I'm the last one to arrive, which is fine by me. It means less time fielding questions about my relationship with Cass.

Small arms wrap around my hips, and I crouch down to preschooler level. Odessa's wearing a puffy red dress that, unsurprisingly, already has questionable food stains on it. "Hey, chicky. Did Santa spoil you rotten this year or what?"

I'm not a Christmas guy, but I can put on a good show for Odessa and Rhett.

Her palms squish against my cheeks, holding me in place so she can excitedly yell directly into my face. "Santa got me a Barbie with a horse!"

"You sure you deserve all that?" I raise an eyebrow and smile at her. "I could use a new horse. Maybe I'll borrow yours sometime."

"Uncle Red!" Odessa shrieks with laughter, scrunching her nose. "You're too big to ride him. He's for *Barbie*."

"Well, shoot. Guess we'll send Barbie out to check cows, hey?" I slowly straighten my knees to stand. "I'm starvin'. Let's go see what your mama cooked up."

"Did you bring your girlfriend?" Her question stops me in my tracks. "I want to see the baby."

"Well, the baby's still in her tummy," I say. "You can meet her as soon as she's born, though."

"She's pretty," Odessa states.

"My . . . *girlfriend?*" I clarify. Odessa's eyes light up at the word—she's Kate fuckin' junior. "You're right—most beautiful girl I've ever seen. Aside from you, of course." I tousle her hair and send her on her way, finally taking a moment to look at all the other people here.

Ranch hands, the Wells family, Kate's parents, and another older couple who I assume are Cecily's parents. There's not a single empty space on the counter or twelve-foot kitchen table; the girls must've been cooking and baking for days to create this spread. The women of Wells Ranch sure have a way of showing their love with food. The smell of smoked sausage makes my stomach rumble, and I slip in next to Jackson at the large island.

"Hey," he mumbles through a mouthful of food. Before he's done swallowing, he's already reaching for more. "How'd it go out there?"

"All good. Everybody's fed, except me. Looks delicious." I grab a plate and begin piling the food on, taking one of everything within arm's reach. I can't wait to fall into a food coma in a couple hours.

Jackson slides a beer across the counter to me, and I set my plate down to crack it open. Then I guzzle. Not because I'm trying to be the drunk asshole on Christmas. The initial drink always needs to go down fast, like ripping a bandage off, because that's the drink that scares me. I'm aware it's stupid, but the first one feels like it has the potential to be a switch—somehow triggering whether I become an alcoholic like my dad or not. Whether I'm suddenly filled with rage like him or not. That first beer down the hatch takes the worry along with it. Then I'm okay . . . *okay-ish.* So I like to get it over with as fast as possible.

"Take it Cass couldn't come?" Jackson asks, bringing his beer bottle to his lips.

"She's with Dave . . . so, no." In a different world—where I was a different guy—I'm sure Cass and Dave would've just come here. She said they normally eat store-bought appetizers and watch movies, and I saw a tinge of sadness in her pretty blues when I mentioned how the Wells family likes to celebrate. I know she would love every second of being here.

"Next year."

"Next year, what?" Denny suddenly appears on the opposite side of the island. No plate for him—he's struggling to balance a small mound of sausage and cheese in his open palm. His eyes dart between us as he pops a chunk of cheddar into his mouth.

"Cassidy will be here next year." Jackson's tone makes it

sound like he has the authority to decide that she'll be here, whether she wants to be or not.

"Is she coming tomorrow for leftover-extravaganza?" Denny asks.

Dubbed "leftover-extravaganza" when we were kids, December 26 was the day when the Wells family used to celebrate Christmas with the ranch hands. Back before Kate decided we might as well come over to the big house for Christmas Day. Grandpa Wells kept a bonfire going all day, liquor flowed freely, and the Wellses' insane amount of leftover food was set out for everyone to devour. We'd toboggan, ride snowmobiles, and roast marshmallows well into the night. The only part of Christmas I've ever truly enjoyed.

"No, she's leaving in the morning to visit Blair in Vancouver."

Denny blinks, and his face blanches like he's seen a ghost. *Weird.*

"Oh," he finally says, after taking a strangely long pause. "I didn't think she still had friends here. That's . . . cool." Tipping his beer back, the muscles in his neck work overtime as he gulps. And gulps. And gulps.

Yup. He's being fucking weird.

Saving me from any more of this awkward conversation, my phone buzzes in my pocket. I pile food onto my already heaping plate and slide into the seat next to Austin, so I can eat and text my Cass in peace.

Cass: I want you to describe all the food you're eating in graphic detail.

Cass: Erase the cardboard-flavored mozzarella sticks from my brain forever

Red: You have a food kink or some shit, don't you?

Cass: Nvm I'll text Denny then.
He'll help me out

I glance over at Denny, who seems to be acting normal again, competing with Odessa to see who can fit more cheese cubes in their mouth.

Red: Cranberry and brie on some sort of homemade bread. Bite-size and the bread's a bit crunchy.
Cass: Fuck me
Red: Right now? On my way
Cass: Why would I want that when you're talking about cranberries and brie?
Cass: Get it together and tell me what else is there.
Red: You could always come over, you know
Cass: Friends-with-benefits don't do Christmas together.
Red: Your fave: scalloped potatoes. Also Nanaimo bars, butter tarts, and something Odessa is calling puppy chow?
Cass: Your work here is done. Thank you.
Red: If you touch yourself to these texts, I better get a fucking video

I ate too much last night to properly participate in leftover-extravaganza, but my only other option is to sit around stressing about Cassidy driving to Vancouver. She insisted my offer to drive her was ridiculous, and maybe it was. But I would've happily driven to Vancouver, spent a few days alone—hating every second of being in the city—and driven back home with her. Just so I'd know she was safe.

She didn't want that. So I pull up a folding camp chair next to the fire and sink down. Watching the crackling orange embers, sipping hot cocoa, and relishing the warm sun rays on an otherwise brisk day. Just beyond the fire, Odessa's tugging Rhett around on a small toboggan, running as fast as she can up and down a well-worn footpath. It's a matter of time before he falls face-first into the snow but, for now, he's belly-gut laughing at his big sister. Next Christmas, that could be Little Spud. Assuming Jackson's right, and Cassidy is willing to come here.

"Hey, man." Speaking of the devil, Jackson pulls up a seat next to me, holding out a snowflake-shaped shortbread. "Cookie?"

I shake my head. "I ate enough yesterday to get me through to next year."

Cass had wanted descriptions of everything, and who am I to say no? So I ate. Texting her details until well after midnight.

He chuckles. "Fair. I think once you become a dad, you gain the ability to eat more than ever before."

"It's because you eat all the kids' leftovers on top of your own." Kate slips into a chair next to his, propping her feet up on a rock in front of the fire. "Your stomach's used to a bonus snack after every meal."

Jackson pats his stomach. "Well, when a woman cooks as good as you."

I didn't even notice Denny sneak in on the other side of me until he opens his dumb mouth. "Red doesn't need to worry about getting a dad bod, then. He doesn't have a woman cooking for him."

"Good," Kate says, glaring at Denny. "It shouldn't have to be the woman cooking all the time, *Denver*."

"Jesus. Put more words in my mouth, why don't ya."

Denny throws his hands up in surrender. "It's not that only women should cook, I'm just saying he doesn't have a woman, *period*. He's too scared to make it official."

"Shut the fuck up, Den." I'd love to tell him he's wrong, but he's not. Cassidy's after-sex speech has made it obvious she has no interest in dating. And, as much as it kills me, I can't say I disagree with her logic. We're having a baby together, and a messy breakup is the last thing we need. She's hormonal, I've never been in a relationship before—the odds of us lasting are low.

"Red, you just gotta do it." Kate adjusts in her seat, wiggling closer to the hot flames. "It's scary, but if you don't say anything, you run the risk of losing her entirely. Ask Jackson all about that."

Jackson throws her a look, clearly not appreciating being dragged into this.

"I had to tell him to ask me to be his girlfriend," Kate continues. "After their mom passed, he was going to let me leave here and move back in with my parents."

"I was not!" Jackson protests.

"No? That's why the night before I was supposed to leave, I confronted you and asked why the hell you weren't asking me to stay. Sounds to me like you were letting me go."

Jackson grabs her hand and kisses it before placing their clasped hands in his lap. "Nah, I just knew you weren't serious about leaving."

"Okay, but Cassidy isn't going anywhere." I sip the hot cocoa, ready to be done with this discussion. It seems every conversation around the ranch circles back to talking about us.

"She's staying in Wells Canyon, sure." Kate leans forward to look past Jackson, staring me down in a way that says there's no sense arguing. "But there's other men out there. You like her, and I'm pretty confident she feels the same. And you're gonna lose her if you keep fucking around."

Cassidy

This babymoon, getaway, girls' trip, whatever you want to call it, could not have come soon enough. With the exception of two days over Christmas, Chase has slept at my house every night for weeks. Honestly, I think my vibrator's starting to feel a bit put out.

Having him around has been good . . . dangerously good. So good I'm struggling to remind myself that we're nothing more than friends. Because I know friends don't look at each other the way we do.

If he was just coming over for a booty call, there's a chance I could manage to keep my emotions tightly guarded. It's the rest of it. Cooking dinner together, cuddling on the couch to watch TV, talking until long after we should be asleep. It's feeling completely comfortable wearing baggy clothes and no makeup when he's around. Being with him is effortless in the same way breathing is. I don't have to think when he's there. We fit together—there's no denying that—but some part of me is terrified we're not like puzzle pieces. Maybe he and I are broken chunks of glass Mod Podged together; we fit well enough for now but are bound to fall apart eventually.

We *really* need these few days apart to reset, then we have to set boundaries. Because, as of right now, the only rule is no kissing. The dinners, cuddles, sex, sleepovers . . . I know it's a bad idea. That's not how I operate. I like rules. I like feeling in control. Having sex with somebody I'm not dating, playing fast and loose with my heart—two things that are *so* not me.

Blair buzzes me into the building, and I move as fast as my tired feet, sore back, and extra twenty pounds will allow me. She briefly stopped by the Horseshoe on her way into town for Christmas, mostly because my dad would never forgive her if she didn't at least say hi. But this is the first time we're having a proper reunion, and I throw myself into her as soon as she opens the apartment door.

"God, I missed you." I clutch her tight. "Please can we never go this long without being together again?"

"Never." She lets go of the hug to caress my stomach. "You've grown over half a human since the last time we hung out."

"Again—concerned that you work in medicine. She's a *full* human, just . . . small."

"You know what I meant." She rolls her eyes, caressing my stomach like a fortune teller with a crystal ball. "How's my future best friend? Come in and sit."

I follow her inside, tossing my duffel bag to the ground. Despite spending hours seated in the car, my spine's on fire, begging for a break from the weight of my stomach and boobs. So I sink into the plush white couch next to her.

"She wants me to eat all the time and then gives me killer heartburn. Makes me constantly tired, but I can't sleep. Our relationship has a lot of ups and downs."

"Typical parent and child shit, then. Speaking of which, how are things with your dad? When I was there it seemed . . . tense." She plucks at a loose thread on the hem of her shirt.

"Still tense. Christmas was weird. We watched a *lot* of movies to avoid talking. And he insists that he's fine when I ask, but he's clearly super disappointed. It's like the time I got a C in grade ten math and he sighed every time he looked at me for two weeks."

I pull my legs onto the couch so I'm sitting crisscross and slowly rub my sore knees. I've had chronic joint pain for as long as I can remember, but everything hurts even more these days.

"He wasn't this dramatic about you getting pregnant in the first place. Is it because of Red?"

I side-eye her. "*Of course* it's because of Chase. Dad tried talking me into setting these ridiculous rules with him—like enforcing supervised visits where he has to pass a breathalyzer first and getting child support payments in writing now. I told him neither of those would be happening over Christmas dinner, and now he's even more butthurt."

"Chase?" She prods a finger into my fleshy thigh, a deviant grin sweeping across her face. "You told me you guys were casually hooking up, not that you're falling in love."

"Because I'm not. We're friends, and he likes me calling him Chase. It's called being respectful to the father of your unborn child."

He told me he likes when I call him Chase, but I didn't need him to. The way his eyes glimmer is evidence enough. And when I call him Chase during sex? It's like kicking him with spurs, encouraging him to push harder, give me just a bit more.

"I bet he does." Blair raises an eyebrow. "Because everyone knows calling a guy by his real name instead of his nickname means a girl's in love."

"Everyone does *not* know that. It's completely casual. There could be a thousand red flags, and I would look right past them because of how horny I've been lately. Not a good headspace to be in if I wanted to start a relationship. He's scratching an itch because he got all possessive and said I couldn't sleep with anybody else while I'm pregnant. It's literally just sex . . . like, we don't even kiss."

"Ah, yes. How Vivian Ward of you. Super logical to be fine with his tongue everywhere except your mouth. That's a good place to draw a line in the sand, dummy."

"I know we need to stop sleeping together before it gets messy, but it's been so nice. Not just the sex. It's nice having somebody to eat dinner with, a warm body to sleep next to, y'know?"

"No. I don't know because I am *very* single. But thank you for rubbing in whatever weird not-dating thing you have going on." Her palms skirt along her thighs as she moves to stand. "Nonalcoholic sparkling juice?"

I nod and watch as she strides across the expansive eleventh-floor apartment. In high school, we spent countless hours talking about sharing a place like this one, with exposed brick, impossibly high ceilings, and a small balcony so we could people-watch while drinking wine. I spent so much time daydreaming about it, I might've actually manifested this entire building.

But Blair had big goals, and I could never find a good enough reason to leave our hometown. I spent my twenties telling myself the time would come. I'd find my calling. Surely it couldn't be working at my dad's bar, one day taking over when he retires. Now I'm thirty-one, single, pregnant, and visiting my best friend in our dream apartment. Though I've been here plenty of times, it's hitting harder this trip. Because even if I found something that was worth leaving Wells Canyon for, I can't skip town now. Leaving on a whim is something my mother would do—*did do.*

Trying to clear the negativity like an Etch A Sketch, I turn and watch Blair pouring sparkling juice into two wineglasses. Even in matching purple loungewear, no makeup, and long brown hair up in a claw clip, she's elegant. Maybe it's due to the influencer-esque apartment with perfect natural lighting.

"Enough about my weird life. What's going on with you? How was your Christmas?"

"Um . . ." Her face falls as she walks over and hands me a glass, her own clinking down on the glass coffee table. "So you know how I said my mom seemed *off* when I visited during the summer? Lots of inconsistencies in things she'd say, and she couldn't keep track of her schedule, money, car keys. . . . I guess my parents were actually lying to me then. Back in the spring Dad got her to see a doctor, and she . . ." Tears pool and dampen her lashes. "Um, so turns out . . . she has early onset Alzheimer's."

"Fuck, Blair." I set down my glass and slide across the couch to wrap my arms around my best friend. "You sat here listening to my bullshit and waited to tell me this? *Shit.* How are you? How are your parents taking it?"

Jesus Christ. Blair's mom, Faye, isn't even old. I try to remember how long ago we had her fiftieth birthday party . . . maybe eight years ago? She's an elementary school teacher, and I know Blair's parents have been eagerly looking forward to enjoying their retirement as snowbirds in a few years.

"I don't know what to think." She exhales, relaxing into our embrace. "Neither of them seem too worked up about it. But they've also known for months, and I assume they had suspicions before then since they decided to see a doctor about it. My sister knew, too. They just didn't tell me because they 'didn't want me to worry.'"

"I'm so sorry, Blair. How . . . advanced is it?"

"It's already so much worse than it was last time I saw her. Back in June it was mostly little things—misplacing stuff, repeating questions, forgetting to pay bills, struggling to remember some people's names. When I was home for Christmas she asked me how university was going. . . . Like she had completely forgotten that I've been out of school for literal years."

"*Holy shit.*" I press a finger to my tear duct, simultaneously squeezing my best friend's shaky hand. "I'll have to go visit them. It's pretty terrible how little I see your parents considering we live in such a tiny town."

"You should." She smiles halfheartedly and picks up her glass, taking a slow sip. "I know she'll want to snuggle your belly."

"Blair, I appreciate your solidarity with the nonalcoholic juice. But please go pour some real fucking wine in that glass. You need it."

She sighs, her shoulders dropping. "Thank God. I wasn't going to drink anything while you're here, but this stuff doesn't even taste good."

She peels herself from the couch and heads back to the kitchen. Then dumps the juice down the drain and uncorks a bottle of white wine, swigging directly from the bottle as she curls up next to me.

The next day, I yawn into my coffee mug before taking a long sip, praying the caffeine will perform a miracle. As expected, I struggled to sleep without Chase . . . or maybe it was only because I didn't orgasm. Either way, I tossed and turned throughout the night. Half-asleep, I felt Blair leave the bed to go to the gym shortly after six o'clock this morning, and I slunk into the kitchen after the slam of her apartment door. It's quiet, calm, and too easy to pretend like this is my life. That this is my apartment—my white aesthetic couch, my elegant vintage decor, my view of . . . well, it's not a great view, admittedly. A grungy street peppered with miserable people traveling to work, and boring buildings taller than this one, which block the real view.

I wonder where Chase lived when he was here with his family.

I nearly blow coffee out of my nose at the image of him anywhere in this city. Cleaned up in his dark blue jeans and a plaid button-up, he could probably pass as a hipster. Nobody in Vancouver would bat an eye. But to me, he'd be hilariously out of place. I tuck my feet under me, pull a cozy blanket across my legs, and stare down at the street below.

Cass: Did you dress like a cowboy even when you lived in the city? Or did you try to fit in?

Red: I wasn't wearing chaps around town, if that's what you're asking

Red: I dressed like I do now . . . why?

Cass: I was trying to picture you here

Red: Just can't get me out of your mind, hey?

Cass: No, no. I was laughing at the image. Don't get it twisted.

A door creaks open long after I've finished my second cup of coffee, and Blair's roommate, Max, pads down the hallway wearing nothing but an oversized Van Halen T-shirt. Her crimson-red bob is messy from sleep and, even though it's not the right shade, I hate that seeing a redhead instantly makes me think of Chase. It's nearly eight o'clock now, and there's enough daylight I'm sure he's already on horseback somewhere, in winter gear and a thick Carhartt coat—maybe the one I used as a blanket in his truck.

"Oh my God. Good morning, baby mama!" Max shrieks, quickly veering from her path to the coffee machine to scoop me into a hug. "Look at you. Holy shit, this baby bump is so cute."

"Thank you. I finally look like I'm pregnant, instead of PCOS bloat," I say, hugging her back. "Where were you last night?"

With a coy smile, she tucks a lock of her messy hair behind

her ear. "Oh, you know. Went for drinks with a pretty girl from Tinder, then went back to her place to *hang out.*"

"Valid excuse to bail on me and Blair, then. Pregnancy has literally made me so horny, I'll skip the most important fucking plans if I think there's an orgasm in it for me."

"Too bad you won't listen to me and switch teams. We could've had a great time here last night. But I guess now you're a bit committed to straight men." She jokingly gags on the last words. "Tell me about him."

"We aren't together or anything. Just friends."

"Blair told me. She also told me he's a hot cowboy, there are benefits to your '*just friends,*' and you had a raging crush on him when you were younger."

"Jesus Christ. Like I told her, I also had a crush on Max from *A Goofy Movie* back then. My taste wasn't exactly refined."

"Mmm, Roxanne, though?" She bites her bottom lip jokingly. "I'm happy for ya, babe. You're going to be a great mom, and even if he's not quite Goof material, I'm sure you picked a good one."

"He's actually turning out to be better than I anticipated."

He's so much better it scares me. Before the rodeo, before the positive pregnancy test, before the anatomy ultrasound, I thought I had him pegged. Red was a dirty, rough, arrogant cowboy with a drinking problem and too many notches on his bedpost. That was an easy box to shove him in—there are a *lot* of local guys in that box. The problem is, he's consistently doing things to make me question whether I've been viewing him wrong this entire time. And with him wandering untethered in my brain, popping up in my thoughts constantly, I'm in trouble.

Despite a two-hour nap, I'm exhausted by the time we get ready, have dinner, and make our way downtown. All I want to do is hop back on the train to Blair's apartment and go to bed, but I didn't visit my best friend to sleep the trip away. Especially knowing how much hard shit she's been dealing with on her own. She deserves a few hours of fun to take her mind off her mom, which is why I'm shivering in the lineup for a nightclub with back pain and a plastered smile.

I'm officially too old and pregnant and sober for this. At least I look cute, with full hair and makeup, and a red babydoll dress that's flowy enough to disguise the baby bump. The last thing I want is everybody staring and awkwardly whispering about the pregnant girl in the nightclub.

When we finally push through the front door, I'm blown back by the smell of alcohol, perfume, and body odor. Holding on to the contents of my stomach with the same death grip I have on Blair's arm, we weave through the bodies. I order cranberry juice—if there's an upside to being sober at a club, it's juice and pop being free—and we head deeper into the crowd.

The part I hate most about nightclubs? The dicks. And I'm not talking about men with bad personalities. Evidently, the loose dress and club lighting have magically made my bump invisible. There are inescapable erections dragging across my ass when I'm simply trying to dance with Blair and Max. The last thing I want is a random man touching me in any way, and if they lay a finger on my stomach, I might have to deck them. Above all, the attention from other men is making me wish I was home with Chase more than I'd like to admit. I'd kill to feel his warm, rough hands right now.

Damn it. Quit thinking about him for one second.

"Hey, looks like your drink's almost empty. Let me help with that," a voice croons in my ear, tearing me away from thoughts of Chase. I swivel my head to see a tall, broad-shouldered, clean-shaven man. A *hot* man. A man I would normally love to accept a drink from. A smile lights his face when our eyes meet, and he cocks his head toward the bar. "What's your poison?"

"Plain cranberry juice for me tonight." I have to lean in close enough I can smell his spicy aftershave to be heard over the pounding bass.

"Being responsible tonight, eh? Hopefully not *too* responsible, though." He winks and places a hand on the small of my back, ushering me across the sticky club floor before I have the chance to turn him down.

Fresh drink in hand, I scrunch my nose and say something that's neither true nor necessary information to share right now. "I have a boyfriend."

"Okay?" He smirks, not giving a shit whether it's the truth or not.

"And I'm pregnant." I tap my fingernail on the side of my nonalcoholic drink, smoothing my free hand over my stomach to pull the dress taut.

"Oh, *shit.* Okay. Cool," he says in a tone that very much indicates it's not okay *or* cool. "Well, hey . . . have a great night and, uh, good luck."

Boyfriend. In the moment, I didn't stop to think about how it felt to say. It definitely didn't feel like I was lying . . . there was no anxious fidgeting, change in my voice, or racing heart.

I sidle back up between Blair and Max. "Pro tip, if you want guys to leave you alone, tell them you're pregnant."

"Or"—Max runs her fingertips down her torso—"dress like a masc lesbian."

"I like the engaged trick." Blair flashes her very large, very fake engagement ring. "Ten dollars at Claire's. My fiancé, Mark, is a wealthy plastic surgeon. He says I don't need any work done because I'm perfect."

"I like Mark." I laugh. "Does he have a brother?"

"Girl, you already have a real boyfriend who's hot and sweet. Leave the fictional ones for the rest of us."

"He's not my—"

Blair pinches my lips shut between her fingers. "Quit lying

to yourself. You're hanging out all the time, you're having sex, he's spending the night. *You're having a baby together.* I bet he thinks of himself as your boyfriend. If you're serious about not wanting a relationship, you can't keep leading him on."

I down my entire glass of cranberry juice, dreaming of a double vodka cran. She's right, and I hate it. I can't keep doing this.

Given how fatigued I felt the entire night, it's rather rude of my body to be wide awake as I lie in bed next to Blair at quarter-to-four in the morning. When I get home, I'll tell him this needs to stop. It's already too convoluted, and feelings are bound to get hurt if we continue. So we can't. But right now, I'll ignore the tangled mess I'm in for the sake of hearing his voice.

"Hey, you." His sleepy voice answers on the second ring.

I slip out of the bedroom, carefully shutting the door so I don't wake Blair, and curl up on the couch. "Hey, I couldn't sleep."

"Oh yeah? I think we both know what you can do to fix that."

"I'm sharing a bed with Blair. And anyway, I didn't pack a vibrator."

I naively assumed I'd be okay to go a couple days without anything in or around my vagina, given the amount of sex I've had in the last few weeks.

"Where are you right now?"

"Her couch." I pull the forest-green blanket up to my chin, peering at the dark street below.

"I'm guessing your fingers work fine since you called me. So why'd you call, Cass? Is it because you need me to help you fall asleep? You can't come without hearing my voice now?"

"Fuck off, that's not why I called you."

Why did I call him?

"It's okay to admit you're ruined for anybody else, sweetheart."

"You're an ass." I roll my eyes. The nerve of this guy to suggest he's so incredible in bed I'd never want to be with anybody else. Don't get me wrong, he's great. Best I've ever experienced, truthfully. But the last thing he needs right now is an ego stroking. "I'm not *ruined*, and definitely not by you, of all men."

"As much as I love how sexy you sound when you're cussing me out, I need to get ready for work. Unless . . . there's something you need."

"Well . . ."

"That's what I thought." His tone is arrogant, and I'm torn between being incredibly aroused and wanting to hang up. "All right, I'll help you."

"Tell me what you want me to do," I whisper.

"Fuck, Cass. You're incredible. Okay, uh . . . I want you to softly touch the skin right at the crease of your thigh, where your panties would sit. That's my favorite spot to kiss. I'd kill to be doing that right now."

I look around the room, confirming what I already know—I'm alone—then slide my free hand under the waistband of my pajama pants. A warmth washes over me from hearing him talk about his lips on my skin.

"Okay." I swallow hard, waiting with bated breath for his next instruction.

"Touch your clit. Just barely. One finger, baby. Tell me how sensitive it is." He sounds needy, and I can picture his cock strained against his boxers. I follow his direction, grazing my clit with my finger and letting out a soft whimper.

"Really fucking sensitive. How hard are you?"

"Mmm, rock fucking hard. I wish it was the tip of my cock teasing you instead of your finger. You'd be begging for me to fill you with it." I hear him shifting things around, most likely pulling out his cock and giving it a slow tug. My thighs clench together at the thought. "Tell me how good it feels to play with your clit, Cass."

"Pretty good."

"Pretty good? That's not enough, sweetheart. You deserve amazing. If I was there, I'd push your thighs apart, licking my way up each one. I'd check to see you're nice and wet for me. Knowing you, you'd be dripping after a few light flicks of my tongue."

My finger's working faster, and I shimmy my pajama pants down past my knees for easier access. I shut my eyes and sink deeper into the couch, pretending it's his work-worn hand between my legs.

"You'd be such a good little slut, eager to let me fuck you with my fingers where anybody could catch us. My fingers would be so deep inside you, thumb playing with your clit until you were squirming right off the edge of that couch—your tight pussy gripping me, wetness running down my fucking hand. I'd make sure we ruined your friend's nice couch." He moans into the phone, and I nearly fall apart. My finger becomes more frantic on my clit, until I'm so close to coming it's painful.

"You'd like that, wouldn't you, sweetheart?"

"So fucking much. I want that so bad." The truth spills out of me in a low moan. "Chase, I'm gonna come."

"Don't you fucking dare. Not until I tell you to."

Lost for words, I nod instinctively, knowing he can't see me.

"Slow down, baby. *Breathe.* I'm not done telling you what I'm picturing doing to you. All the ways I want to destroy that beautiful cunt of yours."

I pant. "Tell me."

"I'd bend you over the back of the couch, slip my cock between those sweet pussy lips. Slowly give you inch by inch until you're begging me to slam balls deep into you. I know you love having my thick cock filling you, pounding you so hard you feel me the next day. Right there in your best friend's living room, I'd make you wake her up with your screams. Show her what a fucking slut you secretly are. And, Cass? I would ruin you for any other guy. Just like you've ruined me."

"Fuck, Chase."

"Slide inside your pretty pussy and tell me how wet you are. Get those fingers drenched and play with your clit again."

"Soaked. I'm so wet thinking about your cock inside of me." I gulp. "I wish you were here."

Shit. I can't believe I just admitted that.

"Me too. You'll be coming on my cock again in a few days, sweetheart."

Good, he thinks I only meant it in a sexual way.

"I can't do this on the couch. Shit. I won't be able to clean it."

"Slide that sweet ass to the floor. I want you to make a fucking mess. Don't hold back." He's quiet as I do exactly what I'm told, sliding off the couch to the hardwood floor. Basking in the glow of city lights, I let my knees fall away from each other as my fingers continue exploring my pussy.

"Spread those legs wide. Now how does it feel?"

I moan hearing the wet friction over the phone as he jerks off. "So fucking good. Oh my God."

"Taste yourself, Cass. Tell me what I'm missing out on right now."

"I . . . uh . . ." I hesitate, then slowly bring my hand to my lips and curl my tongue around my finger. The hold he has over me—making me do things I never would—is astounding. "Sweet . . . maybe a bit tangy?"

"You taste like you're mine, don't you?"

"Mmhm," I whimper.

"Good girl," he rasps. "Fuck your fingers until you come. And I want to hear you say my fucking name when you do."

My hand keeps moving over my clit, the pressure becoming firmer, tempo frenzied. Until I'm so fucking close the edges of my vision are going black and the arches of my feet cramp as I fight to keep from becoming jelly.

"Fuck," he says with every whimper and moan I let free. I'm trying—and failing splendidly—to stay quiet. If I wake Blair and Max up, so fucking be it.

"I wish I was there watching you come. I bet you look so goddamn sexy gushing all over your fingers."

"Chase." I barely get the word out before I come completely undone. My knees straighten with a convulsion that rocks me from head to toe. I squeeze my eyes tight, letting myself pretend his heavy breathing is right in my ear instead of over the phone.

"*Fuck, Cass.* I want to be coming inside of you. How big of a mess did you make, sweetheart?"

The skin from my neck up to my cheeks burns as I touch the wood floor beneath me. "Oh, God. Bad."

He lets out a huff. "If only I was there to clean you up and get you to bed."

"I wish you were." I close my eyes, leaning my head back against the couch and losing myself in a daydream of curling up against his naked body. It's quiet, save for the sounds of our slow panting and city traffic. I hold a hand to my chest, feeling the steady drum of my heart. If I try hard enough, I might be able to pretend it's his thunderous pulse against my palm. What I wouldn't give to be snuggled up next to him right now. The warmth of his flushed skin against mine, his callused hand petting my hair, and his slowing breath as he drifts to sleep.

"How's your trip?" he asks after a few moments of silence.

"It's been fun. Clubbing is a lot less fun sober, but spending time with Blair and Max has been great. Blair and I are going baby shopping tomorrow, too."

"Max?" I swear I hear his spine stiffen through the phone.

"Short for Maxine. Calm down. You think I'd call you if I was hanging out with another guy?"

"No other guys—that's the deal, remember?"

If I rolled my eyes any harder, they'd come out of the sockets and bounce down the hallway. "No, the deal is no sex with anybody else. Quit the possessive shit. We're not a couple—I can hang out with guys."

Not the time or place to confess that I actually turned a guy down tonight by saying I had a boyfriend because I'm actually not interested in anybody else. The problem is, I don't know if I'm truly interested in Chase, either.

"We could be . . . a couple."

I sit straight up, a jumble of Blair's words about leading him on swimming through my orgasm-hazed brain. A couple? Shit. Shit. *Shit.* I should have ended this weeks ago instead of giving him the wrong idea. I knew a friends-with-benefits arrangement was stupid. Damn hormones got the better of me, and now I'm in over my head.

"Chase, I told you I didn't want to risk fucking things up between us. Honestly, things are probably too messy as it is, and I wasn't trying to make you think this could turn into something more. I'm sorry for making you think we could be . . . I'm not in the right headspace for a relationship with anybody. I need to focus on the fact that I'm having a baby in a few months. I know we keep saying it's the last time, but I'm serious now. I think it would be best for Little Spud if we just be friends . . . nothing more. No more benefits."

"Okay," he mumbles. He's lying. I know him well enough to know the tone in his voice means it's not okay, which absolutely guts me. "Just . . . if you ever decide you want to date somebody, consider giving me a chance? Get some sleep, Cass. Sweet dreams."

I'm crying before the line goes dead. I know we need to set boundaries to be effective co-parents. I refuse to trap him with a baby, force a relationship neither of us would've wanted if it weren't for Little Spud. Getting together only because I'm pregnant will lead to resentment, detachment, and a future broken home.

So, as painful as it is, pushing him away is better. We'll both suffer for a while, but one day we'll realize that sticking to being friends was worth it. It's what's best for Little Spud. I know I can't lead him on, and I know we can't be together. Those words play on repeat in my head, the silent mantra behind the tears.

Red

Thirty weeks (baby is the size of a loaf of bread)

Cassidy texted me to say she made it home safe and we should have a talk about boundaries after the holidays—then silence. I know we're apparently done hooking up, but after four days apart, I genuinely expected she would give in. Even if not, we're supposed to still be friends . . . and this feels like I'm not even somebody she'd make polite small talk with in the goddamn grocery store.

I should've kept my big fucking mouth shut instead of admitting I didn't just want to be whatever the hell we were. *I can't believe I suggested we be together.* Hell would freeze over before Cassidy would be interested in dating me. Her dad hates me. Her friends are probably indifferent, at best. And even though she calls me Chase now, I'm still Red deep down. I'm still a fuckup kid from a fuckup family. A wave of ruin, liable to destroy the future she deserves. Unworthy of somebody so incredible, so bright, so beautiful.

Denny chucks a log onto the bonfire—our thrown-together New Year's Eve celebration, since going to the big party at the Horseshoe isn't an option. "Who wants a turn against the reigning champ?"

"Yeah, me." I take a long pull of whiskey to stay warm, then hand the bottle to Kate. Jackson climbs onto the snowmobile with a devilish look, and I know he's not going easy on us. The kids are in bed and all bets are off.

Denny and I hop onto our GT snow racers—sleds meant for small children, with tiny plastic seats strapped to three ski blades. We're seriously testing the weight limits, and my knees are up to my chest when I sit down. We must look ridiculous. But towed behind a snowmobile at high speeds, they're fun as fuck. At the very least, it makes for a great temporary distraction.

I barely have time to give the nod that I'm ready before Jackson's taking off, sending us jolting forward with a sharp yank of the tow ropes. We're floating across the snow-covered hayfield, guided by the headlights on the snowmobile. The bonfire at the far end of the field is a faint orange glow, and I struggle to make out Denny on the other sled. Until he veers the tiny, barely functional steering wheel on his snow racer and heads right toward me.

Motherfucker.

The object of the game is to knock your opponent off. Denny's been the champ three winters in a row because, apparently, his experience as a saddle bronc rider is actually good for something. He has surprisingly good balance.

Just before the front ski of his sled crashes into mine, I kick my foot out and give him a hard shove. He shoots away with an echoing, goofy laugh, and I make chase. Cranking the tiny plastic wheel and tearing after him. Jackson turns the snowmobile, helping give me the upper hand as I glide across the fresh powder.

Neither of us is prepared for a sudden acceleration when our sleds make contact. I'm thrown backward, reflexively grabbing Denny's arm and dragging him down with me. In a giant cloud of powdery snow, we tumble onto the ground.

Denny jumps to his feet with a grin. "I win that round, you fucker. You hit the ground first."

Jackson swings the snowmobile around to pick us up. "Nah, that was a tie. You went off at the same time. Tie-breaker?"

I shake my head and brush the snow from my coveralls. "I need some more alcohol first. *Shit*—falling off hurts more and more every year."

Back at the bonfire, the ranch hands are playing beer pong on the flat deck of Colt's pickup. Somebody's cranked the truck speaker so loud the bass comes out scratchy. And I snatch the whiskey bottle from Austin for another long pull. "Are we getting too old for this shit?"

"Definitely." Austin shakes his head, holding Cecily tight on his lap. They kiss, and it feels like I've taken a bull horn to the sternum.

Cass was never mine to start with. Even when we were fucking and sleeping in the same bed every night, she made it clear we were nothing more than friends-with-benefits. And, apparently, friends-with-benefits don't kiss under any circumstance. Who the hell am I to argue? I'd follow any bullshit rules she gave me if it meant being in her life.

At midnight, I watch the couples kiss and text Cass to wish her a happy new year, knowing she likely won't reply. I don't know what else to do. I've never cared about somebody enough to be put in a position where I might have to fight to keep them. And losing this girl isn't an option.

The rest of the night's filled with mayhem, alcohol, and singing country songs at the top of our lungs. I can't go more than two minutes without thinking of her—no amount of liquor seems to erase the constant missing her. It does nothing to ease the dull ache in my chest or the weariness in my bones. But, damn it, that doesn't stop me from trying.

Even with all the cowboys working together to dethrone

Denny, he comes out on top. Reigning champ four years in a row—and he won't let us forget it, either. Kate presents him with a purple-and-gold crown from Odessa's dress-up box, which is still firmly on his head when he passes out on the bunkhouse couch at three in the morning.

Cassidy

Closing the Horseshoe's front door behind me, I turn the deadbolt and stroll past the bar to my dad's back office. He's here early to do payroll, which means it's the best opportunity to get him alone—before the kitchen staff have shown up, after the grocery and liquor deliveries.

In Dad's mind, I should be having a baby completely on my own. And, while I don't know exactly what Chase and I are to each other, I know he's going to be in my life. There can't be any conflict between the two of them when the baby arrives. I haven't found the words I want to say to Chase yet, but I can work on my dad in the meantime.

My knuckles rap twice on the door before his voice beckons me in.

"Hey, kiddo. Why are you here so early?"

I toss my purse on the faded-orange armchair, which has a worn-out floral pattern straight out of 1975. Then I plop down, eager to take some pressure off my lower back, and look around at the depressing, undecorated space. After owning the bar for close to thirty years, you'd think he would add *something* to the office he spends hours in every day. Instead, it's just dingy white walls, a desk overwhelmed with unfiled paperwork, a filing cabinet, and this old chair.

I take a deep breath. "I need to talk to you about something."

My hand finds its way to my stomach, which appears to be growing exponentially now after a slow start. I always thought pregnant people rubbed their stomach for attention, but now I understand it's an unconscious habit. If my hands aren't preoccupied, they're probably on the baby bump.

"Okay." He sets down his pencil and pulls the reading glasses from his face, setting them on a teetering stack of paperwork. "What's up, buttercup?"

"Dad . . . we need to talk about Chase—Red. I know you're choosing to pretend he's not part of this, but he is. I'm sorry I didn't tell you about him sooner. I didn't mean to lie to you, honestly. You just assumed about Derek, and I lied by omission." I gulp, watching his forehead wrinkle more and more with every word I say. "You were already so disappointed in me, I didn't want to make it worse. I also never expected you to find out the way you did . . . that was the first time he stayed over, and it was honestly because of the storm."

"First time . . . not only time. So he's stayed over since? In the house I own?"

Shit.

"Yeah." I rub my temples vigorously. This conversation is already not going the way I'd rehearsed a dozen times over the past twenty-four hours. "I need you to hear me out, though. You have valid reasons to be wary—I get it. But he's been all in with this pregnancy since the day he found out. Chase checks in on me constantly and does anything I ask. When I was sick, he made sure I was eating every day. He's driven me home when Shelby was too boy-crazy to care when I was tired. He's been to my appointments and made me feel better when the doctor was a jerk. Is he perfect? No. But there's no questioning his love for this baby. That's all I can ask for."

Tongue tucked in his cheek, Dad rolls his office chair closer to me. "You were too young to really see what kind of guy Joe Thompson was when he still lived here. And I see the same issues in Red. I don't want you to be stuck dealing with that shit."

"So you think I'm the same as Mom? I'm gonna ditch this kid when I decide I'm tired of being tied down, right? Because when you talk shit about Chase and his dad, the little voice in my head tells me"—I wipe the tears clinging to my eyelashes before they mess up my work makeup for tonight—"you're probably wondering the same thing about me. You're just too scared to say it. I grew up with a crappy mother. He grew up with a crappy father. I don't think—*I fucking hope*—that doesn't mean we're destined to screw up this baby girl."

"Cassie, you're nothing like your mother."

"Aside from the fact that half of my DNA is hers."

His fingers interlace behind his neck, and his gaze turns to the ceiling. "I understand you're a grown woman now, and I can't tell you what to do. That said, I don't think involving him is a good idea."

"My child is gonna be lucky enough to have two parents who love her—I'll *never* deny her that. I don't think you really understand how hard it was for me to not have both you and Mom growing up. I know you did so much, and I'm so thankful for you, Dad. But don't you honestly wish that—even with her issues—Mom had been more permanent? I know it killed you when she walked in and out, too."

He sighs, rocking back and forth. For a minute, there's nothing but the incessant squeaking of the spring on his ancient desk chair. "If you insist on involving him, I still think you need to get him to—"

"Jesus Christ, Dad. I'm not making him sign child support papers or a custody agreement right now. I trust him. If anything changes, I'll deal with it then. Be as disappointed as you want in me, but please stop trying to convince me to do everything the way you want it done."

His tongue darts out to wet his lips, then he leans back in his chair, arms crossed against his chest, and blinks at me. I continuously wipe the tears before they can run but, judging by the mascara smeared on my fingers, my makeup is already too far gone. Vision blurred, I strain to read the tiny numbers on his desk clock. At least there's time to run home and freshen up before my shift.

"Are you two together, then?" Dad finally breaks his silence right as I'm running out of things to look at in his cramped, messy office.

"Not right now. This isn't the 1950s, so I'm not rushing to the altar. I just . . . I'm taking the time to get to know him before I make any judgments. It would mean the world to me if you'd do the same. Like it or not, you and Chase are the most important men in my life right now. And when this baby comes, I refuse to be the mediator between you. You'll have to act like adults and figure it out."

Hearing me say Chase is right there next to him on the list of important people in my life makes him wince like I stabbed him with a leather skiving knife.

"I can be civil. That's all I can promise. I love you, Cassie, and I'm not disappointed in you—I could never be. Even if I don't necessarily agree with your choice." He picks up his reading glasses and turns to his payroll again. Sorting through a stack of time cards because he refuses to update to computerized bookkeeping. "I need to get this done before we open. Lock the front door behind you when you go."

"Thank you, Dad. I love you."

I walk out of the office awash with relief, despite not getting my dream outcome. Sharing my feelings, finally having him listen to me, and getting him to agree to be civil still feels like a win.

I wish I'd waited to talk to Dad because when I arrive back at home to fix my makeup for work, my heart sinks at the sight of a paper bag on my front step.

Chase was here. I'm positive it's from him before even looking at the contents. There's no note, but my favorite snacks and a Tupperware container with dinner in it is all the confirmation needed.

> **Cass:** Thank you. You know you could've brought it inside so nobody would steal it.
> **Red:** Didn't feel right letting myself in.
> **Cass:** Sorry I wasn't home to talk to you
> **Red:** I just don't want you living off whatever random food you find at the gas station
> **Cass:** I enjoy being a trash panda, fyi.

I drop the bag with a *thunk* on the coffee table and pace across the charcoal-gray shag rug. I could call him. Ask if he's still in town and wants to talk before I go back to the bar, so we can talk about boundaries. Or about not having them anymore. Because I'm so fucking torn between what I know I should do and what I desperately want to do.

I pace the house. Stand in the half-decorated nursery. Brain awash with thoughts about this sweet baby girl. Little Spud. She can't be the only reason Chase and I get together. My heart, and my vagina, and my brain *all* need to be on board that this is more than two people trying to make the best of a strange situation.

All the more reason to keep my distance for a while longer.

A few more days to think, decide what I really want. Not be swayed by food or orgasms or whatever other sweet gestures he has up his sleeve. If I see him, smell him, or touch him, I'm a fucking goner. No shot of standing my ground when he's staring me down with a look that reveals how well he can see right through me. Just like every day before my trip, I'll say "fuck it" to any discussion about boundaries and say "fuck me" to him.

No talking. Not yet. Not until I can get my head on straight.

Red

Thirty-one weeks (baby is the size of a tub of movie theater popcorn)

The phone rings, and my chest cracks at the sound. Sitting around the giant kitchen table in the big house is every single person who might call me. Except one. And she doesn't call me just to chat anymore. Hard to believe two weeks ago I was practically living at her house, sleeping in her bed, guiding her through masturbation over the phone.

If she's on the other end of the phone, it's likely not a good thing.

"Hello?" I answer without even looking at the name, letting the back door slam shut behind me.

"Hi, Chasey." The woman's voice is instantly recognizable, despite how much time has passed. *God*, how long has it been? Five years, maybe?

Should've taken a half second to check the call display first.

"Mom." I try, and fail, to swallow the lump in my throat. My legs are wobbly. Too unsteady to be trusted to keep me upright, so I plunk my ass on the porch swing. "What do you need?"

"Sheesh, can't your mother call to say she misses you?"

If we had a relationship, sure. As it stands? There's no way that's why she's calling.

"Sure. What's going on?"

"Well . . ." Her blubbering, whiny voice is cut off by full-on sobs that I can only shake my head at. If any other woman in my life called me like this, I would drop everything for them. But I've been the victim of these crocodile tears a time or two. "It's about your dad."

I snort. "Of course it is. What did the fucker do this time?"

Drunk driving, bar fights, gambling, getting in trouble with the wrong guys . . . it's always something. And if it warrants a phone call from Mom, it probably requires bail money or some shit.

"He's dying—it's his liver. The doctor said less than six months, most likely. Especially since he refuses to quit drinking. I thought maybe you'd want to come visit him. I know you two had your *issues* when you were growing up, but it would mean a lot to him."

Her tone implies we argued about shit like my grades or staying out past curfew. Conveniently overlooking the times he smacked me around when I was too young to defend myself. Too young to have even done anything worthy of being hit in the first place.

"Okay. Thanks for letting me know. Honestly, I have no interest in seeing him. Besides . . . my girlfriend is having a baby in a few months, so I can't get away." I don't know why I add the comment about Cass—who is the furthest thing from my girlfriend, considering I haven't even seen her in weeks. But I have to admit, it feels nice to say something that might hurt my mom. As petty as that is.

"I'm going to have a grandbaby?" Her voice perks up like Little Spud will have an effect on her life. I guess she can brag to her friends about it. She might've been the better parent of the two, but the bar was real fucking low. Even still, I've never doubted she loves me and my four brothers. She just loves our crappy father more.

"Yeah, a baby girl. Maybe after Joe dies, you can visit sometime. Anyway, I gotta go, Mom." I hang up before she has the chance to scold me for calling him Joe, instead of Dad.

The back door squeaks louder than normal thanks to the hush falling over the busy kitchen when I walk back in.

"Whatcha all staring at?" I clear my throat and sit back down in my usual spot.

"Who was that?" Denny asks.

"My mom. My dad's dying, apparently." I shrug, piling more and more rice onto my plate, until Cecily's hand reaches out to stop me, and I realize I lost track. Half my plate's covered. "Anyway, who wants to go out for drinks tonight?"

Nobody answers and all of them are staring. *Fuck*, even Rhett is being perfectly silent, which is unheard of for a one-year-old.

Finally, Cecily speaks up. She's always the fixer. Never shying away from hard conversations—at least, not since her own dark secrets were spilled. "Are you sure that's a good idea? Maybe you should have a low-key night instead of drinking the sadness away."

"It's not sad drinking. I want to celebrate. Fuck that guy."

Kate lets out a loud huff. I'm a little thankful for all the pity, otherwise she'd be tearing a strip from my rear end for swearing in front of the kids.

"Sorry, that was a bad word." I smile weakly at Odessa, who's unfazed. If Kate heard the way everyone—Jackson included—talks when she isn't around, we'd all be strung up. Odessa's dropped her fair share of F-bombs herself.

"Problem, Red. Where we gonna go?" Denny asks. "Can't exactly go to town. . . . There's some liquor in the bunkhouse, but not enough to do any damage."

"I'm fine to go to town," I say.

"*Okay.* Who wants to chip in for bail money now?" Denny grabs his hat from the back of his chair and holds it out like he's accepting donations.

"Red, don't you think this might make things worse with Dave . . . and upset Cassidy?" Cecily's nose scrunches. "Just saying. Maybe think this through for a bit."

"She's right." Kate points her fork at Cecily while giving me a pitiful look. "Getting into an altercation with her dad isn't the way to go about winning Cass over."

If Dave's gonna kill me, he's gonna kill me. It's not like staying away from the bar is any protection now that he knows the truth. He could show up here if he wanted to. Then there's Cass . . . *fuck.* She's already made it clear there's nothing I can do to win her over. It doesn't matter that I busted my ass for her. That I followed every asinine rule. That I *love her.* None of it matters.

"I don't give a shit about that. It's too late."

Eerily silent, everyone stares. From his seat next to mine, Jackson places a firm palm between my shoulder blades. "Maybe you should hold off for the night?"

"I want to go for drinks with my friends, and that's the only bar in town. You're the ones making this into something bigger."

I'll go to the bar, have a couple drinks, eye-fuck Cassidy from across the room, and play it cool. *Easy peasy.*

"Well, what if I go in and talk to Dave first? Feel it out before you roll in and start shit," Denny says.

"Fine, let's do that." I nod, shoveling a scoop of rice into my mouth, since apparently that's all my dinner will be tonight. At least it'll soak up the alcohol.

The bar parking lot is busier than I would've expected for a Thursday at eight o'clock, and knowing there's a crowd inside almost makes me change my mind. I just want to listen to music and have some drinks with my friends. Of course, both Dave's truck and Cassidy's car are in the parking lot. Knowing she's here makes me more anxious than thinking about seeing Dave for the first time since he practically walked in on me fucking his daughter.

Colt, Sundial, Levi, and Rob sit on the flat deck of Colt's truck with me, waiting for the verdict from Denny. The air's cold and crisp, with a brutal wind, but I'm sweating. Unable to focus on the guys' conversation.

Denny crashes through the bar's front doors with a grin and practically skips over to us. "We're allowed in, but you"—he juts his finger into my chest—"need to be on your best behavior."

"Great. We're fucked." Colt throws his hands up.

"Shut the hell up." Walking toward the double doors, I stick my boot out to trip him. Thanks to the amount of road pops he drank on the way, Colt barely manages to stop himself from face-planting into a pile of dirty snow. Giggling as he rights himself and carries on.

My hand lands on the door handle, and I stop breathing. With the flip of an imaginary switch, my body mindlessly goes through the motions—walking into the warm building and across the worn floorboards guided by muscle memory. Despite the edges of my vision getting foggy, I keep my eyes trained on the table along the back wall. Our usual spot. When I sit down next to Denny, I stare at the knots and dings in the shiny wood table. If I lift my head, I might see Cass. And as much as I want to see her, I'm terrified of how I'll feel when she makes it obvious she doesn't want to see me.

There's not much time to panic before she's there. Right fucking there at the side of our table. Hair in a high ponytail, sparkling eyes, and . . . *shit*, her tits have probably doubled in size since I last held them. Either that or she's wearing a serious push-up bra. All I know is I'm immediately envisioning them pouring out from my hands while she's on top of me. And there's no denying she's pregnant anymore.

How has so much changed in two weeks? Two weeks I should've been there for.

"Hey," she says softly.

"Hey," I reply. The other guys may as well not even be here. "You look beautiful."

"Liar." She tugs at the hem of her dark-green long sleeve, tilting her head to hide a small smile. When she looks back up, our eyes meet for a split second before she redirects her focus to the rest of the guys. "You guys need a round of beer?"

"Yeah, thanks," Denny says. "You do look great, by the way."

"Thanks. I'll be right back with your drinks."

I watch her walk across the empty dance floor, stopping to grab a few empty glasses from another table, then putting in our order with Dave. He doesn't so much as glance at her—shooting daggers at me as he pours pint after pint. I'm fully prepared for him to hurtle his body over the bar top and charge at me. Maybe pull a gun from under the bar and take me out with a quick head shot.

But he simply fills the glasses, then turns away to do something else. Whatever Denny did or said to convince him to let us in here, I'm impressed.

Thank God it's not long before she's back with a round of beer. Then a second. Then a third. The boys are doing some heavy drinking to make up for lost time, since most of them have avoided this place for as long as I have. Cass flutters around the place like a hummingbird, never stopping for longer than necessary. It's no wonder why her back hurts and she's always so damn tired. I should be going home with her to massage those aching muscles tonight.

After setting down the fourth round, she lingers with a yawn. Her hands rest underneath her stomach, cradling it as she leans against the table. "You all better tip good. It's rude to make the pregnant girl hustle back and forth all night because you insist on sitting the furthest from the bar."

"We can move," I offer. But, looking around, there's nowhere else that can seat all six of us. "Or not . . ."

Denny beams at her. "We love you, Cass. I'm sure Red would be more than happy to show our appreciation in other ways."

"Wow, is that all my time and energy is worth? Serving really is a thankless job." Her hand finds the back of my chair, seeking stability so she can lean between Denny and me to grab a pair of empty beer glasses. Her tits are so damn close to my head it makes my dick hurt. Then her fingertips graze my back, sending a shiver up my spine. It's likely my imagination getting the best of me, but I swear her fingers stay where they are for longer than necessary. The simple touch rushes through me with a buzz and, when she pulls away, I can't breathe.

"I'd offer my type of thank-you, but I think the big guy would kill me." Denny winks at her before slapping me on the back, restarting my heart. If any other guy made a similar comment, I would remove his testicles with the dirty work knife I keep in my pocket.

She chuckles—the sweet version, not her true laugh. I hate knowing what her laugh sounds like and not being able to hear it every day.

"That's the most unappealing proposition I've gotten all night. And Toothless George told me he has a pregnancy kink while he had a dollop of ketchup on his ZZ Top beard." She walks away, arms loaded with empty pint glasses.

Toothless George. He's been old, toothless, and permanently drunk for as long as I can remember. He's gotta be at least ten years older than my dad. How is it Joe's going to drop dead of liver failure any minute and this fucker will probably spend the next twenty years slumped over that bar? Not that my dad doesn't deserve to have his liver fail . . . but still. It's bullshit that the world works this way.

"You good, bud?" Denny elbows me. "You look spacey."

"Yeah, yeah. Just thinking about Toothless George."

"Afraid he's gonna steal your girl? I heard he has a big inheritance. Can't say I'd blame her if she gets the choice between you two."

"Fuck right off. I'm thinking about why he gets to live another day."

"Hey, man, being part of the sick parent club fucking sucks. I've been there. . . . Just a heads-up, the dead parent club isn't great either." He gives my shoulder a quick squeeze before picking up his beer glass and downing it.

When his mom died, it hit me hard, too. Obviously, I would never try to compare my grief to that of Denny, Jackson, and Austin, but Lucy Wells was more of a mom than I'd ever had. She taught me how to cook a steak, how to ride a horse, and how to add fractions. My mom taught me that fictional men are apparently always better than the real version, the proper way to roll a cigarette, and the lyrics to every single Fleetwood Mac song—not saying those aren't surprisingly useful life skills.

Knowing my dad is dying doesn't feel like it did when we found out Denny's mom was dying. There weren't any conflicting emotions about losing her. It was pure misery for every person who was blessed enough to know her—the entire town was devastated. With my dad, I'm torn between relief from knowing karma is finally kicking that son of a bitch in the ass, anger that he couldn't even be bothered to tell me himself, and disappointment because he'll never have the opportunity to turn his life around. Despite everything he's done, there's always been a tiny part of me hoping things could change.

I rub my hand up my bare arm, feeling the scarred skin under my palm, and follow suit with the beer chugging. If anything, at least both of us sitting here with empty glasses will get Cass back to our table faster.

Like she has a sixth sense for men in need of a beer, she almost immediately turns back up next to me and plunks down into the empty chair. "Sorry, I need to sit for half a second."

"Are you okay?"

"My back feels like it's about to spontaneously combust, and if my feet could talk, they'd be screaming bloody murder. Oh, and I think she's parked right on my bladder." She points a finger angrily at her stomach, like she can somehow intimidate the baby into moving. "But, yeah, peachy. I'm fucking peachy keen."

"Give me your feet."

"I have to work and also . . . no. Gross. I've been running around all night. They're sweaty."

"Give me your fucking feet, Cass." Unblinking, I stare her down. She doesn't move, narrowing her eyes right back at me. So I reach under the table to grab them myself. Her heels fall onto my lap, and I untie each sneaker before pulling them off.

"You really shouldn't," she protests before sinking into the chair with a relaxed moan when my thumb presses into the ball of her foot. "*Fuuuck*, okay. Can you do my back next?"

"I would. You know I would." If she would invite me over, I'd do anything. Fucking *anything* to be allowed back in her world for a single night.

"I need to get back to work, though." She pulls her leg, and I grip her foot tighter. "Your drinks won't refill themselves, will they?"

"No. But I have two feet and a heartbeat. Take a break, all

right? I got it." I stand up, setting her socked feet down on my empty chair, and grab the empty glasses from the table.

Apparently, I'm about to have my first interaction with Dave since that morning at Cassidy's house. Letting out a slow exhale, I walk across the bar floor. Feeling the weight of Cass's stare on my back and the crushing fear from Dave's looming presence on my chest.

"Hey, Cass needed a break. Where do you want these?"

Okay, now we wait to be murdered.

I wince when his mouth opens. "Through those doors, chuck 'em on the rack."

What the hell. What the hell. What the hell.

There's no way he was that chill. *Nice, even.* I follow his instructions and decide to push my luck by ordering another round. Again, nothing.

"Is she okay?" Dave asks, looking up from the quickly filling pint glass to where Cassidy is still sitting at our table, talking to Denny and twirling a fallen strand of hair.

"Oh . . . yeah. Just said her feet and back hurt."

"Right. I told her I'd be civil, and I will be." He hands me a round black tray and starts placing full pint glasses on it. A monotone voice and zero expression in his face. Refusing to look at me as he speaks. "Until you hurt her. If you treat her with any less respect than she deserves. If you break her heart . . . I will fucking end you."

"All due respect, if anybody's going to end up hurt, it's me. Cass is the one with all the control here." I struggle to balance the tray as he places the last glass for our table on it.

Jesus, how does Cass do this every day?

"What else do you need me to do so she can stay off her feet awhile longer?"

He eyes me suspiciously. "Clear off that table over there. And see if anybody needs a round."

I sidle up to our table and start passing around beers, to

the boys' delight. Not a single one of them will let me get away without chirping me.

"Damn, what a fuckin' downgrade in the quality of staffing here." Sundial—the shittiest cowboy we have on the ranch—chucks a handful of peanuts into his mouth, then adjusts the backward ball cap on his long hair. Just for that, I take a long chug of his beer before handing it over.

"Shut up. He's got diapers to buy. Let the man earn some extra cash." His brother, Colt—an infinitely better cowboy and probably the sole reason Sundial's still employed—smacks him on the arm. "Hey, Red. If you show me your tits, I'll tip you extra."

"Colt, the only person I'm showing my tits to tonight is your mom after I'm done here. Fuck off." I smack him on the back of the head and carry on.

Denny doesn't fuck around. Jamming a five-dollar bill in the waist of my jeans before I can set the tray down to stop him. "No offense, Cass, but I might like Red being our server even more than I like you."

Cassidy laughs. *The real kind.* "No offense taken. I like it better, too." She reaches into the black server pouch tied around her hips and pulls out a bill, waving it at me like we're at a goddamn strip club. "Will you show me your titties, or are they fully reserved for Colt's mom tonight?"

"Sweetheart, you know you're the only MILF I want seeing my tits. I'll give you the VIP treatment, even."

Denny grimaces. "Cool it, Romeo. I already know enough about your guys' sex life. Save the cringey dirty talk for later."

"Would you rather hear the non-cringey stuff?" Cass looks up at me with a smile so big I bet it can be seen from space. Her hands lightly, absentmindedly rub over her baby bump.

Before I say something stupid—one of her many rules I still find myself trying to follow—I leave to do Cassidy's job so

Dave doesn't lose his shit. Do I tell every table I pass to go place their own damn orders at the bar? Absolutely. Wouldn't kill most of them to get some exercise, anyway.

Things are going smoothly. Dave seems less likely to kill me with every trip to the bar. Regardless of how much he hates me, he's not going to force his pregnant daughter to get back on her feet when I'm capable and willing. We both want what's best for Cass, and right now, that's drinking a root beer and talking to Denny.

"You gonna be bitch boy for her all night?" says a guy who's best described as the crusty cum sock under a teenage boy's bed. Landon Wiebe. Twenty-eight years old and desperately trying to become a rapper. Somehow he hasn't realized nobody gives a shit about rap lyrics from a punk who's never left his mom's basement in small-town Canada.

"Whaddya need, Wiebe?" I slip my hands in the front pockets of my jeans because it'll buy me a few seconds to think about my actions if the next words from his mouth are deserving of a punch.

"Bro—*just sayin'*—I heard Cassidy fucked a few guys at the rodeo. Now she's got you trapped with a baby that's probably not even yours."

I crack my neck and tighten the fists in my pockets, wishing Cass was here to calm my inner demons. The way she did when I wanted to hit that arrogant ex of hers in the grocery store parking lot. "Keep her *fucking* name out of your slimy mouth, skid."

I look at her briefly. Carefree, relaxed. I should walk away—go to her. Wrap her in my arms, inhale her sweet perfume, and ignore the crap spewing from this loser's mouth. But it feels like my feet are cemented to the floor, and no amount of electric zaps from a cattle prod could get me to move.

"Bro, I'm just sayin' what I heard." He shrugs and looks

over at his equally stupid, ugly, wannabe-rapper friends. Then he laughs. "I heard she's a slut and, like, fucked a whole load of dudes. Guess if it comes out a ginger, you'll know for sure, though."

I want to give him a final warning. I do. Because every rational part of my brain knows I shouldn't do anything to piss off Cass or Dave. But I can't give him another warning because the alcohol and the rage combine in my stomach, burning me from the inside out. So I snap, seeing red. The pockets do nothing to stop my hands from grabbing the front of his hoodie, yanking his pinner body closer to mine.

"You wanna talk about the mother of my child? I'll make sure you don't even make it to the hospital, *bro.*" My words land with spit droplets against his ugly face. Then my fist makes contact with his jaw, right as his friends strike from all sides.

My tunnel vision's smaller and smaller. If time's moving, I'm unaware. Soon, all I can see is a fist—I assume mine—hitting Landon Wiebe's narrow nose. And I don't feel anything until there's a hand on the back of my shirt, pulling me backward, out of the brawl. My ass slams onto the sticky bar floor.

Maybe it's been ten seconds, maybe ten minutes. Maybe I only hit him twice, maybe we're both bloody messes. I have no idea.

Blinking to clear my vision, I see my friends fighting the skids. And the person who yanked me out of there still has a firm grip on my shirt—Dave.

Fuck.

Send me back into the middle of the donnybrook full of flying fists, knocked-over chairs, and spilled drinks. I'll take that over whatever fury Dave is going to unleash.

"My office. *Now.*" He points toward the double doors leading into the back, then stalks toward the group to break them up.

My heart's hammering inside my chest and my skull at the same time, threatening to beat so hard it seizes completely. With Dave's back turned, I could slip out to the parking lot or jump back into the fight. A lot of good either of those would do when I'm stuck with Dave just as much as he's stuck with me. Our worlds revolve—and collide—around Cassidy's sunshine.

I stand up slowly, too afraid to search for Cass and see whatever emotion she's feeling right now. Disappointment, anger, fear, worry. I can't handle any of that. I don't remember the last time I worried about anything other than winning the fight. My reputation's long been ruined, and impressing people was the lowest priority. Before she came along and gave me a reason to want to be a decent guy. Although my Cassidy-induced good behavior hasn't changed anything—I'm still here, pining over a girl who doesn't give a fuck about me and fighting guys who talk shit about her. Nothing has changed.

Keeping my eyes trained on the dirty, worn flooring, I push through the doors and locate Dave's small office. In total contrast to Cassidy, who has everything neatly organized and clean, Dave has this place looking like somebody let a wild animal run amok. I pick up a pile of papers from the shabby armchair and set them on an empty patch of floor before sitting.

The seconds drag on, bringing me back to never-ending strings of days where I sat like this in my high school principal's office, waiting to be told if I'd be paying for my stupidity with detention or suspension. At least I was fairly confident Principal Thiessen wouldn't walk in and stab, shoot, or punch me. Can't say the same for Dave Bowman.

I'm dragging my boots back and forth across the dusty floor when Dave storms in some time later. Immediately, I sit upright, tucking my hands deep into my pockets, ready to face my punishment like a man. Whatever he thinks is a fair consequence.

"What the fuck was that?" He slumps into his rolling desk chair, dragging a hand down his face. "Let me get one thing clear, Red. I knew your dad pretty well back in the day. And I refuse to sit back and let you drag Cassidy through that kind of bullshit. She won't be bailing you out of jail, dragging your sorry ass home after a rough night, or taking care of your kid while your ass is on my bar stool so often I should charge rent."

I nod, refusing to make eye contact with him. Counting the pens sitting in a mason jar on his desk instead. Five blue, three black, one red. And a worn-down pencil with purple hearts on it, which seems like it probably belonged to Cass before ending up here.

"Denver told me about your dad. Frankly, that's the only reason I'm talking to you instead of calling the cops—got it? Take this as a win and clean your fucking act up. Be a goddamn man. Don't go starting bar fights in front of the mother of your child." He knocks his boot hard against mine so I'll look at him. His brows are tight, forehead wrinkled, and eyes narrow as he assesses me. "Cassie's relentlessly trying to convince me you can be a decent guy. And I don't think she would say that for no reason, so be that man. If not for yourself, do it for the baby. You don't need to become your father, Red. But you sure as hell will if you don't figure your shit out."

Clearing my throat, I say, "Thanks for not calling the cops. Is that all?"

"Yup."

I rise from the chair despite my entire body feeling numb, tingling with TV static. And the walk of shame I do through the bar, past Cassidy, and out to the parking lot feels worse than the handful of times I've been dragged out in handcuffs. I'm like a kicked dog, tail between my legs, rushing across the icy parking lot. Desperate to get far away from this place.

I would say this entire night was a bad idea, but the truth is that it wasn't. I got to see Cass. Talk to her. Feel her fingers graze my body. Hear her laugh. Flirt.

Then I had a rude awakening.

I can't do this anymore.

Cassidy

"What the fuck was all that?" I hand Denny a bar towel wrapped around ice for his busted lip. Most of the bar emptied immediately after the massive fight was broken up. Partially because it was almost closing time, but mostly because they didn't want to feel inclined to help clean up.

Thankfully, the rest of the ranch hands from Wells Ranch are sweeping up broken glass, mopping spilled beer, and righting tipped tables. I've witnessed my fair share of bar fights, but tonight there's an anxious hum under my skin and my hands haven't quit shaking since I watched Chase's fist make contact with Landon's face.

"How am I supposed to know? They were about to be five on one, so we had to jump in for Red." Denny dabs the cold cloth on his face. "All I know is some greaseball clubbed me right in the moneymaker with a beer bottle."

"They must've said something, right? Do you think he punched Landon in the face for the hell of it?"

He wouldn't, right?

It's scary not immediately knowing the answer. For all the bar fights he's been in while I've worked here, I've been too removed from the situation to know or care what started it. My primary concerns were whether tabs were still getting paid and the offenders were kicked out. Too often, that meant kicking out Red . . . Chase . . . Red . . .

Even if he had a legitimate reason tonight. What about all those other fights? I convinced myself that wasn't who he was. That he's *Chase*—not Red.

He's both.

He's always been both. And I think I've been falling in love with Chase . . . but I'm not sure about Red.

Before Denny can answer, the double doors behind me swing open, and I turn to see Chase walk out. He stalks toward the front doors without bothering to look around at the damage, his friends, or me. His eyes are firmly fastened to the ground as he blows by.

"Chase," I say, leaning to try and catch his arm over the bar top. I'm sure he hears me, but his gait doesn't slow as he storms out to the parking lot, letting a cold blast of winter air chill me to the bone. For the first time since the fight broke out, I notice a sad, twangy country song blaring through the speakers. *Seems fitting, honestly.*

Without a word, I brush past Denny and out the front doors. The hair on my arms stands at attention, and I wrap my arms around my stomach, desperately trying to conserve body heat. Leaning against a tailgate, Chase hangs his head low, one hand keeping a tight grip on the cowboy hat held at his side, while the heel of the other digs into his forehead. When he hears the crunch of my sneakers on the crusty snow, his eyelids snap open.

"The fuck was that?" I'm shivering but no longer cold. Instead, my blood's boiling as it rages through my blood vessels. I charge across the white ground until I'm no more than two feet from him. His hands drop to his sides and he looks up at me.

"I can't fucking believe you would come here tonight and do *that*. After all the shit I've been through trying to convince my dad you aren't a total piece of shit, you show up and act like a total piece of shit."

"I didn't mean for this to happen."

"So tell me you had a good reason for punching him. Tell me your actions were justified and I shouldn't be mad at you."

He shrugs. *Fucking shrugs.*

"Great. *Great.*" I stare off at a lonely streetlamp in the distance to discourage the angry tears welling in my eyes. Snow flutters past the warm glow before settling on the empty street. "I told you we needed boundaries and I wish you could've respected me enough not to come here. Especially when you showed up only to act like that. What the hell happened? How can you go from being so sweet and helpful to beating the shit out of somebody? Like . . . *shit.* If Landon doesn't press charges, I'll be amazed because he was *fucked up* when he left."

My jaw clenches, and I watch the muscles in his throat repeatedly work to swallow while he looks anywhere but at me.

"It fucking sucked when it felt like I didn't know who you were a few minutes ago. Sure, I've seen you get into fights, but it feels different now. *You* feel different to me now. I don't like this and I didn't like you back there."

"Cass." He breathes out my name, and there's no stopping my tears now. I tug the sleeve of my shirt over my fingers and press the thin, soft fabric to the inner corner of each eye.

"I don't know what the hell you want me to say," he says quietly. If it weren't eerily still in this empty, frozen parking lot, I wouldn't have even realized he was speaking.

"I want you to tell me if I've been wrong in thinking you're a good guy. Thinking you aren't the kind who goes around punching people for no good reason, and then just fucking walks right past me like I don't matter. If that's who you are, we're done here. So tell me that's not who you are."

"Yeah . . . it's who I am. Don't pretend like you didn't know that already. You know me. Nothing has changed."

"I thought—"

"You thought wrong. I'm the same piece of shit I've always been."

Fighting back tears, I turn toward the front doors. "Go home, Red."

Once I'm finished rage-cleaning the bar, I poke my head into Dad's office. "All cleaned up out there. I'm gonna head out."

"Come sit."

Shit. Apparently, I should've left without saying anything to him. I'm exhausted, ready to go cry in my bed over Chase, and the last thing I want is a lecture. Yet I sink down into the chair; the quicker he gets this out of his system, the quicker I can go home.

"Cassie, I really don't like this." He massages his temples.

"Yep, I know you don't."

"He started a bar fight for no good reason tonight. *That's* the kind of guy you want in your life? I thought I raised you better—did a good job of showing you how men should act."

"You did. Honestly, you set a great example, Dad. I'm not saying he'll be anywhere near as good of a dad as you are, but I want my baby to have both parents around. He's a different person outside of this bar, and I wish you could see that side of him."

"Doesn't it concern you that he has *sides*?" Dad raises an eyebrow, pinning me with a stare as I meagerly shrug. "So when he's here, he punches people for no good reason, but I'm supposed to trust when you say he's capable of treating you with respect elsewhere? You could've gotten hurt tonight when the fight *he started* turned into a brawl. You think he would've even cared? Or noticed? Seemed like you were the last thing on his mind when you should've been the first."

"I'm not saying what happened tonight was okay. And I

don't know how I'm going to handle this, but the last thing I need right now is to fight with you, too."

Dad's jaw tenses. "Did you fight with him? What did he say to you?"

"*Nothing.* That's the fucking problem." I rub my teary, exhausted eyes. "I tried to get him to tell me what happened. Maybe it's my fault—I'm the one who wanted boundaries. To keep it a strictly professional co-parenting relationship."

"And he doesn't like that."

No, he doesn't like it. But that's because he asked me to date him and I bluntly turned him down. And before the fight, I spent all evening kicking myself for it.

"He's not the terrible guy you make him out to be, Dad. I don't think he always makes the right decisions in the heat of the moment. But . . . *clearly,* neither do I." I glance down at my protruding stomach. "When we're together, he's completely different. Chase does anything I ask, and usually I don't even need to ask—he's already taking care of it for me. He's really good to me, Dad. *Too good.* Like maybe somebody I might even love, which scares the hell out of me. That's why I told him we needed boundaries. I was scared about what might happen if a relationship with him imploded. Which . . . I guess it kind of did tonight."

I rest a hand on my anxiously bouncing knee and let a free fall of tears run in rivulets down my cheeks. Falling from my chin, they leave wet patches on the dark-green shirt barely containing my stomach. After a minute or so, I sniffle and look up at him through the tear-induced haze, expecting him to continue the lecture.

"I know I can't tell you what to do. But you need to decide if this is the situation you want to be in. I have a gut feeling this won't be the last time he has you crying in my bar if you try to make any kind of relationship work with him."

"Maybe you're right. But . . . *I* have a gut feeling something else was going on when he punched Landon. The guy is a total loser, for one. And then the stuff between us . . . I don't know. I need to think."

He nods slowly. "Good. Think about all of it, Cassie. Remember, you're making decisions for your child now, too."

"Oh, I know. This shit wouldn't be so complicated if I wasn't thinking about her."

Cassidy

And he wasn't even mine to begin with.

He could've been. Almost was.

I should accept that he's a broken, angry man and it's not my responsibility to fix him. He's been this way for as long as I can remember, and it's silly to think he would suddenly change because of me. The sex is amazing, but it's not as if I have a magical vagina capable of solving decades of emotional trauma. In fact, I can't shake the feeling that I played a small part in breaking him.

"Is this an intervention?" I look at Shelby, then Blair.

Over the last two days, I've watched approximately four hundred episodes of the reality TV show *Intervention*, so I know one when I see it. Shelby sets an armload of snacks down in front of us and sinks into the couch. She's dressed cute, in leggings and a ripped band T-shirt, hair tied up with a hot-pink scrunchie. I, on the other hand, am the village troll. Most of my normal clothes no longer fit, so I'm wearing a pair of oversized sweatpants, a men's XXL T-shirt I got for free with a case of beer, and Chase's hoodie. My hair's in a messy bun, but not the cute kind.

"If that's where your mind jumps to when your two best friends want to do a girls' night, you probably need one." Blair smiles on my phone screen, which is propped up on the coffee table opposite Shelby and me.

"We wanted to hang out before you return to your senses and start ditching us for your baby daddy again," Shelby says, pouring us both a fizzing glass of root beer. "Which we're fully supportive of, by the way. You two are good together."

"I don't know if we'll ever even be friends again. There's no world in which he and I would've ended up together if I didn't accidentally get knocked up. And I thought he had changed, but maybe it was all an act."

"Hear me out." Blair pops a chip into her mouth and chews it thoughtfully. *This is undoubtedly an intervention.* "What if he's a nice guy who made a mistake? Or, even crazier, what if he hit Landon Wiebe because he deserved it? Like . . . why are you siding with a piece of moldy cheese over the guy you're in love with?"

"I'm not siding with the moldy cheese. I don't exactly have the best track record at picking decent men to date. And now with the hormones and him being around all the time . . . maybe those are the only reasons I like Chase."

Blair shrugs. "Yeah, maybe. But what if that's not the case and you're self-sabotaging because you're scared of being hurt again?"

"Ooooh . . . she's got you there," Shelby adds, gripping my shoulder to give it a little shake. "Some guys are cheating assholes—that's all there is to it. Don't swear off all men because you're scared, though."

"It's not that I'm scared he would cheat on me. It's . . . I don't want to be with somebody if I don't think I can trust them one hundred percent."

"Fair, but also . . . people screw up sometimes. I don't think one big mistake means you should totally write off the man you're having a baby with." Shelby pulls a face, squinting at me as I pull a throw blanket tighter over my legs.

"Having a baby together isn't a good enough reason to date somebody. And I'm doubtful we would both be feeling this way if there wasn't a baby involved."

Shelby clears her throat like she's preparing to lay into me. "I think it's safe to say your feelings are way deeper than you're giving them credit for. You're depressy without him, and we hate seeing you like this. You need to go get him back."

"I'm not *depressy.* I'm pregnant and fat and my back always hurts and it's winter. It's perfectly acceptable to sit on the couch and binge-watch reality TV all day."

Following a frustrated exhale, Blair says, "Cass, I mean this with all the respect and love in the world—shut the fuck up. You might be delusional enough to believe your own bullshit, but you can't lie to us. You were so much happier when he was around. And you'd be the first one to call us out if we were acting this pathetic."

"We literally couldn't have a single conversation without you mentioning him and all the nice shit he was doing for you. Girls would kill for that. Hell, *I* would kill for what you have," Shelby says.

Eyes shut, I sip my root beer and ignore the two of them as they continue listing the reasons I'm stupid not to jump at the opportunity to date Chase. Which is *in-fucking-sane.* Not long ago, they would've had an intervention to talk me out of dating him, had I mentioned wanting to.

In spite of myself, I like him. If I let myself, I can picture loving him, too. It's utterly, devastatingly terrifying. I was supposed to end up with a nice guy from out of town—with his own house, a job that doesn't leave him smelling like sweat and hoofed animals, and zero desire to be involved in a bar fight. A guy I wouldn't have to convince my dad to tolerate.

Blair's voice drifts back into focus. "He also technically doesn't break your three rules. He hasn't slept with either of us, you've known him since elementary school, and he doesn't go to the Horseshoe."

I roll my eyes. "Doesn't count, and you know it. Elementary school is practically still in diapers. And he was a regular at the bar until we slept together."

"If anything, that should count for more. There's only one bar in town and Red stopped going there just to keep you happy." Shelby scrunches her nose, eyeing me to see if their tactics are working.

I suck in my lips. "Until the other night . . . and he acted like an asshole."

Red

Thirty-two weeks (baby is the size of a box of donuts)

Nearly everything we do around the ranch, we do on horseback. In part because it helps protect the soil, the sensitive native grasses, and the numerous streams we cross daily. But mostly because Grandpa Wells would kick our asses six ways to Sunday if he found out his cowboys weren't being real cowboys.

The one exception is calving season. When it's thirty below zero, I'm thankful for the shitty ranch pickup—with torn leather seats, a staticky radio, and a chunk of cardboard zip-tied in front of the radiator to help the truck build heat. Sitting in the passenger seat, Denny's struggling to keep his coffee from spilling as the old jalopy rumbles down the dirt road.

"Nobody teach you how to drive?" He holds his coffee mug out in front of him, trying to guess where the next pothole might be in the dim glow of our crappy headlights.

"You're the one who wanted to ride bitch. I'll trade you so I can fucking sleep for an extra five minutes. I've been lucky to get three hours a night lately."

The truck careens over a large rock, splashing hot coffee down Denny's arm. *Maybe* it was somewhat on purpose. He slams the cup into the cupholder, shooting me a death glare that's impossible to take seriously with the way his lip curls upward.

"I still don't get why you're spending all this time on a Christmas present—almost a full month after Christmas, I'd like to point out. I thought you two haven't talked since you punched Landon Wiebe?"

"We haven't. But I still want to do this for her. She's so sure she'll have to give everything up because of the baby, and I don't want that. She deserves to have the things that make her happy. Even if she never wants to talk to me again, I want to do nice things for her. Sure, it's a lot of fucking work to build this thing from scratch, but she's worth it, man."

Even in the dark, the bunching of his eyebrows is obvious. "Careful. You might break your back trying to kiss your own ass like that. You can say you're making her this extravagant gift to win her back. I won't rat you out."

"Sure. Let's just say that's why I'm doing it."

A few kilometers up from the main ranch entrance, Denny nearly loses his coffee again when the truck rattles across a cattle guard approaching the calving barn.

"So you want to be with her? Be a couple? Make it official? Not see other people?"

Stepping into the brutal cold, I slam the truck door behind me with a shiver. A deep inhale makes my nostrils freeze shut for a second. "Jesus, how many ways can you ask the same question?"

"Oh, I can keep going." He throws open the heavy barn door, and while the air isn't much warmer inside the old building, it cuts the nasty wind. "I didn't see this shit coming. You and her. You and anybody. Now I'm stuck chasing buckle bunnies with Colt as my wingman."

"That's the real reason you're invested in my love life."

"*Love life?* You got it that bad for her?" He side-eyes me as we pass calving pens filled with cows and their brand-new calves.

I nod. I'm a total goner. "She's everything."

Colt yells our names from the end of the aisle, cutting the conversation and grabbing our attention. "Mornin'. Think you guys might want to help this one. When I was out at midnight she was just getting started, but she still hasn't calved so I brought her in."

Typically we let nature work. When things are going well, it's better for everyone involved not to intervene with birth—mamas do it on their own, and we try not to jump in to assist unless absolutely necessary.

"Great. Red needs his practice delivering babies, just in case." Denny ducks before I've had the chance to process what he said. Turns out my brain struggles to function at five a.m. when I didn't get to sleep until well after midnight.

"You're a dipshit." I lazily swing my arm in his direction. "Go grab the chains, Colt. She likes to throw big calves—likely needs a good tug on the calf from our end."

"Hope you don't talk about Cass that way when the time comes," Denny says, quickly hopping out of arm's reach.

Colt shrugs. "Hopefully she's an easy calver."

"Colt." I raise my voice. "Grab the fucking chains like I told you to. You're both idiots, and I'm gonna go back to bed if you want to be pains in my ass all morning."

Settling in on the bunkhouse couch shortly after five p.m., I can already feel my eyelids growing heavy. I'm close to finishing Cassidy's present, and with her still not wanting to speak to me, I can afford to take a night off. Get a decent sleep, for once. Well . . . *decent-ish*. I haven't had a restful night since the last time I slept with my arms around her.

Rob, the obnoxious old son of a bitch, sits in the recliner and leans back, chugging from an amber bottle. Seconds later, Colt flops next to me and holds an open beer in front of my face.

"Nah, I'm not drinking." I nudge his hand away. "Told you, I quit that shit."

"Sorry, bro. Forgot." He grins. "More for me."

Rob snorts. "Not drinking. As if that's gonna last long."

I could drink it. Not like it fucking matters. It's been a week since my last drink at the Horseshoe, and nothing has changed. I haven't suddenly become a new person. Cass hasn't reached out. At least a few drinks would take my mind off how miserable I am for a few hours.

I shouldn't drink it. Because, on the off chance Cass wants to talk to me ever again, I want to tell her I'm trying. And mean it.

Retreating to my room like a child hiding from my alcoholic dad again, I grab my phone out of habit. I expect her to ignore me, since that's the way all of my other attempts at contacting her over the past few days have gone.

Red: You had a doctor's appointment today, right? How did it go?

Cass: Baby's good. I'm good.

Red: I should've been there

Cass: Yeah

Red: I'm sorry. Really fucking sorry.

Cass: I know. I just don't know what to do with that right now

Red: Talk to me?

Cass: Sunday? I have the day off

Red: Sunday. I'll bring dinner.

Sunday. Today is Friday, and somehow I need to make it to Sunday. Then I can try to fix this. Not a fucking clue how to fix it, but I need to. There's no other option.

I toss the phone onto my bed and pace, my mind reeling

with ideas of what I could possibly say to make things better. I pace across the room. Pace the hall to the shared bathroom. Pace downstairs in the kitchen. Back upstairs. In circles around my bedroom.

"You good?" Denny asks from the couch when I'm on my third tour around the bunkhouse.

"Maybe. No. I don't fucking know. I need air." I strain to get the words out around the lump in my throat and an agonizing inability to get a lung-filling breath. It feels as if a boulder is crushing my sternum; the fear of blowing my one shot at getting Cassidy back suffocates me.

Suddenly, I'm throwing on a coat and trudging down the moonlit road to the stables. Compact snow crunches under my boots—the only noise on an otherwise silent ranch. Pulling open the barn door, I see the soft red glow of heat lamps. With the flip of a switch, the ceiling lights begin to hum, gradually warming up until the entire place is lit with a midday glare. A few horses blink wearily at me from their stalls, and I head straight for Heathen, my favorite mare.

She's misunderstood, with her hot temper and rash decisions. Quick to throw me if I push her buttons. Even quicker to apologize after the moment has passed. We butt heads, and I threaten to send her to slaughter on a daily basis. But when I need to get my head on straight, she's the horse I come to, not any of the nine other mounts I rotate through for work.

"Hey, girl." I pull a mint from my jacket pocket—a peace offering for being the asshole who woke her up. She happily accepts, then thoroughly sniffs my pockets for more. "I don't know if I'm cut out for this shit. Being a dad. A boyfriend. The two things I want to be more than anything else in this fucking world, but I know I'm going to screw it up. I already have. And now I might have an opportunity to fix it, and no idea where to start. They deserve so much better than me."

Heathen stares, unblinking and still working on the hard mint, like she understands when nobody else cares to.

Cassidy

Shoving my phone in my back pocket, I lean on the counter and wait for my dad to finish closing out a bar tab. With Freddy heading out, it's only Toothless George holding down his permanent spot at the end of the bar.

"Cool if I leave a bit early since it's so dead in here?"

He glances around the empty establishment and nods. "Sure, kiddo. Go get some rest."

The bitter wind hits hard, ripping down my neck and back despite my winter coat. Tugging the downy, puffy jacket up around my ears and nose, I shuffle across the ice to my car. The engine and I shiver in unison as it rumbles to life, and I grab my phone from my pocket to reread the string of texts that prompted me to leave work early.

Denver: Whatever is going on with you and Red, can you please figure it out?

Denver: Starting to get a bit worried, honestly.

Denver: First he found out his dad's dying. Now you two are having issues. He's barely been sleeping. And he's been down at the barn by himself for hours.

Denver: I'm not the type to get involved in this shit, but I think you're the only person he might talk to about what he's got going on

Denver: Maybe give him a chance

He found out his dad's dying and he didn't tell me. The dull thud in my chest becomes complete, despairing loss as my heart falls into the pit in my stomach.

Before I put up walls and shut him out, we talked about everything. In the late night, the hazy euphoria of my bed—just after sex and just before falling asleep—we'd share our secrets. He knows all my fears of becoming my mother and of never amounting to anything. I know the origin of every scar on his body. *Twenty.* Twenty visible scars are a direct result of his father. There's no telling how many he carries around in his soul.

I know all that, and now I don't even get to know about something as big as his dad dying. But why would he tell me? I forcefully pushed him away the second things started feeling too real.

I stare at the phone for less than a heartbeat before tapping my frozen fingers against the screen.

Cass: Let me know if he leaves the barn. I'm on my way.

Without a second thought, I roll straight through the single stop sign in town and onto Wells Ranch Road. Thirty kilometers of rough, snowy road that I'm praying my car can manage. No music—I need to focus. My studded winter tires crunch and creak over the thick snow, climbing the hill out of town and chasing the distant moon. The headlights bounce off snowy blankets cloaking the roadside trees as the road winds across the mountainside.

Chase made this drive nearly every single day. For me. For the baby. He busted his ass, doing manual labor and riding a horse from sunup to sundown. Drove on this bumpy, windy road to get to my house. Made dinner. Helped clean up. Gave me the best orgasms of my life. Then woke up before dawn to drive back to the ranch. Repeat. *For weeks.* Never complaining or asking me to come to him instead.

"I'm a fucking asshole." I smack my hand against the steering wheel. My fingers curl around the leather and grip until my knuckles turn white.

I was grateful. I knew what he was doing for me was a big deal and I wasn't trying to take any part of him for granted. But following in his footsteps—driving this distance to see him after a long day at work, and fully intending to cater to him when I get there—has me realizing how terrible I am for pushing him away.

I've never been to Wells Ranch, despite growing up in Wells Canyon. Which, *obviously,* shares a name with the family that built both the ranch and the town. The Wellses' reach extends far beyond the sprawling cattle ranch Austin, Jackson, and Denny operate. They have extended family involved in nearly every facet of Wells Canyon, and there's always at least one Wells kid in both the elementary and high school at any given time.

My car crests a knoll, and the ranch comes into view. A swinging wooden sign hangs suspended at least twenty feet in the air and spans the width of the driveway, bearing the Wells Ranch name and brand—the same brand Chase has scarred deep into his chest. I've traced it so many times with my fingertips, I can perfectly picture the feel of his soft skin on mine.

The driveway winds past a large white farmhouse without a single light on inside. It's still decorated for Christmas; garland and twinkle lights encase each banister of the front porch railing. Then my car crawls past a two-story, partially finished house, which must be Austin and Cecily's new place. The lights are out in every building—not surprising, given the fact it's after midnight. I'm just about ready to turn around and go home, pretend I didn't drive out here uninvited like a deranged person, when I notice an orange glow around the edges of double barn doors. I pull my car up next to Chase's truck and step out into the cold night.

With less than a dozen streetlights in Wells Canyon, we have a great view of the starry skies. Certainly better than I've seen when visiting Blair in Vancouver. But out here? Unmatched. Like God got carried away while painting the stars—flicks of white leaving little blackness in the sky. The moon's hung low, kissing snowy treetops and lighting my route to the barn.

I tuck my jacket around myself, following a well-worn footpath. I'm unsure if I'll find Chase, and equally unsure what I'll say if I do. But I have to try. When I give it a tug, the metal handle on the barn door sticks to my clammy hand. It shimmies open a bit, so I pull harder. The overpowering smell of horses nearly knocks me down as the clunky door slides along the overhead rail.

Even with his back to me, I know it's him by the auburn hair and the way he leans against the stall. It's the same stance he frequently has while standing in my bedroom doorframe. Popped hip, hand in his pocket, sinking all his weight into the wall. In my house, he usually wears a cocky smirk while he watches me get dressed . . . or undressed, depending on the time of day. But tonight I doubt he's smiling, and his voice is barely audible as he talks to a horse.

"Chase." I pull the door shut behind me.

He spins to face me with a halfhearted, wavering smile. "Hey, you."

Chase makes no move toward me, relying on the wall like

it's the lone thing keeping him upright. I rush down the cement barn alley to him, then slide my arms inside his unzipped Carhartt jacket and around his waist. His hand combs through my hair, moving to grip the back of my skull and tugging me into him. A move he's done so many times before. I bury my face in his neck and allow myself a deep inhale. The smell of his skin calms me in the same way coming home does. Steadying my heart rate and removing all the weight of the day. If somebody had told me that one day I'd be driving all the way to Wells Ranch to breathe him in, that one day this man would be responsible for me feeling so many big feelings, I'd tell them they were crazy and kick them in the shin for good measure.

"You came all the way here," he says. "I thought you weren't free until Sunday."

"Of course I came. Denny told me about your dad." I rest my cheek against his collarbone. "I'm sorry. Sorry you've been dealing with it alone. Are you okay?"

"Yeah. Fine."

Bullshit.

"Are you okay?" I repeat, lifting my head to look at him. "Honestly."

Eyes dropping to the floor, he draws in a long breath before speaking. "I don't know if I am. And I fucking hate that."

"It's okay not to be okay. Even though he wasn't who you deserved him to be . . ." Letting a hand leave the warm space inside his coat, I run my palm across the rough stubble of his jaw, begging him to look at me. "You can be angry with him and still be sad about him dying. It doesn't have to be black-and-white."

"Yeah, it's definitely not that." His tongue darts out, leaving his bottom lip glistening.

"Nothing ever is." I lean into him, relishing the rise and fall of his broad chest, his hand cradling my head against him.

"Do you think I'm like him?" He whispers the words

against my hair. The warmth of his breath travels down my neck with a quiver.

"No." The answer comes quickly because, no, I don't think he's like him. Not a single sliver of my heart believes he's like his dad. I wrap the fabric of his T-shirt around my fingers, wanting him closer. "Do you?"

He swallows, and I feel the bob of his Adam's apple on my temple. His voice is heavy and ragged. "I don't know. Maybe. It's not black-and-white."

"Why did you hit Landon Wiebe?"

He's quiet. The only sound around us is the slow snoring of sleeping horses.

"Chase, tell me. I don't want to believe you did it for the thrill of a fight. But I need to know why. I deserve to know, after all that shit. I've been struggling to give you the benefit of the doubt because you were so quick to shut me out that night. Please tell me the truth."

"He said some disgusting shit about you, us, Little Spud. I warned him, but . . ." His voice quakes, his breathing suddenly uneasy, as if he's reliving that god-awful moment. "Anyway, I'm sorry. I'm not sorry for hitting him because he's a motherfucker and deserved it. But I *am* sorry for starting a bar brawl, pissing your dad off, and leaving you to deal with my bullshit. I should've dragged his ass outside first. I shouldn't have left afterward. I acted like an asshole and a goddamn coward."

His hands wrap around my forearms, and he places them at my sides. Taking a few steps back, he leaves me alone and cold and worried it was a big mistake coming here. Maybe I waited too long to talk to him.

"Dave said some shit that might not have been entirely true, but he got into my head. And I just . . . I just couldn't face you right then. Maybe I'm not quite as bad as my dad—at least, not yet—but I'm not flawless." Chase shrugs half-heartedly, letting his shoulders slump even lower than they were before. He looks close to becoming one with the cement floor, his body too worn down to bother continuing to stand. I want him to let me hold him up. "If you weren't pregnant, you wouldn't take a second glance at me. Hell, *even now,* you could walk away and find a guy who would be perfect for you. Somebody who can give you everything you want. Somebody without a fucked-up childhood and a shitty reputation. That's what you and the baby deserve. Anyone but me."

I swallow the saliva that's been building up in my throat the entire time he was talking. His eyes are so vast and wistful and full of love. He runs a hand through his hair, then leaves it resting on the back of his neck, not breaking eye contact for a single second. And I can't remember what Joe Thompson looks like off the top of my head, but I'm confident he's never looked at anything except liquor with this much passion.

With a step toward him, I open my mouth. "You're—"

"Cass, please. I'm not done. I just . . ."

I nod slowly but don't step back. The space between us is warm. Wrought with emotion. If I stumble forward slightly, I'll crash into him. If I swing my arm anxiously, our hands will touch. "Okay. Take your time, and I'll talk when you say you're done."

"I'm not drinking anymore. The night at the Horseshoe was the final nail in that fucking coffin—haven't had a single sip since then. I know it hasn't been very long yet, but I swear I'm done for good. Not because I think I'm addicted like my dad is. But I don't like how similar I am to him when I've been drinking, or when I'm in your dad's bar. I know I have a temper on the best of days, and there's something about that atmosphere—I'm unable to stop myself. I just . . . black out. And every time I drink, there's this little voice in my head questioning if this is it. If *this* is the beer that pushes me over the edge and makes me become him. If one more beer is going to make me an alcoholic like him or make me drunk enough to hurt somebody I love. And . . ." The corded muscles of his neck tighten and bob with a hard swallow. "I can't live with that fear anymore. I don't want Little Spud to be embarrassed by me. Definitely don't want *you* to be embarrassed or have to deal with my shit. None of this bothered me before. It didn't matter what anyone thought of me. I was fine being a letdown . . . a fuckup . . . a loser."

"That's not—" I start, but his narrowing glance cuts me off. I make a motion like I'm zipping my lips and nod for him to continue.

"Sorry. This shit has been running through my brain for fucking ever, and I want to say it out loud to somebody other than Heathen here." He tilts his head toward the horse in the stall next to him. After a long, shaky exhale, he continues, "It's just who I was, even though I didn't always like it. I didn't give enough of a shit to change. But then, you told me you were pregnant. Now I don't want to be those things anymore—really don't want to do *anything* my dad would. I'm not saying this to win you over or make you feel bad for me, by the way. I just want you to know I'm sorry and I'm trying to be better."

I press my fingers to my tear ducts, holding back the sob rising in my throat. Biting my lip to stop it from quivering, I stare at him through my eyelashes. Waiting for the gentle nod to indicate he's done.

"I didn't come here because I wanted an apology. I'm here for you. To make sure you're okay. You might think those things about yourself, but I don't. I know after the night at the bar, I didn't seem sure. Well . . . honestly, I wasn't sure. And that was fucked up of me because I know you—the you most other people don't bother getting to know. I should have trusted you wouldn't do that for no good reason."

"I didn't tell you the reason because it didn't matter. No excuse would make it okay that I put you in that situation. Having you hate me felt like a deserved consequence after I embarrassed you, hurt you, and then walked away."

"I wish you'd told me. Not because I think it would've

made me less mad. But I deserved to know . . . to have you talk to me." A chill scatters over my skin.

"Really? Because you weren't talking to me either." His eyes are red and glassy when they meet mine. "Where have you been?"

"What?"

"Before the shit at the bar, you weren't around. So, sure . . . I guess I could've talked to you about shit when you cornered me in the parking lot, but you made it clear we didn't have that kind of relationship anymore. You went on your trip and basically fucking disappeared. I get it—you don't want to date me. Your rejection didn't come as a shock, even if it didn't feel great." His face scrunches like he's just torn open a fresh wound. "Shit, you didn't even want anyone to know we slept together until it became nearly impossible to keep a secret. But I don't blame you 'cause I know I'm not your first choice." Chase's hands fall against his sides with a resonating thud.

I swipe a tear from my jawline, continuing the path upward to massage my temple slowly. If I hadn't panicked and cut him out entirely, things would still be good. We'd be friends. We'd be having amazing sex. And I would still be painfully pretending I'm not falling in love with him.

"Just because I didn't want people to know before doesn't mean I feel the same way now. I know I should have been honest about us a lot sooner instead of making you think I was ashamed. Because I'm not."

"Can I be honest?" His tongue darts out to lick his lips, and his gaze burns clear through me. "I *never* wanted to be your fucking friend or your friend-with-benefits or your goddamn co-parent. But I would settle for any of those titles if it meant going back to cooking you dinner and watching crappy reality shows on your couch, and falling asleep with you. Being *at* your doctor's appointments, glaring at Dr. Dickhead—not getting a text message after. I want to be holding your hand when you have our baby and see your eyes light up when you hold her for the first time. I want to take care of you so you can take care of her. Hell, I even want to change a shitty diaper at two o'clock in the morning."

I blink down, letting tears splatter on the dusty floor.

"And it fucking sucks to know I maybe had all of that before I opened my mouth and suggested something as laughable as—" His voice falters with a flustered, sharp inhale. A fist comes up to cover his mouth, and he exhales hard through his nose.

"I wasn't trying to hurt you. I was trying not to muddy things more than we already did. And to get back to the way we were before we started sleeping together."

"If that were the case, I could deal with not having things work out the way I wanted. Like I said, I didn't expect you to agree to more in the first place. But we haven't been friends. Haven't even been fucking co-parents, honestly. You texted me an 'all's good' after your doctor's appointment and that was pretty much it."

I'm chewing the inside of my cheek to shreds, fighting with myself over what to tell him. Considering I've had multiple days alone—and an hour-long drive to the ranch—to think about it, I should have a vague idea of what I want to say.

Instead, I'm still sitting on a jagged, splintering, wobbly fence. No way of knowing which way I'll jump or fall. Whether he'll catch me, or I'll crack my head open Humpty Dumpty–style on the concrete.

"I'm sorry," I finally croak in the nick of time before the tears spill. I wipe frantically at my eyes, smearing black mascara across my hands and, likely, my face.

Before the fence crumbles beneath me, I leap to the side that feels right. Where there's a reasonable probability of landing safely. Comfortably. And in his arms.

"I don't want to be friends. I want . . ." A fluttering breath rattles my chest. "All the same things you do. I said I needed boundaries because I like you, and it scared me. When you mentioned being together, I panicked when I should've talked to you. But I was so worried I only liked you because of the pregnancy hormones, or you were being nice to me because I'm carrying your baby. Or we're forced together by circumstance and like each other because we're stuck together. I didn't want Little Spud to be the sole reason behind us being together. After the bar fight, I was scared—not of you. Scared I would need to keep those boundaries up forever because, *God,* I didn't want to. I just needed time to sort out all my emotions and determine if my fears were unfounded. And they are . . . aren't they?"

The seconds between when I finish my sentence and he opens his mouth are a free fall. I've never been skydiving, but I imagine this stomach in your throat, whirlwind in your skull, and panic in your chest are what you feel while plummeting to the Earth.

He sucks on his teeth. "You tell me."

"I think we wouldn't have ended up here if it weren't for Little Spud, but that's not why I have feelings for you now. We work and make sense and *fit* in a way I've never experienced. You're my first choice. You're good enough, Chase."

My eyes drop from his for a fraction of a second. Then his hand's on my jaw, pulling my chin upward with a sharp movement. Begging me to look at him. "Maybe you *are* just hormonal as fuck, because I think every single person we know would agree I'm not good enough for you."

"Why does it matter what anybody thinks outside of you and me? I wish I'd gotten to know who you really are sooner. I'm sorry for that."

He shakes his head skeptically. "I don't even know if I'm capable of being a good man. I've never given a fuck about much . . . until you. But I want to do better for my girls. One day I want to be deserving of you."

His words make my heart race until I'm unable to stop my

body from moving into his. My belly hits first, and I cringe, preparing for it to ruin the moment. With a contented sigh, Chase leans into it, spreading a hand across my lower back to keep me close.

His eyes shutter, holding back whatever thoughts are running through his mind. Vapor from our breaths fills the quickly narrowing space between us and, despite that, I don't feel cold in the slightest. Hot embers spread under my skin, ignited by his touch and growing hotter by the second. When he leans down, my arms instinctively swing around his neck, pulling him the rest of the way.

His mouth hovers over mine, stopping fractions of a centimeter short. "The kissing ban needs to end."

"Mhm." My brain may be screaming *kiss him,* but my body's moving in slow motion. His close proximity has me paralyzed, wrought with overwhelming emotion and need.

"It was a stupid fucking rule to begin with." Slow and with attention to detail, his lips brush mine like watercolor, further blurring the harsh lines—the boundaries I was sure we needed.

"Agr—" Before I can get it out, he swallows the word with a passionate, knee-buckling kiss. A soft moan escapes my throat and his fingers tighten against my back. It's nothing similar to the awkward kiss on the rodeo dance floor. Or the torrid, rough kiss on the car hood. This time, it's full of care—a kiss we've been envisioning, waiting too long for. Tonight, we're both committed to doing this moment right.

Cassidy

His free hand slides past my ear and tangles in my unkempt waves. Cradling the back of my skull, he holds me close enough there isn't room to take a full breath. And he's kissing me like I'm his sole source of oxygen.

The hair at the nape of his neck is soft under my fingertips. As is the skin under his shirt, when I slip my hands underneath it to stroke his stomach. His groan catches in his throat, and his hips grind into me. I'm pulled closer by strong hands on my ass until his thigh is tight between mine. Pressing into me with each gentle rock of my hips, but not giving quite enough friction to satisfy my craving.

By the time we break apart, my fingers are beet red from the cold and my lips tingle. The buzzing, roof-mounted space heater isn't doing nearly enough to keep my extremities from turning into popsicles. And I'm numb down to the bone—except for the fire deep in my core, which is telling me to fuck Chase in the barn and worry about frostbite later.

"Sweetheart, we should get out of here. You're shaking like a leaf, and your teeth are chattering." His hands vigorously rub my arms and shoulders, lips pressing softly on my forehead.

I don't want to go home. More than anything, I want to stay here. Hell, I'll even sleep in his Boy Scout Camp bunkhouse if it means not leaving him. "C-can I stay with you? I'm tired and it's a long drive and the roads are—"

"Obviously you're staying here." He smiles, then kisses the cold tip of my nose. "Even if things hadn't gone the way they did just now, there's no way in hell I'd be letting you drive home tonight."

"Yeah, right. Where would I sleep? I don't have the heart to kick Denny out of his top bunk."

Chase laughs, keeping a tight grip on my waist as we move toward the barn door, practically joined at the hip.

"You realize we all have separate bedrooms . . . with normal beds, right?"

"Damn, that's boring." My tongue catches between my front teeth in a cheeky grin. "Bunch of hot guys all sharing a room sounds more fun . . . more *erotic*. I'd pay good money to see that. In fact . . . think we can convince the guys to make some videos for the internet? We're sitting on a gold mine here."

"Jesus, woman. A month without a good dicking and this is the sick shit you think about?"

"G*ood* dicking is a bold statement." I shrug impishly, then shriek as he grabs my shoulders and pushes me up against the barn door. Even through my winter coat, the cold wood chills me to the bone. His hands move to either side of my head, caging me in. His predatory gaze pinning me in place. And that only makes me want to tease him more. He's worried I'll view him as violent or mean or aggressive. But I *want* the fire in his eyes and tick in his jaw. If I weren't pregnant, I'd run just to see if he'd make chase. Find out what happens once he catches me.

A frozen breeze flutters through the crack in the door, making even Chase's body tense. "We should get you somewhere warm."

"I think I'd rather stay here, frozen and catching wafts of

horse shit, over finding out what your bunkhouse looks and smells like."

"The girls keep it clean, actually. But anyway, I want you to myself tonight. Cecily's old cabin is empty. It might not be much warmer than here, but I'll start a fire." He grabs my hand and flicks off the barn lights, pulling my hood up over my head before tugging me into the snowy night.

It's so cold, the air feels frozen in place. A stillness has settled over the ranch—the sharp crunching of our feet down the compact pathway the only noise. I thought my world was the only one tipped upside down tonight, but a light snow is falling as if the universe flipped Earth like a snow globe. Swirling, dancing, meandering snowflakes float through the air like specks of glitter before settling on our heads and coats, gathering in clusters on the frozen ends of my hair.

"I'm just gonna grab an armload of firewood," he says as we approach a towering pile of split timber. Hesitantly letting go of my hand, he begins to pile wood into his arms.

"Let me help." I follow suit before he can argue, grabbing as many pieces as I can, afraid I'll drop them because I can't feel a single thing. Whether the numbness is from the cold or the emotions surging through me, I'm unsure.

Arms loaded, our steps fall perfectly in time as we continue past our vehicles, past bunkhouses, to a small log cabin. Chase steps ahead to clear snow from the porch steps with a sweeping foot movement. Then he swings open the door and leads me inside.

He was right. It's not much warmer than the barn. Not that it would matter—I'm frozen inside and out. It's game over for me. I'll thaw when spring comes. Though it's not warm, the small one-room cabin has the potential to be cozy.

"Get comfy." Chase holds a steady grip on my shoulders and sits me down onto a vintage, well-loved couch. Evidently aware I'm too cold to do so myself, he snags a thick wool blanket from a basket on the floor and wraps it around me. "I'll get the fire going and it'll be warm in here shortly."

Within minutes, there are vibrant flames dancing in the stone fireplace, casting an orange glow over the small room. He turns to me with a proud smile, his shoulders sitting a tiny bit taller than they were in the barn. "If we're lucky, the heat tape on the pipes is working—which means running water. We could take a bath and warm up?"

Warming up and easing my aching joints in a bath sounds like a dream. Being naked with Chase does not. Regardless of how badly I want him to kiss me, touch me, and chase me through a wooded forest, then fuck me against a tree . . . he hasn't seen my body in a month. In normal life, that would mean absolutely nothing. A month during pregnancy—especially in the third trimester—is an entirely different story.

"Oh, no. I can't have hot baths." *Good cover-up.*

"I know. I'm not trying to cook Little Spud. We'll keep it warm-ish. It's nicer than sitting here while we wait for the room to heat up. It'll feel good on your back and feet, too."

"I'm honestly good here." I give him a thin-lipped smile, pulling the blanket tighter around myself. My entire body convulses when an icy chill runs down my spine, and he cocks an eyebrow.

"Don't bullshit me. I know you like taking baths. If you don't want me to come, you can go alone. . . ."

"It's not that I don't want you to." *It's absolutely that I don't want him to.*

"So then let's go." He grabs hold of my wrist, tugging until I'm forced onto my feet with a groan.

"It's that . . ." I draw wide, attention-grabbing circles around my stomach with my hands. "I'm pregnant."

"Shit, *really*? Who's the father? Somebody I know?" He snorts, a cloud of steam escaping his parted lips. "Jesus, Cass. *Duh.* I'm aware you're pregnant. What's your point?"

It feels both stupid and incredibly vulnerable, so I squeeze my eyes shut and let the question fall out. "A-are you still . . . um, physically attracted to me? You know . . . since I actually *look* super pregnant now."

"Cassidy." Chase grabs my hands, interlacing our fingers, and steps in so our stomachs are touching. I'm trying, and failing spectacularly, to focus on him, rather than the fact that my belly now sticks out farther than my boobs. "I am so *fucking* attracted to you. When you showed up here tonight, it took everything in me not to immediately start kissing and touching every inch of you. Every time I see you, I think you can't possibly get more beautiful. And you somehow keep proving me wrong. . . . I told you before that I'll always find this"—his hands smooth over my stomach—"beautiful. I meant what I said. Your body is fucking perfect in my eyes. Pregnant, not pregnant. So please come with me. I know you want a bath."

I reluctantly allow him to pull me into the bathroom, where there's an old claw-foot tub under a small window. The outside frost has tooled intricate designs in the windowpane. And he playfully insists we cross our fingers as he turns the hot water knob.

"Thank God!" He exhales dramatically when water comes pouring out, instantly creating swirling steam in the frigid air. "I would've been pissed with myself for talking you into this if the water lines ended up being frozen."

"Can we maybe not have the harsh ceiling light on?" I scrunch my nose. If he's really insisting on me being naked, the lighting and ambience need to at least be somewhat flattering. Preferably deceiving.

Without a reply, he leaves for a moment and returns empty-handed. "Fuck, if I'd known you were coming I would've bought some candles or something. There's nothing in the cupboards." He pulls his phone from his pocket, turns on the flashlight, and sets it on the counter. "Best I can do."

"It's perfect." I pull him to me for a slow, explorative kiss.

Now that I've had his lips on mine, I hate knowing I could've had this all along and chose not to.

Wasting no time, he's unzipping my coat. Shimmying my pants down. Delicately pulling my shirt over my head. Unclasping my bra. Until I'm wearing nothing but a shadow cast across the wall.

I gulp, watching him intently for any hint of disgust or disappointment. The slightest tinge of regret. Anything to confirm what the monster inside my head is telling me, that he won't want me anymore. I pushed him away and now, seeing me naked for the first time in a month, he'll realize it was better that way.

"You're a fucking dream," he says with a wanton rasp, eyes raking over me.

With his support, I settle into the tub—filled to the brim with water that's the perfect temperature to ease my muscles and warm my bones. It's squishy with us both in here, but he doesn't seem to mind me between his legs, my head laid back on his chest. And for a long while we sit in perfectly comfortable silence.

A sensation I'm sure I'll never fully get accustomed to lights a smile on my face. I grab hold of Chase's hand and press it firmly against my skin. Holding it flat on the cold part of my belly sitting just above the water. Within seconds, she kicks again.

"Holy shit, Cass. *Holy shit.* Was that?" His fingers spread wider automatically—trying to cover as much of me as he can.

"Little Spud. You were the first to feel it—like I promised. It's been getting hard to dodge hands on my stomach lately, but you deserved to feel her before anybody else. She goes wild every time I have a bath, so I was hoping you'd get this."

His lips press to the top of my head. Over and over. Soft kisses as his hand holds tight to my stomach. "Remember when you told me not to say nice things or you might fall in love?"

"Mhm." I stroke my fingertips over the back of his hand.

"We never talked about what'll happen when I fall in love with you."

Red

I should *not* have said that. Cass's heart is pounding so hard and fast, I swear it's causing ripples across the water. I swallow hard. It's too late—*obviously.* I'm already so far gone for her. Offering up a *what-if* scenario was merely a test to see how she'd react.

I'm not ashamed to say I'm wrapped entirely around her pretty little finger. If she asked me to, I'd give up cowboying to start a fucking potato farm so she can eat them endlessly. I'd build her dream house with my bare hands. Hell, I'd even move to the goddamn city, if that's what she truly wanted.

Yes, sweetheart. Anything for you, sweetheart.

But Cass's thundering heart rate makes me think it's not the night to tell her the truth. Not the moment to express that I love her beyond words.

"I don't mean—"

She cuts me off, tilting her head to look back at me. "I know what you mean."

Her wet hand slides up to my cheek, and she kisses me. Soft, slow, in the dim light of my phone's flashlight. For a month, I've been craving the feel of her hands on my skin. For longer, I've been desperate for her kiss. So it doesn't take long before my cock's rock hard, pressed into her back.

Her lips smile against mine. "A little kissing too much for you?"

"When I'm kissing the most gorgeous girl around? Abso-*fucking*-lutely."

"Should we get out?" She plants kisses between each word, unable to take a break for long enough to form a single sentence.

"What's the rush?" I stroke her hair, letting my knuckles brush along her jaw, then trail down her wet skin until I'm cupping her tit. Rolling my thumb over her hard nipple. "We have all night, and if I get lucky, maybe the snow will trap you here for a few days."

My hand trails lower, slipping between her legs, and her moan gets lost in my throat. Circling her sensitive clit, my fingers send her hips bucking, sloshing water over the edge of the tub. She's writhing in my arms, thighs fighting to press together for more friction. I won't let them—my free hand holds her knee firmly against the porcelain.

"I missed you," she whispers breathlessly. Hopefully it's not only the orgasms she's been missing. I silently—selfishly—pray she's been as devastated to be apart as I have.

"You have no idea how much I've missed you." I snag her bottom lip between my teeth, sucking it into my mouth then releasing it slowly. "So fucking much, Cass."

Her fingers wrap around the tub edge, gripping as her hips lift buoyantly. Even in the water, there's no denying how aroused she is. I could lift her hips a few more inches and slide my cock right in. No doubt her bouncing on my lap in the warm bathwater would have us coming in minutes. But I want to take my time with her, let her enjoy herself, savor her, and prove how I feel about her. She fills the air with a soft whimpering sound. My cock's rock hard against her back, and I swear I could come just from the noises she makes.

I smooth my finger over her clit, and her fingers dig into my forearm. "This what you missed, sweetheart?"

"Chase, I missed *you*." Her hooded eyes meet mine for a split second before they're forced closed by my frenzied movement over her pussy. The wave of an orgasm flows through her, and her grip slips from the tub as she falls apart in my arms. The sweetest relaxed sigh leaving her lips and allowing every muscle to slacken.

When we finally drag ourselves from the cool water, we're stuck dripping and towel-less in the small bathroom. Tiny goosebumps spackling her skin.

"Shit. Sorry. Guess we should've stopped and grabbed some towels." I comb my fingers through her damp hair, giving a tug at the same moment her lips crash back into mine.

"Mmm. I'm too relaxed to care," she mumbles against my mouth.

When my eyes open, I'm greeted by a view of the curve of her back and her thick, round ass in the foggy mirror over the sink.

"Cassidy, turn around for a second. Look at yourself." She blinks up at me, then slowly—warily—spins. Her nose scrunches at her reflection, and I take my cock in my hand, waiting for her gaze to snag on it in the mirror before speaking again. "You're the hottest fucking thing I've ever seen. The next time you start to wonder if I'm attracted to you, I want you to remember what you do to me. I'm so fucking hard for you all the goddamn time. The whole time you were gone, I couldn't even *think* about you without needing to fuck my hand. You kill me. And I know it's hard for you to watch your body change, but on the days you hate it, I'm going to love it enough for the both of us. You're incredible, sweetheart. And I'm obsessed with you—with this *perfect* body of yours."

Letting go of my dick, I run my hands along her flushed, damp skin. Kissing her shoulder as I hold her tits. They're full and soft. As expected, they no longer come close to fitting in my hands.

"These fucking tits. Are you kidding me? *Shit.*" I rub my thumbs over her nipples. So much darker than they used to be, and I can't wait to have them in my mouth when I spin her back around. "If you aren't careful, I'm going to keep putting babies in you so I never have to give these up."

"Don't you fucking dare." Her hard glare meets mine in the mirror. "I'll castrate you myself."

My chest to her back, I pull her tight against me with a quiet laugh. "Okay, okay. Definitely one more, though."

She rolls her eyes, but there's no hiding the half smile.

"You're better than any fantasy I've had about you." I trace the curve of her stomach, the ticklish spot over her hip bone, down between her legs. I can't stop staring at her face—at her eyes following my hand as it roams her body, the freckles on her cheeks, and her kissable lips.

"Sweetheart, you have the most beautiful pussy I've ever seen."

She mumbles a halfhearted disagreement as my tongue slides across her shoulder to her neck.

"I swear to God, I could come just from thinking about it. How wet you always are for me. Your pussy lips hugging my shaft. The way your greedy cunt grips me when you come. It's fucking heaven." I bite her earlobe and her neck instinctively crooks, giving me more.

"And this? *Fuck.*" I draw across the soft skin where her ass meets her thigh. A raspy breath leaves her parted lips when I run the tip of my hard cock between her ass cheeks, pre-cum marking her skin.

"Look at what you do to me. You own me." I grab her hand and wrap her fingers around my cock. "You are everything I need, Cassidy. I want to spend the rest of my life telling you how perfect I think you are. Have you all to myself to worship every day until you stop questioning every compliment I give you."

"I want that, too." She strokes slowly from base to tip, then notches the head at her entrance, gripping the sink with her free hand so I can slip inside her with a groan.

"*Fuck*, sweetheart. Look at us—look at how perfect we

are." I fill her deeper from behind, watching us in the mirror. The sound of slapping, damp skin as I fill her to the hilt. "How well I fit inside you. I was fucking made for you."

She moans, meeting the reflection of my eyes. "You make me feel so good."

"C'mon. It'll be nice and warm out there now. You can get comfy, and I'll keep making you feel good." I reluctantly pull out, knowing she won't be comfortable standing for much longer, regardless of how hot it is to watch us fuck in the blurry bathroom mirror. Not letting my hands leave her body for a single second, I urge us toward the bathroom door and into the small living space. As I expected, it's damn-near tropical out here.

We fall together on top of the dark-green quilted bed-spread, and I slide a hand up her thigh, squeezing and tugging it over my waist. A needy sigh escapes as she rocks her hips into me. Palm sliding down my cock, she begins stroking with an unrelenting fist.

"Easy," I groan. My fingers wrap around her wrist, halting the tugging motion. "Like I said—I want to make *you* feel good. Relax and let me."

Usually, we fuck. Rough, loud, sloppy, and with the constant threat of it being the last time. And while that's incredible—the best sex of my life, easily—I don't want it tonight.

Despite everything in my body wanting her hands all over me, I remove her fingers from my dick and gently place her arms at her sides. "No more touching, got it? This is about you."

She purses her lips with annoyance but nods slowly. My hands find their way to her tits without hesitation. After so long without her, the feel of them spilling out around my palms makes my cock twitch against her thigh. I follow the curve of each breast with my tongue, then lick and suck her dark nipples. My lips drag down her stomach, leaving a soft kiss where earlier I felt Little Spud kick for the first time.

When I reach her upper thighs, she's lifting her hips off the bed and aggressively gripping the quilt beneath us.

"Quit torturing me," she whines.

"Breathe, baby." I rock forward to kiss her before moving back down to the warmth between her creamy thighs. "I know how you love being treated like a slut, but tonight"—I swipe my tongue along the soft skin of her inner thigh, forcing an arch in her back—"you're my queen. I might not be good enough for you in a lot of ways . . . this isn't one of them. I *know* I can fuck you better than anyone. One day you'll come to your senses and find a better man, and you'll think of me every damn time you're in bed with him."

I kiss her clit softly to distract myself from the thought of her with somebody else. It's a heavy, smothering weight on my chest—the seemingly inevitable future where Cassidy and our baby are being taken care of by someone other than me. Where I'm condemned to a life of watching another man give Cass the things she deserves. If I think too hard about it, I can't breathe.

"Chase." She grabs my hair, but not to push my face into her pussy. Instead, she yanks upward, forcing my eyes to meet hers. "I don't want another man. I want you. *Only you.* The way I've acted lately was shitty, but it had nothing to do with who you are. No matter what happens, how complicated this gets, I'll still want you."

"Then let go of my hair and let me pretend to be worthy of you for tonight." I slip a finger inside her wet entrance while I kiss her bare skin with a moan.

"Fuck," she whimpers when I pull away.

"Get comfortable, sweetheart. We'll be here for a while." Her arousal coats my tongue with a single swipe, and my self-control is quickly fading. I talk a big talk about making this last. About wanting to *make love* instead of fuck. But the soft moans, her writhing body, and the delicate taste of her is pushing me to the brink of coming already.

Alternating between attentive licks and gentle kisses, I don't stop until she's pulling my hair with so much force I might be bald when we're done. Her hips buck against my face as I home in on her swollen, glistening clit. Sucking. Grazing my teeth across. Fingers crooked deep inside her, coaxing her to make a fucking mess of me. I lick in rapid, tight circles until she's flooding my face with her cum. The most spectacular waterfall I've had the pleasure of bathing in.

"Atta girl," I say, finally coming up for oxygen with a dopey, drunk smile on my face. "Never make me go a month without you again."

"Deal. Even when I meet my future husband, I'll keep you as my side-piece." She squints down at me with a devilish grin. The orange flicker of the fire dances across her skin in time with my wandering hands.

"God, you're such a brat."

And I fucking love you.

"You love it."

I smirk. "I do."

And you. I love you.

To shut myself up, I kiss her stomach—a reminder of why I can't rush my confession and risk losing her again. *Maybe for good, this time.* Her nails rake across my shoulders and down my arms. Over the scars, bumps, imperfections in my flesh. She sees me. She knows me. And, somehow, she's here in spite of it all.

"Are you comfortable?" I ask, grabbing her ass and pulling her to meet me. Seeing a contented expression on her face, I wrap her creamy, smooth legs around my waist.

The head of my cock glides up her slit with ease, forcing drops of pre-cum onto her clit with each slow thrust forward. "Rub that in for me, baby."

Her dainty fingers find their way to her clit, massaging the beaded liquid into her skin. I notch the tip inside her, then hold still. My cock's pulsing with anticipation, desperate to feel her everywhere. She's so fucking tight, clenching around the head as her fingers work over her pussy. My girl's a soaking wet mess.

"Quit teasing." She rolls her hips to force my cock a tiny bit deeper.

"I'm just watching. I fucking *love* watching you play with yourself." I touch her, collecting her wetness and spreading it down my shaft with a slow stroke. Then I bring my fingers to my mouth to lick them clean. One by one. Taking pleasure in the sweet taste of her cum, the needy look in her eyes, and the pink blush traveling from her cheeks to her chest.

"Oh, yeah?" She picks up the pace, punishing herself with her fingers and arching her back. Driving my cock deeper yet. It's no longer just the tip—I'm halfway inside her, and her muscles are working overtime to draw me all the way in. I groan, fighting to keep from fucking her senseless.

"How can you question if I'm attracted to you when you do things like that? You're the most gorgeous . . . most sexy . . . most incredible woman I've ever seen."

I thrust my hips forward, matching her loud moan as I fill her. Soft and warm, she stretches around my cock, taking all of me so fucking well.

I might not be good enough for her, but she's perfectly made for me.

I stroke her thigh as my cock pumps in and out. For the first time, I wish she didn't have a pregnant stomach in the way. Because I want her to see the way her tight pussy fits around me. See that our bodies are made to be connected this way. But more than that, I want to kiss her while we make love.

The movement's so relaxed and natural, it feels like I'm dreaming in slow motion. The world's hazy and disorienting, and it's hard to remind myself not to tell her I love her right now. Our bodies rock together, making her gasp with each thrust. She grabs my thighs, urging me deeper, closer.

"Can you . . . hold me?" she asks breathlessly. A request I didn't expect but definitely won't say no to.

"Lie on your side, sweetheart." My entire body's falling apart the moment I'm not inside her, like a piece of me has been torn away. I move to press my lips to hers with a slow, explorative kiss. Letting our tongues brush, holding her bottom lip hostage between my teeth, feeling her whimper travel down my throat.

She can't roll to her side fast enough before I'm cuddling in behind her and slipping my cock back into its warm, safe home. And now, without her stomach between us, I can hold her. I can love her properly. With my hands caressing her boobs, my lips on her neck, and my chest pressed to her back. The fiery glow illuminates her soft curves. The smell of her shampoo fills my nostrils, and there's only the sound of crackling fire in the room. With unhurried, effortless thrusts, I hope this is as magical for her as it is for me. Because, *fuck me,* I love her with every part of my soul.

She looks back at me with a small smile, and I'm smiling back like a love-drunk idiot when I feel her muscles tense around my cock. Her fingers work her clit in a frenzy to draw out an orgasm. The tingling starts in my balls, engulfing me with an intensity that makes my legs numb and my breathing weak. I gasp when I crash into her for one final time. We fall apart together, and my cum fills her completely. Leaking out around the edges of my cock, which I refuse to pull out. As far as I'm concerned, we can stay exactly like this forever.

"You're so good to me." Her fingers weave between mine. "I'm sorry for pushing you away."

"Shush. I'm the one who fucked this all up." I push her hair away from my face and kiss the smattering of freckles on the back of her neck. One upside to the variety of sex positions we've been in is learning every intimate detail of her body. The freckles she doesn't even know she has. The small scar on her left inner thigh. The soft blond hair on her lower back, which I'm sure she would hate to find out I've noticed. "And despite me being a huge idiot, you came back. If I had to lose sleep over something for the last month, I'm glad it was you."

She's quiet for a moment, scratching her nails up and down my forearm that's draped across her. "I'm done being scared of this. I want to be with you, if the offer still stands."

"What if I let you down again?"

"Then we talk about it. Which is something we clearly both need to work on." She rocks her hips so I regrettably slip out of her. Then rolls onto her back, a sated smile appearing on her lips. Blue eyes shining in the dim fire glow. "Speaking of talking, I want us to have dinner with Dad. I need things to be good between you two."

I seriously doubt anything I do will make him think I'm better than my dad. But if Cass wants me to be her man, I'll die trying to prove myself. As long as she thinks I'm worthy, the rest of the world can go to hell.

"You're right. I need to apologize to him, too. I'll cook?"

She kisses me, pulling my hand down between her legs. Gripping my middle finger and guiding it gently over her clit. Drawing teasing lines up and down.

"You're incredible, you know that? Now . . ." Her sentence trails off with a moan as she increases the pressure. "Slow and intimate was amazing. But it's been a month, and I *need* you to fuck me. *Please.*"

Jesus Christ. I love her.

"You should probably be punished for driving me so goddamn crazy for the last month, shouldn't you?"

She grins. "Definitely. Do whatever you want to me—I'm all yours."

"Guess fucking you until you're so sore you can't do anything tomorrow without thinking of me will work. Are you still full of my cum, baby?"

Her nose twitches, eyebrows lowered in confusion. "I assume so."

"Squeeze your pussy, sweetheart. Use those tight muscles you love to grab my cock with. I want to see how good of a job I did marking you as mine, watch my cum drip out of you."

I push up to my hands and knees, eyes racing from her blushing face to the perfect V between her legs. Her hands clenching her thick thighs, spread wide in front of me. And when my cum flows out and down the crease of her ass, I swipe it with my fingers and spread it over my rock-hard shaft. Shoving my cock inside her with a strangled, feral moan. Then I fuck the ever-loving hell out of my girl until our muscles are too fatigued to carry on and we fall asleep tangled on top of the bed.

Cassidy

Thirty-three weeks (baby is the size of a bag of ketchup chips)

Sun beaming in through the frosty window wakes me up from the *best* dream. Until I look around, seeing the forest-green quilt barely covering Chase's naked body and the glowing red embers and small flames crackling in the fireplace. This is the dream. A fairy tale. Nothing that happened last night feels real—like a blurry, pieced-together memory after a night of drinking.

I fell in love with him.

As easily as the snow fell around us last night. Not falling so much as floating, swirling around before settling in like a comfortable blanket over everything. Despite how long I spent drifting, loving him was as inevitable as the January snow.

Standing up, I snag a spare blanket and wrap it around myself for the five paces to the bathroom. On the way back, I wedge a log into the fire, waiting until it ignites before spinning to face the bed. Chase is propped up on his elbow, watching me with a tilted head. Wearing a crooked smile and glazed, sleepy eyes as he pats the bed. I pad across the wooden floor, plunking onto the mattress and falling against his chest with pure contentment.

"This is the warmest and coziest I think I've ever been." I

nestle into the crook of his arm, wrapped in warm sheets and topped with the weight of a handmade quilt. "Let's never leave, deal?"

"So the reason you're normally pissy in the morning is because you're cold? You're somethin' else."

"Definitely has nothing to do with the fact that you're usually waking me up at four in the morning." I relax further into him, turning to putty as his knuckles stroke my thigh.

"I told you I'd slip out. You even gave me a key to lock the door behind me," he says. "It was your choice to wake up with me."

"'Cause it feels like a booty call when you're trying to sneak away before I wake up."

"I came over, fucked you, and left first thing in the morning. That's a booty call." He laughs under his breath. "Thank God you've finally figured out what I've known all along."

"Oh, yeah?" I look up at him, and his lips brush against my forehead. "What's that?"

"You're mine. From the second you spread those gorgeous legs on the hood of that car, you were mine."

"Boy, somebody sure is cocky for"—I pick up my phone and squint at the time—"seven o'clock in the morning. You don't own me. I'm not an object."

"Still mine." The muscles in his arms flex around my chest, squeezing until my breathing becomes wheezy and I'm tapping out. My hand smacks against the scarred skin next to his elbow—remnants of a twenty-year-old wound nobody bothered to care for properly. Every time I think about his past, I want to smother him with kisses and find a way to mend his heart. After last night, at least I'm finally able to do the first one. I kiss his cheek, the rough stubble on his jaw, his soft lips, the hard ridge of his nose, his forehead. Neck, chest, shoulder, clavicle, ear. I don't stop until he's laughing and repeatedly asking what the hell is wrong with me.

"Bring back grumpy morning Cass. At least I know what

to do with her. You're in too good of a mood this morning." His moistened lips leave a trail of sleepy kisses down my neck and across my collarbone.

"I just . . ." *Love you?*

My stomach thunders through the room, cutting me off before I say something big and scary.

"I said I want grumpy Cass, not *hangry* Cass. I need to feed you and Little Spud before you turn feral." He's quiet and perfectly still for a moment, his lips hovering above my skin. Either he's deep in thought or he just malfunctioned. "Um. Problem. Either we go to town, we eat whatever random shit we find in the bunkhouse, or . . . we go to the big house." A small ripple of wrinkles forms on the bridge of his nose as he says the last words.

"I'm not responsible for the troll I'll turn into if I can't eat anything until we get back to Wells Canyon. What exactly is 'the big house' and why did your tone make it sound daunting?"

"It's Jackson and Kate's house, technically. But it's more of a general hangout for everyone. At minimum, Kate, Cecily, and Beryl will be there. Good chance of seeing Austin, too. And God knows who else."

The wind's knocked out of me. Seeing everyone makes this real. Makes us real. "Oh."

"I know you said you were open to dinner here a while back, but making you deal with them first thing in the morning isn't exactly the same. I think there's probably some cereal or Pop-Tarts or something at the bunkhouse, and I doubt anybody is there."

"The big house has real food?"

"Yeah. Maybe not full-on breakfast, but there's always pastries, bread, fruit. . . ."

"You had me at 'yeah.'" I sit up and reach for my clothes. As uncomfortable as it may be, I want to show him that the hiding and booty calls are over. I'm choosing him. "Let's go."

It was easy to forget how cold it is outside when I was surrounded by the dry wood heat. *Holy shit,* is it ever cold out. My nostrils stick together with every inhale, but I don't dare breathe through my mouth because the icy air hurts my lungs. The big house seems so much farther away on foot than it did when I drove by last night, and I clasp Chase's large hand with both of mine to maintain balance on the icy pathway.

Covered in snow and timeless Christmas decor, the massive white farmhouse is something plucked from a *Better Homes & Gardens* magazine.

"God, this is my dream home," I say.

"Noted." Chase squeezes my hand.

We climb the front porch steps, and I can so easily picture summer nights sipping a glass of wine right here. Overlooking barns and fields and . . .

Never mind. Now I'm envisioning spending winter nights inside. Chase opens the door and we're greeted by the scent of fresh bread and coffee. The foyer's warm and, despite never having been here, it feels like home. Inviting and clean and so immaculately decorated with gorgeous antique pieces. Peeking into what appears to be the living room, I see oversized armchairs littered with blankets next to a roaring fireplace. That's exactly where I would spend every cozy, wintry night.

Following the lilting sound of voices, we traipse down the long hallway with photo gallery walls and step into the expansive kitchen. As someone whose cooking expertise doesn't extend beyond a grilled cheese sandwich, I can't say I've ever dreamed about a kitchen. But if I did, this would be it.

"Mornin'." Chase announces our presence.

Cecily and Kate, as well as an older woman—Beryl, I assume—turn to look our way. News of me being here must've traveled fast this morning because none of them seems surprised by my presence. Austin looks up from his magazine for only enough time to give a gentle nod. And at the far end of the table, Odessa and Rhett are armpit deep in Play-Doh.

"Hi." I give a meek smile. Maybe I was invisible before I spoke. My little voice is all it takes for the room to explode with so much energy I grab Chase's arm on impulse, as if the shock wave from their collective excitement might blow me over.

"Come sit down." Cecily wipes her hands on a tea towel and points to the dining table. "Are you hungry?"

"Do you want coffee? Tea? Water?" The gray-haired, tanned-skin woman putters toward a cupboard, looking back at me the entire time.

"Oh, um. Coffee would be perfect. Thank you." I walk toward Cecily and the empty chair she seems to be holding out for me. And by the time I've sat down, a plate heaped with food is in front of me. Followed not long after by a large white mug full of coffee. "Wow. I could've made my own plate . . . thanks."

"If you're not careful, these three will keep cramming food into your face." Chase sits down next to me and rests his hand on my thigh, filling my chest with butterflies. *We're really doing this thing.* It's possible nobody can even see his hand under the table, but it feels like a public declaration.

"Oh, shush." The old woman sits down opposite us, flanked by Cecily and Kate. It seems a lot like the start of an interrogation. Austin even lowers his magazine to side-eye them before shaking his head and returning to whatever he's reading.

"I'm Beryl." She confirms my suspicions with a warm smile that crinkles the skin around her eyes. "So thrilled you finally came out here. I've been hearing nonstop about you for months, honey."

"We're all excited you finally came here." Cecily beams brightly at me. She and Austin aren't exactly regulars at the bar, but they've come by enough times for us to be familiar with one another. "And thrilled you two are . . ." She trails off, sipping her coffee and flicking her wrist to gesture at the two of us.

"How are you feeling?" Kate leans in. "You know when I gave you my number I honestly meant you could text me anytime."

"Um, I'm feeling pretty good. I mean, there's a lot of joint pain and—oooph." A small body crashes into me with a hug. Glancing down, I see Odessa in a futile attempt to wrap her arms around me in a hug, and not for lack of trying, as she smooshes and stretches to reach.

"God, I don't miss being so uncomfortable all the time," Kate says.

Odessa's climbing right onto my lap now, nudging Chase's hand away with her bony knee. Staring into my soul from barely an inch away, her head blocks the three women from my view. So close I can smell the Cheerios on her breath.

"The baby is *still* in your belly?" she asks, clearly shocked I'm still pregnant so long after seeing her at the winter fair.

I nod slowly, trying to back my head away from her as much as I can. I hoped it would be easier to connect with her this time—it's not. For the love of God, I hope Chase was right and I won't feel so uncomfortable with our baby. That the maternal instincts will kick in. Chase taps my foot, and when our eyes make contact, he gives a small wink like he can read my mind.

I clear my throat and look at Odessa. "Yeah, she is. For a few more weeks."

"You're having a girl?" Odessa shrieks, eyes bulging with excitement as she bounces slightly on my lap. "I get to have a girl cousin?"

"You do. That's pretty fun, hey? You'll have to teach her everything you know."

"I'm going to be a bull rider when I grow up, and I can

teach her how. I'm really good at riding on cows—except when I fall off sometimes. But then I get a cast on my arm, and I'm allowed to draw on it." She beams at me like breaking her arm is the biggest thrill of her life.

"Maybe we don't teach your little cousin *everything* you know." Kate pinches the bridge of her nose, biting back a smile.

"You can probably teach Uncle Denny how to ride," Chase says. "He falls off all the time."

Her tiny face scrunches with disgust. "He's not cool enough to ride cows. Just horses."

"Oh, I can't wait to tell him you said that. You're gonna get a whoopin'." Chase grins, and Odessa leaps from my lap with a squeal. Not fast enough, though. He loops an arm around her waist and hauls her into his lap. Tickling her stomach and mussing up her hair, which elicits more high-pitched squeals. Rhett, who's been playing politely with the Play-Doh until this point, screams in harmony with his big sister.

Chase stands up, slinging Odessa over his shoulder and scooping Rhett up with his free hand. They spin in circles around the kitchen, Odessa's curly brown hair flying in every direction, and laughter filling the room. Somewhere in the distance, I can faintly make out muffled voices as the other women chat. But my focus is entirely on him.

I wish he could see himself now—he's nothing like his father.

While all of this might've started as a mistake, it's far from that now. Didn't expect to hook up with an obnoxious cowboy at a rodeo and end up falling in love with the man I'm having a baby with. But here we are. And I'm so glad it's him.

I'm so lost in my own world, I miss the conversation entirely. Although it's apparently reverted back to me because all three women sit quietly. Watching me expectantly for the answer to a question I didn't hear.

"Sorry, I missed what you said." My eyebrows pull together

as I fight to keep my gaze from shifting back to Chase and the kids.

"Oh, we were talking about setting up a food train for when the baby's born. The last thing you want is to be worrying about cooking for yourself with a newborn," Cecily says while the other two eagerly nod. Chase snorts, clearly finding the humor in them suggesting I would bother to cook for myself.

"And are you having a baby shower?" Kate asks. "What sort of things do you still need to get? I have a *ton* of stuff I can give you. There's basically an entire baby store set up in the attic. Honestly, take everything you need."

"Wow, thank you. That's super generous." I pick at the plate in front of me. "Um, I don't think I'm having a shower. My best friend can't get here until right around when I'm due, so maybe we'll do something small after. I'm not sure. . . . Anyway, I think I have most of the essentials, so it's not really necessary. And my dad and I set up a nursery." I reach my hand under the table, resting it on Chase's knee as he sits back down.

"You did?" He turns to look at me, the hurt that flashes across his face making my chest ache.

"Yeah." I gnaw the inside of my cheek, pushing hash browns around on my plate. "Sorry."

"Anyway." Beryl's chair scrapes across the hardwood, cutting the tension. "We have a lot of bread to get baking. I'm glad I finally got to meet the girl who's stolen our sweet Red's heart. He's a good boy."

"The goodest—and the prettiest—boy." I squeeze his thigh just in time to feel his phone start vibrating in his pocket.

He pulls it out and walks away to answer. Then returns a few minutes later and places a rough kiss on top of my head. *Definitely out in the open now.* "Jackson's having issues with a tractor and he's out by the North Creek field. I gotta grab some parts and go give him a hand. Are you good to stay here?"

"I should head home. Change into some clean clothes, take my meds . . . that stuff." Not a single part of me wants to leave him, or even wear clothes, period. But this is the life of a ranch hand, I guess. Even when it's supposed to be his day off, duty calls.

"Come back? I'll make us dinner, and, besides, I still haven't given you your Christmas present."

My face and shoulders fall in unison. *It's Saturday.* "I have to work tonight."

"Shit, right." He scrubs his jaw with the palm of his hand. "Okay . . . um . . ."

"We'll figure it out. Go do your work."

"I'm sorry about this. Text me when you get home."

He starts to walk away, but I grab his hand, tugging him back toward me. My palm races up the length of his arm, holding to the back of his neck and pulling him in for a slow kiss that causes my heart to skip a beat. I hope everyone is watching and, more important, I hope Chase can tell what I'm feeling, even if I'm too nervous to say it out loud.

Cass: Home, safe and sound. And going to take a bath in a very lonely tub

Chase: About to quit my job so I never have to miss out on seeing you naked

Cass: Or you can have the best of both worlds

Without a second thought, I snap a photo of my naked upper body. To be honest, that's the *one* thing that's working in my favor these days; if nothing else, my tits are the fullest and perkiest they've ever been. He replies instantly with a string of various emojis to depict all the emotions he's clearly going through, followed by the words, "*Cass, you're my fucking dream girl.*" And I melt into the warm bath.

I've never been the type to send nudes, but having somebody genuinely appreciate them—appreciate me—has me rethinking my stance.

Before I reply with words I won't be able to take back, I call Blair. My mind's flooded, and I need somebody who can help me wade through it.

She picks up on the first ring. "Psychic twin powers strike again. I was *just* about to call you. Phone in hand and everything."

"What's up?" I ask, pulling a cluster of bubbles over my breast and thinking about Chase's hand there last night.

"You go first since you beat me to the phone call."

"I'm in love with Chase." The words flow from my tongue so easily it's astonishing to think this is the first time I've said it out loud.

Blair cackles. "No shit—I knew that months ago. What made you suddenly realize it, though?"

"Technically, I think I realized it when I visited you at Christmastime. I've never felt this way before, and I was freaking the fuck out. Last night Denny texted me." I've said his name thousands of times, but not to Blair. That's one topic we *never* discuss. "Um . . . he was worried. Apparently Chase's dad is sick, and he's been acting off or something. I couldn't sit at home worrying, so I went to the ranch, and it cleared a lot up for me. Mostly that I've been stupid."

"I'm glad you finally realized it, dummy. I guess if I have to give up my co-parent status to anybody, I'm content with it being him. I know I haven't actually seen the two of you together, but you're good for each other. I can tell. What's your plan with your dad, though?"

I groan, sinking deeper into the bath until bubbles line my

chin like a beard. "I'm going to tell him the three of us need to have dinner and talk, so . . . pray for me."

"Thoughts and prayers." She laughs. "Any other news you need to share?"

"No, just something that apparently wasn't actually new or shocking information to anyone except me. Your turn."

"Well . . . as much as I love hearing you and Red worked things out, I still expect to share in some of the co-parenting benefits. I get first dibs on babysitting for all your date nights, and I'm coming over for newborn snuggles anytime I want." She clears her throat, and the sound of her fingers tapping a drumroll comes clear across the line. I have no idea what the hell she's on about, and my lungs fail to function as I wait for her to finish the train of thought. "Because I'm moving back to Wells Canyon."

My entire body jolts, a lightning strike of adrenaline buzzing under my skin. "Oh my God. You are? What? Why? When? You swore you'd *never* come back here."

"Yeah, well . . . That was before Mom's diagnosis." *Shit. Of course.* "Dad can't do it all by himself. My sister's hands are full, since her baby daddy sucks, so I doubt she'd be much help with Mom. I reached out to Dr. Brickham, and he was ecstatic to be able to off-load some of his patients. Maybe start slowly retiring."

Dr. Brickham has been the only doctor in Wells Canyon for longer than I've been alive. He's ancient and crotchety and makes house calls in a beat-up old pickup truck. My first memory of him is from when I was about five years old; I ate the cheesiest poutine of my life while watching him fix a guy's dislocated shoulder in the middle of the bar.

"He has to be close to two hundred years old now. It's about time his immortal, ghoulish self retires."

"Yeah." Blair sighs. As excited as I am for my best friend to come back, I know how torn she must be. The one thing worse than dealing with feeling stuck here like I've been for the last thirteen years is finally getting out of the small town you were born and raised in, only to be forced back to care for your sick mother. If I wasn't going to have a baby to take care of soon, I'd be packing my bags and moving into the Harts' home so Blair didn't have to.

"When are you moving?"

"I gave my notice at the hospital for the end of February. So . . . first week of March." Her voice perks up a bit. "At least I won't have to miss a single moment of my niece's life. Honestly, getting to see her all the time makes the thought of moving back hurt a lot less. So thank you for getting knocked up."

"Glad my messy situation is helping with yours. Shit, I wish I could help you move but . . . for obvious reasons, that's a no go."

"It's all good. It's not like I need to bring a lot to move back into my childhood bedroom."

"I'm sorry, Blair."

"Is what it is. As much as I love my life here, I need to be there for my parents. I want to spend time with Mom while I can . . . and Dad refuses to admit he needs help, but he does."

"Selfishly, I can't wait to have you around. I know this isn't at all what you wanted for your life, but maybe it'll turn out to be a good decision. Lord knows we need some better medical care around this place."

She laughs under her breath. "What? You have a problem with Brickham doing sutures out in the hayfield?"

"Prime example of why my doctor is in Sheridan. That crypt keeper isn't welcome near my vagina or my baby."

"She's the size of a pineapple now, by the way."

I jokingly dry heave. "We've officially reached the point where the size references are so big it makes me terrified knowing she has to come out one way or the other. Stop."

Blair cackles. "Girl, a pineapple is *nothing.* Just wait."

Red

Thirty-five weeks (baby is the size of a foot-long sub)

I replace the wad of chewing tobacco tucked into my lip and nudge Heathen's side with my heel to move her along faster. If there's any hope in hell I can shower and get dinner started before Cass gets here, this damn mare needs to cooperate for once in her life. I swear she understands my anxious need and is purposefully ignoring me.

With the afternoon sun heating my back, turning my Carhartt jacket into a personal sauna, I hop out of the saddle. Knowing we're so close to home—and dinner—she finally picks up the pace. Leading her into the barn, I come face-to-face with Austin heading down from his office.

"Hey, boss." I drop the lead rope and begin untacking. "Thanks for babysitting Odessa and Rhett tonight."

I was smart enough to go directly to Cecily with my request to babysit in order to give Jackson and Kate a date night. All so I'd be able to use the nice kitchen in the big house for dinner with Cass. It would've been a lot easier and more convenient to have dinner at her house in town like usual—the routine we've fallen back into since the night she showed up here—but I can't give her my super-late Christmas present unless we're here. Though try explaining that to Cassidy without blowing the whole thing.

"You owe me." He follows behind me to the tack room.

"Yeah, yeah." I toss the saddle down on the rack with a dusty thump and turn to him. "Just trying my best to make this work out, y'know?"

He snorts. "Yeah, I know that feeling."

"I know ya do, boss. Right from the day Filly showed up here, you only had eyes for her. And that's how I've felt about Cass since that rodeo."

"Better go get your shit together, then. She's gonna take one look at you like this and run the other way." He gestures to my appearance—filthy jeans, shit-covered boots, and a wrinkled long sleeve. He's right. I have a lot to do and not much time to do it if I want tonight to be perfect.

"Hey." Cass's voice travels ahead of her. I've been so wrapped up in cooking, I didn't notice her headlights beaming down the driveway. A few seconds later, she turns the corner, wearing a low-cut, flowy red dress I've never seen before but I'm hoping I get to see *very* often from now on. Her hair's braided loosely, resting on her shoulder.

"You look . . . *fuck*." No words.

She smiles, wrapping her arms around my waist and rising onto the balls of her feet to kiss me. Her lips taste like cinnamon gum, and she melts into me for a moment. "Thought I should get dressed up, since this is technically our first date."

"Every dinner has been a date to me." I tuck a few strands of loose hair behind her ear, even though they don't seem to be bothering her; I'm constantly overwhelmed with the need to touch her in any way I can. And now that we're officially together, I'm allowed to. Which is something I will never take for granted. "You're sexy as hell, no matter what you're wearing . . . or not wearing."

"We'll get to the 'not wearing' portion of the evening

later." Her teeth tug on my bottom lip, pulling me into a slow kiss.

I can't help myself. I run my hands down her waist and—just like that—I'm under the short hem of her dress. Fingertips tracing the smooth skin of her upper thigh. "Cass, do you always skip underwear on first dates?"

"Never know when my date might need easy access." She shrugs with a sultry smile.

My tongue follows the path of her jawline to her ear, and I whisper, "Such a fucking slut."

The sweetest, softest whimper slips from her lips and brings me to my knees. *Fuck dinner,* I'll eat her. I lift her dress, smiling to myself at the way she instinctively spreads her legs for me.

"Chase," she moans when my tongue makes contact, dampening the skin and making her thighs quiver on either side of my face. "What if somebody comes in?"

"Guess they'll get a show." I kiss her bare pussy, letting go of the balled-up dress fabric in my hands so I can push her legs farther apart. "Spread wider, sweetheart."

She obeys—of course she does. She only protested a tiny amount because she probably felt like she should. But our flirty text messages all day prove she wants this. I bury myself deeper, spreading her with my finger and thumb, running my tongue across her warm, wet entrance. The dress fabric around my head muffles her moans, and she buckles, struggling to stay upright as I slide two fingers deep inside her.

"I can't," she pants, knees caving in.

Pulling back to check on her, I find her hands clutching the slick quartz counter edge, knuckles white to stay steady. It's not going to be enough to keep her from collapsing when an orgasm shatters her.

I stand up with a low growl and swipe my forearm across the kitchen island, shoving the dinner prep out of the way.

The clang of metal mixing bowls hitting the wood floor echoes through the room, followed by the dull thuds of a dozen or more potatoes falling to the ground one by one. A glass measuring cup shatters, and I slap my hand on the cold counter. "Get the fuck up here."

She stares at me like I've lost my mind. And maybe I have. But my hands grab her ass, and she doesn't fight me as I boost her onto the edge.

"Lean back and let me taste you, baby. Get comfortable."

She leans back on her elbows, keenly watching me lift the skirt of her dress. I duck my head under, running my flattened tongue up the inside of her soft thigh until I reach her wet heat.

Maybe it's because I'm intoxicated by her, but Cassidy Bowman tastes like she was made for me. Like her last name might not stay Bowman if I have any say in it. She's more addictive than any alcohol, and instead of making bad decisions when I drink her, I'm wanting to do so fucking good.

Arching her back, she must flail an arm because something flies off the counter with a loud crash. She moans, thighs battling against the weight of my forearms as she tries to press them together. Still I hold steady, keeping her in place so I can fuck her pussy with my tongue and fingers. Circling her clit and drawing my fingertips against her inner wall, begging her to orgasm. The vibrations from her shaky legs radiate through me and she rocks her hips, forcing my fingers deeper.

"You want it so bad, don't you? Fucking my hand to make yourself come?" I nip the delicate skin of her inner thigh, and her muscles contract underneath me.

Clenching my fingers with her tight pussy, she breathes out an irritated moan. "Somebody has to make it happen."

"You're such a shit." I grip her thick thighs, pulling her off the counter and spinning her around. She reaches for the counter edge, and I draw her hips toward me until she's bent in half. With the weight of the baby pulling on her spine, this position might not be comfortable for long. Good thing I know how to make her come quickly. "Think I can't make you come? You're such a slut for my cock, I bet your cum is running down your legs within seconds. Hold on to the counter—I'll show you."

"Okay, Daddy." She smirks over her shoulder at me.

Fucking hell, I love her.

I can feel her racing heartbeat against the palm I have pressed to her lower back as I scramble to unbuckle my belt one-handed. The head of my cock's pressing into her before my jeans have even puddled around my ankles. She's soaking wet, glistening and perfect with my cock notched at her entrance. Cass moans when I drive into her, letting her head fall forward until it's touching the shiny island.

I finally do the thing I've thought about every damn time I see her hair in a braid. I grab it, gripping the soft golden mane in my closed fist like a bronc rein, and give a little tug. Nothing too hard. Not at first. She moans, sinking back onto her heels so my cock drives deeper. And I pull again, harder this time.

"You love being used, don't you, Cass?"

"Only by you." She whimpers, palms pressed against the island to support herself. "You can do anything you want to me. I'm yours."

Mine. Somehow Cass is mine.

I inhale deeply. "*Fuck.* I'm obsessed with you."

Clenching my jaw to fight the urge to come, I fill her repeatedly, watching her head loll side to side. She moans under her breath, and the feeling of her strangling my cock has my balls tightening with a tingling warning. I can't hold back—not with Cass. Coming too soon was never an issue before I met the woman who drives me completely wild with desire. From the moment I slide my dick inside her, it's a losing battle.

Who am I kidding? It's a losing battle from the moment I touch her.

My fingers find her clit, desperately swishing across it until her legs begin to shake and her spine stiffens. And then I let go, closing my eyes and snapping my neck back, succumbing to the shuddering relief that starts in my groin and explodes out through my limbs. Her pussy tightens in waves around me, drawing out my orgasm as she comes. Cass's forehead falls to the countertop and, for a moment, we stay perfectly still in stunned silence.

Tugging my pants up, I kneel behind her and gently lick my way around her pussy. My fingertips gripping her thick ass, I clean our mess with my tongue and revel in the trembling of her thighs against my cheeks.

"Can't say I've ever experienced that on a first date," she says when I stand back up, tucking loose hair behind her ears with a satisfied smile. Attempting to smooth out the creases in her dress. Her cheeks are rosy, hair mussed up, eyes hooded, and she's the most beautiful thing I've ever seen. If I were a painter or a photographer or a writer, *this* is how I'd want to capture her: leaning her elbow on the counter, free hand cradling her stomach, and a slow rise and fall in her flushed chest.

"Should've let me ask you out a long time ago, Cass. Clearly all those other first dates were a waste of time."

"They fed me dinner, though. And you . . . have no food anywhere in sight." She bites her lip and scans the now-empty counter space.

Grabbing her shoulders, I turn her in the direction of the long wooden dining table and gently push her forward. "That's enough out of you. Go sit down and let me clean up, then I'll feed you before you get any meaner."

Broken glass, potato shrapnel, and an assortment of cookware litter the floor. By the time the kitchen's cleaned up and dinner's served, it feels like there's a ticking time bomb in the center of the table. I don't want to be here when Kate and Jackson get back and, based on how quickly Cass inhales her mashed potatoes, I think she feels the same. And this confirms why I *need* to talk to Austin about moving into his place when their fancy new house is built—it may only be one bedroom, but it's better than the bunkhouse. Maybe I'll temporarily stay in the empty cabin where Cass and I spent the night while I wait for his place to be available. I'm sure I'll be at Cassidy's house most of the time after Little Spud arrives, but I want her to feel comfortable coming here if she wants to.

Holding a firm grip on her hand, I lead Cass along the snowy driveway from the big house to the barn. Even with her knee-length puffy jacket, she's trembling. I should've warned her we would need to go outside—I'll run her a bath and hold her all night after this. We move slowly so she doesn't slip, following the beam of light from a flashlight clipped to my chest pocket. Finally, we stop in front of a small shed tucked around the back side of the barn.

I turn to her. "Ready for your Christmas present? Close your eyes."

She gives me a wary head bob, eyelids drifting closed, and I unlatch the shed doors. Once I'm sure her eyes are fully shut, I reach inside the door and flip the singular light switch. A small ceiling light glows across the wooden work benches and casts shadows onto the snow through the window and open door.

"Okay. Open."

She's completely silent, her mouth agape, as she takes in her present. A small wooden shed, complete with handmade work benches, a wall of drawers and storage shelves, and even a plush light-blue rug that's the same shade as her eyes. I'm not a carpenter, but I think I did a damn good job.

"Chase . . . what—I thought you said a small present. What *is* this?" She lightly bounces in place, trying her damnedest to hide her excitement.

"Well. It started small, with that leatherworking tool you said you wanted but were too cheap to buy."

A memory dances across her face. "The fancy maul, yeah."

"Anyway, it turned into this entire workspace. Guess I got bored and needed a way to pass the time, with you ignoring me and all." I nudge her gently with my elbow, and she rolls her eyes. "I don't want you to have to give up something you enjoy. So this way you have a place to do it, and I'll make sure you get the free time."

Cass heads inside, letting her fingers glide across the work-top. She opens drawers, a wide smile making her squint, as I continue explaining. "It has a small heater, and we can do a window AC unit for summer. Figured we could put it in your backyard over the unused garden beds. I also have twenty cowboys with pretty extensive orders placed . . . belts, chaps, headstalls. I think Jackson wants to talk to you about some custom artwork on a saddle for Kate's birthday." I pull out the notebook where I've been keeping track. It started with a bit of coercion to get every single ranch hand to order a belt. Once the ball started rolling, it got away from me pretty quickly.

She thumbs the pages. "That's a *lot* of orders, and I won't have a lot of time."

"They're all okay with things taking as long as you need. You're too talented to box up your supplies and call it quits."

"Chase, I . . . thank you." She launches toward me, wrap-ping her arms around my neck and pulling our bodies tight. Suddenly the collar of my shirt is damp, and I press a kiss to her hair.

Before I can catch myself, I whisper the truth that's been pestering me for months. "I love you."

Her sniffling breath stops. Time stops, I think. I can't feel the hum of her heartbeat through all of our clothing layers so, hopefully, she can't feel the way my own is hitting my chest like a jackhammer.

"Cass, please don't freak out. You don't need to say it back . . . *ever.* I didn't . . . *fuck.*" If asking her to go out with me was enough to scare her off a few weeks ago, there's no way this isn't going to bring out the easily spooked wild horse in her. "I didn't say it because I expect you to say it back. You don't ever have to. I-I've never loved someone before, so I don't know how to do this sort of shit. But you're the only one for me, and I can't keep lying to you. Can't keep pretending I don't feel this way. Whether you want it or not, my heart belongs to you. *Please* don't hate me for it."

With a shaky exhale, her fingers tighten against my back, drawing us closer. "Thank you," she whispers, looking up at me. Her cheeks are tearstained and eyelashes drenched, but the smile she gives me is real.

She loves me. I'm sure of it now.

I never need to hear her say the words, as long as she keeps smiling at me like this for the rest of my life. That's enough for me. It means enough.

I swipe away her tears with the pad of my thumb, then hold my lips to her forehead, her nose, her cheek, and her mouth. And repeat. And repeat. Until the tears stop and her face is pink from my scruffy facial hair, not from crying.

Cassidy

Thank you? What the hell is wrong with me?

He told me he loved me. Three words I've been struggling to hold in and, when it was finally the perfect time to say them, I didn't. Words have never been an issue for me. When a guy at the bar makes an inappropriate comment, I can turn it back around on him on a dime. But the man I love says he loves me for the first time, and my brain turns to oatmeal.

Pregnancy brain. It's gotta be.

We walked to the cabin in silence, with me holding tight to his arm and even tighter to my emotions. Knowing my tears would probably freeze before they had the chance to fall was the only thing keeping me from falling apart. Then he stoked the fire inside the log cabin and said he was heading out to grab more wood.

I stare at a pile of perfectly stacked firewood—more than enough for the night, I'm sure—and reach for my phone.

Cass: EMERGENCY. He told me he loves me and I said thank you.

Shelby: THANK YOU?!

Blair: Cackling. Maniacally. Thank YOU for this.

Cass: Very helpful, assholes

Blair: Okay, okay. What did he do when you THANKED HIM?

Shelby: Didn't you tell Derek you loved him after like 2 weeks? Why the fuck are you suddenly gun shy?

Blair: Because this time she means it. Also, she's a dumbass.

Cass: Rude.

Shelby: Doesn't deny it though

Blair: Quit talking to us and tell him how you feel

Shelby: Say it louder for the dumbass in the back

Blair: GO TELL HIM

Cass: Fuck both of you.

Snagging my thick puffer coat from the couch, I race out the door, careful not to slip down the icy front steps. The path to the woodshed isn't much better, and I hold my arms out to keep my balance.

Probably could've waited until he got back to the cabin, dumbass.

"Chase!" I skate toward him, unsure if the somersaults happening in my stomach are from the baby or my nerves. Hearing my voice, he drops the wood bundled in his arms and charges toward me.

"What's—are you okay?" He grips my forearms, searching my eyes to figure out why I'm out here. In the cold. In a dress. I'm sure the look on my face is conveying panic, too.

"I love you," I blurt out. "I don't know why I didn't say that earlier. *Shit,* why I didn't say it weeks ago, but I do . . . love you."

"And you had to race out here to tell me right this second?" He raises a brow—a smug smile popping up on his face.

"Sweetheart, I already knew. You didn't need to chase me down when I was coming right back."

Fuck right off. I shake my head. "Bullshit. You're going to stand here and tell me you knew how I felt before I did?"

"After the rodeo you told me to ignore you like I usually do. But, Cass, I've *never* ignored you. Sure, we weren't exactly friends, and I didn't know you like I do now. But I didn't ignore you."

I pull my jacket tighter around me and stare at him without speaking. I'm entirely unsure of what point he's trying to make.

"You had a friendship bracelet business in elementary school, remember?"

I laugh, and steam from my breath clouds around us. "Until I got shut down for giving one to Sophie that said BITCH. She *was* a bitch, though—still is."

His tongue pokes the inside of his cheek, and a smile extends well beyond his eyes. "She fucking deserved that, for sure. I convinced Grandpa Wells to pay me for doing extra farm chores so I could buy your bracelets. I was a goddamn eleven-year-old boy—I had no need for *friendship bracelets,* but I wanted an excuse to talk to you. This"—he holds his wrist up and twists the leather bracelet in the moonlight—"means the fucking world to me because of that. I think part of me was already in love with you back then, even though I didn't know what love meant. In high school, it didn't seem to matter to you that you were smarter and funnier and cooler than everybody else. You tutored for free, helped show new kids around the school, volunteered for all kinds of projects. I thought you were fucking incredible, and it was also very clear you were *way* out of my league. You were so nice to everybody, but you never looked my way."

My eyebrows scrunch together, and I open my mouth to protest, but he stops me with a smirk. "You know I'm right. I'm not trying to give you shit, Cass—I'm just saying, I've always paid attention to you. You didn't notice, because you didn't give a shit about me, and I don't blame you at all. I wasn't exactly doing anything to help my case, even though I've liked you for years. Maybe it was selfish of me to agree to hook up at the rodeo when you didn't know all of this, but how could I turn it down? My dream girl was finally giving me a shred of attention beyond the sassy comments I lived for every time I saw you. Then you told me you were pregnant, and it felt like I finally had my chance. I've been busting my ass ever since because I want you to see me."

He brushes a snowflake from my eyelashes. "So I had my suspicions. Because, despite all the bad—all the reasons why you shouldn't give me the time of day—you're here. Looking at me with these big, beautiful eyes and a smile I've never seen you give anyone else. That's more than I ever dreamed of having. I didn't ever need to hear you say the words."

"Thank you for being patient with me. I know I'm a mess and I suck at telling you how I feel. I'm sorry. I wish I'd found you sooner. I wish I didn't fuck it all up when you said you wanted to be together."

"You didn't fuck anything up. We're here now." He kisses me deeply, with a hand holding tight on my jaw. My cheeks are damp, and I'm not sure if I'm crying or if the warmth between us is melting the falling snow.

"I love you, Cassidy." He whispers the words directly into my kiss-drunk mouth.

I shut my eyes, focusing only on the feel of his lips hovering over mine—not expecting or demanding a response, but patiently hoping. "I love you, Chase."

The kiss that follows has me turning into molten lava, hot and barely able to stop myself from becoming a puddle on the floor. I don't know if we're kissing for five minutes or five hours. My mouth feels bruised and I'm tingling from head to toe, but I can't let go—wouldn't want to if I could. But slowly he pulls back and nods toward the moonlit path.

"C'mon, sweetheart. I can't risk you getting frostbite or pneumonia. Let's continue this inside."

I nod, struggling to remain upright without his steady, thick body holding me. "Why did you leave me alone in the cabin?"

"Could tell you were nervous. Thought you needed a minute to panic alone, text Blair, figure out if you should admit to feeling the same, maybe consider running—I would have stopped you if you tried to leave, by the way."

He might know me better than I do.

"I didn't consider running, but I did the other three."

He laughs under his breath. "And what did Blair say?"

"She said I was a dumbass and I needed to talk to you."

"I always knew I liked her." He leans to pick up the blocks of wood scattered across the snow.

"Well, good. She's moving home in a couple weeks, so you'll be seeing a lot of her." Grabbing hold of his thick bicep, I walk beside him back up the dark path. "We might need a bigger couch to fit all three of us for our reality TV binges."

"No way. You're the only person on Earth allowed to know I watch that shit."

I scrunch my nose at him. "Too late. She knows you're a big sucker for dating shows. I think you might've watched enough seasons to officially be considered a superfan. Hope you know I'm buying you merch for your birthday." A brilliant idea flows into my brain, and I squeeze his arm tight. "Holy shit. I'm buying us matching T-shirts to wear while we watch the season finale. Why haven't I thought of this before?"

He laughs. "What part of not wanting people to know I've watched that stupid show makes you think I want a T-shirt?"

"Told you that you'd regret making me fall in love with you."

"I don't regret it for a single second, sweetheart. The T-shirt is living permanently at your house, though—can't risk any of the guys seeing."

"So you mean we can't take a cute couple photo for social media?" I tease, nudging my elbow into his ribs. "*Kidding.*"

I'm not kidding. I'm taking a photo.

"Bullshit—you're not kidding. You're really putting in effort to make sure I have regrets, eh?"

"Doesn't matter. You're stuck with me." My free hand rubs over my stomach, and I've never had so few regrets in my life. Everything feels perfectly in place.

The room's still dark when I wake with a jolt. A painful cramping sensation rocketing through my pelvis.

Maybe I just held my bladder for too long.

By the time I've pulled myself from the bed, it's gone. I shuffle to the bathroom, refusing to open my eyes more than a sliver so I don't fully wake up, then back to the bed, tucking a pillow under my stomach and throwing an arm over Chase's torso. Warmed by the wood heat, I'm in a half-asleep daze when the pressure forces my hands to my stomach.

What the fuck. What the fuck.

Before there's too much time to spiral, the discomfort dissipates. I lie perfectly still, taking controlled breaths and feeling my pulse bang against the palm spread across my stomach.

Rolling to my other side, I pick up my phone to check the time: 4:54 a.m. Chase's alarm will go off in six minutes. Then I can have him reassure me I'm being crazy. I'll take some painkillers or something. It'll be fine.

Sleeping is out of the question. Staring at the small digital numbers is the only thing I feel confident I *can* do to prevent myself from having a full panic attack. One minute until his alarm. Then he'll ease my . . .

Nope. I haven't had a baby and I should have taken Kate up on her offer to chat. Because this can't be. Can it? There's still a full month left. No. I'm making the executive decision. It's not happening. Simple as that.

"Wasn't expecting you to be awake." Turning off his phone alarm, he rolls over and kisses my shoulder.

"I'm just . . . really uncomfortable, for some reason. Like everything is super tight."

His lips leave my shoulder, concern washing over his sleepy face. "Should we go to the hospital?"

"I'm sure it's nothing. Probably from sleeping without the pregnancy pillow. Or I need to drink some water. Or it's contractions. Or it's from the sex last night. Or I don't know."

"Cass. You can't throw 'or it's contractions' in there and breeze past it. Is that what's happening?"

"I mean . . . maybe. It *is* pretty consistent. . . . But I've never done this. What the hell do I know?"

"*Jesus.* Why didn't you wake me up?" He tosses the covers off and scrambles out of bed, throwing his shirt and jeans on within seconds. Then he stares at me, like I'm the insane one for not trying to break a world record with how quickly I can haul my ass out of bed and get dressed. "Come on. It's a long fucking drive to the hospital. I'm not messing around here so we can end up having a baby—an *early* one—on the side of the highway."

"Okay," I say, exasperated. "You're right. Let's go. But if this is something super embarrassing, like I need to pop an antacid, you don't get to laugh at me."

"No laughing. Only celebratory French fries if that's what this turns out to be. Get dressed, I'll go start the truck so it can warm up." He slips out the door, leaving me to freak out.

My brain's foggy, but somehow I manage to get dressed and sit myself on the edge of the bed to wait for him. I've been so wrapped up in our relationship—or lack thereof—I forgot about all the parenting shit. I don't have a hospital bag. We haven't picked out a name. I haven't fully decided if I want an epidural—*no, I absolutely do.* We haven't talked about whether he's allowed anywhere near the foot of the bed during the birth. I don't know if I can do this.

"Hey." Chase is suddenly crouched in front of me with his hands on my knees. "It's all going to be good. The truck's warm, I have a bottle of water for you to drink, and we can stop at your place to grab whatever you need."

I lick my parched lips. "I don't have anything packed. I made the list but I haven't . . ."

"That's fine. I'll grab stuff. Come on," he says with a soft smile. Even softer voice. Taking my hands and pulling me to my feet.

"I couldn't bring myself to pack the bag . . . because it made me think about having to do this without you."

His lips graze across my knuckles. "Sweetheart, you got me. I'm here. You aren't doing this without me."

The drive into Wells Canyon is painfully slow, thanks to the actual pain in my stomach every five to six minutes and Chase driving at funeral procession speed.

"Sorry, but why are we moving slower than molasses? We'll be lucky to get to Sheridan by my actual due date at this rate." I place my trembling hand over his, which is resting comfortably on my thigh. Just the simple calming weight of his palm has me thanking whatever higher power is out there that I have him. I'd be in a full-on panic attack if I were alone.

"Because this road is bumpy as shit, and I don't need to jostle Little Spud right out."

"You know what's funny." I wedge my toes against the heat vent. "We've known she's a girl for *months* and haven't bothered to name her."

"You mean she can't be Little Spud forever?"

"Yeah, and be bullied relentlessly."

His grip on my thigh tightens. "I'd love to see any kids fucking try."

"You can't beat up children." I give him a disapproving sideways glance. "Anyway, you're missing the point here. She needs a name."

"Rhett and Odessa can do it for me." His grip loosens,

thumb slowly rubbing across the top of my thigh and sending warmth through my veins. "I assume you have a whole list of names. What do you like?"

I pull my phone from my pocket. "Thought you'd never ask." I tap away, pulling up the list I've been curating since I was approximately thirteen years old. "Ivy, Poppy, Hazel, Eloise, Noelle, Fiona, Ada—"

"Whoa," he says, tapping his hand on my leg. "Slow down. How the hell am I supposed to even think if you—was one of those names *Noelle*? Like Christmas?" He raises an eyebrow but doesn't look at me, unwilling to take his eyes off the road for a single second.

"It's pretty," I protest. "Do you have anything better?"

"I honestly haven't thought about it much, so give me a second." The truck turns onto my street and pulls in front of my house with a lurch. He pops open his center console to grab my house key, and I can't help but notice multiple cans of Skoal chewing tobacco.

"I thought you quit chewing?"

"What?" He closes the console, giving me a confused look. "Nope, definitely didn't quit."

"I never see you with a dip in." To think of it, I don't remember seeing him with a tobacco-stuffed lip since that first night.

"Because you wouldn't kiss me with tobacco in my lip, and I wasn't about to risk losing an opportunity. Besides, I don't really feel the need to when I'm with you."

All that time he was waiting to kiss me, and I was too trapped in my head, stupidly ignoring the incredible thing right in front of me. All the little sacrifices and the caring gestures day after day—the way he was loving me better than anyone ever has.

"Oh, you have a *big* crush on me, eh?"

"You have no idea. Okay, what do you need inside?"

My packing list is longer than the baby names—and I

rattle it off faster, too—but he seems to have no problem keeping track of it. Leaving the truck running and the heater blasting, he jogs up to the house. Listening to the idling diesel engine, I breathe through the uncomfortable thing that keeps happening—well, *clearly* they're contractions, no denying it now—and try to keep my mind off the thought that that's what they are because we aren't ready for this. She's not supposed to be ready yet, either.

Less than five minutes later, he's tossing the bags and car seat—which is still in the stupid box—into the backseat. "I grabbed everything you listed, plus the body wash you love and my hoodie you stole and the fuzzy blanket from the couch. Because hospitals are cold and you basically require a heat lamp on you at all times. And your names are beautiful, but we should wait until we see her to decide. I think we'll just know."

His hand immediately takes back its spot on my thigh, holding tight as he pulls onto the quiet street leading to the highway. Thankfully, now that we're on smooth pavement, he's getting the truck to go a little faster. Definitely not breaking any speed limits or performing any risky maneuvers, but there's a chance we'll get to the hospital in time.

"Thank you for being so amazing this morning." I bite my lip, blinking back tears. "What are we going to do if this is actually happening right now?"

His pinky finger loops around mine. Glancing over at me, he says, "Then we have a baby girl who's beautiful and strong, just like her mom. She's clearly ready to take the world by fucking storm, so I bet she's going to be a handful. But we'll figure it out—together." He pulls our hands to his mouth and presses a soft kiss on the back of mine. "You're going to be the best mom this little girl could ever hope for. And I'm going to do my best to be everything you two need me to be."

"I thought pregnancy was only supposed to make *me* sappy and emotional." Sniffling, I frantically wipe away the tears with my free hand. "Stop, or I'm going to look even worse than I already do by the time we get there. All this crying."

"Sweetheart, you look like a dream."

"Stop," I jokingly whine, rolling my eyes with a smile. I went twenty-something years mostly ignoring him. Ruling him out. Wasting time with boys who wouldn't know which of the ten bottles of body wash in my shower is my favorite. Who looked at my body forty pounds ago like it was something I should be ashamed of. Who didn't have the trauma that Chase has, but also didn't have his heart.

What an absolute miracle this baby is—in more ways than I can count.

Naturally, Chase couldn't be bothered to pay for parking, and I'm pretty certain we're parked in a reserved doctor's spot. But it was close to the main entrance and, while the contractions became much less consistent during the hour-and-a-half drive, he insisted we didn't come here to fuck around.

Evidently, the medical staff disagree.

"It could be worse. We have a bed . . . and the privacy of a curtain." I watch him pace in the tiny space between the bedside and the off-white curtain. "Anyways, I'm fine. This is why I told you it was silly to text Dad and Blair. I bet the doctor comes in soon and sends us on our merry way."

"We've been here two hours with no answers. And it's been a full hour since anybody even checked on you."

"Because I'm *fine.*" I gesture wildly toward the monitor—which is connected to a strap wrapped around my stomach—knowing neither of us has any idea what the lines on the chart mean. They mentioned the words *dilated* and *early labor* shortly after we got here, and Chase has been extra jittery ever since. "If I wasn't, they'd be in here. Why don't you go outside and cool your jets for a bit, okay? Get some air. Grab me a snack."

"I'm gonna have some words with somebody out there first." He narrows his eyes at the curtain edge.

"Hey," I say, grabbing his wrist to stop him from storming away. "No fighting any doctors, remember?"

He lets out a dramatic exhale. "Fine. I won't fight anybody—*yet.* If you need me, I have my phone, okay?"

Reaching up from where I'm sitting uncomfortably on the rigid hospital bed, I slide my fingers into his hair and pull him to me for a kiss. He tastes like peppermint, and his lips are soft and cool on mine. I can't help but get lost in him for a minute.

My hands fall to my sides with a thud and he straightens his back. "I'll be right back with snacks."

I slide farther down under the scratchy, sterile blanket and close my eyes. With any luck, I can get a nap in while he's gone. Chase grabs his wallet and phone from next to my feet, giving my toes a quick squeeze through the sheet, and slips between the curtains.

His voice fills the otherwise disconcertingly quiet hospital wing. Not with an angry or irritated tone, but there's a definite rasp of concern that he's managed to hide from me all morning. "Hey, we've been here for the past hour, and my wife's been having . . ."

Whatever he says may as well be white noise with how easily my ears block it out after hearing the word *wife.* There's a knocking in my chest. An insistent smile quirking at my lips. A tremor that has nothing to do with my contractions. Perfect contentment washing over me, like the peace you feel the moment you're falling asleep. And then I do.

Red

I take the stairs two at a time down to the hospital's main floor. The elevator seemed too much of a gamble—if it got stuck, I wouldn't be able to get back to Cassidy. The nurse told me someone would be in to see Cass within fifteen minutes. Honestly, her words sounded like bullshit to me, considering how long we've been waiting. But I need to be who Cass deserves. Not a hothead. Not an asshole. So I thanked her politely and walked away.

The main floor of the hospital is busy thanks to the overcrowded emergency department. Ignoring the knotted feeling in my chest, I weave through the sea of people without taking my eye off a row of vending machines near the exit. I'm so determined, I don't even notice somebody trying to get my attention until they're grabbing hold of my arm roughly, yanking to stop me in my tracks. I spin around, ready to throw down, only to come face-to-face with Dave.

"Oh, hey." I drop my free arm with a relieved breath.

"Where is she? Is she okay?" *Fuck.* Maybe Cass was right and we should've held off on telling him we were coming here. There's worry painted across the grooves in his forehead, and this might be the first time in history when his gaze isn't full of contempt when he looks at me.

"She's good, as far as I can tell. Nobody's checked on her

since shortly after we first got admitted, so Cass sent me for snacks." I point at the vending machine bank.

"You've been here for two hours and nobody has bothered to keep an eye on her? What the fuck do our taxes pay for then?" His face is turning red and, by the last sentence, he's yelling. At least I'm not the only person who thinks this is absolutely bullshit.

"Don't get me fucking started. I'm trying to keep my cool for Cassidy." Plunking change into the vending machine, I buy her Flamin' Hot Cheetos, ketchup chips, and an Aero chocolate bar.

Dave taps the window on the front of the machine. "Coffee Crisp is her favorite."

"Usually, yeah. But she hasn't touched a Coffee Crisp since she ate two in a row and threw up a couple months ago. She still can't even think about them without getting nauseous."

Resigned, his hand drops to his side. "Right. Okay."

I would take the stairs again, but with Dave on my heels, I veer left toward the elevators. When the door shuts behind us, I clear my throat. "Listen, I wanted to apologize for what happened at the bar. What you said stuck with me. The last thing I want is to put Cass through even half of what my dad put Mom through. I know there are people—yourself included—who think I don't deserve her. And you're right. But loving your daughter is the most rewarding thing I've ever done. And I'm willing—no, not just willing. I'm fucking *eager* to bust my ass to be a man she's proud to be with. Because I need this to work more than I need air."

He tilts his head to look at me. "It takes a real man to admit that."

"That's what I'm trying to be. I'm not drinking. And no offense, but I'm not stepping foot anywhere near your bar again. I'm trying to be better."

Questioning eyes scan my face, seeking a thread to pull. Doing his best to unravel what I'm sure he thinks is bullshit. "Cassie deserves the best."

"Couldn't agree more." I step off the elevator after him and point down the hallway toward the maternity ward. "She's right down there."

A mixture of relief and dread sloshes in my stomach at the sight of a doctor talking to Cass. Both women turn toward us as we walk in, and I toss the snacks down at the foot of the bed, needing them out of my clammy hands before they end up scattered across the floor.

"You must be Dad." The doctor gives me a nod hello. I open my mouth to correct her—clarify that I'm the boyfriend and Dave is her dad—when I realize we're talking about Little Spud. And, *shit*, I'm a dad. Based on Cass's smirk, my face must be contorted in a way that makes it seem like this is the first I'm hearing of a baby.

"Oh, yeah." *Why is my mouth suddenly so dry?*

"Perfect. So I was explaining to Cassidy that we'd like baby to stay in until thirty-seven weeks. She's dilated, but contractions have stopped, so I feel comfortable sending her home. That said, for the next couple weeks she needs to rest and stay hydrated. No long walks, limited stairs, no heavy lifting—and pelvic rest, too. So nothing inserted vaginally and *no orgasms*."

Either somebody's cranked up the thermostat or I've developed a fever randomly because I'm burning up. I can feel the flush from my stomach right up to the top of my head, which honestly might have steam coming from it. And there's Dave, listening to all of this.

"Okay," I croak.

"Perfect. So you're all good to go home. Hopefully we don't see you back here for a few more weeks." She gives Cass a squeeze on the arm before ducking around the curtain.

"Hey, Dad. I told you that you didn't need to come all this way."

"You thought I'd sit at the bar waiting to hear if it was an emergency and then drive the hour to get here?"

"Well, it's silly that you drove all the way here for nothing." Legs dangling off the side of the bed, Cass tries to reach for her shoes. Dave and I move simultaneously, nearly head-butting in an effort to be the first to help her. Slipping her winter boots on and tying the laces tight, I glance up to find her loving every second of this treatment. I know she's going to get a kick out of pushing me around for the next couple weeks, not understanding that the harder she makes me work for it, the deeper in love I fall.

"Hey, Dave," I say, still crouched with my hands on the black boot laces. "Why don't you follow us to Cass's house for lunch? I'll cook."

I know the look on Cassidy's face well. I can bet she's internally cursing the doctor for putting her on pelvic rest right now.

"No need to cook. I'll grab us pizza on the way. Meet you two there."

What the fuck, Cass silently mouths at me, her eyes the size of saucers. And the moment Dave's gone, she's tugging me by the shirt collar, forcing my lips onto hers.

Balancing pizza and pop in my hands, I plunk down next to Cass on the couch, handing her the biggest slice of pepperoni I could find in the box.

"You know 'light activity' doesn't mean I can't leave the couch, right?"

"But you don't need to because I'm here."

"What next? You baby-bird the pizza to me?"

"If you're into . . ." I stop myself from offering because

Dave walks into the room. He already witnessed the doctor stare into my soul as she told me I was absolutely not allowed to give his daughter an orgasm for the next two weeks. That's more than enough awkwardness for one day.

We eat pizza mostly in silence. Then Cass assumes her normal position, feet on my lap and twirling loose hair around her index finger. I tuck the blanket around her and press my thumb to the ball of her right foot. We've spent hours sitting exactly like this, watching her reality dating shows, but I feel like a zoo animal with the way Dave's staring us down. Narrowed eyes swinging like a pendulum between his daughter and me.

Thankfully, I don't need to talk, because Cass doesn't stop long enough for either of us to get a word in edgewise. Her eyes shimmer in the warm lighting, and there's an unbreakable smile creating small wrinkles around her eyes. She tells her dad about the shed I built, describing every detail, periodically glancing in my direction. Then she launches into telling him about the lengthy list of orders she already has from all the guys at the ranch—orders she's eager to start on, since she's officially on medical leave from work. His expression is soft, full of love and awe, as he soaks up every word out of her mouth.

When she finally comes up for air, I know I need to say something, even though it's going to crush her spirit. "So I don't know if I'll be able to get the shed moved down here within the next couple weeks. I'll talk to the guys and see if I can recruit them, but it might be tough to get it done in time. I'm sorry."

"Well, what if we don't move it at all?" she asks, startling me so my hands stop massaging her feet. "I-I was thinking it might be easier if I stayed at the ranch with you? If that's okay, of course. *Not* in the bunkhouse, though."

"Of course that's okay. I'm fine coming here, too. You know that?"

"I know. But it's been on my mind since the first night I drove out there. I'll be on maternity leave, so I don't *need* to be in town. Then you won't have to commute, I have the girls there when I need help, and I can do my leatherworking. I know I have Dad here"—she nods in the direction of Dave, who's being unnervingly quiet—"and Blair moves back soon, but they both have to work. It would be nice not to sit here by myself all day, every day."

For a beat, I'm afraid to respond. Waiting for Dave to say his piece. Expecting he'll protest her plan. But he doesn't.

Spending every night wrapped around her in bed and waking up smelling her shampoo is all I've ever wanted. "If that's what you wanna do, sweetheart. Where's the baby gonna sleep, though?"

"She'll be in a bassinet next to the bed for a while. Then we'll figure it out."

"Okay." I nod, not bothering at all to hide how happy I am. Cass rakes her nails up my forearm, signaling she feels the same way. "Okay, I'll see if some of the guys can help move stuff."

"Red, I can help, too. Whatever you need."

"Thanks, Dave." I squeeze Cass's foot under the blanket at the same moment her fingers tighten around my forearm.

Cass is single-handedly making me the man I want to be. She's salvaging the broken pieces from the wreckage, sifting through the bad and finding the good, loving me despite the fact I'm a mess. *Maybe,* a little voice in the back of my head chirps—a thought I've been dismissing aggressively before now—*maybe I can be good enough for Cassidy.* Maybe I can be everything she needs. Maybe I can be her dream as much as she's always been mine.

Cassidy

Thirty-seven weeks (baby is the size of a bucket of chicken)

Sitting at my work bench, I carefully line up and punch holes into the last belt order from the ranch hands. There's still a saddle, chaps, and a purse for Cecily on the docket—but, thankfully, my customer base is essentially family with how they've welcomed me onto the ranch so quickly. They're understanding about a potentially long wait.

As unorganized as ever, Blair's been frantically preparing for her move next week. As a result, most of our calls lately have been like this one. Me working in the shed, and her packing boxes. Sometimes we talk, sometimes we just quietly work within camera frame.

It's during a quiet moment, shortly after a gripping conversation about the logistics of marrying somebody at first sight, that I get a painful cramping in my stomach. I shift side to side in my seat until it dissipates. A few minutes later, again. Then again. All through our debate about whether my best friend is packing correctly—she's not, which is why I should be there to help her. Until it's been an hour, and the agonizing feeling of a too-tight elastic band stretching across my stomach is evidently not stopping. In fact, it's getting worse.

"So, hey, Blair. I think I'm having contractions."

"You're what?" She wipes the back of her hand across her sweaty hairline, pushing the loose hair from her face.

"I'm . . ." The sentence pauses against my will. It takes every morsel of brainpower to push through the discomfort. I bite my bottom lip until I taste iron as the pain radiates across my stomach and down through my groin. After a few seconds, I'm able to breathe again. "Yeah, I'm having contractions."

"Holy shit! How bad are they? How far apart? Is there pressure or only pain?" Blair's face is suddenly super close up, staring at me through the phone.

"They just feel like my period cramps—not that big of a deal. I don't know how far apart, but there's no pressure."

"Cass, you have PCOS and your regular period cramps would bring most women to their knees. You're not a good judge of pain. When did they start?"

"Oh, it's been happening all day. But pretty sporadic for most of the morning."

"Cassidy Bowman!" she shouts. "We've been on the phone for . . . one hour and twenty-four minutes, and you're just telling me this now?"

"I've had random little ones ever since we went to the hospital. I thought it was nothing." I set down the tools, feeling the sensation start to build in my stomach again. It comes on like a wave, slow and building until a thunderous crash of pain engulfs my entire midsection, before receding to nothingness.

"Cass." Blair's voice is quiet as I lick my lips and let out a long exhale on the comedown. "I don't want to alarm you, but that was under two minutes. And lasted a full minute. I think you should track down Red and head to Sheridan."

I blink at her. She's right. She's *definitely* right. God, I wish she wasn't.

"Keep me on this phone until you find him, okay?"

"Okay," I mutter. The walk to the door feels like I'm wading through waist-deep water. My head's spinning as I step out into the sunshine, letting the crisp February air rosy my cheeks. "I think he's at the barn."

Blair presses her fingers to her lips, waiting patiently as I shuffle down the dirt road. I don't make it far before the pain grips me. Nearly sending me crashing into the Earth as my knees buckle.

"Pressure," I blurt out when I'm able to, still fully consumed by the punishing cramp wrapped around my midsection. "So much pressure."

She only says one word, but the tone gives away how much trouble I'm in. "*Fuck.*"

"What . . ." I struggle to breathe, clutching my hand to my chest. "What do I do?"

"We go find Red. Does it feel like you need to push?"

"Maybe." My voice takes on the same panicked tone as hers. "I-I don't fucking know, Blair. But maybe."

Thankfully when I tug open the barn door, I nearly crash into Chase on his way out of the tack room.

"Hey, sweetheart. What's up?" He kisses my forehead. Noticing Blair, he twists so he can wave at her. "Hey, Blair."

"Hey, long time no see—you need to get her somewhere warm and clean before your baby is literally born in a barn."

"What do you—" His question is cut off by my nails digging into the flesh of his bicep, fighting to keep myself from yelling. "Okay, let's get in the truck. The hospital bags are already in there."

"Don't think you have time for that," Blair yells through the phone. "Cass, you gotta try to breathe through it, okay?"

"No." I start to cry while the pain subsides. Gently taking the phone from my hand, Chase wipes my tears with the sleeve of his hoodie. Every ounce of blood has drained from his face, and he stares at me wide-eyed as I ramble. "We need to make it to the hospital. I'll be fine until then. People always say your first baby takes forever to come."

"Yeah, well . . . not yours, honey."

Chase ushers me back outside and up the path toward our cabin. Stopping more than once so I can breathe through the pain and instinctively clench my thighs together to avoid the overwhelming pressure in my groin.

"I want to be able to get an epidural," I whine when the contraction ends, and they both sympathetically smile.

I can tell by the look in Chase's eyes that he's terrified, but everything else about him is so calm.

"What do I do?" he asks Blair, clutching my phone while I slip out of my sweater, suddenly overcome with the need to ditch some layers as sweat prickles my skin.

"Call an ambulance. Let me talk to Cassidy for a second."

Chase hands back my phone, watching me worriedly while he dials 911 on his cell.

"Cass. I wish I could be there right now. But you're strong and brave, and this is going to be a badass story. No original experiences—thousands of women have done this and so can you. Decide where you'll be comfortable. Floor? Bed? Bath?"

"Respectfully, fuck off. I don't give a shit whether other women have done this." Modern medicine exists for a reason, and I planned on taking advantage. I didn't plan for this. Not a single part of me thought a homebirth was appealing—in fact, I promptly shut Blair down with a string of expletives when she mentioned it as an option months ago. "Bath. Definitely bath." My hand's trembling so aggressively it's a struggle to keep my phone from crashing to the floor.

By the time Chase is done talking to dispatch, I'm naked and climbing into the empty bathtub, with Blair left sitting on the closed toilet lid.

"Jesus, sweetheart. Let me help you. Here." He grabs my elbow, lowering my shaky body down. Tears stream down my face, and he kneels next to the tub, turning on the tap and holding his hand under the running water to ensure the right temperature. "What do you need from me, Cass?"

"I don't . . . I don't know. I don't want to do this. It's not how it's supposed to be."

"I know. But Blair's right—you're strong. If anybody can do this, it's you."

"Yes, you can!" Blair's yell echoes through the small bathroom.

I want to tell them to shut up, but my brain is floating somewhere outside of my body. It feels as if I'm tumbling through ocean waves, unable to do anything except focus on getting a breath of air every time I briefly surface. I don't know if I'm not in pain or if I'm in so much pain my body has simply stopped registering it.

Red

She's zoned out, staring at the faucet, knuckles white as she grips the tub edge, face blanched. I don't know if Blair's still on the phone—I assume so—but the air's been terrifyingly quiet since the last contraction ended. I didn't tell Cass that the ambulance estimated it would be forty-five minutes. But I'm sure she knows it won't get all the way to the ranch anytime soon.

"Sweetheart, do you want me in there with you?"

Saying nothing, she scooches forward, and I strip down in record time. Then slip in behind her. Just like last time, when I felt our baby kick and all but confessed to Cassidy that I love her. She leans back, and I whisper against her hair, "I love you."

"I'm so scared," she whispers back.

"I know." It's all I can say, stroking my hand softly over her hair. I'm scared, too. So fucking scared. I know all the things that can go wrong. I've helped with calving a few thousand times—calves die, cows die, they need medical intervention. If anything happens, I will never forgive myself for not forcing her to stay in a hotel in Sheridan for the past two weeks.

She groans, moving her hand from the tub to grab hold of mine and squeezing so hard the bones might shatter.

"Breathe, Cass," I say, because it's the only thing I can think of that might help in this situation.

She braces her feet at the far end of the bathtub. While I didn't know my heart was capable of beating as fast as it has for the last twenty minutes, it somehow finds yet another gear. Slamming against my chest as I hold Cass, feeling her bear down with a guttural moan that reverberates through me.

"I'm so proud of you." I kiss her on top of her head when her body finally relaxes, brushing a strand of hair from her sweat-slicked forehead.

"Thank you—also, fuck you." With another contraction, her nails dig into my forearm, no doubt drawing blood.

Three intense pushes later, I watch the love of my life reach down to pull the new love of my life onto her chest. Small, head full of hair, screaming loud enough I'm impressed glass isn't shattering. And, as expected, the look in Cassidy's eyes while she stares down at our baby girl is the most incredible thing I've ever witnessed.

"You did it, sweetheart. You fucking did it. I love you so much. You're so beautiful and incredible and, *holy shit,* I fucking love you." One hand smooths over her hair, while the other rubs slow circles on our Little Spud's back. My vision's blurred with tears, and the echoing baby cries are the most miraculous sound I've ever heard. And Cass tilts her head to kiss me in a way that makes the world stop spinning entirely.

This time, the doctors don't fuck around when the ambulance drops us off at the hospital two full hours later. Once it's confirmed that Cassidy and the baby are okay, they put us into a proper room. A private one complete with real walls, a pungent sterile smell, and a view of the snowy courtyard—not that I plan on looking at anything but the perfect girls cozied up in the reclined hospital bed.

When the nurse leaves, I tuck the powder-blue blanket around Cass's legs and sit on the edge of the bed to watch my girls. Just as I suspected, Cass is a natural. Even before the ambulance arrived, she had the baby fed and perfectly swaddled in a thick blanket. Honestly, if it weren't for my fear about all the things that could go wrong, she probably would've told the paramedics to stand down.

"Sorry about the red hair." I smooth my thumb carefully over the freshly cleaned, silky peach-colored hair.

"I would've been a little disappointed if she was born with anything but." Her eyes leave our perfect, sleeping baby for only a split second to make contact with mine. She tucks fallen hair behind her ear with a drowsy smile. "I love her so much but, like, she kind of looks like a potato, right? Did I eat too many and make a potato baby? Did we jinx it by calling her Little Spud?"

I laugh and gently cover her tiny ears. "Shush. Hazel's the most beautiful tiny potato."

Cass looks up at me and raises an eyebrow. "Hazel?"

"It was on your list, wasn't it? I like it. What do you think?"

She twirls her hair into a makeshift bun at the nape of her neck with one hand. "I love it. That was always my top choice from the list."

"Perfect baby Hazel. I have a feeling she's going to give us a run for our money."

"Yeah, I imagine you have a lot of karma coming your way." She pushes another fallen strand away from her face.

"Can you sit up a bit?" I stand and rummage through the small front pocket of her suitcase to find a hair elastic. Then wedge myself next to her and comb my fingers through her blond hair.

"What are you doing?" She turns her face toward me, and I place my fingertips on her jaw, lightly pushing her gaze toward the far wall.

"Your hair is clearly driving you nuts. Hell, watching you constantly fucking with it is driving *me* nuts. And your hands are full, so let me fix it." Starting at her crown, I fold sections of hair over one another. She's long since given up on keeping the hospital gown in its right place, so I kiss her bare shoulder as I work.

"You know how to braid?"

"Sweetheart, I was *born* to be a girl dad."

She snorts a small laugh. Tying off the long braid, I press my lips to the skin behind her ear. "I've braided my fair share of manes and tails over the years. Just saying, I'm pretty fucking great at it. This bad boy isn't going anywhere." I give the braid a light, playful tug, and she leans into it.

She tucks her body under my arm, and we become entirely transfixed by the seven-pound-three-ounce miracle in her arms. Tiny, raspy baby breaths fill my heart until I think my chest might burst. She lets out a small whimper, which Cass is quick to calm with a gentle shushing sound. They're perfect. And I know I'm not—far from, really—but I'm working at it. For them, I'll be everything. I'll do everything.

"You saved me, you know," I say with a hushed voice, trying to disguise the lump in my throat and the tears pricking at my eyes.

Cass tilts her head to look at me, and the corner of her mouth quirks up. "Somebody had to—happy it was us."

There's a knock on the door just as Cass is finishing breastfeeding. I jump from the bed, where I've been watching in awe at how incredible of a mom she is already. "I'll tell them you need some more time."

"It's okay—she got too milk drunk and passed out again. They've all been downstairs for hours waiting to be allowed up to visit. Just let me put my boob away."

"You're amazing. You know that?"

"You've only told me four hundred times in the five hours since she was born."

"If I said it every time the thought popped up in my head,

it would be three times that number . . . *at least.*" I can't wipe the smile that's been on my face since the moment I realized my girls were going to be okay. Once she gives me a nod to indicate she's covered, I open the door—a tidal wave of family nearly knocking me on my ass.

So many people in the room, yet you could hear a pin drop with the way they all silently fawn over the sleeping baby.

Denny drops my truck keys into my palm and pulls me into a tight hug. "Love you, man. Can't believe you have a kid."

I jam the keys into my pocket, never taking my eyes off Cassidy, although the people swarming her keep disrupting my view. "You're telling me."

A massive hand smacks me firmly on the back. I turn to find Dave next to me, and my stomach drops—but only for a second. I've never seen a grin quite as large as his, and his eyes are watery when he gives me an approving nod. "Congratulations. She's beautiful."

"Yeah, I think Cass and I spent a full hour staring at her in silence earlier."

"Thank you for taking care of her today. Keeping her safe. I'm sure you were shitting yourself—I fainted when Cassidy was born, and that was in the hospital with doctors and nurses helping. I can't imagine."

"Honestly, there wasn't much time to panic. It happened so fast, and I think I subconsciously knew we couldn't both be freaking out. Plus, Blair was on the phone to walk me through everything during and after. Cass is the one who deserves praise. She did the hard part."

"Well, I'm glad she had you there. I might've misjudged you before—sorry for that." He pats my back again. "I think that baby girl's lucky to have you. Cass, too."

I give him a nod, so taken aback by the shift in his attitude I don't know how to respond. "Thanks, Dave."

He steps in close to hug Cass, then eagerly takes the tiny

swaddled pink bundle into his huge arms. And I get why he didn't like or trust me—I understood it at the surface level before, but now I *get it.* Hazel's only been in Cassidy's and my arms before now. And I know the people in this room will protect our little girl with their lives, but it still makes my mouth dry up watching as everybody gets their turn to hold her. Passing her casually from person to person. No way I'm ever trusting *anyone* with my baby girl.

"Okay . . . even though you said you didn't need one, we planned a little surprise baby shower for you for this weekend," Kate announces, passing Hazel along to Beryl. "But I'm guessing you won't want a party anytime soon. So we brought our presents and . . . are you guys coming back to the ranch?" Her eyes cut between me and Cass until she gets a nod. "Perfect. Well, all the food we made will be in your fridge there."

"Thanks, Kate." Cass smiles. Despite how exhausted I know she is, she's glowing.

Cecily hands over a gift bag full of baby books—unsurprising considering she almost always has a book in her hand. "I don't know which board books are the best, so I might've gone overboard buying anything that looked cute."

Cassidy pulls out a John Deere book about tractors, and Cecily adds, "*That's* Austin's contribution, if you couldn't tell."

Denny laughs, poking Aus in the ribs. "Looks like his reading level."

"Thanks, you guys. This . . . means a lot." Cass wipes the corners of her eyes, pulling the tissue from another gift bag on her lap.

Kate rubs her hand over the blanket covering Cass's legs. "It's the least we can do for family."

· BABY ANNOUNCEMENT ·

Welcome to the world!

Hazel Blair Thompson

February 22

7 lb 3 oz, 2:14 p.m.

Cassidy

Five weeks later

The cabin air's warm and carries a faint smell of cedar. An entire hour in my leatherworking space felt like a vacation, even though I didn't get much work done with my mind constantly wandering to thoughts of how Chase was coping. He insisted they'd be fine—that Hazel would likely sleep the whole time I was gone—and it would appear he was right. He's reclined on the couch watching TV, feet resting on the coffee table, holding her tiny body against his bare chest. Her legs curled up under her diaper-clad bum, tiny fist tucked in next to a chubby cheek, wispy red hair stood on end.

Something about the sight of them together always plucks at my heartstrings. I seriously doubt I'll *ever* get tired of watching Chase hold our baby. While I thought seeing him as an uncle was hot, watching him fall madly in love with our baby girl has made me even more attracted to him than I thought possible. But there are certain moments when the six-week postpartum date cannot come soon enough. Like now, when they're having skin-to-skin bonding time, or when he bounces her to sleep while shushing softly, or when he wears her in a baby wrap while he cooks dinner.

I'm ruined.

I sink down into the worn couch next to him with a contented exhale.

"So, how did it go?"

"I spent most of the time worrying about you two, but that'll probably get better, right? I have to say, it was *really* nice to see something other than these four walls for a change." I tuck my feet under me and peer over at her fluttering eyelashes. "I came back because I'm guessing she'll wake up any second, based on how sore my boobs are."

On cue, she whimpers, lolling her head across his skin. Just before she starts to really wind up, I pluck her from his chest, bringing her to mine. All the worries about not bonding with her seem silly in hindsight. I loved her before she was even born, but reaching down to grab her as she entered this world filled me with an entirely indescribable feeling. Like we share a soul, she and I. I'm not concerned about whether I'll follow in my mom's footsteps—not anymore. And I can't speak for Chase, but I don't think he's scared of becoming his dad.

Looking at our perfect baby girl, it's impossible to imagine how anybody could hurt their child. Hazel has two parents who would do anything for her. Two parents who are so in love time stops when we kiss and shooting stars whizz past when I look into her daddy's eyes.

"You're incredible." Chase leans in so the side of his head is touching mine. These days we spend the majority of our time exactly like this, watching in awe as our perfect daughter simply exists. It doesn't matter if she's eating, sleeping, pooping, or doing all three at once. We're obsessed.

My phone vibrates, and Chase reaches to grab it from the coffee table. "It's Blair. Um, apparently she was volunteering at the rodeo today and Denny got knocked out. So they're heading to the hospital."

"*Shit.* Is he okay? Do you need to go?"

"Um, hold on. I'll ask." His fingers are already tapping out a reply as he speaks.

"Also . . ." I give him a mischievous look. "Denny and Blair are together right now? For the first time in over a decade? Can we talk about that?"

"You're such a shit disturber." He nudges me with his shoulder. "Denny's awake and they're going to run some tests at the hospital. So I'm good to stay here with my girls."

"You know you make my heart melt every time you call us your girls."

He kisses me, then leans down and softly plants a kiss on her head, taking a second to savor her sweet baby smell. "You're my two girls, my world, my entire reason."

Four months later

Lounging by the riverbank, I dip my toes into the cold stream while nursing Hazel under a beach umbrella. Aside from my leatherworking space, where I've been spending hours each week in preparation for my online store launch next month, this is my favorite place to be. Everyone on the ranch takes advantage of this small slice of heaven every chance we get. Which hasn't been terribly often, thanks to the unbearably hot summer so far, with raging forest fires and plenty of days when the skies are too smoky to safely sit outside with an infant.

Cecily's lounged back between Austin's legs, nose buried in a book. Kate and the kids are stacking rocks downstream. A little farther down, some of the ranch hands are splashing and acting like teenage boys while chugging back beer. And Blair's lying on her stomach on a towel next to me, her sunglasses so dark I can't tell if she's simply zoned out or asleep. Either way, she's been perfectly still for at least twenty minutes.

Looking down, I see Hazel's fast asleep in my arms. Taking

my chances that Blair's awake, I say, "Can you watch her while I go see what's taking Chase so long?"

"Mmmm. What?" She tilts her head, shielding the sun with a flat palm, then realizes what I was asking. "Oh, yeah. Yes. Give me my niece." She sits up in a hurry and drags the umbrella toward her, then scoops up my daughter and eases her into her arms with a calming shush.

"Thanks. I'll be right back." I stand and brush the sand from my legs before slipping on my sandals and heading up the hilly path toward the ranch.

I'm taken aback by Chase carrying a loaded cooler down the dirt path. Bulging veins weave an intricate pathway up both arms, from his large, work-hardened hands to his massive biceps. His chest is taut, gleaming with a light sheen of sweat. And the smile he shoots me nearly brings me to my knees.

God. It's cruel how attractive he is.

"Hey, you," he says.

I respond by grabbing the back of his neck and kissing him. Exploring his warm mouth with my tongue, biting his bottom lip to pull him further into me. We don't break the kiss as he bends over, clunking the heavy plastic cooler on the ground. Then his hands are free to touch me. To run down my waist, slip under the summer dress I'm wearing and grab my ass. He toys with the strings of my bathing suit, running a finger over my hip bone.

"Hey, Daddy." I smirk against his lips.

"God, Cass. You know what that fucking does to me." His hips roll, pressing his quickly hardening bulge against me. I know *exactly* what it does to him.

"Auntie Blair has the baby."

"Yeah?" His fingertips press harder into my ass. "Should we go home for a minute?"

"Better idea." I lick my lips. *This* is the moment I've wanted. "How fast can you run, Daddy?"

I don't wait for his answer before taking off up the path, then veering left onto a trail that runs farther down the creek. Even though I got a head start, he's catching up quickly. Admittedly, I wasn't a runner before. But five months postpartum, I'm not exactly in the best shape of my life.

His fingers graze my back, and I squeal, not wanting to be caught and also desperately wanting to be caught. Then they snag on my dress, and I'm brought to a screeching halt. His free hand latches on to my arm, tugging me into him.

"Why you running, sweetheart?" Out of breath, he smashes his lips to mine.

I huff, holding a palm to my burning chest. "Wanted . . . to see . . . if you'd chase me."

"Of course I'd chase you. Always have. Always will." His heavy body presses me into a tree, the rough bark scratching my back as he kisses me deeply. Callused hands glide under my dress, his finger hooking on my bikini string. His hand runs across my lower stomach, inching closer to where I'm throbbing—where I'm aching to feel his touch. We haven't had much opportunity for this since Hazel was born, and it shows in how wet I already am. How hard his cock is against my stomach.

"Touch me," I whimper. "*Please.*"

"Right here in the open? Broad daylight? You're something else, Cass."

"Guess you were right." I get close enough that my lips brush his ear. "I'm a *total fucking slut* for you. What are you gonna do about it?"

He blows air from his nose and digs his fingers into my fleshy hips. "You keep talking like that, and I'm going to fuck you up against this tree, then send you back down to hang out with our friends with my cum leaking out of you. That's what you want, isn't it?"

"Yes. God, yes." I grab his hand, pulling it between my

legs. When he discovers my soaked bikini bottoms, a low rumble resounds in his chest, and I'm pinned between his hot, half-naked body and the tree. Every fantasy I've ever had come to life.

"Have you been swimming, or is this all for me?" he asks with a teasing smile.

"That's *such* a pervy dad comment."

"You love it." A callused finger skims across my skin before slowly sinking inside me. "*Fuck,* you're my everything. How did I get so lucky?"

I muffle a moan with a clenched fist held between my teeth, biting into my knuckles as he slips in a second finger, then a third. His mouth explores every inch of me with ferocity, as if we're on borrowed time and he may never get another chance to have his lips on me. When his hand retreats from under my dress, we fumble together to get his shorts off. And, for a split second, our eyes meet and a spark of fear flashes in his eyes. Or, perhaps, he's simply mirroring the way I feel.

"Are you sure about this?" At the flip of a switch, he becomes the caring, concerned man I love. "If you still aren't comfortable, I get it."

"I started the pill specifically so we didn't need to use condoms forever. At some point we need to trust it'll do its job, right?"

He cocks an eyebrow with a grin before steeling his face again. "Spread your fucking legs like a good little slut. And be quiet, unless you want everybody to know you have a thing for being fucked where anyone could catch us."

Plucking at the bikini string, he exposes me in one move. Clutching the pink scrap of fabric, he wraps his other hand around my neck, pinning me and tangling my hair in the tree bark. And when his cock drives into me, I moan despite the pressure from his fingertips.

"So you do want somebody to catch us?" he asks between

kisses along my jaw, pumping in and out. My dress bunches up, my bare ass dragging across the tree with every jarring thrust.

"No," I whimper. "I just . . . can't be quiet."

Chase tucks his tongue in his cheek. "Open up, sweetheart."

I do as he tells me, letting my jaw go slack. And for a second I'm entirely disgusted, but the look on his face as he gently tucks my bathing suit bottoms between my lips is all it takes to convince me this is the hottest thing in the world. My leg wraps around his hips, my heel spurring him. Over and over. Forcing him deep. Deeper. Until every last goddamn inch of his thick cock is filling me to the hilt. I groan around the soft fabric in my mouth, letting him tear me apart and put me back together—his cock and fingers working to set off a tsunami inside me. If it weren't for his hand on my throat, I'd be falling to the ground. My knees are weak, muscles liquified, and I can't see straight.

"*Breathe,* Cass. Through your nose. Keep coming for me. You look so fucking gorgeous right now. Your cum's dripping down me, baby." He thrusts harder. Faster. The grip on my neck is tight, and the skin along my spine stings with every pump, the rough bark scraping and rubbing me raw. He's so close, I can feel it in the tremble of his hand. See it in the delirious look in his eyes.

As he starts to fall apart inside of me, I yank the bathing suit from my mouth and cram it into his, stifling his roaring moan. Stoking the fire in his eyes as he comes entirely undone.

That. That was worth the risk of skipping a condom.

With a smirk, I pull the fabric from his lips and kiss him, feeling his fingers swipe against my skin before easing into my pussy. My eyes flutter shut and I bite my lip to stifle another moan. I know what he's doing. We both know it's not going to lead to a pregnancy—at least, it better damn well not. But he loves ensuring every last drop stays inside me, and something about Chase marking his territory like this has me wanting to jump him again. I pull him in for a final slow kiss as his hand retreats.

I fight to catch my breath as he bends down to slip my bathing suit back on, pressing a soft kiss to my sensitive skin.

"I don't know if I can walk back. I think you broke me."

"Hop on my back."

I give him a look of disbelief. This man refuses to believe anything negative I have to say about my size. I love that there's no pressure to lose all the baby weight, or to be anything other than myself with him. But that doesn't mean he can carry me down a winding, uneven dirt path.

"Cassidy, let me piggyback you. Or I'll be forced to pick you up against your will and practice the best way to carry you across the threshold for when we get married one day."

"*When* we get married, hey? Bold statement."

"Oh, it's happening. I need to get a ring on that finger before I knock you up again, or I think your dad really will kill me next time."

Reluctantly, I accept the piggyback and all eyes are on us when we turn back up at the riverbank. I sink back onto the blanket next to Blair, and she shakes her head with a knowing smile.

"Hey, Cass." She leans back in her seat, and I feel her delicately stroke my exposed shoulders. "You're gonna want to get Red to slather some Polysporin on your back later. Looks like you had a tangle with a feral cat."

"We could also talk about what it looks like you've been doing." I point at the poorly concealed hickeys on her boobs, and she slaps my hand away with a laugh.

Chase settles in next to me, picking up Hazel from her bounce seat and tucking her against him. His left hand falls to my thigh, and I trace an imaginary line back and forth across his ring finger—cementing a promise I know he understands.

Epilogue—Red

1 year later

A warm summer breeze drifts through the open barn alley, carrying the aroma of fresh-cut hay, and I slip a mint from my pocket to hand to Heathen. She takes it delicately from my palm and crunches while staring me down, ears perked and waiting like the good personal therapist she is.

"See, if you could be this polite all the time, I'd include you today. But it wouldn't be a good look if you tossed me and my bride, would it?"

Her muzzle twitches and she leans in to sniff Hazel, who's tucked against my side in a puffy white dress. She looks like a princess, smiling and trying to grab at the horse with chubby fingers. And, while she has my hair, she's the spitting image of her mama. *Thank God.*

At eighteen months old, she's already a horse girl through and through. Thankfully, Heathen has enough sense to be gentle with toddlers, pressing her soft nose against Hazel's open hand.

"Here, princess. Wanna give her a treat?" I pull another mint from my pocket and press it to her tiny, soft palm. Holding her fingers flat, I guide her hand toward the mare. "Like this, keep your hand open so she doesn't nibble on your little fingers—might think they're baby carrots."

She giggles at the feel of Heathen's whiskers tickling her skin, quickly pulling her arm away with the biggest grin once the mint's gone. I kiss the top of her head, patting the horse and turning to leave.

Cassidy's watching us from the doorway in a wedding dress, and I quickly cover my eyes with my free hand. "*Jesus.* Isn't this bad luck?"

She laughs, and suddenly I feel the warmth of her hands slipping around my waist. She smells so fucking good, and I want nothing more than to open my eyes, drink her in.

"Babe, if we didn't already have luck on our side, we wouldn't be here." Her soft lips press to mine. "Besides, aren't some rules made to be broken?"

Reluctantly, I drop my hand to my side and blink to focus on her. Long blond hair in a braid with small white flowers tucked into the strands, and a glowing smile that sweeps across her face as she peers up at me through thick, dark lashes. Her dress is lacy, flowy, and low cut—and it's going to look phenomenal on the bedroom floor tonight.

She takes a step back, clutching my hand in hers. "What do you think?"

"You're . . . *God,* you're something else. I-I . . ." I lick my lips, unable to come up with a way to express how gorgeous she is.

"Pwetty," Hazel chimes in.

"Aw, baby. Thank you. You're the prettiest girl here, though." Cass squeezes her chubby cheeks, planting a kiss on her tiny nose.

"You're stunning, sweetheart. My dream girl," I say, squeezing her hand. "Both of you are. I don't know how I deserve this, but I'm the luckiest man alive."

"We're lucky to be your girls."

"Speaking of which, I have something I want to show you." I suddenly remember the secret I've been struggling to keep for the past few days. A secret that's incredibly hard to hide when we live in a small house and I like to be naked with my wife as often as possible. "I got it as a bit of a celebratory thing, since I didn't have a traditional bachelor party."

I hand Hazel over to her mommy and work the buttons on my shirt. Cass raises an eyebrow. "What on Earth are you—"

Her sentence stops abruptly, and she bends to examine the fresh tattoo on the left side of my ribcage. Three sets of flowers bound together with leather lacing tied off in a bow. A bouquet inked on my skin, into the grooves of my ribs. The way the two girls represented by the floral design are embedded in my soul.

"I wanted something to represent both my girls forever. So I got your birth month flowers—larkspur and violets."

"Are the white ones your birth month?" Her long eyelashes flutter as she briefly looks up at me.

"They're potato flowers. Thought it was fitting."

"Chase, I love it." Her voice cracks with emotion, and she hugs Hazel tighter to her side.

"I have so many tattoos to cover the pain from the worst moments in my life, to hide the broken parts of me that only you seem to love." I watch as she studies my skin, the corner of her mouth quirking up. "But I wanted something for the best moments. Something almost as colorful and beautiful as my two favorite people on Earth. I wanted to finally have a tattoo that comes from a place of pride, not shame."

"Oh my God, that's beautiful. I can't believe you're doing this right after I finished my makeup." She delicately dabs at her tear ducts and smiles through watery eyes like she's the lucky one here. But because of her, I have more than I ever thought was possible—a reason for waking up every morning, a family to come home to every night, a gorgeous wife, and a baby girl who looks at me like I'm her world.

Today I get to marry the woman who saved my life, on the

ranch that's always been my home, in front of our friends and family—Hazel being the only one I'm *technically* related to. If there's one thing I've learned since getting sober, cemented by a phone call after my father died a few months ago, it's that my chosen family is more important than blood. People who do nothing but love and support me, Cassidy, and Hazel. Who would step in front of a fist to protect us, rather than step aside and watch us take the hit.

"You're the best thing to happen to me. My first choice, my every dream come true. Thank you for being the other half to my broken pieces. I am so madly in love with you, husband."

And she kisses me like we're made for each other, with an intensity I've never had before her. Making me forget to breathe. When my hands glide over the intricate lacework of her dress, it's a reminder that I'm kissing *Cassidy Bowman.* The girl of my dreams. The girl who was so far out of my league for years; the girl who is still too good for me. I kiss her, and my heart fucking skips at the thought, because Cassidy soon-to-be Thompson kisses me back.

Bonus Epilogue—Cassidy

3 years later

Chase stares at me from the couch with a lopsided grin. "Pacing and bouncing around the room doesn't make the commercial breaks go by any faster."

"In my mind, it does. I can't sit still for another second."

"Cass, if I have to watch your ass jiggle for another fucking second, we'll miss it altogether because I'll be hauling you to bed."

"Don't you fucking da—" I squeal as he hooks his arm around me, pulling me into his lap before I can get the sentence out. His thick arms wrap around my waist, and he places a warm kiss on the side of my neck.

For the rest of the unending commercial break, he holds me tight to him; the rise and fall of his chest keeps my heart beating steadily, despite my anxiety making it want to race. I fiddle with the ring on his left hand, spinning it around and around. Turns out, I had no reason to worry about not loving him after the pregnancy and postpartum hormones dissipated. In fact, I'm even more in love with my husband today and I have a feeling I'll only continue falling deeper with time.

"Holy shit!" I gasp and point at the television, feeling Chase's arms loosen so I can sit back up. "Holy shit. Those are my shoes. I can't fucking believe it. You know she's going to win Female Vocalist of the Year tonight, and she's doing it in shoes I fucking made."

I lean forward, staring into the cool television glow, watching as arguably the most popular country singer in the world performs her new hit single on the Country Music Awards stage. When her team contacted me to make custom tooled leather heels for tonight, I think I briefly passed away. Then it took some convincing before I trusted it wasn't a scam. Regardless of the success I've seen over the last couple years—the features in western fashion magazines, the influencers and barrel racing champions wearing my brand, and the fact that my website sells out within seconds every time I open up for orders—this is absolutely mind-blowing.

"Dance with me," Chase says, kissing my shoulder before gently pushing me from his lap.

"You never want to dance. You usually look at me and Hazel like we're the two biggest dorks when we do."

"Yeah, because I need to save my moves for special occasions. If I do them too often, you won't be impressed anymore." Pulling me to my feet, he slips a hand onto my lower back, and we sway to the love ballad.

"I'll always be impressed by you," I say. "I wouldn't be here if it weren't for you pushing me to try. Making me feel like I have something to offer the world. Not to mention, helping me juggle a baby and a business."

"I knew if I stuck it out for the hard times, eventually I'd have my own sugar mama." He kisses me, sending a familiar cascade of warmth over my body. "I'm so proud of you, sweetheart. You're so strong, smart, talented. I'm just grateful you want me along for the ride."

"I love you so much, Chase Thompson."

"Not as much as I love you, Cassidy Thompson."

When the song ends, we don't stop dancing. I kiss him, smiling against his lips as we hold each other. His hand steady at my back. My fingers twirling through the auburn hair at the nape of his neck.

Our feet move over the creaky floorboards of our first home. It's small, cute, situated about halfway between town and Wells Ranch, and it's all ours. Six months after Hazel was born, Dad offered to sell my house and give us the money. After my first big feature in a magazine the following year, I paid him back. Despite my salary these days being enough to buy a house twice this size, this has been plenty for our little family. I know Chase's dream is to have us living on the ranch, since we're already there more often than not. And the more I think about it, the more I wonder if it's time we take the next big leap.

"I've been thinking," I mutter into his neck, letting my head rest against his collarbone. "Maybe we should revisit the idea of a bigger house."

"I thought we had to stay living here forever because of all Hazel's firsts here."

"Well, originally I didn't want to ever leave the cabin because she was born there. But I'm real glad we have our own bedroom—with a door lock—here now. So maybe I'll feel similarly about a bigger house on the ranch, with a bunch more firsts, when we have another baby."

"Cassidy." He pulls me away from him so he can stare into my eyes. "Are you telling me you're pregnant?"

"No, no. I was thinking . . . Hazel is going to be four in a couple months. If we're going to have a baby, I want to do it soon. But I don't know if I can manage Hazel, a baby, and my job."

"*We* can manage it. We make a fucking great team—look at how we rocked dinner, bath, and bed tonight so she'd be asleep before the award show. If you want another baby, let's have a baby. Call me selfish, but I'd kill to see you with pregnant and breastfeeding tits again. You're the most gorgeous pregnant woman."

"So should we?" It's a rhetorical question. I know he's been hoping for another baby for years. It's always been up to me to make the call, but planning for something as huge as a second baby was paralyzing. After our wedding, we started relying on the pull-out method as our only birth control. Considering I got pregnant the first time despite my PCOS and a condom, I honestly anticipated it would happen immediately again. It felt easier to leave it up to chance than having to make the decision myself.

Clearly, that plan isn't working.

"You know my answer. I'd fill this house with a dozen kids if that's what you wanted."

"*Jesus,* let's not get carried away. I'm agreeing to one more."

"Perfect." He smacks my ass, nipping at my neck. "Let's go—I can't wait to get to work. I'm going to knock you up so fucking hard, sweetheart."

He pulls me back down to the couch, making quick work of slipping my T-shirt over my head as I straddle him. His hands cup my bare breasts, and his sweatpants aren't doing anything to hide how hard he already is. I grind against his lap, kissing him relentlessly.

Perfectly on cue, Hazel's raspy voice cries out from down the hallway. Something about a green monster in her closet that Daddy needs to deal with. He groans against my chest.

"You sure you want another?" I laugh and climb off his lap. "It means even less alone time for us."

"She's the best thing I've ever done. The two of you are my reason for being. So, yes. *Fuck yes.*" He kisses my forehead. "Pour yourself some celebratory champagne and relax. When I come back, you're going to be a good wife and let me put a baby in you."

"Well, when you say it like that, how could I say no?" I push him away, watching his muscular back as he strolls down the hallway to our daughter's room.

After twenty minutes of silence, I slowly push the door open to find Chase and Hazel asleep in her tiny bed. His chin resting on top of her head, her arm and leg flung across him. I carefully pluck the teddy bear dangling from her fingers and tuck it beside her. Then pull her pink comforter up over the pair of them and give each a soft kiss before ducking back out.

This wasn't the way I thought my life would go. I was lost and apathetic for so long. Not realizing a single reckless night with an unhinged cowboy named Red would change everything. That the man I'd passed over for years was exactly the person I needed. Now the only future I want to have is one with this perfect little family—the rest is small potatoes.

Acknowledgments

To my very own "Red"—my husband—thank you for sticking it out when I was pregnant and eating loaded baked potatoes in bed every night (10/10 bedtime snack, honestly). And thanks to my daughter, who basically turned me into the real-life Cassidy Bowman—sleeping, shivering, and eating potatoes daily. There's just as much of you two in here as there is me, and I love you for it.

Brittany! This book is for you, even if I thought up the idea before ever meeting you. Your (somewhat extreme) passion for the accidental pregnancy trope kept me going even when I was worried that everybody would hate it. Thank you for reading this book when so much of the story was a hot mess, and for loving it anyway (or being a great liar).

Huge hugs and thanks to my incredible beta reading team: Sydney, Samantha, Albany, Stefanie, and Amanda. Your insight, feedback, and hilarious comments helped make this book into what it is now. Thank you x a billion.

Andrea. I'm so honored to be the reason you had to look up the spelling of thundercunt. Once again, thank you for putting up with my ridiculousness and making this book shine. Sorry for making you cry.

Friend and proofreader extraordinaire, Hannah. Thanks for not murdering me when I climbed into your car without even questioning whether it was a good idea to do so. I can't wait to run into your arms again sometime soon.

I can't mention two of my book club girlies without the rest. Brittany, Samantha, Mimi, Jessica, and Nicole, you're the best group of friends to go for drinks and talk about smut with. Thanks for putting up with me attending book club on the months I haven't had the time to read, for supporting me in every way, and for being so excited to hear all my secret book plans.

Also, WOW. What a change from publishing *Alive and Wells* just a few short months ago. I've been so blessed to meet a ton of incredible authors and readers through Bookstagram/BookTok. I had no idea that I would make this many friends, and I'd be here all day if I tried to name every person who's impacted my life in the last few months. But a special shout-out to the people I can't go a day without talking to: Karley, Kayla, Abby, Chelsea, Danie, Ceilidh, and Sydney. I'd probably get a lot more writing done without our millions of unhinged voice messages, silly TikTok videos, and brainstorming book ideas, but this author life would be significantly less fun without all of you. Also, sometimes I need somebody to threaten to throw me out of a window or come at me with a sword if I don't hit my word count goal.

And a big thank-you to my agent, Carly. I'm *so* grateful for your expertise and your love for this series. Your belief in me has done wonders for my self-confidence. I know we're going to do some really big things, and I'm blessed to have you in my corner.

Thank you to the street team that promotes the ever-loving shit out of me and my books. You make sharing teasers, cover reveals, and all exciting news 100x more fun. And the group chat is one of my favorite places to hang out.

ARC readers: I know I'm writing this before you've had the chance to read it, but I want to thank you anyway. Whatever success comes from this book is largely thanks to you.

Whether you realize it or not, your reviews have a massive impact on my career. I love every one of you.

Speaking of which, you lovely reader, you. *I love you more than potatoes.* Thank you for reading. Thank you for reviewing, sharing with a friend, and reposting my social media posts. It all means the world to me. When I published *Alive and Wells,* I truly anticipated that only a small handful of people would read it. I'm so overwhelmed in the best possible way by the amount of love people have for this world and these characters. All of this is for you. <3

About the Author

Bailey Hannah is a Canadian romance author with a passion for strong heroines and rugged men who aren't afraid to love their women hard.

Born and raised in small-town British Columbia, she always includes a touch of rural Canadian flair (dirt roads, rodeos, and ketchup chips) in her stories. Bailey lives with her husband, daughter, dogs, and chickens. In her spare time, she enjoys reading, spending time in the outdoors, and daydreaming about her characters.

baileyhannahwrites.com
Instagram: @baileyhannahwrites
TikTok: @baileyhannahwrites